T0276415

BISON
BOOKS

An Endangered Species

A Novel

FRANCES WASHBURN

University of Nebraska Press | Lincoln

The University of Nebraska Press is part of a land-grant institution with campuses and programs on the past, present, and future homelands of the Pawnee, Ponca, Otoe-Missouria, Omaha, Dakota, Lakota, Kaw, Cheyenne, and Arapaho Peoples, as well as those of the relocated Ho-Chunk, Sac and Fox, and Iowa Peoples.

Library of Congress Cataloging-in-Publication Data
Names: Washburn, Frances, author.
Title: An endangered species: a novel / Frances Washburn.
Description: Lincoln: University of Nebraska Press, 2024
Identifiers: LCCN 2023028692
ISBN 9781496238672 (paperback)
ISBN 9781496239457 (epub)
ISBN 9781496239464 (pdf)
Subjects: LCGFT: Novels.
Classification: LCC PS3623.A8673 E54 2024 | DDC 813/.6—dc23/eng/20230629
LC record available at https://lccn.loc.gov/2023028692

Designed and set in Arno Pro by K. Andresen

For all those who care about the endangered,
no matter the species.

Pay attention.

AN ENDANGERED SPECIES

Prologue

Bill and Martha were not supposed to be outside their pen, but they escaped for an early morning walk, searching the watery ditches for their breakfast of arrowhead roots and tubers, speaking their one-word vocabulary: hoo-hoo. Martha tugged with her black beak at a particularly tough root, bracing her flat feet, her long neck stretched as the root resisted. The slanted rays of the rising sun turned her white feathers a soft shade of gold as Bill stumped over to help his mate. When the shot came, Bill raised his head in time to see the red flower blossom on Martha's breast, watching as she slumped and fell, the puddling blood darkening a patch of gray-brown road dust. Bill stepped aside, avoiding the spreading wet, looking for the source of the sound, and when he heard no further shots, he tentatively moved closer to Martha, poking at her with his beak, poking again, then again, nudging, silently pleading for her to get up, but she was still and silent as a light breeze ruffled her feathers. He lifted his head, stretched his long neck, fluttered his wings as he strutted back and forth, back and forth and around Martha crying out, "oh Oh, oh Oh, oh Oh."

When he heard the sound of footsteps crunching in the coarse dirt and pebbles of the road, he moved away from the body, stepped sideways, his cries intermittent. The kid walked up to Martha, shoved her with his boot and said, "Huh." He looked over at Bill, less than ten feet away, yelled "Boo," and laughed as Bill stepped away, six foot wide wingspan fluttering as he continued to cry out, "oh Oh!" The kid leveled the shotgun he carried at Bill and said, "Boom!" Bill faced the gun.

The kid leaned over, grabbed Martha by the neck and hoisted her twenty plus pound weight so the body hung over his back, blood dripping from the wound in her breast. He cradled the shotgun in his other arm. Without looking back at Bill, the kid walked away down the road. For a hundred yards or more Bill followed, crying out, louder and louder, until the kid leaped the borrow ditch, awkward with the heavy trumpeter swan over his shoulder, caught his balance, and walked off across the field.

Bill paced on the road side of the ditch, calling and calling, flapping his wings.

1

Tom Warder tried to sleep in the passenger seat as Wayne Finley drove, but the jolting of the old deuce and a half army surplus truck bounced Tom's head against the window glass until he gave up trying to sleep, sat up straight, and stared at the yellow headlights shooting the dark highway ahead. "Want a cup of coffee?" Tom asked.

Finley leaned forward over the steering wheel, turning his torso from one side to other, stretching his tired back muscles. "That would go down good," Finley said.

Tom poured the thick black liquid from the battered green thermos into the silver lid, careful not to spill the hot liquid onto his own fingers as the truck jerked and bounced along. He handed it to Finley with a "Careful, it's hot."

Somewhere east of Gillette, Wyoming, heading toward Greybull, the men and their truck with the load of cages in the back had traveled less than five hundred miles from Red Rocks, Montana, even though they had been on the road for more than ten hours, but 45 miles per hour was top speed in the old truck. John King, the manager at LaCreek National Wildlife Refuge, had picked it up at an auction of government surplus, surprised he got the low bid until the truck was delivered and King saw what he had bought with his allotted funds from the Department of the Interior. Once the big boys upstairs dictated that twenty trumpeter swans had to be moved from the refuge in Montana down to LaCreek, the old truck was the only means King had of collecting the birds. Wayne Finley and Tom Warder were the lucky men who got to make the trip, or one of them thought it was lucky. Finley's parents lived in Greybull, so he thought it a chance to spend a few hours overnight at their place. Warder was indifferent about the excursion at first, but the more he thought about it the more he looked forward to it. The morning drive down from Red Rocks to Yellowstone gave him a chance to see country he had never seen before, but only from the window of the slow-moving truck. With a load of caged birds in the back there was no time to stop and inhale the scenery, and now, approaching eight o'clock on this September night, he saw nothing beyond the hypnotizing passage of dividing lines on the interstate. In 1960 traffic still hadn't reached maximum saturation on the interstate system, especially not on the northern plains with tourist season past. Tom looked forward to getting out of the truck at Finley's parents' home, letting the roar of the engine recede from his hearing, and after a hopefully short conversation with the old folks, a chance to lie flat and sleep.

He was to be disappointed. Mr. Finley senior was a retired Methodist minister who never retired his proselytizing, so Tom politely listened to two hours of Jesus talk while Mrs. Finley, frail with arthritis and a heart condition, insisted upon plying their son and Tom with more coffee. Worse still, Tom wasn't allowed to smoke in their house. When he finally did get to lie down on a pull-out couch shared with Wayne, the caffeine buzz kept him awake. He choked down the runny eggs and burned toast gratefully, signaling the end of the visit to the Finleys' and the beginning of the end of a disappointing trip.

Big as young turkeys with beaks that pinched, the swans demonstrated their unhappiness when Tom and Wayne cautiously opened the cage doors to shove in pans of water before they started up the truck, drove through the sleepy town and onto Highway 434 to Buffalo, where they would get on Interstate 90 for a short stretch until they turned off at Moorcroft. By the time the road crossed the state line into South Dakota, Tom was driving, his eyes feeling like sandpaper, while Wayne's head bounced against the passenger-side window as he slept. They passed through Custer, stopping only briefly for gas and cigarettes, then on down through Oelrichs, where the air smelled oily from the creosote used to coat the fence posts produced by the town's only industry. They drove across Pine Ridge Reservation where Tom grew up, just as the sun sank behind them, creating a glare in the cracked rearview mirror.

When the truck stopped in the headquarters yard of LaCreek National Wildlife Refuge, King was waiting along with the graduate student, Carl Wilson, from South Dakota State, who was interning at LaCreek for the fall semester. King took one look at the exhausted men and ordered them home while he and Carl unloaded the caged birds in the pen prepared for them.

Tom drove the mile and a half to his small frame house, hugged his sleepy wife, looked in on his four daughters, and went to bed. As he was dozing off to sleep, Tom remembered: it was September 15th, his birthday. He was forty-two years old.

Sometime in the early morning, Tom felt a weight on the side of the bed. Anna, his wife, shook his shoulder. "Tom. Time to get up. It's past six already. You'll be late for work," she said.

"No," he said. "King told me not to come in today. I've got a long weekend."

He felt the weight lift from the side of the bed and moments later felt more weight on the other side as Anna slid back into bed beside him, cuddling up against his back for a few minutes. She would have to get up again shortly to wake the girls for school. Her feet felt like blocks of ice. He didn't notice when she slid out of bed again a few minutes later, but he did hear the argument, the same circular one she had most mornings with their second-eldest daughter, Betsy, the one they had nicknamed Little Bit but had quickly shortened to just Bit. As she grew older, it became harder to tell whether she was bitten or whether she bit.

2

Bart Johnson got out of bed about the same time that Tom Warder was getting into his own, but Bart woke up feeling nearly as tired as Tom had when he fell asleep. That sense of urgency that Bart felt at other seasons of the year shouldn't have been on his mind now, in late September, the slack season on his ranch. In a few more weeks, when the cold bit deep and the ground was white with snow, he would feel the urgent need to get up, load his hay sled, and pull it out to the small holding pasture, stopping to fork off the load of sweet-smelling alfalfa to the anticipating herd of black Angus. Spring brought calving season with its own urgent need for him to check the near parturition cows, especially the young heifers that might have trouble delivering their first calves, and in these difficult times, the loss of even one calf was costly. Then came summer, when the sickles on the mowing machines had to be sharpened, ready for a long day of cutting the alfalfa once the dew had burned off so it wouldn't mold when the baler wadded the cut stems into neat blocks to be stacked for the winter season. Now in late September, Bart had breathing space for another month or two until he had to gather the cattle, cull the year's calves, and ship them to the auction barn. This was the time of year when he could sleep in a little, walk down to the big Quonset barn and take his time going over his farm equipment—tractors, hay sled, mowers, rakes, balers, all of it—replacing worn out or broken parts cobbled together in a hurry back in the summer when down time meant money. No, it wasn't the routine cyclical work that kept him awake at night and up early in the morning, but his family. The urgency that roused Bart out of bed very early this September morning was not concern about the ranch, but what to do about Brian.

Bart and Betty married right out of high school, a not unexpected match since both of them were children of first-generation ranchers in the county, both growing up on nearly adjacent plots of land, attending the same church, the same grammar school and high school. People remarked about their wedding picture in the local paper. They said the two looked like kids, and they were, just eighteen years old, but marrying young was common in their part of the Midwest in the early 1950s. No, the community meant they looked like *KIDS*, like twelve-year-olds, and they did: skinny, faces yet unformed, eyes wide and innocent as kids growing up with limited television access and a life lived so far deeply into a remote section of the country.

That wedding picture sat on the polished maple buffet in the dining room on a hand-crocheted white doily, and every time Bart saw it he thought that the community was right. He and Betty had been *KIDS*, naïve in their belief that their world would always be ordered, proceed along an acceptable path, comfortable but not rich with minor bumps until they grew old watching their own kids grow up, marry, and eventually Bart and Betty would become the grand old couple at the town's annual Fourth of July picnic, sitting on lawn chairs while they watched the baseball game between the Catholics and the Presbyterians. Life has a way of seizing you by the neck and popping your head off like a dog killing a snake.

Betty wanted a big family and Bart said the same, but he didn't really care one way or the other, except he did want a son. After that it didn't matter if the kids came or not, or how many. He'd find a way to make the ranch pay enough for everyone, but there were no kids, not in the first year or the second, and by the third the old ladies at their church were whispering among themselves, wondering if it was Bart's fault or Betty's. Of course, their gossiping bothered Betty a lot more than Bart. She had to put up with the old biddies while the women prepared the annual pheasant dinner in the American Legion meeting room to benefit the local hospital, and during the monthly meetings of the Lady's Aid Club when the younger women talked about the latest incident with their own kids and the old ladies smiled sympathetically at Betty.

Bart's friends down at the Legion Club and his buddies at the Wednesday livestock auction were men, of course, and men didn't talk about gynecological matters or what their *FEELINGS* were, except to complain about the lack of rain or the overabundance of rain, or a balky piece of machinery, or sometimes, their wife's cooking. Still, he felt the absence of a son of his own when he went to the local Little League games cheering on someone else's boys.

Six years into the marriage Betty got pregnant, and Bart felt vindicated. He endured, even enjoyed the crude jokes from his friends about the old bull who finally performed just when the owners were ready to ship him off for dog food, but his happiness was complete when Brian was born.

The next time was Susan, four years later, and Bart scarcely noticed except to tell his friends he expected to go broke buying ladies' products and fancy dresses. He mostly ignored his daughter, but he handed out cigars with blue bands around them when his son was born, bought Brian a pair of cowboy boots when he was just a few months old, a baseball bat, toy trucks, took him everywhere, even riding standing up beside Bart on the tractor, a practice that got Betty steaming mad because she said it wasn't safe and he knew she was right, but he couldn't help himself. He wanted his boy to know everything about cattle, about growing alfalfa, about riding a cutting horse when the cattle were gathered in the fall, about helping a heifer in trouble deliver a calf and more. Brian took to it, following Bart, imitating his old man right down to the swagger in his walk. For the first three years, before Brian changed.

3

Bit Warder was only called Bit at home. At school she was Betsy, a name she hated because it was old-fashioned and reminded people of their old maiden aunts. She wished her parents had given her a good modern name, like Linda (there were two of those in her little country school) or Barbara or Susan, like her best friend, who was sweet and kind but really dumb. Bit never said out loud that Susan was dumb; that would be mean. Bit didn't mean dumb like the slang term where it meant someone who wasn't up on the latest anything. She meant dumb as in a person who didn't learn very well, didn't remember what she learned, and sometimes argued from incorrect information. If there had been a bigger pool of kids at her school Bit probably wouldn't have been best friends with Susan, and not just because she was dumb, but because they didn't have much in common.

Susan liked playing with dolls; Bit thought dolls were boring. What could you do with a doll? Dress it up; pretend you were a mommy and the doll was your baby? Bit didn't care about being a mommy. She didn't know what she wanted to do but that wasn't it. She was good at everything except sports. She was good at all her *SCHOOL* subjects, so good that she knew it after the first lesson and found herself frustrated when Mrs. Ellis made her do worksheets of multiplication problems over and over. Drills, the teacher called it. Why would you need to drill something over and over if you got it the first time? Bit was bored, which got her into trouble.

When her boring drill sheets were done, her vocabulary word definitions written out ten times each (using them twice in a sentence), her history chapter read, her spelling words written out, and the main exports of Portugal memorized, she read. Anything and everything, which wasn't much because her school didn't have a library.

Once every six weeks Mrs. Ellis went to the county library, checked out twenty books, and brought them to the classroom. Each of the students was supposed to read one of the books every six weeks and write a book report. Bit read them all. She could have written a report on all twenty, but that was boring too. She wrote her one. The daily assignments took up less than the first hour of each class day, and after that Bit read. Mrs. Ellis didn't like it. Bit was not supposed to be the smartest girl in the sixth grade. That distinction was supposed to go to one of the Lindas or even Susan, any of the kids whose families were white and more prosperous than Bit's family, but Bit was too young to understand why Mrs. Ellis always frowned at her; why the teacher picked at her, why she told Bit the colors she picked for her arts and crafts project were ugly, but when Randall Baker chose the same colors, Mrs. Ellis crowed about how original he was.

Reading took Bit away from the boredom and the daily aggravations of school when her mother wouldn't let her stay home. But reading only lasted so long. She read all twenty books from the county library within two weeks, and after that she fidgeted at her desk. She wrote her name multiple times on the lined notebook paper. She doodled and stared out the window daydreaming of better places and better times, enduring the waiting until she could be grown up enough to leave forever. She got in trouble.

There was that time when she was looking around the room, daydreaming, and spied a row of books on the top shelf of the corner bookcase that she hadn't noticed before, even though they had always been there, a set of maybe twenty or more books, all with dark blue covers. Mrs. Ellis had left the room, probably to the classroom next door—there were only two rooms in the entire school—to speak with Mrs. Thompson, who taught grades one through four. Bit had pushed a chair over to the bookcase, but when she still couldn't reach that top shelf of books, she climbed up onto one of the lower shelves. The books were a series, each one with a title like "Annabelle of England" or "Lita of Peru." Why were these books here, and why hadn't they ever been given these to read? Intrigued, Bit pulled one out and read the first page and started on the second when she felt the sting of the ruler across the back of her legs.

"You. Get. Down. From. There. Right. Now." Every word accompanied another blow of the ruler. Startled, Bit did a little jig dance on the edge of the shelf, slipped, caught herself, and half jumped, half fell to the floor. The bookcase teetered briefly over her head before it righted itself. Mrs. Ellis slashed at her with the ruler as Bit hurried back to her desk still clutching *ANNABELLE OF ENGLAND*.

Mrs. Ellis stood over Bit, the ruler poised above her head ready to strike again as she shouted, "I will NOT have you behaving like a monkey in my classroom! This is not a zoo!" She struck out again with the ruler catching the book so *ANNABELLE OF ENGLAND* flew from Bit's hand, hit the floor and slid until it came to rest splayed like a dead animal against Randall Baker's shoe. Mrs. Ellis stood over Bit a moment longer, breathing hard. Bit sat very still, her hands folded carefully together on the desktop, waiting for another blow of the ruler but Mrs. Ellis dropped her arm, stalked back to the front of the room, sat carefully in her chair, and smoothed her gray hair with one hand.

She cleared her throat and said, "Remember, everyone, today is Friday, when Mrs. Heinz comes for music instruction. She'll expect you to know all the words to 'You Are My Sunshine,' so let's practice that now." She got up, walked to the battered piano at the side of the room, struck a key, and began to sing:

YOU ARE MY SUNSHINE, MY ONLY SUNSHINE . . .

The children joined in on the second line. Bit mouthed the words. The back of her legs stung.

At recess Bit and Susan were the last ones chosen when the kids divided up into two teams to play softball, so they were sent to the outfield where nobody ever hit a ball except Paul James, a red-haired fat boy, strong as an ox, who always hit the ball far over the outfielder's heads and into the cow pasture beyond. As they were strolling over the brown dead grass to the outfield, Bit said, "I don't know why Mrs. Ellis hates me."

Susan stumbled on a heap of dirt piled up by one of the many ground squirrels that lived in the tunnels beneath the playground but had probably already gone into winter hibernation. "If you'd just sit in your seat like everyone else, you wouldn't get into trouble," Susan said. "Mrs. Ellis just wants you to be like us."

No she doesn't, Bit thought. She wants me not to be here at all.

"Tell you what, I've got fig bar cookies in my lunch. I'll share," Susan said, touching Bit's shoulder.

After recess, after math, after lunch, after the spelling test, which Bit only got eight of the ten written down because she wasn't really listening when Mrs. Ellis pronounced the words for the sixth graders to write down, after Mrs. Heinz played the piano and they all sang "You Are My Sunshine" and several rounds of "Row Row Row Your Boat" and a couple of other songs that Bit hated, after one of the little kids from Mrs. Thompson's classroom rang the bell signaling the end of the day and the end of the week, after the very long day was over, Bit asked Susan if she could stop at Bit's house for a while on her way home.

Susan hesitated. "I can't. I'm—I'm going home with Linda Baker," she said, and stopped as if she were embarrassed. "See you next week."

Bit walked the half mile home alone, avoiding the company of her younger sister, who was in Mrs. Thompson's room. Bit's youngest sister was too young to start school. Even though it was late fall, there were no dead leaves to scuff through because there were no trees along the way. Trees on the high plains only grew in two places: naturally, along the few creeks that wandered lazily through the nearly flat landscape, or purposely planted in ordered rows on the north and west sides of farmsteads, planted there in the late 1930s as part of a WPA program started during the Great Depression and continuing for decades afterward. Bit's father told her about that. He had worked for that program when he was only a kid himself.

The Warder house squatted on an acre of land one muddy back street off the paved farm-to-market road that passed through the small village, which boasted a tiny country store, a post office with one employee, and a two-pump gas station slash car repair shop. A white clapboard house, Bit's home looked like a big shed because it had been an addition on another house that was being torn down, so Tom Warder had bought it, closed in the open side, divided it into two rooms, and this was the house where he brought his bride, Anna, home. The family had grown through their marriage but the house hadn't, so the two parents and three girls crowded into the space within in the cold months and spilled out into the yard when the weather was warm. Fall was an in-between season, but Bit's mother must have been anticipating the cold because the house smelled like winter food—beans and ham bone cooking on the stove, fresh hot rolls just out of the oven. Bit inhaled the smell with pleasure, thinking of chokecherry jelly on a buttered hot roll for dessert.

Bit's dad sat at the oil cloth-covered round table, a cup of sludgy coffee left over from breakfast at hand. Bit knew he must be having one of his headaches. The cure Tom Warder had created, which only cured the headaches half the time, was two aspirin and a cup of strong coffee. Bit clasped his shoulder as she leaned over to kiss the top of his head.

"You get caught up on sleep, Dad?"

Bit had missed his quiet presence while he had been gone on the trip to Montana. She knew where that was—the pink state at the top of the map in her classroom. She wished she could have gone with him. "Yeah. And caught another headache."

Bit settled into a chair beside her dad, and asked, "What's Montana like, Dad? And Wyoming. Did you go through Yellowstone Park?"

"Not now," her mother told her, as she took the hot rolls out of the oven. "Your dad has one of his headaches. Go feed the chickens."

"How come Connie can't do it? Or Patty? It's not my turn."

"I'm sending them to the store. We're out of butter. And what's this about 'turn'? Everybody does whatever needs doing when it needs doing."

Bit walked down the path at the back of the property, opened the door on the side shed of the chicken house, and scooped out the feed to put in the split tractor tire that served as a feed trough. The chickens came running, entering the fenced pen. Bit counted them all, and when she got to the twenty hens and two roosters that she knew should be there, she shut the gate. Someone would have to come down later when the chickens had gone to roost and shut the coop door, but it wouldn't be her if she could help it. She cheered up a little as she walked back to the house remembering that it was her favorite night of the week: Friday, with an entire weekend before her when she didn't have to think about school or Mrs. Ellis or why Susan was spending the night with Linda when Bit didn't get asked, and even better, her favorite television show, *RAWHIDE*, came on at six o'clock.

Tom Warder had bought the Philco television just weeks ago, a luxury for the Warder family but a common household fixture for almost everyone else in the community. He put up an antenna, but it was only about twenty-five feet high, so the set only captured one of the two channels beaming this far into the hinterlands. For Bit the television was magic in a beige metallic box almost as big as her mom's wringer washing machine, except the TV didn't have legs. It sat on the stacked wooden orange crates that held her dad's paperback western novels by famous authors like Luke Short and Louis L'Amour and Zane Grey. He used to read a chapter or so from one of them every night while Anna and her girls did up the dishes, but now they watched westerns on the TV even though the characters looked like shadows of people moving through a blizzard. As they sat at the table for dinner, Bit's dad felt well enough to make his usual joke when he said, "Pass the fridge joles," his wordplay on the Spanish word for beans: *FRIJOLES*. Connie and Patty giggled, but Bit only smiled. She'd heard the joke more times than her sisters had. With a cautious glance at her mother, Bit asked again, "What was Montana like?"

Tom chewed the bite of roll he'd just taken, swallowed and put his fork down. "Parts of it look pretty much like it does around here. Wheat and cattle country, nearly flat, and not very many trees."

"What's the other parts look like?"

"There're mountains in Yellowstone Park that we went through to get there. Pretty country, but it was almost dark when we went through on the way up, and almost dark on the morning we came back through. We got into Red Rocks after dark. They got us up early to load the birds, and we left before sunrise."

"What's for dessert, mom?" Connie asked, tapping her fork on the edge of her plate. "Is there cake?"

"No, I didn't bake a cake," Anna answered.

"No dessert?" Patty whined, tapping her fork in imitation of her sister.

"Shut up, you two, I want to hear about dad's trip," Bit said.

"*ANAGOPTOMPE*!" Anna said, slapping her two youngest daughters' hands in turn. "There're canned raspberries that your Auntie Sue brought when she visited last summer. And it's your dad's birthday. He said he'd rather have raspberries than a cake."

Bit brightened up. She loved those raspberries in sweet syrup even more than chocolate cake.

"Those birds," Tom said as he helped himself to another serving of the beans and liberally dosed them with ketchup. "I never knew they existed. Never knew they were so big. When King told us we were going up to Red Rocks to bring twenty of them back here, that intern kid, Carl, got all excited. I thought his eyes would pop out of his head."

"Why?" Connie asked, smiling at the idea of someone's eyes popping out of their head. "What's so special about some big old birds?"

"Carl said trumpeter swans are rare. Almost extinct, he said."

"What's stinked?" Patty asked.

Bit made a face at her littlest sister, and said, "Not stinked, stupid. Extinct. It means none of them are alive anymore. He said they were almost extinct, so that means there aren't many of them left alive anymore, right, Dad?"

"That's right, Bit, but don't be so rude to your sister. Carl said the birds aren't breeding anymore. Not laying eggs, not even making nests. No eggs, no nest, no baby birds, and they go extinct."

"How come Carl knows so much?" Connie asked.

"He's working on a master's degree in wildlife management. I think a master's degree means he's already went to college for four years and got a bachelor's degree first," Tom said. "Carl is excited that he gets to work with an endangered species. King's not so happy about it."

"Why would that be?" Anna put in, as she got up to clear the table.

"I don't know. I think he's afraid of the responsibility. The Red Rocks Refuge people have been trying to get the birds to breed for years, but they don't. The old birds die off, and there aren't any young ones coming along to replace them. The bureau decided that LaCreek has better conditions for raising the birds—better habitat, that's the word Carl used. I think King's afraid LaCreek will fail too, and since he's the refuge manager, he'll get blamed."

Anna set bowls of dark red raspberries swimming in the sweetened syrup in front of everyone, starting with Tom. Bit dug in with delight.

"And there's something else," Tom continued. "King's pulling me off maintenance work. He wants me and Carl to work with the swans."

"That's good, isn't it, Dad? No more rebuilding greasy old motors. Well, I dunno. Maybe taking care of these swans is worse?" Bit offered. She dripped raspberry juice on her jeans, looked down and rubbed the spot. Her jeans were dark enough, maybe her mom wouldn't notice the stain.

"I think King put you on that project so if it fails, he'll have someone to blame," Anna said.

"Maybe. I guess I just won't fail then," Tom said with a little grin.

"I wonder what other animals might be en-dan-gered species," Bit said, sounding out the long word carefully. "Do you think Carl would know?"

"I don't know," Tom said. "If you're talking about birds, probably, because that's what he studies, but other animals—I don't know. You could ask your teacher."

"I'd never ask her anything I don't have to," Bit snapped. "She's mean, and she's stupid, and even if she knew, she wouldn't tell me. She hates me. How come I couldn't go to boarding school like my cousins?"

Anna slammed down her spoon, splattering berry juice on the oilcloth. "We've talked about this," she said. "No. You will never go to Indian boarding school."

"I've read about boarding schools a little. Places where kids get special classes, and lots of books to read, and they have fun," Bit argued. "It couldn't be worse than my school."

Anna grabbed Bit's wrist. "Those boarding schools are not the same as Indian boarding schools. You have no idea what they are like. They're ten times, no, a hundred times worse than the school you've got," Anna said, her voice thick and angry.

Bit breathed in slowly. She didn't know what to say.

"Bit," Tom said calmly, "trust your mother. She knows. She went to Marty Mission, and that's not a good place. I know how it is for you girls in school here. It's not good, either, but you have to go to school someplace, and this is all there is."

For a few minutes, no one said anything as spoons clinked against bowls.

"Anyone want more raspberries?" Anna asked brightly. Bit knew her mother was trying to take the sting out of her words, but more raspberries wouldn't help.

Bit thought about her mom's words and her dad's words as she helped put away the leftover food. She'd heard her mom's views on boarding school before, but never spoken so sharply, and she was amazed at her dad's words. The information about trumpeter swans was interesting, but her dad was usually quiet. Tonight, even though he was nursing one of his headaches, he had spoken more at one time than Bit could remember, except when he was reading, and those words weren't his own.

When offered her choice of helping wash the dishes or going down to shut up the chickens for the night, she chose shutting up the chickens, and for once her sisters didn't argue. They would always rather do inside work than outside work.

As she walked down the path, she swished her arm through the dying horse weeds and Russian thistles that had grown back since her dad last mowed the yard. The crisp air made her wish she'd put on a jacket. Frost would come within the next few nights, she knew, because her dad's birthday had just passed and the weather usually turned cold right after that. The Russian thistles were dry and brittle, and soon, when the wind blew, they would break from the roots and roll across the land spreading their seeds as they went, piling up in fencerows and against the sides of buildings, tumbleweeds.

She thought about her dad, wondering how old he was now. Birthdays were not particularly special in the Warder family. There was never enough money for presents, but her parents always remembered to say happy birthday to each of the girls when they woke up on their birthday, and Anna would bake a cake, but that was all. The kids at school always came in talking about the gifts they'd been given bragging to each other about it. Bit was glad her birthday came in the summer so she never had to tell anyone that she didn't get a present.

She entered the chicken pen, peeking into the door of the coop. The moonlight didn't provide enough light to see inside, but the chickens sat on the tiered roosts shuffling a little. One of them made a sleepy clucking, burring sound. She shut the door, stuck the stick through the hasp on the lock, and hurried back up to the warmth of the house.

4

After supper, Brian Johnson watched *RAWHIDE* on television while his mom clattered dishes in the kitchen and his dad sat in his recliner reading the local paper, which Brian knew his dad had already read the night before, right after the paper came out. When his dad folded the paper, got up and walked out the door, Brian waited a minute before he tiptoed to the window, twitched the curtain aside an inch, and peered out. Bart walked down the path toward the Quonset building with that odd stride he had where his heel bounced up again as soon as it touched the ground. The increasingly more prominent strands of gray in his hair glinted silver beneath the yard light. Brian waited a minute longer before he slipped out to follow.

Bart walked through the big overhead doors into the Quonset, flicked on the light switch, and looked back over his shoulder toward the house, but Brian knew he wouldn't be seen where he stood in the shadows behind the overgrown lilac bushes, even though they had begun dropping their leaves. He was glad their Australian Shepherd dog was gone. Shep—really unique name—hated Brian, probably because Brian hated the dog, but despite their mutual distaste, the dog would have followed and given away Brian's hiding place.

He watched his dad walk farther back into the building, past the big tractor standing on the concrete floor with half its guts torn out. His dad was rebuilding the motor or something, Brian didn't know what. He took no interest in the farm equipment or the farm animals or anything about the farm. He slipped from behind the lilac bushes toward the side of the Quonset, listened a moment. Hearing no sound from within, he slipped through the double doors, along the side of the building between the tractor and the curving wall, avoiding the big pan on the floor, half full of oil and parts put in to soak. He paused at the wall, which jutted out from the side of the Quonset at a right angle. His dad had created a little space there at the back of the building and put in a heater for the cold winter days when he had to work out there. Cautiously, Brian peered around the wall.

Bart stood at the workbench against the far end, his back to Brian, a bottle glinting in his right hand. Brian watched his dad raise the bottle and take a long swallow. Brian pulled his head back, his hand over his mouth to keep from laughing. He had found the bottle months earlier, hidden in the bottom drawer of the workbench behind a bundle of clean rags. Jim Beam, two-thirds full. After Brian drank it down an inch, squinting and choking, he filled it back up with water from the hydrant outside to where he thought it had been before taking a drink. That bottle had gone empty within a week, as Bart drank the increasingly weakened whiskey, but another bottle replaced it, and Brian continued sampling and adding water with each new bottle. This one had less than three inches left in it, and that was likely half water. Bart wouldn't get much relief out of this last bit. Besides the bottle, Brian had also found three magazines in the same drawer that he knew his mother would not appreciate.

Listening, Brian heard nothing from the other side of the wall. Had his dad got out the magazines? Brian risked another peek around the wall. Bart sat on an upturned bucket, his head in his hands, moaning. When he lifted his head suddenly, Brian ducked back again behind the wall, but Bart was facing the side of the building, not directly toward Brian.

"Fuck it, just fuck it. Fuck it all!" Bart snarled and kicked the bucket he had been sitting on. It bounced across and hit the metal wall of the Quonset with a metallic crash. When he heard the sound of his father's footsteps, Brian ran as quietly as he could, but his foot caught the edge of the pan of oil and parts bumping it against the tractor tire with a muted clunk as the parts inside jostled together.

"Who's there? Anyone there?" Bart called out.

Brian ducked under the tractor behind the man-tall tire, hunkering down on the floor, hoping his dad wouldn't notice the oil that had sloshed from the pan onto the concrete floor, but he saw his dad's feet walking toward the front of the building on the opposite side of the tractor. If Bart glanced to his left and down, Brian would be in plain sight. He duck walked under the tractor, trying not to bang his head, over to the other tire, and sat holding his breath. He saw Bart's worn brown cowboy boots slow, then stop as Bart listened.

"Anybody there?" Bart called out again. After a few seconds the boots moved on, the overhead lights went out, and Brian heard the sound of the overhead doors as Bart pulled the chain to lower them.

Brian sat in the dark for a few minutes, waiting until he was sure his dad was inside the house. He rose to a half squat and moved out from beneath the tractor, holding onto the tire for balance. He stood a moment as his eyes adjusted to the dim light coming through the three cobwebbed windows on the Quonset wall. When he heard no further sounds, he stood up, crossed to the unlocked side door, let himself out, and walked quietly back to the house. He peeked through the window into the living room. His dad wasn't sitting in his recliner, so Brian let himself in. *RAWHIDE* was over; the credits rolling, but he sat anyway and watched the next show without really absorbing it. His mother must have gone to bed early, but the kitchen light was still on, his dad sitting at the table with piles of paper scattered before him, frowning as he sorted through them.

Brian knew his dad was worried about money. Bart didn't say that, not even to Brian's mother, but Brian saw his father's lips thin and tighten whenever his mother came through the door burdened with bags full of stuff, mostly clothes, sometimes things for the house—new bath towels, a special pan that she put under the counter and never used, talking in that chirpy voice about all the bargains she had found. Brian didn't understand what the big deal was about his mother buying pretty things. He was proud of her, knew she was the best-dressed woman around, even though he would never tell her so. Tall and thin with rich brown hair, she didn't wear the frumpy cotton house dresses like most of his friends' moms wore, but stepped out in tailored slacks, one of the few women to wear them unless you counted Old Lady Peterson, who appeared in public wearing bib overalls or high waist denim pants, probably salvaged from her dead husband's wardrobe. She wasn't really an old lady, but she wasn't a respectable person either. After her husband died, Mrs. Peterson ran their farm herself, hiring and firing help when she needed it, driving the tractors, slopping the hogs, and failing to go to church. There were rumors that she was having an affair with the husband of the county librarian, a man who seemed to have no visible means of support except his wife's county salary. Brian had overheard the local women talking about Mrs. Peterson the last time the Lady's Aid Club held their monthly meeting at the Johnson house.

Lady's Aid! The name was so silly. The women never aided any one. The membership consisted of wives of the most prosperous local farmers and ranchers with a few wives whose husbands ran small businesses in town, and while the club was supposed to be open to everyone, in reality no one joined unless they were invited. Brian loved it when the meetings were at his house. Each of the women brought a dessert—a pie, a cake, cookies, something—but they all only nibbled because the real treat was the bottle each woman brought buried in the depths of her handbag, and left the treats at the hostess's house. Susan the pig came in for her share, but Brian was always first off the school bus and home fast enough ahead of her that he could hide a good bit of the food, but he had to be careful to eat it or dispose of it. A few months earlier, his mother had found his moldy stash under his bed. There had been words. Brian told her to leave his room alone and quit snooping around. His mother argued that *SOMEBODY* had to clean it, and just as Brian had been close to hitting her, his father intervened. Now his mother stayed out of his room, but he still had to be careful. Sweets drew ants. Ants drew attention.

When the news came on the television, Brian got up and switched it off. He had no interest in current events, local or national, and after the news there was nothing on either channel but a test pattern until six o'clock the next morning. As he went up the stairs to bed, Bart still sat at the kitchen table, shuffling papers.

Brian woke before sunrise, turned over and tried to go back to sleep, but sleep wouldn't come, so he got out of bed, pulled on his jeans and an old pair of lace-up boots, and crept downstairs. The house was quiet. In other seasons his father would be the first one up, dressed and out the door to feed the cattle in winter or get an early start in the alfalfa field in the summer. After a while his mother would get up and cook breakfast, wake up Brian and Susan, and when his father came in from the early work, they all sat at the table and ate together, mostly in silence, except for Susan, who never seemed to understand the value of shutting the hell up.

In this season, out of sync with the rest of the year, Bart slept in, and this year it seemed he slept in later and later. Brian slipped on an old jacket, took the .410 shotgun from the rack behind the door, and walked out into the cool morning as the eastern horizon grew lighter. He strode down the steps and around the back of the house, crunching through the fallen cottonwood leaves, hoping his dad wouldn't insist on Brian raking them up. He imagined the conversation. Bart would put out that same argument that it was about time that Brian earned his keep, and when was he going to take some responsibility. Brian walked north for several minutes to the edge of the Johnson property, the boundary between Johnson land and the wildlife refuge. A seasonal creek divided one from the other with a four-wire fence on the refuge side. Old rotten posts with a few strands of rusty barbed wire still clung to the Johnson side of the creek, something that Bart sometimes commented that he was going to clear out. Someday. Brian stepped over a rusty coil, hoisting the gun to his shoulder as he slid sideways down the steep bank. Walking along the creek bank, he looked for pheasant runs in the tall dry grass. The birds didn't know the fence marked the difference between protection for them and possible death. The refuge was, of course, off limits to hunting. Every year, groups of local hunters with their dogs walked the perimeter, or part of the way around the perimeter of the refuge, hoping some of the fat pheasants would wander outside the protected area. Sometimes they did. Sometimes they nested on the Johnson side of the line. Pheasant season was still a couple of weeks away.

Occasional cottonwoods, dry grass, and a wealth of dry brush lined the creek banks on both sides. Brian manouvered through it, careful not to stumble on hummocks of dried mud heaved up in wetter times over the past year. He came upon an old pheasant nest with a few eggshells from the spring hatch that he had missed. He hoped for an adult pheasant, a cock rooster would be best, better yet one with very long tail feathers. One of the clothing shops in town gave a gift certificate to the hunter who brought in the longest tail feathers. There was a pair of boots in the store that Brian coveted but his dad wouldn't let him buy. He could bury any pheasant he shot today, keeping the tail feathers until after hunting season officially started.

The sun was well up when Brian turned back the way he had come without finding anything, not so much as a jackrabbit or cottontail, but as he was starting to climb the bank on his way back to the house, his foot turned over a small bird, a sparrow, likely dead for a week or more with maggots crawling on it, surprising that maggots could still be active this late in the fall. He picked it up by the feet, looked at it a moment and snickered as he walked back to the house swinging the dead bird in one hand, the shotgun in the other.

His parents were up by then, his father silently drinking coffee at the kitchen table while his mother flipped bacon at the range. Brian dropped the bird at the edge of the porch, walked in, and put the gun away. "Brian? That you? Breakfast is about ready, so go wash up," his mother called.

Well, who else would it be? Susan was staying overnight with one of her bratty little friends. He went to the bathroom and washed the stink of dead bird off his hands, came back and sat down at table. "I really appreciate you rebuilding that tractor engine for me," Bart said. "I'm sure you've got it all together and humming like a top."

"Bart," Mrs. Johnson cautioned as she slipped several slices of crispy bacon onto Brian's plate. "It's a lovely morning to go for a walk." She smiled at her son.

"Yes, it is," Bart countered. "Especially if our son walked down to the Quonset and did a little work."

Brian's ears turned off as his parents' conversation went back and forth. He ate the bacon and two pieces of toast liberally smeared with grape jelly from one of those pretty little jars that his mother liked because they were pretty little jars. Several of them sat in a row on the window sill with bits of dying greenery in each. Starts, she called them. Some kind of violets that she always tried to get rooted in water but they always rotted first. When Bart had polished the last egg yolk from his plate with a piece of toast, he abruptly got up, dropped his plate in the sink with a clatter, and walked out. Mrs. Johnson finished clearing the table.

Out on the porch, Brian looked for his father, but Bart had disappeared probably pretending to work on the tractor while he read his magazines, Brian thought. He listened to his mother washing up the dishes, bent over and retrieved the dead bird. Holding his arm down by his side with the dead bird in his hand, he went back in the house, up the stairs and down the hall to his sister's room at the end. Her door was partially open, the sun coming through the window where the shade was only halfway pulled down. She had a pink ruffled bedspread. Pink painted walls with posters of kittens. Dolls wearing pink dresses on the bed. He flipped back the bedspread, lifted the pillow, and deposited the maggoty bird on the sheet, replaced the pillow and smoothed the bedspread over top. "Surprise, surprise, surprise," he said.

5

Bit woke to the sounds of "Polka Parade" playing on the radio.

> *I DON'T WANT HER, YOU CAN HAVE HER,*
> *SHE'S TOO FAT FOR ME, OH, SHE'S TOO FAT FOR ME.*

She knew her dad would be standing at the washstand wearing the dark blue bib overalls that he called his dress up clothes, one strap hanging down as he shaved and listened to the music. It was Saturday and they would be going to town, the entire family to do their weekly grocery shopping. Tight Shoe Day, she'd heard people say, mostly the men who owned the shops in town—Berkman's Hardware, Jackson Clothiers—those people. An old joke, it assumed that poor farmers in the area went barefoot during the week, only putting on their shoes when they came to town on Saturday. It wasn't true. The poorest farmers might have only one pair of shoes, leather cracked and worn, but they wore those shoes seven days a week. Farmers and ranchers were classed differently with farmers considered lower on the socioeconomic scale unless the farmer was lucky and successful. Only a few farmer families had that status. The rest of the farmers took out mortgages on their land in the spring to buy seed and fertilizer, counting on a good crop in the late summer to pay off the mortgage, live through the winter, and have a little ahead so they wouldn't have to take out another mortgage the next spring. For most of them that rosy dream never came true. Their crops got the rust fungus when it rained too much, dried up when it didn't rain, or got hailed out in one or more of the many summer storms, so they could only pay the interest on the mortgage in the fall and maybe a tiny bit on the principal, and renewed the mortgage for the following year. Tom Warder used to be a small farmer, one of those the townies sneeringly meant when they referred to Saturdays as Tight Shoe Day, until he got offered a temporary job on the wildlife refuge. He had struggled on for a couple of years longer trying to farm part time, but eventually when his job was converted to permanent employment at the refuge, he gave up farming the 160 acres of marginal land that his family had been awarded through the Indian Allotment Act a generation earlier. He still owned the land, couldn't sell it, so he leased it to Bart Johnson since Tom's land adjoined Johnson's on the west side, the poor side. Tom's relatives used to own land on the good side, the wet side of Johnson's land allotted to them, but they had lost it when eminent domain took it to create the refuge. Now Tom worked for the same refuge that took his relative's land, a wage earner with a salary barely enough to keep ends together let alone tie up the ends with comfort, but the job was secure.

Bit knew this family history, though most of it had happened when she was too young to remember. She did remember one thing: a summer hailstorm, her mother holding a pillow up against the screenless window, fearing the giant hailstones would shatter the glass, but the window held. Her father, sitting at the kitchen table, his head in his hands, her mother saying maybe the storm went around their field. But it didn't.

Bit rolled over in bed expecting to bump up against one of her sisters who shared the bed with her, but they were already up. She sprang out of bed, dressed quickly, and went to the kitchen. Her mom was just putting a platter of pancakes on the table. The family ate quickly, and while Tom checked the oil in their '56 Ford, then checked the tires, Bit and her sisters helped with the dishes while their mother changed her dress and gathered the pail of three dozen eggs to sell in town. The hens laid more than the family could eat, so Anna sold the excess to the local grocery store. The money wasn't much, just twenty-five cents a dozen, but better than letting the eggs go to waste for nothing. Get the money while she could, Anna always said, because when cold clamped down, the hens would quit laying one after the other until they'd be lucky to get two eggs a day.

Jackson had no stoplights and no need for them, except maybe on Saturday nights when the teenagers drove their cars up and down the three blocks of main street, turning a U at the west end in front of the Presbyterian church. Fifteen miles from the Warders' little village of Taylor, the dirt road between the two wound here and there past a couple of farmsteads, uphill and down, passing fields of stubble, the grain harvested weeks ago, and ready for the fall tilling—summer fallowing it was called. One farmer on a tractor waved at the Warder car when it passed, the light breeze kicking up the dust as the discs of the trailing implement dug into the short, dry grain stalks, flipping them under to provide organic material for next year's crop.

Tom Warder waved back, a little vein in his temple throbbing, his eyes turning quickly from the farmer back to the road. His wife reached across and clasped his hand briefly as it rested on the steering wheel. In the back seat, the three girls scuffled over who was taking up more than her fair share of the space. Anna Warder responded in the classic way of most parents: "If your dad has to stop this car to settle you three down, you won't like what happens next. But," she added, "you break any of those eggs, and you'll be in even more trouble."

The girls responded in the classic way as well, whispering and elbowing each other the last few miles until the family car reached the outskirts of town, passed the Jackson Auction Barn where cattle, hogs, and a few sheep were sold every Wednesday at noon. They passed the newly built Jackson Motel with its eleven units that nobody except traveling salesmen and livestock buyers ever stayed in, and at the junction where the highway continued west, Tom turned right, drove a couple of blocks north, then another left onto the main street.

Most of the parking spots in the town center were occupied with farm pickups, dusty and muddy because most folks didn't care much about a spit shined car, but there were a few sedans as well, family cars mostly driven only to town and church on Sundays. Tom found a spot in front of the courthouse, pulled in and stopped, shifting to get his wallet from his back pocket. He handed Anna two tens and a five-dollar bill to buy groceries and, reaching into the front pocket of his bib overalls, handed each of the girls a dime. A candy bar cost a nickel and a pop was a dime. Her two younger sisters always debated and debated about whether to buy a pop or two candy bars, but it was never a question for Bit. She bought one candy bar and saved the other nickel. Back home in a washed-up mayonnaise jar she had $2.85. She was saving to buy a horse, but she knew that might take years. She had her eye on a lady's cowboy hat in the window of Samson's Dry Goods. The white straw body of the hat looked just like the men's summer cowboy hats, but the ladies' version had a blue hatband ribbon that trailed down the back. The price tag read $3.98. Bit was afraid summer would be over and the hats would all be gone, sold or withdrawn or something, before she could save up enough nickels to buy one.

Anna Warder put the cash in her wallet and the wallet back in her purse just as someone leaned in the open window on the passenger side. "Ain't it a beautiful morning, Anna?" The woman had a crooked smile but an infectious one.

Anna smiled back. "It certainly is, Mary, but it started off chilly. We had a light frost last night," she said as she opened the car door. "That's the last of the garden, but maybe it will bring on the beans. The vines are loaded. How's your garden?"

After the bean bushes had been picked over two or three times for fresh green beans, and Anna had canned several quarts for winter use, she left the last crop to dry, collected the pods, shelled them out, saved some for planting next year and some for boiling up with ham. The ones they'd had for supper the previous night were an early gathering of the crop.

"Oh, my garden's been gone long since. What the bugs didn't get, the hail did," Mary Bechtol said, waving her arms so the flabby flesh of her upper arm jiggled and flopped beneath the short-sleeved cotton dress. A big woman but hardworking, so you'd think she would be trim and muscular. She milked four cows every morning by hand, and her fingers and hands were strong from the work, but the rest of her flesh drooped on her bones. Anna privately thought Mary had a hormone problem, and so did Mary's other friends, but nothing was to be done about it and Mary was a good sort.

Mary motioned to the wide bench on the courthouse lawn. "Come sit with me a bit before you go do your shopping," she said.

"I will, but first I need to turn in my eggs at Andy's Market," Anna said. "Walk down with me."

Tom got out of the car folding the seat forward. The girls scrambled out, Connie clawing her way over Bit who had sat in the middle. Patty emerged first, taking off at a trot up the street toward Jackson Drug and the soda fountain.

Anna turned back toward the car. "Hey, you girls! Don't be getting into anything, you hear?" They heard but didn't acknowledge.

Bit sighed and mumbled, "Okay."

Tom Warder caught her by the shoulder. He looked directly into her eyes and said, "Mind your mother, now, Bitsy."

Bit pulled away. "Don't call me that."

"Meet back here in a couple of hours, okay?" Anna called but got no response. The words were a formality said every Saturday, so they all knew the routine. The girls would find a friend from school, sit at the soda fountain and gossip, examine the latest Tussy makeup hanging from pegs on the side wall opposite the soda fountain counter and complain that their mothers wouldn't let them wear lipstick yet. Or shave their legs.

Tom walked two blocks to the far end of the business district where the Frontier gas station boasted two pumps, an ethyl and a regular. Doc Paine had run the gas station in the old run-down building for twenty years or more. His cramped little office inside served as a gathering place for men from the country and a few townies for almost as long as the station had been operating. The men bought bottles of lemon soda from the cranky pop dispenser, peanuts from the rack on the counter, dumped the peanuts into the pop, waited until the peanuts swelled a bit, and downed the mess over a period of an hour or so while they discussed politics, the weather, and gossiped about their neighbors. The better sort of men—ranchers, the wealthier farmers, the town's business owners—gathered in the bar across from the two-lane bowling alley in the basement of the Legion auditorium, sipping their beers or something stronger while they talked about politics, the weather, and gossiped about their neighbors.

Tom Warder enjoyed a beer once in a great while, but he never felt comfortable in the Legion. Most of the Indians of the area didn't. They were welcome as long as they were spending money, but more than a few times an Indian who had only had a couple of beers had been accosted by the sheriff or one of his deputies as the Indian came up the steps from the bar, accused of drunken disorderly, arrested, and put to work on the city garbage route. Even if they had the cash to pay off their fines, the sheriff never allowed it. For Tom a cold beer wasn't worth the risk even though he doubted it would happen to him. He had earned the respect if not the friendship of the local elite. He took care of his family, worked hard, and minded his own business.

His steps slowed when he saw that Old Man Bennie Black Hawk was inside sitting on one of the two battered folding chairs. Bennie had to be eighty, maybe more, or maybe he looked older than his years. He was a kind old man, had seen a lot of history between his own Indian people and the whites who moved into Dakota territory at the end of the late-nineteenth century when his people had been moved onto reservations and their vast stretches of prairie land confiscated through shady treaties that had opened up the land for white settlements. Then the reservations had been broken up by the Allotment Act, each Indian deeded a piece of the land and the huge number of leftover acres sold off. Bennie's allotment had been one of the pieces taken later by eminent domain to create the wildlife refuge where Tom worked, and he never let Tom forget it. In his quiet way old Bennie accused Tom of being a sell out Indian, that Tom should be fighting against white men like Crazy Horse had done. Tom's response was always the same even though phrased a bit differently every time: "Even Crazy Horse gave up when he saw that there were many, many more white men than Indians, and those white men had guns, more guns and better guns." Of course, Bennie's response was: "Then you take it to law. If you don't have guns, you use law." Tom came back with "Law doesn't work either. Ask the Cherokees. They tried that, and they won. John Marshall's Supreme Court said they won, but Andrew Jackson said, 'John Marshall has given his opinion. Now let's see him enforce it,' and the Cherokees lost anyway. White people have more guns than Indians, and they have more law too."

That shut Bennie up, sort of, but he would continue mumbling objections for a few minutes longer before he changed the subject, usually to tribal politics. Bennie might be an old die-hard, never give up kind of man, but he was a canny politician. Anyone who wanted to serve in an elected tribal office needed Bennie on his side because the old man knew about horse-trading—get someone to vote for you and you vote for something they want. Nothing much changed for the better with tribal administration, but Bennie's people kept a firm grip on power.

Well, what the hell, Tom thought. He wasn't going to let an old man's favorite subject of argument spoil his Saturday morning raw jaw with his friends. There wouldn't be many more of these warm fall days before he would be lucky to buck the snowbanks to town, get groceries, and scoot back home again. He quickened his footsteps.

Bit followed her sisters down to the drugstore. Connie and Patty sat at the counter with a couple of their friends from school, turning themselves around and around on the red vinyl topped stools while they tried to make up their minds whether to buy a soda or a pair of candy bars.

"Hey, Bit," Connie called out, "lend us a nickel apiece so we can each have a candy bar and a soda."

"Why would I give you two my money?" Bit said.

"Because you've got a whole jar full of nickels at home in your dresser drawer, and I bet you brought some of them with you," Patty said.

Bit narrowed her eyes. "How do you know about my jar of nickels?"

"Because we had to fold and put away the clean clothes last week, when *YOU* were supposed to do it, but you took off down to the creek," Patty said.

"Listen, you two little shits," Bit said, grabbing Patty by the wrist and squeezing until she felt the wrist bones crunching together. "Keep your little grub hooks out of my stuff. Got it?"

"Oww, oww, let go or I'll tell Mom," Patty cried out.

Bit let go. "Besides, you think I'd carry all that cash around with me?"

She walked down the aisle of hair care products to the back of the store, to the racks in front of the pharmacy counter where comic books were displayed. She liked them all, *SUPER MAN* and *SUPER GIRL*, but especially the Donald Duck ones that had stories about Richie Rich living a life she could hardly imagine. Red-haired, freckle-faced Paul O'Brien stood at the racks, idly turning them around.

"Hi, Bit," he said with a grin. Paul was one of the three O'Brien brothers who used to attend the same country school as Bit, but this year his mother had moved herself and the boys into a nice house in town. Rumor was that Mrs. O'Brien had left her husband because even though he was a prosperous rancher, he was also a mean drunk who beat her. She was Catholic so she put up with it for years, but finally Father Schmidt had conceded that Mrs. O'Brien could live apart from her husband without committing a sin as long as she didn't file for divorce.

The O'Brien brothers got a weekly allowance of fifty cents, and Paul, like his brothers, spent most of it on comic books, which he read only once before passing them on to Bit. She had stacks of them under the bed she shared with her sisters. They were not allowed to touch her comic books under pain of death, she told them with a low, mean growl, which they took seriously. Bit read them multiple times. Especially the ones with Richie Rich as a character.

"Want to go play pool?" Paul asked.

"Yeah, but I promised my dad I'd stay out of the pool hall. I got into a lot of trouble the last time when someone tattled."

"Your dad never goes in there, so how would he know?"

Bit hesitated. "But if someone sees me and tattles . . ."

"Here," Paul said, pulling off his green John Deere cap. He held it out to Bit. "Just like we always do. Put your hair up under the cap and no one will know you're a girl."

They entered Bob's Pool Hall through the side door that opened onto the alley. Four pool tables sat in the middle with one more in an alcove in the back. The other side of the back was the men's restroom. Bob leaned on the counter at the front where he sold snacks and served free coffee. Most of the men snuck in a can of beer, but Bob never said anything about their beer as long as they were discreet about it. A couple of men leaned on the other side of the counter having an argument with Bob over the upcoming general election even though they were all Republicans who would vote for Nixon no matter what. Another ten or more men stood around, some of them playing pool while the others sat at the mismatched tables and chairs along the far wall. No one was at the pool table in the back. They had all complained to Bob at one time or another that the table in the back wasn't level. He argued with them. They argued back and boycotted that table unless the others were all occupied. If a man lost, he could always argue that the game wasn't fair because the table wasn't level.

Paul led Bit to the table in the alcove, where she stood with her back to the room. "You got the money to pay for a game?" she asked. A game cost fifteen cents. Paul carried three comic books that cost fifteen cents each, so he should only have a nickel left.

"Sure. I swiped the change out of my mom's purse while she was taking a shower," Paul said with a grin.

Bit had a good day. Within ten minutes she had taken most of the shots, putting the ball she indicated in the pocket she stated, while Paul had scratched twice. A few minutes later she had won the game. Paul didn't have enough change for a second game. Bit was not going to chip in her dime.

"Hey, kid!"

Paul and Bit started out the side door, but Paul turned back when the man called out again. Bit kept her face toward the door. If she got caught in the pool hall and kicked out, she'd really get it from both her dad and her mom. "Not you, kid. Your friend in the John Deere cap," said a big burly man with a red beard who might have been Paul's father, but wasn't.

Bit turned around slowly. "You're pretty good with that pool cue. Care to give a grown man a shot?"

Bit hesitated.

"Come on, kid. You win, I'll give you a buck. How about it? Think you can beat me? I doubt it."

Paul nudged Bit. She took a deep breath and said, "All right, mister. Rack 'em up."

Bit won the game in less than ten minutes. It was like magic. Time flowed like honey as she made shot after shot. When the game was over the man handed Bit a crumpled dollar bill. "You won fair and square, kid," he said sheepishly. "How about a rematch? I win, you get another dollar. You win; you give me back my dollar."

Again, Bit hesitated, but before she could agree, Richard Packer, the man she knew owned and ran the local steak house, spoke up. "How about giving a real expert a chance? Come on, kid. I bet I can whip you up one side and down the other."

Bit shook her head. "I was just lucky that time. I can't win again," she said.

"Aww, come on, kid," Packer urged.

Paul grinned and nodded at her to go ahead.

"Three dollars," Bit said. "I win, you pay me three dollars. I lose, you get one dollar."

"What kind of a deal is that?" Packer demanded.

Bit shrugged and started for the door.

One of the other men started clucking like a chicken. The other took it up until the place sounded like Bit's mother's henhouse when one of the chickens laid an egg.

"Okay, okay, kid. Three bucks if you win, one buck if I win," Packer conceded.

The men gathered around the back table as Packer racked the balls, and the game began with the same result as before. Bit tried not to grin as she folded the bills and tucked them in her jeans pocket. Outside in the alley Paul pounded her on the back. "You sure showed those guys," he crowed.

"Shut up, shut up, shut up! If any of those guys tell my dad, I'll get an ass beating," Bit said.

Paul sneered. "No, you won't. Your dad never whips you. He just gives you that funny look," he said.

"That look is worse than any beating. And you know what happens after the look? I get hauled over to my grannie's next door, and she makes me listen to one of her old stories."

"Really? What kind of stories? That's got to be better than an ass whipping."

"You haven't had to listen to those stories."

"What's so bad about her stories?"

Bit thought a minute. "They're mostly about Inktomi, the spider, and how he does something bad and it turns out all wrong," she said. "I'm supposed to learn a lesson from that. I never will."

"Still doesn't sound all that bad to me," Paul said.

Bit wondered if the rumors about his drunken father were true and maybe he beat the boys besides beating up on Paul's mother.

Back inside the pool hall, the red-bearded man asked Bob, the owner, "Whose boy is that?"

"Nobody's," Bob said with a smug little grin.

"That's stupid. Kid has to have a father," Packer said.

"Oh, there's a father all right, but the kid is a girl." Bob polished the old wooden counter with a dirty rag, his grin wider.

"You're shitting me," Packer said. "You lying bastard."

"Not lying," Bob said, not very happy about being called a liar. "That's Betsy Warder, Tom's oldest girl. She and that O'Brien kid have been sneaking in here to play pool for months now. She's pretty good."

"How come I never noticed before? How come you let a girl in here?" the red-bearded man asked.

Bob shrugged his shoulders. "Kid never bothers anybody. Wouldn't have bothered you, either, if you didn't know she was a girl."

"She's gonna be a hell-raiser in a couple of years," Packer said.

The room was quiet for a few minutes before the laughter started. "You guys got your asses handed to you by a little girl!"

"Stop it. Everyone knows that pool table ain't level."

Back at the drugstore, Bit added in her head the four dollars she had won onto the $2.85 she had in the mayonnaise jar at home plus the ten cents of her allowance still in her other pocket. She had enough. She could buy that ladies' cowboy hat if she wanted to, but maybe she'd save a little while longer to buy a horse.

6

Bart went to bed early and had only just got to that place of neither sleeping nor dreaming, when the mind jumbles images and conversations into a fractured puzzle that seems all quite normal as it plays out in the brain. The screams he heard folded the sound into his dream until Betty shook him awake. "Bart. Bart! You need to come straighten out your son right now," she said.

Bart rolled onto his side, slid his legs off the bed, pushed himself into a sitting position. He resented the wake-up. He had drank just enough Jim Beam so he wouldn't have a hangover in the morning but his mind would quit running around like a rat in a barrel. The figures on his bank statement wouldn't matter and the approaching date on his bank mortgage would recede into a meaningless date on the calendar, sometime after Thanksgiving but before Christmas. Now it all came back. The family savings was gone. The checking account balance crept lower with every statement. November 30th would come.

"Bart! You've got to do something," she said, as she stood in front of him, giant pink curlers creating a monster shadow of her head on the wall.

"What the hell is the matter?" Bart said, louder than he intended. He stood a bit unsteady, pushed Betty aside, and walked to the door, tugging at his blue pinstriped boxer shorts.

Susan sat in the hall outside her room, her knees pulled up to her chin, sobbing loudly.

Bart paused, squatted beside her and touched her shoulder. She jerked away, screaming. "Honey, what's the matter? Did you have a nightmare?"

Susan turned her body against the wall away from her father.

"Susan? I can't fix it, if you don't tell me what's wrong!"

He heard the soft padding of Betty's slippers on the hardwood floor. When he looked around, she had her arms crossed, an angry expression on her face.

"Susan! Enough! Stop your caterwauling and tell me what the hell is the matter!" Bart shouted. He felt like slapping her, felt like he often did: a stranger in the family who was never told anything but expected to fix everything.

Susan lifted an arm and pointed at her room, muttering something unintelligible.

Bart turned to his wife and said, "If no one is going to tell me what the hell the problem is, I'm going back to bed. You sort it out!" He knew if he went back to bed, he would've lost that little boost into sleep. He would lay there long after Betty began that soft snoring, like a kitten purring.

"Just check under her pillow!" Betty snarled.

"No, it's not there anymore. I knocked it onto the floor," Susan said clearly through the blubber and the snot.

"Just go look!" Betty said.

Bart paused at the door and flicked on the light. The pink assaulted his vision as if he had fallen through a pond and settled to the bottom as a pink curtain was flung over the surface. He detected a faint smell of decay.

The bird, barely recognizable as a bird, mauled into a mess of feathers, dried blood, and stench lay on the floor beside Susan's bed, a pillow flung down beside it. He bent over for a closer look

A single maggot wormed around in the bird's breast. He felt the whiskey in his belly wanting to erupt. He turned his head away. "Bring me an old towel," he called out.

"What?" Betty called back.

"Jesus, do I have to do everything myself? Bring me a goddamned old towel, a rag, a torn-up old sheet, anything!"

Did a bird fly into Susan's room somehow, lie down and die? He stood up, pulled aside the curtain, lifted the roller shade, and slid the window sash up. Cold air rushed in. The screen was intact, a bit rusty in spots, but he found no holes or gaps. Somebody put the bird in Susan's room. Bart knew who. He turned as a faded no-color rag was flung into the room. He wrapped the bird in the rag, maggot and all.

Out in the hall, Betty knelt beside her daughter holding her while Susan sobbed quietly. "It's okay, honey, your dad is taking care of it. No more dead bird," Betty said.

"I'm never sleeping in there again. I hate that room!"

"Oh, no, you love your pink room. I tell you what, you can sleep in the spare room with me tonight, and tomorrow we'll wash your sheets and pillowcases and it will be like it never happened," Betty soothed.

Bart walked past the two, holding the rag-wrapped bird at arm's length, down the stairs. He unlocked the back door, carried the mess out to the barrel where they burned their trash, lifted the wire mesh cover and dumped it in, old rag and all. Somewhere in the dark an owl hooted. His hands stank. He washed them with dish soap at the kitchen sink, letting the hot water run to flush out the sink afterward. Brian.

Susan's sobbing had halted as Bart pounded back up the steps, bellowing, "Brian! Brian! Get out here!"

Brian appeared in the door to his room at the end of the hall, standing on the threshold, leaning against the doorjamb. He was still fully dressed: jeans, T-shirt, flannel shirt with cuffs turned up, old lace-up hiking boots on his feet. Bart took long steps down the hallway, stood in front of Brian, and glared at him. "What the hell did you do that for?" Bart demanded.

Brian's face was expressionless. He said, "Do what?"

Bart poked a finger in the kid's skinny chest. At sixteen Brian was nearly as tall as Bart. In the dim light the pupils of Brian's eyes looked like dark pools. "You know goddamned well what I'm talking about," Bart said.

Brian shifted from one foot to the other, leaning on the opposite side of the door. After a minute he flung his arms down at his sides, hands in fists, leaned into his dad's face and yelled, "It was a joke! Just a fucking joke! No one around here has any sense of humor!"

Bart slapped him across the face, so unexpected that the kid's head cracked against the doorjamb. "A joke! A joke! That's the least funny thing I ever saw. That's sick! What the hell is the matter with you?"

A trickle of blood ran from Brian's nose. He dabbed at it with a finger, wiped it on his shirt front, and lowered his head to his chest. More blood dripped onto his shirt, onto the floor. He turned his head sideways, a little smile curving up the corners of his mouth as his eyes looked up at his father.

Cold chills chased themselves down Bart's spine. The kid didn't look human, but like a character from one of the scary movies they showed at the Inland Theater in town around Halloween. He never had any interest in those, but they didn't scare him either. His own kid scared him. What happened to the pudgy baby boy they brought home from the hospital? The little boy toddling around in his first pair of cowboy boots? When did this monster appear? Bart hated himself for wanting a son. He had wanted children, a son, maybe two boys, but this kid was not what he planned. He wanted a boy who took an interest in the land, went with him to the Farmers' Co-op in town, went over figures with him to figure out the yield in tons per acre of alfalfa, how much they should keep for their own cattle, what they could afford to sell. After he was about three years old, Brian never had a single second of interest in the farm, or the animals they raised. He never felt the surge of life that Bart felt when the first calf was born. Brian went to the cattle auction barn with Bart a couple of times, but he fidgeted; he demanded a pop; he cracked his knuckles over and over; he disappeared without explanation.

Brian laughed a low, nasty chuckle.

Bart grabbed Brian by the front of his flannel shirt, dragged him down the hall. He wanted to throw the kid down the stairs. He wanted to stomp the little bastard into the throw rug at the bottom until his head looked like the dead bird planted in Susan's room, but Betty stood at the bottom, her hands over mouth as if she were blowing into them to warm them. He dragged Brian down the stairs, the kid unresisting, his feet only touching about every other step, through the hall and out the front door with Betty calling after him, "Bart, don't!"

The yard light cast a blue-white light. This late in the season not a single moth circled. The evening air was cool, but not cold enough for frost. Heavy dew had settled on Bart's black Chevy pickup, on Betty's new red Impala. The Quonset loomed darkly across the graveled driveway, beyond the yard light and, next to that, the new-just-this-past-spring hog house, really a farrowing barn that Bart had gone into debt to build a year ago. He planned to diversify, raise a few hogs, but then he decided to go in big. He bought a hundred gravid sows, fed them up and farrowed them out in the hog house. The building was built up to date with modern concrete floors and faucets to hook up the hoses and wash the shit out. He'd sold the hogs, sows, and piglets a week ago, what offspring there had been. Each of the sows had farrowed out an average of ten pigs, but eight of the ten had died of some mysterious hog disease; the bottom fell out of the hog market and he sold the sows and the pigs at a loss. He'd meant to give the hog house a final hosing out but couldn't bring himself to step foot in the place. The smell of hog shit reminded him of the shit he'd dropped himself into. He told himself that as the weather grew colder, the smell would dissipate. He'd clean it out then.

He stopped at the graveled driveway with Brian's shirt still wadded up in his fist. The kid gasped and breathed fast but didn't fight back. Bart dragged him across the gravel and down to the hog house, through the aluminum gate, switching on the overhead lights. The place still stank. At the first farrowing stall Bart opened the half door and flung Brian inside. The kid staggered, righting himself against the far wall.

"Tomorrow when you get home from school, I want your ass out here. I want you behind a shovel and a hose cleaning out this barn," Bart said. "And don't think you're getting out of school tomorrow either. I want you waiting at the stop when the school bus pulls up."

Brian's nose had stopped bleeding, but the blood trail between his nose and his mouth gleamed a dark maroon scab color in the light from the overhead bulb.

In a conversational tone of voice, Brian said, "I've been meaning to ask, Dad. Can I have the pickup to go to the football game next Friday? It's Homecoming you know."

Bart stepped forward, grabbed Brian again and flung him into a deep pile of aging hog shit at the side of the small pen. When Brian started to get up, Bart leaned over and shoved Brian's face into the half dried shit. "What do you think of that? Huh? Funny? Big joke? How about a bite?"

It took him a minute to realize that Betty was tugging at his arm, trying to drag him away from the kid, now curled into a fetal position on the cement floor.

"Bart, Bart, stop it! Stop it, you'll kill him!"

Bart slowly relaxed, stepped back to the door of the pen. Betty ducked under Bart's arm, went into the farrowing stall and, leaning over Brian, helped him to his feet, wiping the shit from his face. Bart stood aside as Betty walked Brian out of the pen, out into the corridor, out the door and onto the driveway, gravel crunching beneath Brian's hunting boots. Betty still wore her bedroom slippers.

Bart watched them cross the driveway, go up the sidewalk, climb the steps to the front porch, and disappear inside. He shut off the lights, turned and walked over to the Quonset.

At breakfast the next morning, Susan asked, "Mom, how did that bird get under my pillow? Did it just fly in there, crawl into my bed and die?" She had paused with a spoonful of oatmeal halfway to her mouth.

Brian snickered.

Bart put his fork down and stared at Brian, as the smile faded from his face. He crunched a strip of bacon loudly, bouncing a knee so it bumped the table leg.

"Stop it," Bart said.

"Mom? What about that dead bird?"

Betty patted Susan's wrist. "Don't worry about it, Honey. It's just one of those things. It won't happen again," she said.

"No, it certainly won't," Bart said, his voice stern while he stared at Brian, who picked up another strip of bacon.

"I just love hogs," Brian said.

When the two kids had left on the school bus, Bart finished his last cup of coffee as Betty cleaned up the kitchen. "I'll be going in to town in a little bit," he remarked.

"Oh. Well, you'd better be back in time for an early lunch. The girls are coming over for club this afternoon at one o'clock. I'll have something in the refrigerator for you," Betty said.

Bart hated it when Betty was the hostess for club, as she called the monthly Lady's Aid meeting. He hated the women sitting around pretending to do something useful while they drank iced tea, liberally laced with bourbon or whatever they put in it. None of them smoked, and he was glad of that. Real ladies don't smoke, but neither should they drink alcohol. Well, maybe a little spiked punch at the co-op Christmas party. He didn't particularly like sweets either, and he especially didn't like the skimpy lunches Betty prepared on club day. Usually one of those lunches was a bologna sandwich and a little pile of potato chips on a paper plate carefully plastic-wrapped and stuck in the refrigerator, and supper wasn't the meat and potatoes that a working man needed but the sweets the ladies left behind while Betty went to bed early with a headache. Bart already felt a headache coming on, but arguing with his wife wasn't worth the trouble.

He got a shower, put on his best gray dress pants, white shirt, and black boots, took the key from the hook beside the door, and drove off in his black pickup. It was Monday, so there shouldn't be many people in the bank, just a few local businessmen depositing their Saturday receipts, but no farmers or ranchers in to talk to the loan officer. They usually came in on Wednesdays, when they were in town anyway to sit in the bleachers at the cattle auction and gossip, which was why Bart decided to come in on Monday. This year his calf crop had only hit 85 percent—that is, eighty-five calves born to every one hundred cows when a rancher needed to hit 95 percent or higher to make money. Only 85 percent calf crop, a down market for spring feeder calves and a total failure of his hog venture for which Bart had taken out a mortgage for the first time. Every other year, he'd made enough money over the season that he had never had to take out a loan.

He angled his pickup into a parking spot in front of Jackson National Bank. Only five other cars were parked on the side street, and two of those were bank employees. He didn't recognize the other three as belonging to people he knew, and since they were sedans and not pickups, he doubted if there were any farmers or ranchers in the bank. The only bank in the county, Franklin Moorhead had chartered it forty years earlier, but after a heart attack three years previously, his two sons, Richard and Jerry Don, ran it now, both of them acting as loan officers. The two were so different no one would guess at a glance that they were related.

Richard, tall and dark-haired, dressed in boots and wore a big hat, was jovial and easygoing, generous in allowing local farmers and some few ranchers to pay only the interest and renew their loans for another year. Richard hunted pheasant every fall on Bart's property, belonged to the Masonic Lodge with Bart, and never seemed out of sorts. Jerry Don was short, fat, and balding with a permanent scowl. He fancied himself a bit above anyone local, and every year he took his family to Omaha to a performance of the symphony. The symphony, of all things. Bart had heard tales about Jerry Don's reluctance to renew loans, hemming and hawing when someone asked to do it. No one ever said Jerry Don was unfair; he did renew the loans, but he made the borrower feel like a sinner who got into heaven by mistake. You never knew which one of the men would be available on any given day. There were rumors of bitter rivalry between the two brothers, rumors that each one wanted to be the sole heir to the family banking business and that their father, with his health conditions, wasn't long for this earth. Richard had approved Bart's loan. He didn't want to deal with Jerry Don. He couldn't tell by the cars parked out front which one was in the bank today because they lived on State Street just two blocks from the bank and walked to work.

Taking a deep breath, he opened his pickup door and walked into the bank. Just inside to the right in a corner stood a stuffed polar bear up on its hind legs. The thing must've been seven feet tall, and it served a very useful purpose; besides speaking to the power of Richard, the beast scared little kids into behaving themselves while their parents were doing their banking business. Richard had bagged it on an ice floe in Alaska a couple of years earlier, a hunting trip that Bart would loved to have taken but didn't feel he was prosperous enough—yet—to afford. He wondered now if he would ever get to bag a bear.

"You wouldn't believe it," Richard had said. "We took a helicopter out to the ice. The guide spotted a bear and the pilot set the chopper down. I shot the damned beast from inside the chopper, never even set foot on the ice. The guide and his helpers winched the thing aboard and we lifted off. I swear we weren't on the ice floe for more than twenty minutes, half an hour at most. Damnedest thing. I thought it would be more exciting."

Bart would love to have been let down like that.

Except for Barbara Kelly, who ran a local dress shop, and an Indian woman with two little kids in tow, there was no one at the teller windows and no one sat in the row of seats outside Richard's and Jerry Don's offices. He approached the teller windows as the Indian woman and her kids left. Angie Wicker, head teller and office manager, got up from her desk reluctantly, as if Bart was the least important customer in town. At thirty-five she kept her figure trim, her clothing conservative, and her makeup correct, but she was well on her way to being an old maid. Maybe that condition contributed to the permanent sour look on her face.

"I'd like to see Richard," Bart said.

"Mr. Richard is out of town this week, but Mr. Jerry Don is in. I'll tell him you're here," she said, lifting the access panel in the counter and walking through, her black high heels clicking on the stone tiled floor.

"Never mind—" Bart started to say, but Angie was already leaning around the open door to Jerry Don's office. She carried on a murmured conversation, then turned to Bart and called out, "Mr. Jerry Don will see you now," like she was a receptionist in a doctor's office and Bart was a patient with venereal disease.

Bart took off his white straw cowboy hat as he stepped into Jerry Don's office. Jerry Don fussed with papers on his desk, moving them from one pile to another and back again, snatching one set of papers back, scrutinizing them as if they held the secret to everlasting life, pretending he didn't see Bart come in.

"Jerry Don," Bart said without any pleasantries. He should have begun with some small talk, he knew, but he couldn't stand the fat little toad and the feeling seemed mutual.

"Bart, good to see you," Jerry Don said, looking up with a brilliant smile. "What brings you to see me on this lovely fall day?"

Bart sat in one of the two leather upholstered chairs in front of Jerry Don's dark wooden desk. The thing was massive, like a coffin in the middle of the room. He turned his hat around and around in his hands. He felt like a kid hauled before the preacher to explain why he said that word in Bible school class.

"I usually deal with Richard on these matters," Bart began, thinking he might put off this conversation until Richard was back at work.

"Oh, Bart. You know, this is a family business. Whatever Richard knows, I know as well. Either of us can adequately address your—" Here he paused, before continuing, "address your particular—concerns."

Bart gazed at one of the pair of windows in the wall behind Jerry Don's desk. The hedge outside masked any real view of the street. The little bastard knew Bart's dilemma, had to know. Everyone in the entire town, hell, the entire county knew about Bart's big fling on hogs, knew about the disease that had killed most of the baby pigs, knew Bart's calf crop turned out much less than expected, that both the hog and cattle markets were down, and knew that Bart had a loan with Jackson State Bank that he couldn't repay, not this year, maybe not for the foreseeable future. Bart had come to the bank on an off day, not because his money problems were secret but because he didn't want the people he met on the street, at church, at the co-op, to see him grovel to the bank. They'd know about it, but Bart could ignore that knowledge if he didn't have to see it in their faces on the day he did the groveling. Jerry Don knew all the particulars, probably even figured out why Bart was here on a Monday, but he wanted to make Bart squirm. Well, he was getting his wish. Bart took a breath and looked directly at Jerry Don's old-fashioned eyeglasses. "I came in to discuss my loan. It's not due until November 30th, but I thought it best I address the situation early," Bart began, and continued, "I've had a tough year, so I thought I'd pay the interest and renew—"

Jerry Don held up a hand. "It's been a tough year for a lot of folks in Jackson town. And Jackson County. Why, I expect we will have half the farmers for miles around sitting in those chairs out there, waiting to discuss continuing their loans. You have company," Jerry Don said.

Bart didn't want to "have company"—not that kind.

Jerry Don tilted his leather chair back, folding his hands across the top of his belly. "I expect you're here about your loan with us. I assure you, it's not a problem. I'll have Angie draw up a new loan agreement. You can come back this afternoon and sign it." He tilted his chair back forward, his earnest eyes on Bart's face. "Unless you're here to pay it off?"

Bart kept a neutral expression on his face. From out in the lobby he heard the booming voice of Gary Kendall, the most successful farmer in three counties and the most vulgar in the language he used, the ideas he promoted, in every way the kind of man that Bart hated but had to tolerate. Kendall loved to gossip, not openly, but he was given to making crude oblique comments in public places so everyone knew the object of his derision. So far Bart had not been an object; he preferred to keep it that way. If he could tough out a few more minutes in Jerry Don's office, Kendall would go on about his business and not even know Bart had been in the bank on a Monday morning talking to Jerry Don about renewing a loan he couldn't pay off.

"No. No. I'd like to renew," he said.

"That's fine. On your way out, you might ask Angie to step in here," Jerry Don said.

Through the open door, Bart could see Kendall leaning both elbows on the teller counter, talking in a low voice to Angie, probably telling an off-color joke. "She seems busy at the moment. I can wait," Bart said. "What about Richard? I hear he's out of town. Is he off to kill another bear?"

"Oh no, no, nothing like that. He's taken his eldest—that's Richard Junior, you know—he's taking him on a tour of college campuses. Junior got accepted to five schools, great ones, all of them. University of Nebraska, Colorado, Kansas. South Dakota State and University of South Dakota, of course. Smart kid, great kid. He could have had a football scholarship, one was offered, but he decided that would take too much time away from his academics."

"That's great. That's terrific," Bart said with a genial smile. Brian barely passed his classes, couldn't be convinced to try out for any sports, not even track, and had played hooky on the day his classmates took the college entrance exams. Bart had not been pleased or proud of his kid. "Does he know what he wants to study?"

"Oh, he definitely wants to be a doctor. Or maybe a lawyer. Whichever one, he plans to come back here to live. Contribute to the community, you know," Jerry Don, the proud uncle, said. He might fight his brother over the family business, but he would support any family member that contributed to the family prestige.

Bart heard heavy boot steps on the lobby floor receding as they moved toward the bank's front door, but the footsteps paused, grew louder, determined.

Jerry Don ran on about the benefits of taking a medical degree as a general practitioner, better for a small-town doctor, you know, where a doctor has to treat all kinds of health problems. You can't be a heart specialist and not know how to deliver a baby in a small town.

The footsteps stopped, then went silent as Kendall walked out of the bank. Jerry Don pressed a button on his phone console. "Angie, would you come in here a moment?"

Figures, Bart thought. The bastard could have called her on the intercom anytime to come to his office, but no, he wanted me to be an errand boy, run out there and ask her into Jerry Don's office. Bart stood up, and said, "I'll be back in next Monday to sign the papers. Tell Richard hello for me when he gets back."

He was so relieved to have the matter handled, the loan in the process of renewal, that he strode out of the bank, looked up at the sky to check for rain and, when his gaze lowered again, it was centered on Gary Kendall, half leaning, half sitting on the hood of Bart's pickup, smiling. "Hey, Bart, what you are doing in town?"

"Oh, I had to come into town for a tractor part. Damnedest thing. I'm thinking about just buying a new one, going with Allis Chalmers this time instead of John Deere," Bart said.

"Funny, I didn't know they sold tractor parts in the bank," Kendall guffawed.

"I just stopped in to visit with Richard for a minute, but I forgot he's off on that college campus tour with his kid."

Kendall squinted at him, but stopped laughing. "How's about having a drink with me down in the Legion? They should be open for business just about now. Say, you'll never guess what I heard."

Well, why the hell not, Bart thought. Maybe he'd hear about someone in worse trouble than he was himself. Or maybe he could give Gary Kendall something else to talk about other than Bart's financial woes.

7

Tom Warder sat in the break room of the refuge headquarters at 6:45 in the morning, doodling idly on a pad of paper fastened to a clipboard. Intern Carl Findley, and Keith Ford, second maintenance man, sat at the wooden table, everyone drinking their ritual morning cup of coffee before the hands on the clock moved around to 7:00, and time to go to work. King, the manager, sulked in his office as he had done for the past few weeks, ever since Findley and Tom had brought in the truck with its load of young caged swans.

The days had gone long and gray as winter approached in mid-November, although the only snowfall so far had been a thin skift that didn't bother to cover the ground. The coal-burning stove in the office didn't do much more than take the chill off, but it was enough for everyone except Findley, who would spend his days inside, tallying and refiguring the numbers from the fall bird counts. He would have to submit his report soon, and that report would reflect the number of birds taken in the annual pheasant hunt as well as the ones that had been taken by animal predators and those that had died of unknown causes. That report, really an inventory of sorts, along with the spring brood count, would be used as the basis for determining what the hunting limits were at the next fall hunting season for pheasants, grouse, and ducks. Finley was the nervous sort who worried about making a big mistake. King wasn't worried about that. An off count could be explained away: winterkill was worse than expected, or less than expected, wild food hadn't been available, some other natural cause other than human error.

King was worried, however, about the trumpeter swan project that he felt had been forced on him by upper management. Red Rocks Refuge management had failed in all their attempts to get the birds paired off and nesting. King was a manager, but not a wildlife expert, exactly. He'd gotten promoted for his ability to manage budgets, not animals, and he never wanted to be assigned to a migratory waterfowl refuge in the first place. A new mustang refuge had recently been created out in Nevada, and he had wanted that job, but it went to some bureaucrat who thought he was a cowboy whose father had been a major donor to the in-party's political efforts in the off-year elections. The kid intern, Carl, now. Carl's specialty was birds. He was excited about the swan project, so King let him run with it. If it all went belly-up, well, Carl would be back sitting in a classroom in corn country Iowa with no way to know what King put into the report when the project failed. King was sure it would.

Tom sketched a flock of ducks flying into a rising sun with a range of hills in the near ground. He only had an eighth-grade education, but he read a lot, the western paperbacks that he traded around with a couple of neighbors, stuff from the county library, including a battered old book on drawing. He practiced by drawing guess-what pictures for his girls: an airplane as imagined from above, a cat with its nose buried in its tail so you couldn't tell which end was which, the oddly crooked-looking back leg of a horse, and sometimes he would get one of the girls to tell him a little story, then he'd make up a comic strip to go with it. Those were Bit's favorites. The clock hands moved five minutes. Ten minutes to the beginning of the workday. They'd been sitting there for twenty minutes and Keith still hadn't said anything more than the grumpy "Morning" he'd said when Tom had walked through the door.

Tom wondered if maybe Keith wasn't pissed off because Tom had been put full-time on swan watch, which meant sitting outside the swan pen for eight hours a day, observing their behavior and making notes. That situation left Keith as the only maintenance man in charge of all the repairs to the buildings, the truck, the tractor they used to mow the dikes around the series of little lakes the refuge encompassed and everything else that went wrong. At first Tom wouldn't have minded trading places with Keith, but as the days wore on from September into late November, Tom found himself enjoying the work, the solitude. He learned to distinguish each bird from the others in the flock, saw individual actions, and had come to believe each bird had a distinctive personality. None of them had formed a pair-bond yet, but he hoped they would. He did want this project to be successful; he wanted to see the swans pair off, mate, lay eggs, and hatch them out.

Carl had ideas, and some of them might be realistic, but Tom felt many of them were classroom exercises that made no sense to the swans, like the nests Carl had insisted upon, which Tom thought were dumb. Tom and Carl had spent over a week piling mud up into truncated pyramids and topping each one with a huge tractor tire filled with hay. That had been part of the problem up at Red Rocks, Carl said. No available nesting material in the sites that corresponded to what swans preferred, or so Carl's theory went. It seemed not many people, if any, had seen an actual swan nesting in the wild, so Tom wondered how Carl knew what swans preferred. He didn't think the birds preferred tractor tires in the wild.

The pen encompassed a couple of acres in a wet area of tall grasses with a wide stream meandering through it. Wire mesh fenced the place with more of the same stretched over the top to keep any swans with ideas of freedom from taking wing. The birds had their wings clipped, too, when they were first introduced into the pen, but they were starting to grow out again. Tom didn't relish the repeat chore of capturing the big birds and clipping their wings. They hissed and flapped and used their beaks like pliers to pinch any human flesh they could reach.

The clock hands moved up to start time. Findley got up, walked back to his office, and shut the door. Tom set his coffee cup on the sideboard. "You coming, Keith?" Tom asked.

Keith sat for a minute longer before he stood up, pushing his chair back with a grating noise on the tiled floor. He stalked to the door, opened it, and walked out, slamming it behind him.

Tom took a breath. He'd asked Keith before what was the matter and got nothing but a grunted "Nothing" in response, and he was damned tired of it. He went outside, where the rising sun over the trees in the east sent lemon yellow rays across the brown and gray lawn. Keith stomped along the path to the equipment barn.

Tom followed, grabbed Keith by the shoulder and spun him around. "What the hell is the matter with you?" he demanded.

Keith lowered his head like a mad bull and took a step toward Tom, who didn't back up but put his hand on Keith's shoulder and shook him. "Listen, man. I don't know what the hell is going on with you, but I'm trying to help. You sit around sulled up like an old toad frog. I can't help you if you don't talk to me. If I can help, I will. If I can't, I'll sympathize, but we've been friends for too many years for you to shut me out."

Keith's shoulders slumped slowly like a tire with the air being let out of it. He raised his eyes and squinted into the sun. "I've got a lot on my mind," he said.

"Like what?"

"Family stuff," Keith answered.

Tom thought about the possibilities. "Inez sick? The kids?"

Keith shook his head.

"Money problems? Man, we all got that."

"Not money problems. Well, no more than usual."

"Come on. Don't make me drag it out of you. Quit playing games and say what the hell is on your mind," Tom said sternly.

Keith pressed his lips together as if to keep the words in. He looked up at Tom and said, "I'm thinking about how to say it. This ain't easy for me, Tom. You know I'm not one to complain about things I can't help. It's just . . ."

The office door opened behind them. "You men need something?" King called out.

"No, we're okay," Tom said.

"Let me think about it this morning. Bring your lunch down to the machine shed at noon. Okay?"

"Okay."

Keith turned and walked away. The office door shut.

Down at the swan pen, a three foot square piece of old plywood leaned up against the wire fence. Tom pulled it away, dropped it flat, and sat down on it. He wore long johns and a long sleeved shirt under the regulation tan coveralls with a heavy parka over all, but he had to sit on the damp ground to observe and write up his comments. The chilly wet seeped through to his bones. If his butt was cold, he was cold all over. The plywood square didn't provide much insulation, but it keep out the wet.

The birds roosted in the short willow trees inside the pen, waking up at first light to forage for roots among the grasses. The pickings seemed to be getting slimmer. How much forage area did a swan need? No one knew, but Tom thought they would need to provide supplemental grain throughout the winter, a suggestion that Carl rejected. "Grain isn't natural food for trumpeter swans," Carl argued. "We can't make them dependent on humans."

"I can't see us walking up and down the ditches digging out roots to pitch over the fence for them," Tom answered. "Better they get dependent on people than they die of starvation."

"We'll see," Carl had conceded.

Tom wondered what Carl would title his master's thesis. Maybe "How to Kill an Endangered Species." The internship would end in May, and after that Tom hoped King might listen to ideas other than Carl's. If they could get all the birds through the winter alive, some of them might pair up and nest in the spring. Already Tom thought he saw signs that some of the birds were expressing preferences for one other of them—he was sure they were a male and a female—and were never far from each other. Something about the female's fussiness, the ways she constantly groomed the male, followed him, shoved him in the direction she wanted to go, and the male's subservience reminded Tom of a bossy aunt and her cowed husband, so he named the two Bill and Martha after those relatives who had died when Tom was still a child. This morning Bill and Martha foraged for roots where the streambed had cut into the bank close to the fence. He watched Bill dredge up a root, saw Martha bump Bill, snatch the root, and stand there as if defying Bill to protest. Tom made notes, his fingers clumsy in brown jersey gloves. Even with the sun up the air was still chilly. He wished he had a cup of hot coffee.

At eleven thirty, he fetched his lunch from the front seat of his car and walked down to the machine shop. This was Monday, so he knew the menu: a pair of tuna sandwiches, a small can of pork and beans, four fig bar cookies, a Jonathan apple, and a waxed paper twist of salt. The hipped roof of the black lunch box held a thermos of coffee liberally laced with evaporated milk and sugar.

Tom didn't expect much from the conversation Keith had promised. The two had known each other since they were kids in the local elementary school, the same one Tom's girls attended now, but Keith had dropped out in the sixth grade, while Tom continued through the eighth grade, which was as far as the school went. The only high school was in Jackson where kids from the country either boarded with someone in town or got their driver's license at fourteen and drove to school every day. There were no school buses back then. Tom's family couldn't afford either choice, so he went to work on his dad's quarter section of land, dryland farming where they got a good crop one year out of five and supplemented their income by trapping the muskrats that thrived in the creek bordering the east side of the property. The muskrat pelts weren't as highly valued as the minks that lived in the same creek but farther north where the creek flowed into one of the small lakes on the refuge.

When Tom was still a kid, the land for the refuge was confiscated through eminent domain, which Bennie Black Hawk still complained about. Tom remembered when he and his dad trapped minks farther up the creek from their land, back before the Civilian Conservation Corps had hired unemployed locals to put in the system of dikes through the wetlands, which created the series of ten lakes making up the refuge complex.

Tom still kept in touch with Keith as his friend, and just after Pearl Harbor the two of them enlisted in the army together, figuring that as an Indian and a poor white kid they would be drafted soon anyway. They thought enlisting instead might get them some choice in where they got assigned, but that was a vain hope. They went through boot camp together in Texas, but Keith got sent to Europe while Tom went to the Pacific—Guadalcanal, some islands in the Philippines. Neither ever rose above the rank of PFC, but that mattered only because of the pay, because neither of them planned to make a career of the military.

Keith married Inez the week before they shipped out, and didn't meet his first daughter until three years later, when he was discharged. Tom didn't find Anna until a year after he came back from the war, back to dryland farming with his dad and then the temporary job on the refuge, which most of his family and relatives hated. Both men were the fathers of girls, no sons, a fact that Keith complained about, but Tom didn't. Sons, daughters, Tom didn't care as long as they were healthy, an expression many men of his time uttered but didn't mean. Tom meant it. Keith never used the expression. He loved his girls, but he blamed them for not being boys, and they acted as if they knew it. Tom suspected that the troubles Keith had on his mind had to do with one or more of his four girls.

Keith had the machine shop's coal stove glowing and had already pulled a stool up to the greasy workbench when Tom walked in. Already Keith seemed in a better mood as he took a bite of his sandwich and waved. Tom pulled up the other stool and sat.

"How's the dickie bird-watching going?" Keith asked.

"It's going; it's going," Tom said. "They're really not your usual dickie birds."

The term had been around for a few years, applied to the big shots from D.C. who came out every year or so on inspection tours carrying binoculars and gazing around at any bird that appeared. Few of them knew anything about wildlife conservation let alone the migratory waterfowl the refuge had been created to protect and preserve. The refuge had hosted a contingent of curious gawkers the previous summer, and when their ignorance and inane questions had become nearly intolerable, King offered them a chance of a lifetime opportunity to see thousands of birds on Pelican Island, a tiny lump of land in the middle of lake ten where pelicans had nested for decades, contributing to the island's height above water level with ten feet of bird shit.

The big shots enthusiastically agreed to the visit. To his disgust, King designated Keith as the pilot for the boat to take them there. Keith tried to steer the boat upwind, but the wind didn't cooperate, nor did the temperature, which had climbed nearly to a hundred degrees, and as the boat came near, the ammonia stench from the hot bird poop got stronger until the men's eyes watered so badly they could barely see the half dozen pelicans that sat incubating the last few nests of the hatching season.

Tom opened his lunch box, took out the small can opener, and cracked his can of pork and beans.

"Swans are just bigger versions of the usual dickie birds," Keith said.

Tom didn't answer. He wondered if Keith was going to pretend he never mentioned telling Tom about his troubles, but Keith put down his sandwich, dusting the white bread crumbs from his grease stained hands. "I don't know how to get started telling you this," Keith said, staring at the pegboard of hanging tools on the wall above the workbench.

"Start wherever is easiest. If I don't understand something, you can backtrack until I do," Tom said. He wondered if Keith expected him to play question-and-answer, where Tom had to keep guessing until he hit on the subject, but Keith started talking, haltingly at first.

"The problem is Mary Ann," he said. "Well, one of the problems."

Mary Ann, Keith's firstborn daughter, red-haired and freckled like a goose egg, she had been a chubby little girl with a permanently snotty nose but had grown into a pretty girl, country fresh and wholesome looking. Her attitude about everything, though, spoiled her charm. Tom thought she had a permanent grudge against the world, and maybe Keith's obvious disdain for girl children had a lot to do with the girl's attitude. She had barely earned grades good enough to graduate from high school and gone to work at the steak house in Jackson, and earned a reputation for being a good waitress but a fast woman.

When Keith didn't say anything more for several long minutes, Tom sighed and gave him a nudge. "Yeah. What about Mary Ann?"

"She's not been herself recently," Keith said, pausing again.

"How do you mean?"

Another long pause, and just as Tom decided he wasn't playing the game anymore, even if Keith never said another word for the rest of their lunch break, Keith opened up and let words out, not in a rush, but steadily, like pouring molasses out of a jar that had been refrigerated. Tom felt like he could have said in a few sentences what it took Keith nearly their entire lunch break to get out.

Mary Ann was pregnant. Inez had known about it for a couple of weeks but kept it from her husband. When he confronted his daughter about her condition, she refused to tell him who was the father. He suspected Inez knew, but she wouldn't tell him either. Keith was embarrassed for the community to find out, but he didn't believe in abortion and didn't know any doctor who would perform one, even though he thought that might be the best choice considering the circumstances. Mary Ann was going to have a girl child, Keith was convinced of it, and the thought of raising an illegitimate grandchild that was a girl as well—well, it made him angry, but he didn't know what to do about it.

"Any chance the father might show up and marry her?" Tom asked.

Keith laughed and said, "Hell, no."

"Any idea who the father might be?"

"Hell, no. I didn't even know she had a boyfriend," Keith said. "What worries me is that she might have gotten knocked up last summer by one of those guys who came through on a harvest crew." He pinched his face up and hesitated. "What if the kid comes out Black? I mean, a half-Indian kid would be bad enough." He caught himself then, gave a quick glance at Tom, who continued eating as if Keith hadn't said something awful. "I shouldn't have said that."

"No, you shouldn't have said that," Tom said. This wasn't the first time or even the tenth time that Tom heard such racist talk, but he wasn't surprised to hear it from Keith. He knew Keith didn't really mean what he said, but that kind of attitude was the built-in common denominator in the white community, never mind that the white community considered Keith and his family in the same category as Indians, Negroes, and the gooks they had fought in the war.

"I'm sorry," Keith said. "I mean, if you'd had a son and he'd wanted to marry one of my girls, I wouldn't have thought anything about it. I mean, I wouldn't have minded."

Tom poured the last of the coffee from his thermos. Nothing he could say or do would change attitudes or behavior of anyone. He had to live with these people, so he just got on with it. "I think you should give it some time," Tom said.

"How much time do I got? Takes nine months to make a kid, and I don't know where to start counting from. Maybe she don't either, but it won't be long until every tongue in Jackson and the entire county will wag."

"So what?" Tom asked.

"What do you mean?"

"I mean, so what? Are you really worried about helping your daughter raise another girl, or are you worried about what people will say? Come on, man. Every year, there's three or four have-to weddings around here, and probably that many or more girls who go spend a few months out of town at their auntie's house in Omaha or Denver, and the families of those girls are some of the leaders of the community. Happens in every family," Tom said.

Keith's eyes were fixed on a pair of red-handled pliers halfway up the pegboard behind the workbench. "Auntie in Omaha, huh?" he said thoughtfully.

Tom drained the last of his coffee, put away his thermos and closed his lunch box. "I'm going to the john and then I better get back to my dickie bird-watching," Tom said, as he stepped down from the stool.

"Yeah. Dickie bird-watching," Keith said in a reverent tone of voice.

As he walked back down to the swan pen, Tom remembered that Keith had said his problems were with Mary Ann and other things. He wondered what were those other things. Tom and Anna sat at their kitchen table enjoying their weekday late afternoon ritual of coffee in the winter and iced tea in the summer. "Where's the girls?" Tom asked.

"Playing cowboys and Indians with the neighbor boys. Guess who's the Indians?" Anna said with a smile.

"Our girls?"

"Nope. The boys!" Her smile turned into a laugh that Tom joined.

"You remember I said Keith has been like a bear with a sore head recently? Well, today he told me why," Tom started.

"Mary Ann's pregnant," Anna said calmly, taking a sip of coffee.

"You knew?"

"Inez told me a week ago. She asked me not to talk about it, but since Keith had already told you, I can say now."

"Keith is worried the father might be some guy who came through on the harvest crew last summer," Tom said.

"Couldn't be. Not possible," Anna said, shaking her head. "She's only a couple of months along, so that means she got pregnant sometime in September. The harvest workers were all gone the first week in August."

"Doesn't matter, I guess, but I don't know why she wouldn't say."

"I do," Anna said with a grimace. "You know Keith. He'd go after the guy with a shotgun."

"Well, only if screaming and yelling didn't work," Tom asserted, as he shuffled through the pile of mail from the table: the electric bill, a political advertisement for a candidate who'd already been defeated in the election a couple of weeks earlier, and a handbill from the local theater listing upcoming attractions for the month of December.

"Did you get the check from Johnson for the annual lease payment?" Tom asked.

Anna shook her head, and said, "Hasn't come. I wondered about that. This is—what—the fifteenth? He's always paid it around the first of November."

"That's odd. Bart Johnson has leased that land for the past ten years, and always paid right on time every year. I know some of the other landowners have complained for years that he was late or paid them short, but you know one of the complainers is Bennie Black Hawk. He's only got that eighty acres left, but he's probably forgot and thinks he should be paid for a quarter section."

"You think Bart wouldn't forget something like the annual lease payment," Anna said, a little worry creeping into her voice. The lease payment wasn't much, less than two dollars an acre, but the family counted on it to help pad out the grocery bill and for Anna, the most important benefit, Christmas money. Most of the money went for necessities, but every year she kept a minimum of twenty-five dollars to buy Christmas for her girls. She never admitted that Christmas was as important to her as to the girls. She wasn't particularly religious; they rarely attended Mass. She loved the bright lights, the evergreen smell from the Christmas tree, the carols playing on Jackson streets from the loudspeaker mounted outside the drugstore, and the excitement. They always had the same thing for breakfast every morning—pancakes—but Anna liked to make Christmas morning breakfast special. She bought orange juice, something she considered too expensive any other time, real maple syrup for the pancakes, and link sausages that the girls called little pigs.

"You think I should get ahold of Bart and ask him about it?" Tom wondered as he heard the girls arguing outside, and one of them, likely Patty, yelling "I'm going to tell Dad!"

Anna got up, stretching her back. As the girls burst thought the door, still arguing and accusing, she said, "We'll talk about it later."

After supper was over Tom helped the girls with their homework, which they were glad to get finished so they could watch *DRAGNET* on the television, a show he didn't really pay much attention to, preferring to pull out one of the paperbacks and read. Usually he got more westerns in trade, but one unusual one had gotten mixed into the last batch he swapped with the guys at Doc's gas station in town. It was a small book, thin, and Tom preferred a big meaty story, but this one, *CANNERY ROW*, was not only not a western in the usual sense of the word, but also wasn't very thick. He planned to look for more Steinbeck books at the county library.

Neither Anna nor Tom talked about the late lease payment from Bart Johnson that night, as if speaking about it might bring on more trouble. When Tom went to bed in the second room of the two room house, the bed he shared with Anna and the girls' bed jammed so close together that they could barely walk between them, he tossed and turned, debating with himself the merits and demerits of approaching Johnson about the late payment.

8

On the first Wednesday in December, Bart Johnson drove home from Jackson through a snowstorm, flakes whirling in front of his headlights in a monotone, hypnotic kaleidoscope. Occasional wind gusts broke up the swirl, driving the flakes against the windshield. He'd gone to town for the weekly cattle auction, but also because Betty's December club meeting had been switched from Monday to Wednesday just for this Christmas month. The ladies wanted a meeting to discuss creative new ideas for wrapping Christmas presents, and they were going to make door wreaths, Betty said.

The sales had been light at the auction barn since most of the local ranchers had already sold off their spring calves; there were only a few cattle buyers present from the big feedlots in the eastern part of the state and from Omaha. The animals coming through were canners and cutters—dry cows, a few spring calves missed in the ranchers' general roundup and sales, a couple of bulls well past their prime, one with a broken horn that had been on the prod. The old Hereford had been so unhappy with his situation that he charged the man in the ring, who was so surprised he nearly tripped in his hurry to climb the pipe fence out of the bull's charge.

When the sale ended, Gary Kendell approached Bart from behind, slapping him on the back in a move that wasn't friendly but aggressive and invited Bart down to the Legion for a drink. "First one's on me," Gary said, spreading his arms wide. "Second, third, and all those thereafter are your problem." He laughed as if he'd made the funniest joke ever.

Bart agreed, not because he wanted Gary's company or a free first drink, but because he *WANTED* the first drink, and all those thereafter. If he said no, he'd have to go home anyway because the Legion bar was the only bar in town. A couple of other local ranchers whose wives were also members of Betty's club joined Gary and Bart, but after half an hour and one drink, they went home leaving Bart to suffer Gary's bullshit alone. Mostly Bart only nodded and laughed at what he thought were the right moments. Gary didn't notice, as his eyes summed up the only waitress, a past her prime bleached blonde whose husband had died a year earlier in a farm accident, leaving the woman to raise three kids on her own.

"What do you think, huh?" Gary nudged Bart in the ribs a bit too hard.

"About what?" Bart asked, absently stirring his Scotch and water with the unnecessary white and red short straw that for some unknown reason always got included with every drink.

Gary pointed at the woman with a middle finger, and said, "Her. Verda."

"Oh, I don't know. Never thought about her much. I guess she's doing the best she can since Eddie got killed," Bart said.

"No, no! I mean, would you take a run at that?"

"What?"

Gary punched Bart's shoulder. "Would you fuck that? What's the matter with you? You drunk already? Would you fuck that?"

Bart recoiled. Eddie and Bart had been goose hunting buddies, lying on the cold ground in fencerow, waiting for a flock of geese to fly low enough to shoot. Verda used to belong to the same Lady's Aid Club as Betty. Bart respected her, thinking she was only about half as silly as the rest of the women. Since Eddie died and Verda had to work, she had dropped out of the club. "Never thought much about her, one way or the other," Bart equivocated.

"What's the matter with you? You a steer? Be a bull! A man without ideas ain't no better than a steer. He ain't good for nothing but hamburger. Be a bull!"

"Maybe I like hamburger," Bart countered.

Gary laughed, and said, "Maybe your old lady would like a steak now and then. Being married is a good thing 'cause you don't have to chase it down; it's right there beside you every night. Just reach over and rip off a piece. But a little chasing keeps a man on his toes, you know? Know what I mean?"

Bart nodded and smiled. Reaching over to rip off a piece would be impossible for him. Since the night Brian had put the dead bird in his sister's bed, Betty had been sleeping in the spare room. He ordered another drink.

Around ten o'clock, as he weaved his way back from the men's room, Bart decided he'd better slow it down or he would have to take a motel room in town, a move that would get tongues wagging for a month. Besides, the bartender had taken a look outside and announced to the entire bar that anyone wanting to get home better start because a blizzard was blowing in. He poured a 7 Up on top of his gurgling belly, resisting Gary's urging for just one more. At eleven o'clock, Bart climbed the steps from the basement bar. The frosted window in the bowling alley door across the hall from the bar had no light on, indicating no one was there. Likely the Jackson Business Man's Wednesday Night League had finished or shut down early.

The cold flakes settled on his dark coat like huge flakes of dandruff as he walked to his pickup. The windows were frosted and half an inch deep with snow, but he didn't feel like freezing while he scraped it off, so he turned the heater up on full blast and waited, but after five minutes the heat in the pickup cab started to make him sick. He turned it off, turned on the wipers, and rolled down his window. He drove home, the speedometer barely registering 30 miles an hour, feeling like he was creeping into an endless white night. At times, when the wind whipped up, he couldn't see either side of the road, so he steered by guess and by God, as his father used to say, nearly missing the mailbox where he had to turn off up the narrow lane to his house. Just as he made the turn, he thought he saw a dark object come out of nowhere. He slammed on the brakes; the truck skidded and slid into the deep borrow ditch coming up with a jolt against the bank on the right-hand side of the lane. The motor died, but the headlights continued shining into the white chaos, the wipers flicking back and forth. He cranked the engine and put the gear in reverse, but the truck was well and truly stuck. Getting it out would take his tractor and a winch. He'd fixed the tractor, but he didn't relish getting it out tonight, and he'd need Brian or Betty to steer the pickup while he pulled with the tractor. He didn't relish walking the 200 yards to the house in the cold and the wind, either, but that seemed like the best choice.

As he walked, the wind cut through his gray Stockman's dress pants and jacket. The snow would stop as soon as the temperature fell, he knew, and it was falling—he could tell from the way the moisture inside his nostrils felt like it was freezing. He tucked his hands under his armpits and walked, head down against the wind. He'd have to feed in the morning, too, after or maybe before he pulled out his pickup. But he couldn't feed until he loaded the low hay sled with bales from the hay yard. The more he thought about the receding chain of necessary events to be completed before he could get to the most important thing to be done the madder he got. His entire life felt like that. Maybe Gary was right; maybe he was just an old steer, like one of those canner and cutter animals he's seen pass under the auctioneer's hammer at the sale barn. Maybe the delay in having kids had been his fault; he wasn't bull enough for Betty, or any woman, not even Verda. He was an old broken-horned bull who should have been sent to the slaughterhouse and made into dog food years ago. Not that Betty was any prize.

Betty, the cheerleader, the homecoming queen, the girl every boy in high school wanted on his arm at the prom, and Bart was the one who got her. He should've let someone else have her, maybe Eddie or Gary, the bull. Gary the bullshitter. Gary got the quiet girl, Pearl Allison, the one who always made A's in math and science, the one named Most Likely to Succeed in the Jackson County High School yearbook. Now she was even quieter than she had been in high school, a mousy little woman who followed one step behind her husband and her four big sons, always looking like she expected to be hit and maybe she'd had practice in dodging Gary's fists. As many times as Bart felt like it, he had never hit Betty, not once.

The kids, now. Susan wasn't any beauty and would never take any prizes handed out for brains, but the girl would be okay. She'd get married and have kids, and she'd be fine, but Brian was the problem. What the hell was he going to do with that kid? Arrogant, lazy Brian, and Betty always stuck up for him, protected the little bastard. He tried to think who in the family Brian might have took after, but no one on his side had ever been anything but hardworking, moderately successful people. Churchgoers. Hunters. Cattlemen. Pretty much the same on Betty's side, so where did Brian come from? Maybe Brian wasn't his kid. Maybe he'd been a cuckoo in the nest. Maybe even Gary's kid.

Bart knew better than that, but he comforted himself with the fiction of it. Betty never had any use for sex, except as a means to get a child, and even sometimes then and always no, when he approached her, she put her hands on his chest, pushing him away, turning her face to the side with a disgusted expression. He couldn't remember the last time she'd come to him willingly. There had been sex grudgingly consented to, but she'd lain there like a sack of feed until he lay across her rigid body, limp and spent. She shoved him hard, and said, "Are you quite finished now?" After he'd rolled off, she got up and stalked to the bathroom. There hadn't been even that lately, not with her sleeping every night in the spare room.

He hurried the last hundred yards, the snow cushion keeping his boots from crunching on the gravel driveway. The metal latch on the front door burned his bare hands like a hot coal as he flung the door open so hard it bounced against the wall. He stood for a moment listening but heard no one stirring from upstairs. His stomach felt nasty, still gurgling. He thought maybe if he put something it in, he'd feel better.

Plastic-wrapped plates and bowls crowded the refrigerator shelves, but most of the covered stuff looked like cheesecake. One plate held little rounds of white sandwich bread with some kind of orange spread on top that looked like it had pickle chunks stirred in, and on top of each, a little red twist of something. He lifted the plastic wrap, took a round and popped it into his mouth, expecting maybe something sweet, but it tasted like beautiful vomit. His stomach rebelled. He ran to the kitchen sink, opened the door beneath, pulled out the trash bag and spat, leaning on the sink a minute until his stomach stopped threatening to bring up all the booze. He reached up and turned on the faucet, stuck his head beneath, turned his face and let the cold water flush out his mouth. As he started to shove the trash can back under the sink, he saw an empty half-gallon bottle with a Jack Daniel's label nestled in a mess of crumpled festive Christmas napkins. Where did that come from? Had Betty drank half a gallon of whiskey at her club meeting? Probably not, no, the bottle probably hadn't been full to start with, and the contents had probably been shared out among the nearly dozen club ladies. No wonder they never ate the sweet desserts they brought. He couldn't imagine anyone eating cake and chasing it with whiskey.

As he shut the refrigerator door, he glanced down at his feet. Melting snow from his boots had made a muddy puddle on the white linoleum. He walked back into the living room and leaned against the wall while he pulled off his boots and set them by the front door. The room smelled different. The Christmas tree was up. The ladies must have helped Betty put it up this afternoon in between drinks. Tinsel glistened in the light coming from the blue-white yard light, amplified by the still-falling white snow. Presents—big, small, many—sat under the tree, piled up to the first branches, and on the coffee table, a pile of clothing with the tags still on them. Betty had gone shopping sometime recently while Bart hadn't noticed, even though he had told her to spend light on Christmas presents and hold off on any other spending until after the new year. He didn't know why he'd said after the new year because there wouldn't be a sudden infusion of cash into his bank accounts.

No, more money would flow out, as a matter of course, when he had to spend on gas and oil to run the tractors during haying season next summer, possible vet bills for any heifers with calving problems, the regular living expenses of groceries, electric bill, and whatever else might come up. The money he cleared from selling this year's calf crop wasn't going to last until next year's was calved, raised, and sold. And he nearly forgot—the monthly payment on Betty's new Impala was due, and even though he had warned her to go light on the checkbook, Betty had been out spending money he didn't have. No way around it, he'd have to go back to the bank on Monday and get a sweetener added onto his loan. The three hundred dollars due to Tom Warder for his lease payment seemed a nothing in comparison to the more than two thousand he owed on other lease payments to Indian landowners.

He jumped as the door banged open behind him, but it was only the wind. He hadn't gotten it pushed tight enough to latch. After he shut the door, he picked up one piece from the pile of clothes laying on the coffee table, a soft white sweater maybe. He deliberately blew his nose on it and flung it at the Christmas tree. Some of the balls tinkled together with the impact.

His stocking feet made no sound on the stairs, but at the top he saw Betty in the doorway of the spare room at the end of the hall. "Bart? Decided to come home, did you?"

He walked swiftly to the end of the hall where she stood, steady on his feet, cold sober. He shoved her in the middle of her gut, pushing her backward into the room. She gave a little gasp of surprise as he shut the door behind them. This was the coldest bedroom in the house, the one that still had only a tiny little register to push in heat from the basement furnace. He felt a little waft of warm air on his left foot where it rested on the vent.

"Bart? What's the matter with you? Go to bed!" Betty said, stepping away from him, back toward the bed. She wasn't wearing curlers, but she had teased and sprayed her hair into a matted, lacquered nest on her head, and after sleeping on it a few hours, it had formed into a lopsided mat. Bart stepped quickly forward, pushing her into a sitting position on the edge of the bed.

"What do you want, for god's sake?" The words were aggressive, but the tone was fearful, nervous.

"I want what you never give willingly," Bart said as he began pulling off his clothes. The zipper on his pants stuck, so he ripped at it until he heard the metal teeth snap, stepped out of them, feeling his penis rising, twitching.

"And I'm not willing now! Bart, get out of here. Go to bed in your own room." Betty's voice rose with her panic.

Bart slapped her across the mouth, knocking her so hard back against the bed that her body bounced against the mattress. "Shut up. You'll wake the kids."

Bart tried to rip her flannel nightgown, but the fabric was too tough, so he pulled it up as high as he could around her neck and knotted it in one hand, while she fought him, paddling at his chest. When she started making gagging, choking sounds, he loosened his grip with one hand, fumbling for his penis with the other, pushing against her crotch, shoving aside the cotton panties.

"Be still, goddamn you. You never moved when we did it before, so why start now?" he growled.

She turned her head and sobbed, but Bart didn't care because he didn't want to kiss her anyway. He smelled booze in the warm breath between them, not sure if the smell came from him or her. He entered her rapidly, jamming against her so hard and fast that her body slid upward and back on the bed. After a minute or so, he slowed, wanting to make it last as long as he could, wanting to prolong this, wanting to make her feel something, even if it was pain or rage or disgust, wanting to fuck some sense into her, wanting her to pay for that new red Impala, for the pile of presents downstairs, that pile of clothes, the pile of shit of a son she had produced, which maybe, hopefully, goddamn it all, wasn't his kid after all. Feeling his body urging him to climax, he shoved faster, harder, the top of her head now banging against the solid oak headboard, until he felt the surge emptying him, pouring out of him, and with the product of his loins his stomach gave up its contents at the same time, splashing down in a stinking gush onto Betty's face.

He held himself reared over her for a minute, his head hanging almost to her breasts, his upper arms pressing against her upper arms, pinning them to the bed. She sobbed. After he rolled off, Betty continued sobbing for a long while, and as Bart was about to fall asleep he felt the bed shift as she tried to get up. He reached out and grasped her arm. "No. You lay in the bed you've made," he said.

9

Tom sat on his chunk of plywood outside the swan pen, feeling the cold, even though he had added an extra shirt and pants under his coveralls and brought his thermos of coffee to sip while he observed the birds. The swans huddled together in the lee of the far bank making small talk among themselves as they groomed each other with their beaks after eating the grain Tom put out. Carl had conceded.

Tom hadn't written a comment all morning, but instead had filled the yellow-lined page with sketches of the birds, the bare branch of a tree, a half-hearted attempt at drawing Anna's face, but he wasn't any good at drawing people. He wanted to give her a happy face, replace the sad expression she had worn for the past couple of weeks or longer since Tom had confronted Bart Johnson about the lease payment.

Tom had seen Bart in town several times, but Bart always managed to disappear into a store or the Legion Club or drive off in his pickup just when Tom was about to catch up to him. He was avoiding Tom, and Tom knew it. Never the pushy kind, not even assertive, Tom finally decided he'd have to go to Bart's house. He hated the idea of dunning someone, even if the money was owed to him. He'd had to do it once, back in the war, in the army when a soldier in his unit who he barely knew had borrowed fifty dollars and not paid it back. When Tom confronted him, politely, Tom thought, the guy looked at Tom as if he were a worm, not worthy of attention, and had said, "What's a *PERSON* like you doing, thinking you can demand anything of me?" Tom knew he hadn't demanded. He made a point thereafter of never loaning anyone money. He gave it freely or he said no. Not that many people ever asked him for a loan; most everyone he knew understood that Tom didn't have any money to lend. Just recently, back on Veteran's Day when the legion members sold paper poppies on the street, Tom and Bennie Black Hawk had been standing on the sidewalk, Bennie delivering one of his usual lectures when Gary had approached them to buy a poppy. Tom bought one for himself at fifteen cents, but Bennie said he didn't have any money to spare, so Tom bought a poppy for Bennie. Tom smiled. More than a month later Bennie still had that paper flower stuck in his hatband.

Tom drove out to Bart Johnson's place early on a Sunday morning, knowing that would be the most likely time to catch the man at home, early, before they left for church. Betty had come to the door when Tom knocked, looking puzzled as to why he would be standing on her front porch on a cold December morning. "Good morning, Mrs. Johnson. Is Bart home?" He asked.

Betty said a funny thing then. "Barely. Come in. I'll get him."

Tom stood in the cozy living room, staring at the Johnsons' Christmas tree with presents heaped underneath, while Betty called up the stairs. "Bart! Bart, there's someone here to see you."

She stood a moment looking up the stairs, then came back into the living room. "Would you like a cup of coffee to warm you up? It's pretty cold out there."

"No, thanks, ma'am. I'm about coffeed out this morning."

"Well, all right then," Betty said hesitantly. "Can I—can I take your coat?"

"No ma'am, I won't stay but a minute."

They stood there, two people who lived in the same world but taking different paths, seeing different realities, each seeing the other as if on the other side of a wavy glass.

"You think we'll have a white Christmas?" Betty finally asked. The weather always seemed a safe topic, especially in South Dakota where the tired old saying went that if you didn't like the weather, just stick around a minute, and it will change.

"Oh, maybe. You just never know." Tom said. The snow from the last December storm had mostly melted with a little warm-up afterward, although patches still remained in the shade of trees and on the north side of buildings.

Bart clumped down the stairs like a thundering bull, Tom thought, but he stopped at the bottom of the steps, one foot still on the stair above.

"Tom. What brings you out so early on a Sunday morning?" Bart asked, as if he didn't know exactly why Tom was there.

"Just a little matter to discuss with you," Tom said, with a sideways glance at Betty.

Bart strode rapidly forward and pulled open the front door. For a moment Tom thought Bart would order Tom to leave, but his face didn't seem angry. "Let's discuss it on the front porch, okay? Betty, you can go back to your kitchen now."

Betty dropped her head without a word and walked off. Bart gestured toward the door with a swoop of his arm, like he was inviting Tom to dance. Tom walked out onto the porch, half expecting Bart's face to turn angry, expecting the man might take a swing at him, but Bart only hunched his shoulders against the cold and stuck his hands in his pockets. He didn't meet Tom's eye. "About the lease payment," Bart said. "That's why you're here, I expect."

Somewhere down in the adjacent pasture a cow bellowed, a long, lonely sound as if she was dying. "Yes. You've always paid it when it was due. I thought maybe the check got lost in the mail," Tom said.

Bart turned and walked to the end of the porch, looking out at the cows waiting for their morning hay just across the barbed wire fence. Another cow bellowed, or maybe it was the same one, and likely they were announcing that it was breakfast time and would someone please feed them.

"It's been a bad year," Bart said, so low that Tom strained to hear his next words. It's always a bad year for the little farmers here, Tom thought; it was always a bad year for me, and men like you never had a day's worry in your lives. He knew that wasn't true, but it seemed like some men had more than their share of good luck, while others never had any at all. He listened as Bart went on.

"Had a short calf crop this year, and the market was down." He turned suddenly and came back across the porch, anger now showing on his face, to stand too close to Tom for comfort. "Why are you people always expecting something? Who said you have any right to that land anyway? You Indians are all alike, always got your hands out."

Tom didn't say anything, but he stood his ground, and after a minute the angry expression left Bart's face. "Well, anyways," Bart said, running a hand through his hair. "Anyways." His face brightened then into a pleasant expression that Tom knew was acting, covering up his embarrassment that he owed something he couldn't pay and that the man he owed it to had to come dun him for it. He continued, "Tell you what. Next year. Next year I'll pay you for this year. You'll get a double payment. That'll work, won't it?"

"That wouldn't be a double payment. That would be a payment for next year and a payment for this year. One year late. It's like I'm the bank, loaning you money but without any interest charges," Tom said.

Bart shook his finger under Tom's nose. "I'll pay it when I have it! And right now, I don't have it," he said.

Tom could see he wouldn't get any payment today, and maybe not until next year, and maybe nothing next year either. He thought about the Christmas tree in the Johnsons' living room and all the presents piled beneath it and knew there would be no Christmas tree this year for his own kids. The problem with living on the prairie was the lack of trees. You couldn't just drive out in the country and cut down an evergreen tree that didn't exist, except in the planted windbreaks around farmers' homes, and lord knew they would not take kindly to someone cutting down one of their trees. He thought maybe he should report Johnson's failure to make the lease payment to the bureau—the Bureau of Indian Affairs, that is, the agency that oversaw all the payments to Indian landowners from their usually white lessees. Probably one or more of Johnson's other landowners had already reported him. Or maybe not. Wouldn't do any good, he thought. The agent in charge of overseeing the payments only showed up for work a few days out of every month, and his secretary wasn't dependable to take a message.

He could see, though, that he wasn't going to get a penny from Johnson today. He turned without another word and left thinking maybe he should have taken the goddamned Christmas tree and presents as part payment.

He hated having to tell Anna, but he did, and she didn't complain, just set her mouth and nodded her head. The girls had asked for transistor radios for Christmas. The small ones weren't expensive, but even so, unaffordable this year. And there would be no Christmas tree for the first time since Anna and Tom had married, and that might not have been as important to the girls as the presents, but Anna felt the loss.

Tom knew the girls would be disappointed and sad, but they were young, there would be other Christmases with presents for them, but Anna's pain was worse for him. And, of course, they counted on that lease payment to pad out the grocery costs for the rest of the winter. They would eat a lot of beans with no ham hocks for flavoring. They would have the jars of vegetables that Anna had canned over the summer along with the few eggs from the hens, and he could bag a rabbit or two for meat on Sundays. He knew that most of the locals poached a few pheasants during the winter, out of season, of course, and illegal. Bit had told him that her schoolmates brought fried pheasant in their lunches and called it winter chicken. Tom had avoided hunting pheasants out of season, knowing that if he was ever caught, he would likely lose his job on the refuge, even if the pheasants he shot weren't actually on the refuge property, and it wasn't just his job security. He especially hated it when hen pheasants were killed out of season. He thought of each one as one less brood count in the spring, one less mama pheasant hatching out their tiny, fluffy babies. The conservation mentality of the refuge had taken hold of him.

After the girls came home from school, Tom walked down with Bit to shut up the chickens for the night. When the door had been closed and the stick shoved through the hasp to secure it, Tom led Bit around the back of the henhouse, where they couldn't be seen from the house. Blowing tumbleweeds had built up a bank of brown spikey stems. "Bit, I need your help," he said.

"Okay," Bit said suspiciously. Whenever her dad got serious like that, it often meant she had been caught out doing something she wasn't supposed to, but she couldn't think of anything she'd done wrong lately.

"You know how important Christmas is to your mom. She loves everything about it—the tree, the Christmas carols, you girls' faces when you open your presents."

"Yeah, I know." Bit never understood why it was so important to her mom. Bit never believed in Santa Claus, ever, but her dad had made her promise not to spoil the mystery for her sisters. Sometimes she thought maybe her mom still believed in the jolly old fat man.

"We won't have a Christmas tree this year, or presents, or a special Christmas breakfast. There just isn't enough money this time, so I want you not to make a fuss."

Bit really wanted that transistor radio. One of the kids at school had one. It was not much bigger than a deck of cards, but it was magic—no cords. You stuck in a couple of batteries and had music you could carry with you, but she wasn't surprised that there would be no transistor radio this year, and maybe not ever. She was used to going back to school after the holidays and hearing about all the presents her schoolmates had gotten. The first year that happened, when she was in first grade, she had been furious. Her mother had told her that Santa Claus was always watching and that if you were very good, you'd get presents, but if you were bad, you wouldn't get anything. She didn't believe in Santa Claus; she knew her parents bought the presents, but still, they could take them away or not get any just the same. She tried very hard to be good, not tease her sisters, do her chores, brush her teeth and go to bed without a fuss, and she had got presents: a new sweater that she loved because she was always cold in the winter, socks that she needed, and another doll, which she hated and threw in the box with the doll she had gotten the previous year, but still, she had presents. Then she went to school and found out that her schoolmates, who had been misbehaving little demons, as her grannie called them, but the little demons had gotten presents anyway, many more and much nicer than a sweater, some socks, and a doll. Since then Bit tried to be indifferent to Christmas. It didn't matter if you were bad or good, it only mattered if your parents had lots of money. She wasn't going to get that transistor radio.

"I won't make a fuss, Dad," Bit said.

"It's more than that. I want you to talk to your sisters. Get them not to make a fuss either."

"What! Why do I have to talk to them? Why don't you?"

"Because," Tom said reasonably, "because your sisters look up to you. They'll listen to you and if you talk to them and set an example, then it will be so much easier on your mom."

Bit made a disgusted sound as she kicked at the yielding tumbleweeds. Underneath them, back against the hen coop where the sun didn't reach was a patch of dirty snow. "They hate me! They'll never listen to me!"

"Yes, they will. Can I count on you?"

"Why count on me? Why are you always counting on me? Why do I have to be the one that gets extra chores, that makes sure things get done when you're not around or don't want to do something? Why?"

Tom put his hands on Bit's shoulders, but she pulled away and turned her back.

"I count on you because I can. Of all my three girls, you're the one most responsible," he said to her back.

"I don't want to be responsible! How come I can't just be a kid? It's not fair!"

"Bit, nothing is fair. The coyote catches the rabbit, kills him, and eats him, and that's not fair to the rabbit, but that's life for both the rabbit and the coyote."

Bit took a deep breath. "All right," she said, wiping away the tears and the cold snot with a mittened hand. "All right, but I'm doing this for Mom, not—not my—not my siblings." She was proud of that word, siblings, and glad that she hadn't said their names.

"Let's go get supper," Tom said.

At school the next day, Mrs. Ellis had an announcement to make. The school Christmas production was coming up on Friday, the last day of school before the break. Bit and Susan Johnson were supposed to sing a duet, "Silver Bells," but Mrs. Ellis didn't like the way Bit sang it. She said Bit sang too theatrically, so Bit fully expected to be told Susan would be singing the song solo, standing there like a store dummy with her hands cupped in front of her while a monotone came out of her mouth, but no.

"Anyone want to take the Christmas tree home after the play on Friday?" Mrs. Ellis asked. "No sense in it sitting here going dry and brown over the break." Bit put her hand up and said, "I'll take it."

Mrs. Ellis gave her head a quick tilt to one side, her mouth curling up in that way she had when she was displeased. "Oh, I suppose that will be all right," she said, and as always, Bit felt like she'd been granted a favor she didn't deserve, but she could stand that. Her mother would have a Christmas tree.

"And be sure to let me know if any little brothers and sisters who aren't in school yet will be coming. Santa Claus will have a sack of peanuts and candy and a little gift for each of them," Mrs. Ellis said.

Bit wrote her youngest sister Connie's name down on the list Mrs. Ellis handed around. She wondered what she would get in the gift exchange. They had drawn names, and her mother had scraped together enough money to buy the school gifts for the names her two oldest daughters had drawn, and even said it was all right when Bit chose a bottle of hot pink nail polish for the name she drew. Bit knew Susan Johnson had drawn her name. The gifts were all under the tree and from the size and shape and feel of the one with her name on it, Bit knew it was a book, the best kind of gift.

On Friday night the Warder family ate supper early, piled into the '56 Chevy, and drove to the school. With only two days more until Christmas, the weather didn't look like there would be a white Christmas. The stage in the front of Bit's classroom took up the front third of the room, with desks moved in from the little kids' room to provide seating for all the parents and kids. The Christmas tree sat in the back corner, a big one, over six feet tall and strung with decorations the kids had made. Bit thought her dad would have to tie it on top of the car to get it home, which would likely mess up the garlands made up of interlocking circles cut from red and green construction paper, but Bit didn't care. Those were ugly trimmings anyway. She and her sisters would help their mother redecorate it with the big blue and gold Christmas tree balls, hang the silver icicles they had saved from the previous year, and put on the string of twenty-five fat, colored lights.

The school production went as well as Bit thought it would. One of the three wise men tripped on his sheet that had been made into a robe falling face first onto the stage; one of the Lindas who had been overindulged in candy before the event threw up all down the front of Susan's pretty new plaid taffeta dress, and Susan herself froze speechless during the duet she was supposed to sing with Bit, so the duet turned into a solo with a silent sidekick. When the last curtain was pulled shut the parents clapped dutifully, rose restlessly to sample the fruit punch and Christmas cookies on the card table in the back of the room. Someone's father came in dressed as Santa Claus and started handing out the presents from under the tree. Bit's present was a book, the least desirable book she ever saw: *A CHRISTMAS CAROL*.

When all the gifts from the students' exchange had been handed out, Santa/Linda Baker's father drew brown lunch sacks full of peanuts in the shell, candy, and a small gift each from his pack and handed them out to the little kids, the ones too young for school. As he called the names a parade of little kids marched to the front, some shyly with a finger in their mouth, but most smiling in their fancy dresses or long pants and white shirts with bow ties. As they came up one by one, the line grew shorter, but Connie's name still hadn't been called. Bit thought maybe Santa called them in alphabetical order by their last name, so Warder would be last, but Barbara Schmidt got her sack, then Marcy Thompson, and Santa stood up, upended his sack and shook it with a big smile. The parents all clapped as Santa took a bow and walked out of the room yelling Ho! Ho! Ho!

Connie went to her mother, climbed up on her lap, and buried her head on Anna's shoulder. Tom motioned to Bit, gathered up Patty, and led his family out the door. Linda Baker's father, standing in the hall, half in and half out of his Santa suit, gave the Warders a big grin.

Tom turned over the engine on the car, put it in gear, and maneuvered between a pickup with dried cow shit dribbled down the back and over the tailgate and the Bakers' new Cadillac, the one advertised on the *LAWRENCE WELK SHOW* as having a swept wing design. In the dim moonlight Bit saw her father's grim face, that muscle twitching in his temple. Connie cried on her mother's lap in the front seat.

"I was a good girl, Mama, I didn't do anything bad. Why didn't Santa bring me a present?" Connie asked through her sobs.

Bit thought of a dozen reasons; she thought the reason was because Santa Claus wasn't real, but that's not what came out of her mouth. She said, "It's because Santa Claus is a son of a bitch." For once in her life, neither Tom nor Anna called her down for bad language.

As Tom paused the car where the schoolyard met the little road leading up to it, someone came running from the schoolhouse shouting, "Wait! Wait!"

Tom looked in the rearview mirror, but didn't say anything. Mrs. Ellis ran up and knocked on Tom's window. When he cranked it down, she said, "Oh, I'm so sorry. I can't imagine how little Connie's name got left off the list, but we've made up a bag of treats for her too."

Bit remembered that the Warders were supposed to get the school Christmas tree. She leaned forward from the back seat and called out the window, "Can we get the tree now? The program is over."

Mrs. Ellis leaned in the window, dangling the brown bag of peanuts and candy. She said, "The tree? Oh, Alice Schmidt is taking that to put in her store. She thought it needed a festive look."

Alice Schmidt ran the little store alongside the highway that passed through the village, selling mainly the staples that people were likely to run out of but didn't want to make a trip to Jackson just for a box of salt or a loaf of bread. Bit slid back in the seat without a word. Tom snatched the bag, rolled up the window and drove away. Mrs. Ellis stood in the schoolyard with her hands on her hips.

The next morning Tom shaved while listening to *POLKA PARADE* and went to town alone with a grocery list Anna had given him. Neither Anna nor Bit nor her two sisters cared about mingling with happy shoppers on the streets of Jackson while "Silver Bells" and "Silent Night" played on the speakers at the entrance door of Jackson Drug Store.

That night there were Christmas shows on the television, but nobody wanted to watch them so they went to bed early. Bit went to sleep wondering what she would say she got for Christmas after the holidays ended when the other kids were running down their lists of gifts.

She awoke to the usual morning smell of coffee, the *WHOMP, WHOMP, WHOMP* sound of her mother beating up the batter for pancakes. For her this was another Sunday like any other. She hated Sundays because that meant only one more night before she had to go back to school, but she couldn't go back to sleep so she got up, and besides that, there would be a week off school for the Christmas holidays. She poked Connie and Patty to get up too. The sight in the middle of the kitchen table was spectacular. It was bizarre. It was impossible. A round fat Christmas tree, three feet tall, completely decorated with Anna's silver and blue Christmas balls, branches drooping under the weight, silver icicles gleaming from the fat, colored lights. It was strange because the tree wasn't green and didn't smell like pine. It was brown and spikey, and Bit realized that her mother had decorated a tumble weed, and it was beautiful.

Three rectangular presents rested under the tree, one for each of the girls, two wrapped in brown paper sacking, one in newspaper pinstripe and tied with twine. Bit expected a couple of pair of socks, but when she opened it—her mother standing at the stove with a pancake turner in hand, smiling, and her dad hiding a smile behind a mug of coffee—the package contained a red transistor radio. Connie got a dark blue one, and Patty's was gray, but Anna had painted a little pink flower on Patty's with some of the nail polish that Bit had gotten her schoolmate for the gift exchange.

Bit looked at her mother and asked, "How?"

Anna simply smiled and put a finger across her lips. "Santa's secret," she said, but Tom looked at his eldest daughter and mouthed the words, "egg money."

There were no eggs for breakfast, but there was orange juice, little pigs, and pancakes with chokecherry jelly. Christmas dinner was a pair of pheasants baked with Anna's sage dressing, mashed potatoes and gravy, a big bowl of Anna's green beans canned the summer before, and bowls of raspberries for dessert.

Christmas night, Bit put her radio under her pillow, tuned low to KOMA out of Oklahoma City. In between the breathless announcer's pitch for local bands playing in Oklahoma and Kansas, places Bit knew she would never visit, she heard Connie Francis sing "Everybody's Somebody's Fool," and a couple of Elvis Presley's latest hits; the Drifters sang "Save the Last Dance for Me." She went to sleep with Chubby Checker doing "The Twist," and when she woke up the next morning, the radio battery was dead.

10

Bart Johnson felt his anxiety ease somewhat as the new year turned into mid-January. He'd been worried that he had sold off too much of his hay crop and wouldn't have enough to get his own cows through the winter, but except for that one big blizzard back in November, the weather had been dry and not as cold, so the cows didn't eat as much to keep their body heat up. He'd gotten his loan sweetened at the bank—Richard approved it, to his relief, and Betty had finally stopped spending. Brian had been quiet, which did make Bart wonder what he might be up to, but he accepted it as a good sign and didn't question. Susan, well, Susan. Nothing to worry about there except she was demanding a pony. Bart didn't need another animal eating up more winter feed. He'd repaired and done maintenance on all his farm equipment—the John Deere tractor he used for mowing and baling hay, the bigger, heavier Allis Chalmers one that pulled the low hay sled to the pasture and back when he fed his cows. His pickup was still in good shape for being four years old, and if Betty didn't demand another new car next fall, if his calf crop was good, and if the rains came at just the right time, he could be back in the black next November. Betty could demand and be damned, he was going to put his foot down this time.

Since that—situation—back in November, she still slept in the spare room, but she had started speaking to him again after that other incident at Christmas dinner. He'd said, "Please pass the salt," thinking that it was between Betty and Brian, and Brian would pass it, but Brian sat staring into space, so Betty picked up the cut glass saltshaker and flung it at his head. He'd dodged just in time as the shaker burst against the wall behind him. The kids sat silently, eyes as big as saucers, without saying a word. Betty smiled. He supposed she thought she was even then, because after that was when she started speaking to him again, just short sentences about routine everyday matters. Once in a while she commented on the weather. Their marriage would never be what it had been in the beginning, but a man didn't get permanent happiness in life, only a few fleeting seconds here and there. Bart would settle for truce, if he couldn't have peace between them.

He had leisure, too, once the cows were fed in the early mornings, time to rest and relax before calving season hit the first week of March. Used to be, calving time came along in April, but competition for bigger and heavier calves in the fall meant the calves had to be born earlier so they could mature and gain more weight over the summer. Usually the animals were auctioned off at so much per hundredweight, so the heavier they were, the more money in his pocket. Just ten pounds more weight per calf translated into twenty dollars or more each in his pocket, and multiply that by two hundred fifty head of calves, added up to five thousand dollars more or less. The drawback was that calving out that early ran the risk of bad weather. Calves born in cold, wet conditions sometimes died, and that was the reason he'd had so many losses the previous spring. One weekend five young heifers had gone into labor and delivered in the same night. He'd been running from cow to cow helping them deliver, and when the temperature dropped, he knew he had to act fast. They put up with four of the five calves in the bathroom overnight, bottle-feeding them, and then had the devil's own time of pairing the right calf up with the right mother when the weather warmed up. He prayed for a mild spring, but with March still six weeks away, he wanted more snow. His alfalfa fields needed the moisture the snowmelt would provide.

He sat in his recliner drinking his last cup of coffee while he listened to Claude Sauer on KOTA radio giving the weather report. No storm systems moving in today as a big high pressure hovered over the northern plains, but there was hope for next week. When the phone rang, he listened carefully. It was a party line, so you had to listen to the rings to know if the call was for you or someone else on the same line. The Johnsons' was two longs and a short; he heard that and then listened quietly when Betty picked it up in the kitchen. She talked for a few minutes, her voice more cheerful than he had heard it in weeks, probably one of the women from her silly club. Their meeting had been canceled for January; he didn't know why and didn't care. He was only grateful that he would get decent suppers every day of the month.

Betty hung up and walked into the living room. "Ben and Amelia asked us over to play cards on Friday night," Betty said.

Bart felt a surge of enthusiasm. Ben and Amelia ranched down closer to the Nebraska border in the Sandhills. Ben was a quiet sort and Amelia was okay. Well, Ben wasn't exactly a rancher, because only half his livestock was cattle. He ran sheep, claiming they did less damage to the fragile grasslands down in his area of the county. Once the deep grass roots died out from overgrazing, the land turned to a series of dry sandy washouts where nothing grew. Ben claimed sheep were the answer for high plains grazing. He argued that sheep gave two crops a year: a lamb crop and a wool crop, and a good proportion of the ewes had twins, but Bart had been born and bred a cattleman and wasn't willing to switch. The hogs had been his one fling, and he'd learned his lesson. No, from now on he'd stick with raising black Angus calves.

"I think that would be nice," he answered Betty's unspoken question. "So, after supper on Friday?"

"Yes. I already said we'd go," she said, walking back to the kitchen.

Bart controlled his irritation that she'd agreed to the invitation without asking him first.

"Anyone else going, or is it just going to be the four of us?" he called after her.

"Amelia said they were asking two other couples so we could have two tables of four. I've got leftover Christmas fruitcake in the freezer to bring along."

Bart wondered who the other couples were, but he didn't feel like asking.

Only one other couple showed up, which was awkward as hell because six in a game just doesn't work. They ended up switching out with four people playing at a time while two sat out. Bart liked the Bakers, but they had opted out at the last minute, claiming they had the flu. He was not particularly glad to see Gary and Pearl. As the evening wore on Gary lived up to Bart's expectations that the man would always be loud and vulgar. During one round when Bart and Amelia had played whist against Gary and Pearl, Gary had berated Pearl over every card she played, belittling the woman who sat with a nervous smile trying to pretend the insults were good-humored jokes. For the next round Betty and Pearl teamed up with Ben and Amelia, while Gary and Bart listened from the living room, drinking cold beer, which did not go well with Betty's fruitcake.

"What do you think about those trumpeter swans the refuge brought in?" Gary asked, twirling his can of beer in one hand.

"Never thought much about it, one way or the other," Bart answered. "Just some big old birds. We've got enough birds; I don't see why we have to save these."

"Ever see those birds? Man, I went out there a couple of weeks back just to check them out. Those bastards stand five feet tall. Biggest goddamned birds I ever saw."

Bart didn't have anything to say. He took a sip of beer.

Gary nudged him in the ribs. "Hey, you think they'd taste like turkey? I bet there's good eating on one of those."

"Yeah, I guess we won't ever find out," Bart said. "They're protected. Shoot one of those and you'd never get to eat it. You'd be eating slop in Ft. Leavenworth instead."

"Not if you didn't get caught," Gary laughed.

"I'd rather have a steak," Bart said.

"I thought you were a hamburger man," Gary said loudly. "You remember what you said? Remember?"

"Yes. Well, as long as it's beef." He got up and walked toward the kitchen. "Speaking of food, I think I'll take another piece of that fruitcake."

On the way home, Betty was chattier than she'd been in months. "You know what Pearl told me?"

Bart wasn't interested, but he grunted a response.

"Pearl told me that Keith Ford's oldest daughter, that red-haired girl, is pregnant."

Bart didn't care, but he said, "Oh?"

"Yes, she's pregnant. She's not married, you know," Betty continued.

Bart didn't care about that either, but since Betty seemed in a good mood, he didn't want to make her go quiet again, so he said, "Well, I suppose it happens."

"Well, yes, but it's not supposed to happen until a girl is married. And guess what else? She won't tell who's the father."

Bart couldn't think of anything to say.

"I bet she doesn't know who's the father. She's always been a wild one, you know," Betty continued. "Keith and Inez never did get a handle on those girls. Wouldn't surprise me if they all turned up pregnant, one right after the other."

"Don't say that. You never know, it could happen to our daughter," Bart said idly.

In spite of Claude Sauer's dry weather forecast, flakes of snow like big white goose feathers fell on the windshield. He switched on the wipers.

"Bart! Don't say that! That would never happen to Susan. We've raised her right," Betty snapped. "She's a good Christian girl. She'll marry a nice boy and someday she'll have children, but not until she's married."

You better hope so, Bart thought, but he didn't say anything. He doubted if at ten years old Susan knew where babies come from, even though she'd seen the bulls in the pasture mounting the cows, even saw a litter of kittens getting born out in the barn. He loved his daughter he guessed, in a distanced way, a long way from when he and Betty were first married, and he had wanted a son so badly.

Betty went silent for the rest of the drive home along country roads rapidly covering with heavy snow. When they pulled into the driveway, Betty got out and slammed the Impala door behind her, stalked across the yard into the house, and went right up to bed in the spare room. Bart thought he might like his wife better when she wasn't speaking to him.

11

Tom felt relieved every morning at work when he could sit by the swan pen and watch the birds in peace. Keith still obsessed over his daughter's pregnancy, repeating the same complaints and comments whether or not Tom made any comments back. "I never would have known she was pregnant if Inez hadn't told me. She wants Mary Ann to go see Doc Walters, but she won't go. She says people will talk, but goddammit, what if the kid's born funny? And if she'd went to the doc the kid would be okay. It's her kid, but goddammit it's my grandkid. Inez and Mary Ann are in a constant fuss. Every so often, Mary Ann gets fed up and goes over to stay at her Aunt Susie's for a few days, then she comes back and the fights start all over. I can't get any peace at home. Mary Ann's always been chunky built, a healthy-looking girl with a bit of a belly. She looks the same to me now, but I suppose that will change pretty damned soon, and that's when the old biddies who work in the courthouse will start wagging their tongues," Keith said.

Tom didn't tell Keith that the old biddies were already wagging their tongues. The word was out all over the county and, as if people didn't have anything better to do, they repeated the story and gave sideways glances at Mary Ann as she went about her waitressing job, wondering and speculating about who might be the father.

Tom's other coworkers were just as annoying. The manager, King, walked from his house next to the administration building with his head down and back again at the end of the day with little to say to anyone except to snap out orders and demand to know whether his last ones had been obeyed. During the day, he sat in his office fiddling with paperwork that no one knew what it was for. He'd had some disagreement with Carl, but Carl wouldn't say what about. Carl had lost the enthusiasm he had when he'd first come to the refuge as an intern, and now he sat in the break room—the admin building wasn't big enough to provide a lowly intern with an office space—reading textbooks and making notes. Tom thought he might be working on the thesis for his master's degree. The plywood square Tom sat on outside the swan pen was his own refuge at work, a three foot square piece of wood where no one batted words off his ears or made him feel like they had no words to bat, and it was somehow Tom's fault. From observing the swans hours every day, it seemed to him that many of the swans were pairing up, choosing mates. He knew they were two-year-old birds just past that age when they'd been brought down from Red Rocks, but until he asked Carl, he had no idea at what age swans mated.

Carl grudgingly told him that there wasn't much information, but what there was indicated that other types of swans likely chose their mates during the winter of their second year. When Tom asked further questions—When did the female start making a nest? Did the male help with that? When did she lay eggs? How many eggs?—Carl mumbled and shrugged. Tom just observed the swans and wrote down what he saw.

He usually saw Bill and Martha at the place where the slow flowing creek had cut into the bank near the fence, even though the water had frozen over weeks earlier and stayed so frozen that Tom had to chop holes in the ice every morning so the birds could drink. They didn't just drink it, they got in and paddled around even as the low temperatures quickly refroze the creek, forming a thin skim of crackly ice on top, which grew to an inch or more thick overnight. He shuddered thinking of sticking his own feet in ice water, but the birds didn't seem to mind.

He noticed Bill and Martha spending more time by the fence, a bit farther up from the cut in the bank, sitting in a patch of tall rushes, grooming each other, and he suspected, he hoped, that was their chosen nesting site. He paid attention to the others that seemed to be paired off, but he couldn't decide if any of those pairs had chosen a favorite spot in the pen. None of them sat on the tires atop the mud pyramids.

One morning in early February, King stood waiting outside the admin building when Tom pulled into his usual parking spot. He was not happy about something, Tom could tell from the characteristic way King paced when he was put off—three steps one direction, turnabout, pace three steps the other. Tom took a breath and got out of his car, zipping up the overcoat he wore over his usual coveralls.

King didn't bother to answer Tom's civil "good morning" but said, "Warder, you're supposed to be observing those goddamned birds."

Tom's eyebrows went up. He thought that's what he'd been doing, eight hours a day, five days a week, for weeks, even months now, but he only said, "Yes, sir."

King glared before he turned to pace three steps away, turn and come back. "Observing the birds means also observing the pen and everything in and around it," King grumbled.

Again Tom said, "Yes, sir."

King turned and paced, turned and came back. "Come have a look at how bad you've been at your goddamned job," he said, stalking down the slight rise to Tom's usual observation spot, than along the fence to the place where the creek had cut under the bank near the fence, except the bank had been dug away farther until the fence hung suspended over the open place. A fluff of swan feather caught in the fence floated gently up and down.

Tom felt remorse. He should have noticed, but from his position on his plywood square the gap was invisible. He didn't know what the swans might do if they escaped. Would they stay near the pen, or would they try to go back to Red Rocks Montana? He scanned the pen, looking for the pair, and spotted them over against the far fence, standing together, looking like a pair of children who'd been caught at a forbidden activity. "Did any of them get out?" Tom asked.

"Hell, yes, they got out. Goddammit, man, can't you do your job?"

Tom scanned the pen, doing a quick count of the birds. He knew them as individuals by small differences in their markings, but before he could run down the inventory list in his head, King said, "Bill and Martha! They woke me up about sunup. Someone kept knocking at the door, but when I went to look, there was Bill and Martha, pecking at the goddamned door knocker!"

Tom barely controlled his urge to laugh by bringing his hand up over his mouth and frowning. He supposed the shiny door knocker had attracted their attention. He wanted to ask, "When they knocked, did you let them in?" but he pushed that down as well. He had to get control of his reaction. He took a deep breath, and asked, "How did you get them back in the pen?"

"When I started yelling at them to get the fuck out of there, they ran back and crawled through that hole under the fence. That's how I found out how bad you are at your job! I want that hole fixed, and after this, I want you walking the perimeter every goddamned morning so this shit doesn't happen again."

"I'll get that done right now," Tom said.

"See that you do," King said. After pausing a moment for emphasis, he trudged back up the slope to the admin building.

Tom walked down to the equipment shed for a pick to break up the icy ground and a shovel to get the dirt into the gap. Once inside the building, he leaned against the wall and laughed at the idea of King dressed only in his underwear, standing in the open door of his house yelling at a pair of five foot tall birds.

King dressed him down on a Friday, and after Tom had walked the perimeter, he spotted a couple of other places where, with a little industrious digging at the bank, the swans could escape and search outside for roots to eat. He decided fixing them all would require more time and heavy equipment, so he fixed what he could with the pick and shovel and volunteered to come in on Saturday after Keith had finished maintenance on the little caterpillar tractor.

After the family had come home from the weekly trip to Jackson, Tom changed into his regular work clothes. Bit begged to go with him, but he hesitated. There was really nothing she could do except get in the way, but she promised to sit quietly and take notes for him while he worked, so he gave in. Anna and the girls had been out to see the birds right after they were brought in, and Anna had been amazed at how big they were. Bit, too, was interested in learning about them but disappointed that Tom had so little information to give. The younger girls were far more interested in climbing the fire tower, a small structure perched a hundred feet up on a timber frame. During hot, dry summers, the men took turns up in the tower with a pair of binoculars, watching for prairie fires. Bit asked Tom from time to time about the birds, and he told her what he'd seen. Together they wondered about the things that Carl hadn't been able to answer.

Tom handed Bit the clipboard with the yellow lined table and a pencil, showed her the plywood square to sit on, and went to get the cat. While he pushed dirt up around the pen's perimeter, Bit sat quietly, watching, writing occasionally. The work took a few hours, but Bit sat patiently, and when Tom had finished and put the cat away, he came back to the pen.

She moved over to give him space on the plywood and handed him her notes.

"Dad, I saw something strange. You see those birds over there? Not Bill and Martha, those two nearby?"

He nodded. "Okay, but they don't look strange to me."

"No, no, not how they look now, but what they were doing. I think they were—I think they were mating. They were in the water grooming themselves. I mean not each other, themselves, dipping their beaks in the water and rubbing it on their own feathers. Then they started doing it faster and faster. Pretty soon, a few minutes later, they kind of wrapped their necks together, staring at each other. Then one climbed on top of the other. I thought at first one of them was trying to drown the other one, because they were almost under water, but then they both stretched their wings out a little bit and they did it."

"You've just seen a pair of swans mating," Tom said, a little jealous that on her first day of observing the birds, Bit had seen something he hadn't seen after weeks of watching.

"Really? Now they'll lay eggs?"

"I suppose they'll make a nest first, but I would guess they'll mate several more times."

"Dad, that's the most interesting thing I've ever seen," Bit said, smiling. "Does that mean they'll hatch babies? That someday they won't be an endangered species?"

"That's the idea," Tom said, pleased that his daughter had taken an interest beyond what seemed like her previous casual questions.

They sat at the pen hoping to see Bill and Martha mate until the sun went down making it too dark to see. As they were driving home, the car heater on high to warm their cold feet, Tom remarked, "You know, Bit, you've seen something that very few other human beings have seen. A pair of trumpeter swans mating."

Within the next week, Tom observed Bill and Martha's mating dance several times, as well as three other pairs. He watched carefully, but so far none of them appeared to be making nests. Perhaps captive birds wouldn't complete the entire cycle from pair bonding to mating to nesting to hatching the eggs into cygnets. Maybe the eggs wouldn't be fertile; maybe there wouldn't be enough room in the pen to accommodate the territorial requirements of each pair. Another thing he noticed: the birds' wing feathers had almost completely grown out from when they had been clipped the previous fall. He mentioned it to King, but the manager had retreated back into his original indifference and resentment of the swans. Tom continued patrolling the perimeter fence at least once a day, looking for gaps in the fence.

Toward the end of February, the wind blew a chinook melting the last snowfall and drying up the mud from the snowmelt. Tom surprised Anna and the girls one Sunday morning by asking if they wanted to go for a drive, but Anna and the two youngest girls were making cinnamon rolls, so Bit and Tom drove away through Jackson and nine miles west turned north at a junction, taking a graveled road up through the little town of Kyle, then west down to Porcupine, where they stopped at the little crossroads gas station and store for Cokes and Penrose sausages that the proprietor wrapped in bits of waxed paper.

Bit knew where they were going. Once a year Tom made a pilgrimage to the tiny village of Wounded Knee, the site of a massacre in the late-nineteenth century, when a group of Indians returning from an approved off-reservation fall hunt had been caught by Custer's old Seventh Cavalry unit and were massacred on the spot. After that the Lakota people had discovered a new spiritual and political movement called the Ghost Dance. A Paiute visionary named Wovoka had a vision that indicated if Indians wore special shirts they would be protected from bullets, and if they danced in a certain way all the white people would disappear and all their ancestors killed by white men's guns and germs would come back to life. The movement had spread across the Great Plains with dances held at multiple locations including the country home of Sitting Bull, one of the last surviving war chiefs.

Some local whites who didn't understand were convinced the Indians were performing war dances preparing to massacre white settlers, so the Indian agents forbade dancing, but the Indians persisted. The whites called on the army to protect them. Sitting Bull was killed during a dance he hosted when a group of tribal police and military showed up at his camp to stop the dance. An Indian tribal policeman named Bull Head dealt the fatal blow, but the death of Sitting Bull only created more fear among the settlers, who were fearful of reprisals from the Indians. In response, the army and the Indian agents ordered all Indians who were off reservation for any reason to return immediately.

Chief Big Foot and his group didn't get the message, but with winter rapidly setting in, the group was en route back to their agency when the cavalry was sent out to round them up. They were found and forced into camp at Wounded Knee, only a few miles from the agency. Some young troopers in the Seventh Cavalry, either from ignorance and fear or desire to avenge Custer's death, fired on the Indians in the middle of the night. When the sun came up, the dead bodies of Big Foot's people extended for a mile or more up the narrow creek bed where they had tried to flee. A blizzard moved in before the bodies could be moved. When the storm ended the bodies were discovered frozen in bizarre positions. Photographers recorded many of the bodies, particularly that of Big Foot, which is still pictured on postcards at various souvenir stores in the Upper Midwest.

The dead were taken to the local Catholic church at the agency, where decorations from the recently celebrated Christmas Mass were still on display. One banner above the altar read "Peace on Earth, Good Will Toward Men." Many bodies were buried in a mass grave in front of a small church on a hill at the massacre site.

Bit knew the story. She had been to the site at least once a year since she could remember. Sometimes her mother and sisters came too. They didn't pray in the little church but sat mostly silent on the narrow cement rim that encircled the mass grave. Tom Warder had ancestors buried in that mass grave. He didn't talk about them much; once he had told the history to the girls when they were small. He came to honor the dead and to remember, not to preach.

This was the first year that only Bit had come to the site with her father. They parked the car and climbed the hill through tall reddish brown grass, dead remains from the previous season. While the air was warmer than usual, on the Great Plains of South Dakota, warmer than usual in February only meant a daily high temperature above freezing.

Tom sat down on one side of the narrow cement line that formed the rectangular perimeter of the grave, patting the ground beside him. Bit bent her knees and sat on the cold ground. "Dad? Are all those people really buried under here?" she asked. "It doesn't look big enough."

"You'd be surprised how many people you can put in the ground if the hole is deep enough. And if you fling them in any old way," he answered, looking not at the grave but at the cloudbank building in the west. "Shhh. Listen."

The wind rising and falling found a voice in a loose shingle on the church roof, whistling and howling. Down on Route 27 an old Chevy station wagon with a loose muffler bumped over the potholes in the broken blacktop, going south.

Tom lifted his cap, letting the wind ruffle his gray-streaked hair, reached out and tousled his daughter's hair. "Why are we here?" he asked.

Bit knew he expected her answer to be more than the casual, factual. "Because we come up here every year." She remembered other visits over the past years of her life, walking up the hill through snow ankle deep, or slipping in mud, or when the grass was green and a breeze blew softly upon her face, her sisters running and jumping alongside her father, and her father, rarely speaking, always sitting on the rim of the grave, asking that same question: "Why are we here?"

"Because they were here first," she answered. That was not the right answer; she knew that, she felt like she was getting no closer to what her father wanted her to say: to know, to understand about this sacred place. He asked her that question often, not just here on the top of this lonely hill.

The creek wound around the base of the hill, dry, lined with brittle brush and squat trees with a few tired gray-green leaves still clinging waiting to be pushed off by new spring growth. That was the creek her ancestors had run up while trying to escape, were gunned down and bludgeoned, old men, women, and children, their red blood spilling out on the white snow, their screams and cries carried on the wind.

Bit stood, stretched, moved back to sit on the sun-warmed, cracked cement church step. Half a dozen brown beer bottles nestled in the weeds to one side, the labels faded and peeling. She looked up at the puffy white clouds floating overhead.

"What do you hear?" Tom asked.

The wind howled beneath the shingles on the church roof. "I hear their voices in the wind," she said.

He nodded. "Looks like we won't get any snow," he said. "Those clouds are going around. Let's go."

At the bottom of the hill he stopped where a sign lay on its face, toppled over in the weeds and the dirt, reached down and turned it over. It read only "Wounded Knee Battle Site" in faded black letters on a white background. "Not a battle," he said. "A massacre."

Bit slammed the car door three times before the latch caught. Tom cranked the engine that whined and complained before the motor turned over. He put the car in gear, circled it, and drove slowly away. "I'll buy you another pop at the trading post," he offered.

"Okay," she said, gloating inside a little that her sisters had missed out on the treat. "Dad," she asked, "are we an endangered species?"

"Not yet."

12

Bart Johnson felt very pleased with himself, pleased that he had turned the bulls into the cows earlier, meaning the calves that would be born in a few days would be even earlier than last year's, even though bad weather the previous year had meant the loss of too many of the babies. It was a risk, but he figured the odds were this year the weather would be favorable. Early born calves meant not only greater weight gain over the summer but also that he could market his calves as much as two weeks earlier than other ranchers. The ones earliest to market brought the highest prices. He needed every dime of extra money if he was to pay off that mortgage and not have to extend for another year.

He stood on his porch, letting the warm breeze ruffle his graying hair. Late February and the thermometer on the porch post read 42 degrees at eight o'clock in the morning. As long as the nighttime low temperature stayed above freezing, his calves would be all right. He felt so good that he decided he would go to the Wednesday livestock auction, knowing there would be a good supper when he got home because Betty's club had met the previous Wednesday at some other lady's house. Betty was still speaking to him only in spurts—some days she chatted about her usual inane nonsense with the odd interesting bit thrown in, and some days she stalked around the house, her hands beneath her apron front staring out the window without a word. He'd given up any attempt at civil conversation. If she talked, he talked, but if she didn't he ignored it. Nothing to be done about it, so why fuss?

Bart thought every other farmer and rancher in the county must have decided it was a good day to go to the auction, because the scarred bleachers surrounding the metal pipe central arena in the sales barn were nearly full. He walked up the stairs at one side to the third row finding a vacant spot between old Orville Curtis and Pete Gier, who everyone privately called Gyro Gearloose because he was always inventing some complicated piece of farm equipment that didn't work as Pete intended and because his last name was pronounce as "gear." Only three cattle buyers had bothered to attend this off-season sale, probably as an excuse to get out of Omaha and into the country. They sat on the first row of bleachers in their tailored stockmen's suits, flipping a lazy finger now and then to bid on one or more of the canners and cutters that came through, and canners and cutters were the bulk of the animals for sale—dry cows that had sluffed their calves over the winter or never were in calf to begin with, a few with obvious signs of injury, not worth the vet bills to keep.

Pete nodded to Bart when he sat down and so did old Orville, after peering a moment, half blind, until he figured out who Bart was. Orville had a lit roll-up, taking a puff now and then when he remembered and letting the ashes fall. Ed Glover sat on the second row just in front of Orville, his pants buckled so low over his big belly that his butt crack showed where his shirt had come untucked. Now and then a draft in the building lifted the ashes from Orville's roll-up, swirled them and slowly deposited them in Ed Glover's butt crack. Orville was either too blind to see or didn't care, and Ed's butt was probably so fat it was numb to any heat leftover in the ashes.

Toward the end of the sale a dwarf calf was brought through. The auctioneer made a pitch that the calf might make a good pet for a kid, which it might but only for a few months or maybe a year. Dwarf calves were genetic freaks, usually dying at birth while those that survived usually had some messed-up guts so they died young. Dumb idea to bring one of the dwarfs to the sale because that would signal to all the other farmers and ranchers that your herd had that defective gene somewhere. Bart knew enough science to understand that it took a defective gene from both the bull and the cow to match up for a dwarf to result, and that sent a signal to everyone that it would be a bad idea to buy a young bull or breeding heifer from that rancher's herd. A dwarf might be cute in their oddly misshapen body, but it was one less salable calf to ship in the fall. He looked up at the lighted sign above the auctioneer's head where the name of the consignee appeared. Everyone else saw it too. The calf went to one of the stock buyers, probably going for dog food, and the sale was over.

Bart went for a drink at the Legion Club with Orville and Ed and a couple of other ranchers. When Gary came through the door, Bart half turned his back hoping he wouldn't be seen, but Gary slapped him on the back as he shoved into the booth beside Bart. After finishing their drinks, all except Orville got up and left the bar.

"Hey, Snipe," Gary called out to Verda, who was running back and forth from bar to table carrying trays of drinks or returning empties. "Snipe," he yelled again. "Bring me a CC water back."

Verda sat down her laden tray of empties on the bar, blowing a strand of hair from her eyes. Gary called her Snipe so often that she answered to it. She gave him a wave and called over the buzz of conversation in the bar, "Give me a second, will you?"

Gary nudged Bart in the ribs with an elbow. "Look at those skinny long legs, will you? Looks just like a snipe, huh?"

Bart gave as small a grin as he could in acknowledgment. He slid deeper into the booth. Verda brought Gary's drink, took his money without a word. As she turned to walk back to the bar, Gary tugged at the bow on the back of her bar apron, but Verda didn't notice as she held her loaded tray in front of her. As she walked the apron slipped lower and lower until it tangled around her feet. She tripped and went down face first into the crashing mess, leftover drops of beer and booze flying amid the shards of glass. Gary punched Bart in the shoulder. The bartender helped Verda up, a trickle of blood coursing down her cheek. Maybe she knew why her apron had slipped down and maybe she didn't. She went to the women's restroom, returning in a few minutes with a piece of toilet paper stuck to the side of her face, and resumed delivering drinks and collecting the empty glasses and beer bottles.

Bart stirred his drink with the red and white striped straw.

"You're being mighty quiet," Gary said.

Bart shrugged and said, "Nothing much to say."

"I think you're just playing dumb," Gary said with a sly smile.

"Dumb about what?"

"You know."

"I really don't know what you're talking about," Bart said wearily. The day that had started out so well didn't seem so good now. He wondered what Betty might be making for supper. Wednesdays were usually pork chop nights, and even though Bart was a beef man, he liked the way Betty cooked them, browned a little first, then baked in the oven with sage dressing, green beans with bacon in them for a side dish, mashed potatoes and maybe gravy. Maybe coconut cake for dessert. He wasn't much of a sweets eater, but he did like her coconut cake. He kept stirring his drink.

"Maybe you're more of a bull than a steer after all," Gary said, but for a change he wasn't bellowing so everyone could hear, but he spoke in a low voice.

"What the hell are you talking about?" Bart demanded. Those words brought back the memory of the first time Gary had said something like that.

"I hear someone's got a bun in the oven," Gary said, and now he added a wink to the sly look.

Bart remembered another conversation with Betty after the card party when she told him that Keith's daughter, Mary Ann, was pregnant and not married. Bart knew the girl when he saw her, but he never saw her except when he was eating a burger at the steak house, and he hadn't been in that café in weeks.

"What's that supposed to mean?"

"You stupid or something? A bun in the oven. A pie in the window. *KNOCKED UP!*" Gary said the last two words so loudly that the men at the next table glanced up.

"Who are you talking about?"

"Who do you think?" Gary smirked.

Bart shoved Gary hard, who laughed and put up a defensive arm. "Get out of the way!" Bart snarled, his breaths coming fast so he panted out the words.

Gary stood up, removed his hat and made a mocking bow.

Bart hurried past the other tables, imagining eyes following him to the door.

He drove home without seeing the dry fields, bare of vegetation, ready for the spring planting in a few weeks, past the trees along the creek, limbs stark and reaching for the pale blue sky overhead.

He didn't remember driving up the lane to his own house, didn't remember switching off the ignition on the pickup, wondering who started the rumor that he was the father of Mary Ann's baby, who repeated it, why anyone would believe it. He loved his small, rural agricultural society, working with the animals, the smell of new-mown alfalfa in the early summer, the smack of bugs on the windshield when he drove down the highway, the sound of distant thunder rumbling bringing much needed rain, the pretty black calves, the way iced tea felt sliding down his throat on a hot summer day, all of those things. He hated the small mindedness, the vicious gossip. He wanted to be alone, an unmarried old bachelor taking care of his land, all twelve hundred and some acres of it, except he wished he owned it all, not just the two hundred acres he had inherited from his father. The other thousand acres was all owned by Indians, mostly 160 acres each, not enough to make a living on in itself, but by putting all those leases together with the land he owned outright, he had a nice midsize ranching operation.

He came to himself when Susan tapped on the window of his truck, realizing he remembered nothing about the drive home, nothing at all since he'd walked out of the Legion Club. He consulted his wristwatch: Ten minutes after five. Betty always cooked supper early in the winter, but come summer it would get later and later so Bart could stay outside working as late as possible. "Dad, are you coming in? Mom says supper is on the table."

He said, "All right," as he opened the pickup door and stepped down into the gravel. Susan skipped along behind him as he walked to the house.

He washed up and sat down at the table just as Betty opened the oven, took out a clear Pyrex casserole dish, and set it on a hot mat in the center of the table. He should've known by the smell that it was tuna and macaroni casserole and not pork chops and dressing, but he didn't care. It didn't matter. He dished some of the steaming tuna and noodles with green peas onto plates as they were passed to him, buttered a piece of bread, and ate. Dessert was canned peaches.

Susan chattered on to her mother, begging for a birthday party at the roller rink across the state line in Merriman, Nebraska. Betty was noncommittal, so Susan turned to her father, who barely heard. "Yeah, sure, that would be fine," Bart said at last.

Brian flicked a pea at Susan, who didn't notice. Bart ignored him.

"That's stupid. Roller-skating, how little kid can you get? I hope you all fall and bust your asses," Brian said.

Betty called him down for the remark, but he continued. "Well, really, Mom. How much fun can that be, creeping around and around that old barn of a place on wheels to that Lawrence Welk old fart music?"

"I didn't invite you to come!" Susan said.

"I wouldn't be caught dead in that place," Bart said.

"Good! You can stay home and play with your old guns," Susan said.

Bart caught the last remark, and said, "What guns? What playing around with guns?"

Brian smacked Susan on the arm. "Big mouth."

"Mom, he hit me!"

"Quit fighting, you two, or you will have to leave the table," Betty admonished, but Bart interrupted.

"I said, what guns? Brian?"

Brian polished his empty plate with a piece of bread, swirling it around and around, a pout on this face. "Nothing. She's making shit up," he said.

"Am not!"

"Okay, okay, Susan, shut up," Bart said. "Now, what about guns? Have you been taking my guns out of the cabinet? What are you doing with them?"

"Aw, Dad, I've been hunting rabbits down on the creek. All the guys at school do it. They're paying thirty cents a pelt in Hot Springs," Brian said.

"You didn't ask," Bart said sternly. "Guns are not toys."

"I know that! I just said, didn't I, that I was shooting rabbits to sell. You know, for a little spending money. It's not like you've been doling out big allowances lately."

"What do you need a big allowance for?" Bart said. It was true that since his money troubles, he hadn't given the kids nearly as much weekly allowance as they were used to getting.

"I'm saving up for a car," Brian said. "My friends have cars so they can drive back and forth to school, and I'm still riding the bus with the little kids. It isn't fair."

Bart could understand that, but he also knew that most of Brian's friends lived farther out in the country where the school bus didn't run. It was true that Brian was sixteen, soon to be seventeen, and most country boys got their driver's permit at fourteen and their permanent license at sixteen, but most country boys drove tractors in their father's fields, mowing and raking and baling hay, drove the tractors pulling hay sleds in the winter to feed cattle. They belonged to 4-H and FFA; they raised a project animal that they showed at the county fair and sometimes at the state fair. Brian couldn't be trusted to feed the barn cats once a week as a supplement for the mice they were supposed to catch. While the other boys took hold, lending a hand and contributing something to their family's income, Brian sat in the living room watching television or up in his room doing god knows what for god knows why. Bart remembered how embarrassed he'd been the previous fall when the FFA held its annual slave auction at the sale barns. Each of the FFA boys sold their day's work at auction to local farmers and ranchers. Each boy worked for one day, and the money the farmer or rancher paid went to the FFA treasury. Bart still recalled how he felt when Gary's sons, big strapping boys, had brought the highest prices at the auction, and Gary had asked where Brian was.

Bart shoved his chair back and said, "All right. Go rabbit hunting, but you ask first. Every time you want to go hunt, you ask before you take a single one of the guns."

Brian smiled in triumph.

"You *ASK*. Every time."

Bart went into the living room, switched on the television. *WANTED: DEAD OR ALIVE* had just come on. He watched Steve McQueen as Josh Randall, the bounty hunter, walk along a board-walk, his spurs ringing with each step, stopping at a wall with wanted posters. He glanced over a couple, reached up and snatched one down. The camera moved in for a close-up on the actor's face. Bart thought McQueen didn't look tough like he supposed the director meant him to look. Bart thought he looked sneaky.

This was a man's show, he thought. Rarely were there any women guest acting. Mostly it was Josh Randall running down a bad guy, which would lead to the inevitable shoot-out with Randall fanning the trigger of his big six-gun from a semi-squatting position, holding the pose a few seconds, then walking forward to nudge the dead outlaw's body with the toe of a scuffed boot. Life was so simple on TV, Bart thought. Good guys and bad guys and the bad guys always lost, after a fight, yeah, that was right, but in the end, justice was served. There was no justice in real life.

Over the television, he heard Susan and Brian bickering, then Betty calling them down, and finally nothing but the television, a commercial for GE, and then the show wrapped up. He didn't pay any attention to what came on next. He wished he'd thought to pick up the Jackson weekly newspaper when he was in town. There might have been something in there to distract him from his troubles.

Betty came in and sat down in what she called her lady chair at the other end of the couch. Her green tweed upholstered chair didn't recline; it had a lower back than Bart's recliner, and it rocked. She sat quietly for a minute, her chin on her chest, rocking, then she got up and shut off the television and sat down again, her feet crossed at the ankles.

"What did you do that for? I was watching that," Bart complained.

"No, you weren't. I need to tell you something," she said. She had her hands held together in front of her as if she were praying. She didn't look at him.

After a long minute or so, Bart said, "Well, it can't be any worse than what else I've heard today, so go ahead."

"Bart, I'm pregnant."

13

Tom sometimes felt like he was the only employee at the refuge who cared about the trumpeter swans. Findley was indifferent; Carl's enthusiasm waxed and waned, but added together and averaged out, came out neutral; King's resentment about not being consulted before the project was dumped on him manifested itself constantly, and Keith was so consumed with his family problems that he drowned himself in his own misery down in the equipment shed, only coming up for air now and then. Tom observed and recorded, watching as nearly half of the swans paired up and mated, and he thought he saw signs that Bill and Martha might be making a nest. The indifference and hostility among his coworkers had become so routine that Tom was surprised when Keith came in late one morning, slammed the door of his old Jeep and stalked down to the swan pen, where Tom sat on his usual seat.

"Tom, we need to have a word with King. He has to do something," Keith said, without even his usual grunted acknowledgment to Tom's "Good morning."

"Do something about what?" Tom asked. He hadn't seen Keith this agitated about anything in weeks.

"That Johnson kid!"

Tom had to think a minute to decide what Johnson kid Keith was talking about. He knew Bart Johnson had a son—Brad? Bruce? something like that—and he knew that Keith lived south of the refuge and drove past Johnson's place when he came to work, unlike

Tom, who lived in the opposite direction, north of the refuge. Mary Ann had to drive more than 20 miles to get to her job in Jackson.

"That Johnson kid is walking around with a loaded shotgun, early in the mornings," Keith went on.

"Lot of people carry shotguns. There's no law against it. I know he's got a permit because he took the gun safety class a couple of years ago when King appointed me to teach it along with Bob Hunter. At least there was a Johnson kid there. I didn't remember his first name, but I know Bart has just one boy," Tom said. Hunter was the local game warden. "He's probably hunting rabbits. Lots of people do, especially the local boys. Gives them a bit of spending money."

"Early in the morning? No, most of those boys go jacklighting," Keith argued.

Jacklighting was illegal, but still done because it was an easier way to spot and kill rabbits than walking the snow-choked gullies and prairies in the daytime. The hunters drove along country roads, stopping now and again to turn their vehicle so the headlights shone out across the snowy fields and pastures or used a spotlight that plugged into the cigarette lighter. Rabbits came out at night to feed on the dry plant stems that poked up through the snow, and instinctually froze in place when the lights hit them, making them easy targets for the hunters. "He's walking awful close to the refuge fence. I bet he's shooting pheasants across the fence, probably even coming onto refuge property to do it," Keith went on.

"Do you have any proof of that? He might just be walking the perimeter. A lot of hunters do that."

"Yeah, they do. In hunting season. It ain't hunting season, Tom."

"He might be hunting rabbits, not pheasants, but you ought to tell King," Tom said.

"That's like spitting in the wind," Keith said, kicking at a hummock of grass that had been mashed down from Tom's repeated footsteps in the area.

"Tell you what. Keep an eye out for that kid, what's his name?" The name came to Tom all of a sudden. "Brian, that's it. Maybe come to work a little earlier or a little later than usual, every day. See if you catch him inside the fence. If you do, that's when you tell King."

"All right. But I know that little son of a bitch is up to something," Keith said as he walked off toward the equipment building.

Glad that Keith had found something else to talk about other than his wild daughter, Tom was also disturbed that that Johnson kid—Brian—might be hunting illegally on refuge property. The law governing the refuge was pretty straightforward: not only was it illegal to hunt anything on the refuge, it was illegal to carry any firearm onto refuge property. If one of the hunters who routinely walked the perimeter during hunting season shot a pheasant outside refuge property but it flew back across the line, even a few inches in, technically they weren't allowed to retrieve the bird. Tom was pretty sure that the rule got broken all the time, but he had never heard of anyone—adult or kid—bold enough to carry a gun onto refuge property. Maybe Keith was wrong and the kid was only out for rabbits, jackrabbits or cottontails hunting along the edge of the creek that crossed Tom's land, now leased to Bart Johnson, the creek that ran under the fence and back into the refuge. The kid wasn't illiterate; he must have read the signs posted every quarter of a mile that said clearly: LaCreek National Wildlife Refuge. No hunting. No firearms. Maybe Keith was right. Maybe Brian Johnson was up to something.

Tom had other concerns to worry about. He'd checked the swan pen fences every morning, filling in any questionable spots with dirt dug from a pit a hundred yards up the creek, tamping it in solid, but he worried that the swans might find a hole in the fence covering over the top of the pen, the fence that was now sagging in places. Their wing feathers had almost completely grown out from when they were first clipped back in September. He'd mentioned it to King a couple of times, but King had only grunted a non-reply. Bill and Martha were already hop-flying a short distance inside the pen. Maybe if they made a nest they would settle down.

BIT'S GRANNY WAS BACK. THE OLD LADY HAD GONE TO VISIT her grandson, Bit's cousin Marvin, in Minneapolis right after Christmas. Marvin's mother, now dead several years, was Anna's sister, and his father had long since disappeared. Granny blamed the army. Marvin had dropped out of high school, gotten arrested repeatedly for drunk and disorderly, and finally, when he was suspected of burglary, the justice of the peace had given Marvin an ultimatum: prison or the army. Marvin didn't last through boot camp. He was allergic to the wool in the army uniforms and given a discharge, or so Marvin said. Back home he picked up the odd job or two living with Granny next door until he'd found some girl who would put up with him and followed her off to Minneapolis. The girl disappeared but Marvin stayed in Minneapolis. Granny claimed that Marvin was an artist, so he should be given some leeway. Artists were different, she said. Anna did not approve, but she didn't argue with her mother; she was just glad that Marvin didn't live next door anymore.

When Bit and Patty came home from school, Granny and Anna sat at the table drinking cups of the thick black coffee left over from breakfast, with Connie perched on Granny's lap. Bit pushed a protesting Connie aside to hug her grandmother, who chuckled as she reached over Bit to ruffle Patty's hair. "Girls! Girls, give your granny some peace," Anna admonished.

"When did you get here, Granny?" Bit asked as she sat in the chair next to the old lady. She missed her granny, who always indulged the girls with a bit of peppermint candy or some other treat, even though Bit hadn't missed being taken to her granny every time she messed up a story, a story with a moral, instead of getting a spanking.

"Just an hour or so ago. I caught a ride back with the Black Eyes. They were up there helping out their daughter. She just had another baby, you know," the old lady said.

Bit got up and went to the bedroom. She wasn't interested in babies. She reached under the bed she shared with her sisters for the notebook she kept there. A spiral-bound notebook with a brown cover. Bit had erased the penciled math problems and used the notebook to write down vocabulary words in Lakota that her granny told her. She was trying to learn the language. Not Indian, but Lakota, as Granny called the language. Anna said it was properly called Lakota, that saying "Indian" implied that all Indians spoke one language, and Anna had learned better when she went to boarding school, where there had been Indian kids from a variety of tribes, each one speaking their own language. Bit was smart enough to know that you couldn't just trade a word in one language for a word in another language and that sometimes the words in one language didn't get said in the same order in another language, but she had to start somewhere. She wanted to learn Lakota so she could cuss out her schoolmates and not get punished for cussing because they wouldn't understand what she was saying. Whenever she could get her granny's attention, she asked how to say a word in Lakota, and how to say entire sentences. She hadn't asked to learn cuss words. Not with Anna listening. Besides, if you snarled out words in another language, even if they were ordinary words, the other person might think they were getting cussed at when all you were saying was "corn." *WAGAMAHAZU* fit that. It made Connie and Patty run screaming to tell their mom when Bit had tried it out on them.

"Guess what?" Patty asked, and without waiting for Bit to answer, she said, "Granny is making wojapi for supper."

Wojapi. That meant a kind of pudding made with berries. Usually wild berries like chokecherries, which Bit couldn't stand to eat fresh because they were puckery and not sweet at all, but they made great jelly. Not so good wojapi. "Chokecherry wojapi?" Bit asked.

"No," Anna said, as she sat down fanning herself with her apron tail. She'd been standing over the propane gas kitchen range, stirring the chili she was cooking. "Whew. Feels like early summer, not nearly the first of March," she said.

"In like a lion, out like a lamb. In like a lamb, out like a lion," Granny said. "We'll have some late-spring blizzards."

"What kind of wojapi?" Bit persisted.

"We'll use the last quart of raspberries your auntie put up last summer," Anna said.

"Oh." Bit wasn't sure how she felt about that. She liked the raspberries as they were, packed in sugar syrup, and raspberry wojapi would be just as sweet, only thicker. She started peppering her grandmother with requests for new words in Lakota in between the women's conversation.

"Granny, how do you say 'dog' in Lakota?"

The word came quickly—*SUNKA*—but Granny pronounced it as if it was spelled "shoonka," so that's the way Bit wrote it down. Next she asked for "horse," and Grandmother said *SUNKAKA*.

"That's almost the same as dog, Granny. Are you sure?"

Anna frowned at her eldest daughter. She didn't like it when her daughters questioned an adult, particularly an elder. It showed lack of respect.

"Sunkaka. Yes," Grandmother Richards said. "Long time ago, our people didn't have horses, just dogs. Everything we had we carried from place to place on our backs or the dogs carried them in packs. When we saw horses for the first time, we thought they were just bigger dogs. 'Sunkaka' means something like 'big dog.'"

Bit made a little note beside the new word. History, she thought. Language contains a bit of history if you knew enough to ask the right questions. She got a few more words written down, colors mostly: black=*SAPA*; blue=*BLO*; red=*LUTA*; and so on. She got one entire sentence that took her a while to write down because her grandmother said it so fast that Bit had to ask her to repeat it, slowly. *HO EYES TOKESKE O YAUN YAMPE HEY*. Granny said it through her nose. It meant something like, "So how is everyone doing?," and it was what you said to someone you hadn't seen in a while. That one was her best sentence so far.

Granny squinted up her eyes and asked, "You know what 'Minnesota' means?"

"That's just the name of a state," Bit responded.

"Oh, ho! You are wrong! That's a Lakota word. Or maybe a Dakota word. I forget. But they say it wrong. It should be '*MNE SHOTA*.' See, there's a lot of lakes and rivers up there. Early in the mornings there's a fog that rises off the water. *MNE* means water, and *SOTA* means something like fog or smoke. So *MNE SOTA* means 'smoke on the water.' Isn't that pretty? They just say it wrong. Minnesota. Dumb white people don't even know better."

Bit wrote that down. *MNE SOTA*. So language contains not just history but geography too.

Anna turned her coffee cup around and around, a gesture that Bit knew meant she was getting impatient. Anna lifted the cup for a sip.

Quickly, before her mom could stop her, she asked, "What's the word for honey?"

TIKAMUKA CHESLE, Granny said, and laughed. Anna abruptly sat down the cup of thick coffee she had been drinking, as Granny continued, "fly shit."

Bit wondered which one of the words meant shit. She could use that word, but not around her mother.

Anna got up abruptly to stir the chili. "That's about enough for one day, Miss Bit," Anna said, while Granny continued to chuckle. "Mother, will you help make the wojapi?"

After her dad came home, after supper was over and the dishes were washed, after Anna had gone over to Granny's house to help her get a fire started in her wood-burning stove because even though the days were warm, the night would still be very chilly, after Bit and her sisters had brushed their teeth, each with a glass of water to wet the brush, dip it in baking soda held in the palm of one hand, brushing and spitting in the bucket under the wash stand, after her sisters had gone to bed, Bit asked her dad, "How come mom won't speak Indian? I know she understands it. And she says that one word, *ANAGOPTANPE*, when she wants us to shut up and behave. So how come?"

"I think she's kind of mixed-up about that," Tom said, putting down the Jackson weekly paper he had been reading. "Don't ask her about it. She gets upset."

"I know. That's why I ask Granny instead of Mom to tell me words in Indian. I mean, Lakota."

"You know she went to Marty Mission boarding school," Tom said.

"Yes. She always gets mad when I say I want to go to boarding school instead of my school."

"That's why she doesn't want to speak Lakota. It makes her feel bad when she says even just that one word, *ANAGOPTANPE*. But she grew up speaking it, so sometimes a word just slips out," Tom said, hoping Bit wouldn't ask further, but he should have remembered that his daughter was like a mouse trying to push a corncob through a hole in a board. The mouse would keep trying until it figured out it could chew the kernels off one at a time, and take them through the hole into its nest while leaving the naked cob behind.

"Why did going to boarding school make her want to stop speaking her language?"

"Because every time she spoke Lakota at boarding school, she got punished. All the kids did, so now, whenever she says a word in Lakota, she feels like she's going to get punished."

"How did they punish her and the other kids?"

"It was bad, that's all I want to tell you for now," Tom said.

Bit supposed that was another one of those later-when-you're-older non-answers.

"Mom's a dog," Bit said.

"What?" Tom was horrified, sitting bolt upright in his chair, the newspaper dropped on the floor.

"No, no. I don't mean Mom's a *DOG*. I mean, she's *LIKE* a dog," Bit said, leaning away from her father's anger, speaking quickly to explain before her dad took action. "I read about it. This man, Padlock, he trained a dog. He'd ring a bell every time he fed the dog and the dog would salivate. After a while, every time the man rang the bell, the dog would salivate, even if Padlock didn't feed him. It's called—umm—I think it's called conditioning."

"Pavlov," Tom muttered, easing back in his chair. "Pavlov's dog experiment."

"That's it! That's what's happened to Mom. I think," Bit said.

"Maybe something like that, but let's don't talk about it like she was a science experiment," Tom said, while inside he thought, yeah, Indian kids were a kind of experiment, one that turned out badly for the kids.

"How come you don't speak Lakota, Dad?" Bit asked.

"I know a few words here and there, the ones you already know, but my parents didn't use the language, and they insisted I speak English. They said the reason we got cheated in all those treaties was because we couldn't understand English. They thought if we understood it, we could protect ourselves."

"Did it work?"

"Not really," Tom said. "Now they have laws."

"What's that mean?"

"Bit. It's time to go to bed."

The next morning, before the girls got up for school, Tom finished eating his pancakes while Anna filled his thermos bottle with fresh coffee to take in his lunch.

"Bit's still pestering her grandmother to learn Lakota words," Anna said, as she corked the thermos and screwed on the lid. "I wish she wouldn't."

"Is it so bad that she wants to learn something of the language?" Tom asked.

"That's not why she wants to learn. She wants to show off to the kids at school. She especially wants to learn cuss words, and yesterday, my mother gave her one. *CHESLE*."

Tom remembered his time in the army in the Philippines, how

the soldiers wanted to learn all the dirty words in the native language, Tagalog, Tom recalled, and especially they wanted to learn to ask, "How much for a piece of ass?"

Anna put the thermos in the top half of Tom's opened lunch box, snapped the metal triangle-shaped piece into place to hold the thermos in the lid, and closed it shut. "I suppose I can't stop her from learning it," Anna said. "She visits Mother when I'm not there, and my mother will tell her whatever she wants to know."

"She'll find something else and lose interest," Tom said, "as long as we don't make a big deal out of it."

"I suppose," Anna said. "There's something else."

Tom braced himself, wondering what other mischief his eldest daughter had gotten up to.

"No, no, nothing to do with the girls," Anna said, putting her hand on his arm. "Mother told me yesterday before the girls came home. Marvin's coming back to live with her again."

Tom sat down his coffee cup so hard some splattered out onto the red checkered oil cloth. "When?" he asked.

"Next week. She said he has a couple of things to clear up there first."

"Like what? Serving out a jail sentence for drunk and disorderly?"

"Tom, I know you don't want him around. Neither do I, but he is family. I just thought you should get a warning, and not have him just show up here."

Tom had been glad when Marvin had followed the girl off to Minneapolis. Always in trouble for something or other, nothing big, not violent crime, just petty theft and the like, enough to fuel his alcoholism, but his mother-in-law expected Tom to bail Marvin out of his troubles. There had to be something that Marvin was good at, something that would hold his interest long enough to stay out away from the drink, but Tom hadn't been able to figure out what. "We'll manage," Tom said.

On the way to work Tom thought about the Marvin problem and the less difficult Bit problem, but he pushed it aside to think about the refuge problems, one of which jumped out right in front of him. He had turned off the main road south onto the gravel road that led to the refuge west entrance, over the cattle guard, and half a mile farther onto the refuge proper when he saw a figure walking toward him with what looked like a shotgun propped over one shoulder.

14

Bart Johnson's legs quivered with muscle twitches, his back ached, his head felt like a swarm of bees buzzed inside his skull. He hadn't eaten in hours and his stomach reminded him, but he felt a surge of satisfaction as he leaned against the wall of the calving barn and watched the heifer get to her feet, watching her start to lick the bloodied calf at her feet. The calf scrambled to get its legs unfolded, half stood up and fell back again. Bart would give it another few minutes before he helped the animal stand. The mother cow nudged the calf. At last, the calf stood, wobbly with its front feet splayed. A few steps, then a few steps more, and the calf butted the mother cow's udder.

Bart stood away from the cold metal wall feeling like a wobbly calf himself as his head spun dizzily. He leaned over with his hands on his knees until his vision cleared before he walked out of the calving stall. The last few days—or, really, the last week—had been tough. He'd probably gotten less than two nights sleep in the last seven or eight days, and that had been interrupted. He kept a cot with a sleeping bag on it down in the barn where he slept with an alarm clock set to go off every three hours so he could get up and check on the heifers in the stalls. The barn wasn't big enough to house all the cows ready to calve out, so once a calf was born and the mama cow had let it nurse, he had to turn them out into the big corral, walk the small home pasture for any other cows about to go into labor and shift that cow into the recently emptied stall. In previous years he had hired a part-timer to spell him, but he couldn't afford the labor costs this year. He thought how much easier and cheaper it would be if Brian had stepped up to help. Even on a school night he could have helped, and Bart would have written the kid an absence excuse for the next day, but Bart had become resigned to the idea that Brian would never make a rancher, never take over the place when Bart retired. Maybe Susan would marry a boy who would be a man.

He walked unsteadily back to his cot in the corridor of the barn, sat down heavily on the bed, reached underneath for the thermos, and poured the cap full. It was cold. You'd think Brian or Betty or even Susan would know enough to bring him a fresh thermos of coffee or a sandwich. When the coffee was gone, he stood up, a bit refreshed and went outside to check the cows waiting in the little pasture. He found a couple that he knew were near to calving, so he went back to the barn, rousted out the last heifer to calve and her baby, now alert, tail twitching as it nursed and moved the pair into the big corral with the other new mamas and their babies. He felt good in his mind even as his body was near to collapse. So far, he hadn't lost a single calf.

An hour later, he thought he might have given into optimism a little too soon. This cow not a young heifer, so she shouldn't have had any trouble calving, but she was. She lay on her side, heaving deep breaths, the calf half in and half out, and backward. He could see the tiny hoofs and in a normal delivery, the calf's head would be positioned right between the front legs to be born headfirst. Not this one. He saw the tail instead and knew he would have to turn the calf. He took off his jacket, rolled up his sleeves and sluiced his hands and arms in the bucket of cold bloody water. He was lying full length on the cold cement floor, his right arm halfway into the cow's uterus, when someone shouted his name. He ignored it until the shouting got louder, finally turning his head to see who the hell wanted to talk to him.

The refuge manager, King, leaned on the rails of the calving stall. "Johnson? Need to talk to you right pronto," King said.

The cow's body stiffened as her uterus tried to push the calf out, pressing hard against Bart's arm. He held his breath, waited for the contraction to pass, scooted closer to the cow, reaching with his hand on the extended arm until he grasped a calf foot. He pulled his arm out, pulling the calf at the same time, turning it, turning it. The cow gave a lurch, and he almost lost his grip on the calf's slippery leg. "Johnson? You hear me?"

Bart closed his eyes, pulling on the calf as another contraction pushed helping him turn the calf farther. "Jesus fucking Christ! Can't you see I'm a little busy right now?"

The contraction ceased, but Bart felt sure the calf had turned to come out the right way, headfirst, head on front legs. He pulled his hand out. The cow shuddered and strained with another contraction, and Bart saw a leg with the hoof turned the right way, and the pink skin of the calf's nose. But where was the other foot? He dropped his head and cussed. The calf was the right way around, but it's left leg was folded back at the knee. As the contraction ended, the uterus pulled the calf back until only the one small leg protruded.

Bart dropped down on the floor again, made a fist of his bloody hand and shoved into the cow, feeling for the calf's bent left leg, grasped it and straightened it. He pulled his arm out and slid backward. Another contraction and both the calf's front legs appeared with the head neatly positioned between them, another contraction and the calf slid out in a gush of amniotic fluid and blood. The cow moaned a low groan.

Bart pushed himself wearily to his knees, his coveralls muddy, smeared with blood and shit. He watched for a minute, relieved when he saw the calf's sides rise and fall with its breathing. He sluiced is hands and arms in the bucket of water.

Somebody had called his name. The refuge manager, King, but he had gone now. Bart wearily walked the small holding pasture, but no other cows showed signs of imminent labor. He staggered back to the barn, turned the new cow and calf pairs into the corral. From the looks of his herd he might get a shower, some food, and a few hours of real sleep before he had to be back down at the calving barn. He was on the downside of the work, now, with two-thirds of the cows already done, and the ones left were mostly the older cows, the ones less likely to have trouble. This was going to be a better year, a good year, he promised himself.

When he walked in the front door, there sat King in Bart's own chair, with Betty in her lady rocker. For a little while, Bart thought maybe he had imagined the man yelling his name down in the barn, that maybe that episode had been some sleep-deprived hallucination, but there the man sat.

"Bart! You're filthy. You're going to get that mess all over," Betty said, standing up.

Bart looked down at his coveralls and his filthy boots, caked with blood, mud, and shit. Even though he'd washed his hands and arms, he hadn't rolled his sleeves back down, and he could see that he hadn't gotten the blood all off. His fingernails were caked dark. He stepped back out onto the porch, pulled off his boots and shed his coveralls, standing in the chilly air, and could see that the blood and mud had soaked through the coveralls, staining his jeans, the front of his shirt, and even the white vee of his T-shirt visible above the neck of his plain flannel shirt. He left the filthy clothes in a pile on the porch and walked back into the living room. "Whatever you want, I have to get a shower first," Bart announced.

King gave him a look, but said, "All right. I got time."

Bart stumped up the stairs, one tread at a time. He stood in the shower for an indeterminate amount of time; he couldn't tell because he had been leaning half asleep against the shower wall as the steaming water sluiced over him, coming awake only when his legs started to buckle. He soaped up his hair, rinsed it and got out, toweled off and looked at his face in the mirror. His red-rimmed eyes stared back at him. He walked naked down the hall to his bedroom. The shower had revived him a little, but he knew it wouldn't last. He couldn't think what King might want. He couldn't think.

When he walked back down the stairs, holding carefully to the banister, and into the living room, he said, "Betty, I could use a couple of sandwiches and some hot coffee." She stared at him for a minute, then heaved herself upright and walked off to the kitchen. Bart sat on the sofa. It wasn't comfortable. He reached around behind him and pulled a couple of magazines out from under his butt, held them in both hands, curling them up and apart, up and apart. "What's this visit about?" Bart asked.

"First, I haven't said anything to your wife," King said. "I thought we should talk this out, man to man. Leave the ladies out of it."

"What ladies?"

"Well, lady. Your wife," King went on.

Then Bart noticed the 12 gauge shotgun King had leaned up against the side of the recliner. Why did King have a shotgun? Was it his own gun? Had Brian taken it out without asking and left it leaning up against the chair? Jesus, the kid was determined to try Bart's patience.

"See, it's about your son. Brian," King said, leaning forward with his forearms on his knees and his hands clasped in front of him.

"What's the little shit got up to now?" Bart asked.

He should have known good news couldn't last. The luck he'd had with all the calves born so far, alive and thriving, no bad weather, that had to be followed with something bad to wipe out the good.

"You know it's a federal offense to carry a firearm on refuge property?" King asked, his pale blue eyes drilling into Bart's.

"Yeah. Sure. It's posted on those signs all around the refuge," Bart said, feeling as if he knew what would come next.

"Can your son read?" King asked with a rough edge to his voice.

"What the fuck! Of course he can read. I'm not raising a dummy!"

King stared at him as if he doubted it.

"Get to the point," Bart said, "I'm pretty goddamned busy right now, in case you didn't notice."

"I appreciate that. So here's what it is. Your son, Brian Johnson, was caught at 6:45 this morning walking down the south perimeter road inside the refuge boundaries carrying a loaded shotgun. This one."

Bart flung the magazines down on the sofa, got up and fetched the gun. Yes, it was his. There was that scuff mark on the butt, from when he'd dropped it last pheasant season when he was climbing through a barbed wire fence. His hand had slipped and the wire popped up and caught him in the thigh just as he was stepping across. He'd dropped the gun and had been very glad that he'd followed safety procedures of always unloading it before he crossed a fence, but the gun slid down a rocky slope.

He rubbed a thumb across the scraped mark on the gun butt. Brian must have taken it without asking when Bart had been down in the calving barn.

"When? Yesterday? Day before? When was Brian on the refuge with this gun?"

"This morning. I already said."

Bart broke the gun open and checked. "It's not loaded," he said.

King fumbled in his pockets and brought out a pair of shotgun shells, bright red with the brass ends.

"I unloaded it. I would never bring a loaded gun into my house or any other man's house," King said. "And it wouldn't make a difference if it wasn't loaded when Brian was carrying it. The federal law says no firearms can be carried onto refuge property. Loaded or unloaded. At any time. Period."

"So what's the damage?" Bart asked.

King came to his feet, his hands coiled into fists at his sides. "What the hell do you mean by that?" he demanded. "The damage is that your son is in violation of federal law. I came here as a courtesy to you, to give you a chance to set him straight and see that it never happens again. I could have prosecuted the little shit. I could've—"

Bart held up a hand, and said, "No, no. I don't mean it like that. I mean, what's the damage—I mean, is there a fine to pay? I mean, what can I do to make it right?"

King blinked rapidly, turned his head and stepped away. "Not this time," he said, "No fine. I'm just giving you a warning," but then, unable to let his anger go, he continued, "I'm telling you, Bart. There better not be a next time. The refuge has been a good neighbor to you. Pheasants from the refuge cross over the boundary onto your land, and I know that makes them fair game in hunting season, and I think you've pretty much followed the game laws. But some of the people you invite out here to hunt—your—your GUESTS, well, they haven't been as law-abiding. I know that several times when they've downed a bird on your side and it flapped back over the refuge boundary line, that they've crossed the line to get the birds. I let it go, in the interest of getting along. And I've heard that your son has been known to shoot a duck or pheasant out of season. How do I know? Because he was stupid enough to brag about it to his buddies, who told someone else, and it got back to me. I'm sick of you and your kid. I'm sick of your shit and I'm not putting up with it anymore. You hear me? From now on you follow the law, and I'll follow the law right down the line. YOU GOT IT?" By the end of his speech King's face was red as he spat out the last of his words.

Bart took a step back, bumped into the sofa and fell into a seated position, the gun clattering from his hand onto the floor. He thought how glad he was that King had unloaded it.

King tossed the shells up and down in his hand, pitched them at the sofa and slammed the door as he walked out. Just outside on the porch he tripped over the boots and coveralls Bart had shed, cussed, and stomped off down the porch steps and out to the official refuge vehicle with the yellow and blue circular emblem stenciled on the side: Department of the Interior, Bureau of Fish and Wildlife.

"Bart? What's going on? What's Brian done?" Betty stood in the doorway to the kitchen holding a plate of sandwiches in one hand and a cup of steaming coffee in the other. Her words barely penetrated Bart's ears.

"Never mind. Not now," Bart said.

Betty set the coffee and plate of sandwiches down on the end table, looked at Bart a long moment, and left.

Bart took a bite of the sandwich. Spam. He hated Spam, but he chewed and swallowed and took another bite, but the last one didn't go down. Bart's vision narrowed, darkness closing in until he only saw a pinpoint of light in front of each eye. The half-chewed bite of Spam and white bread with a lettuce leaf came out of his open mouth and tumbled down his shirt front as he fell asleep.

He didn't hear the school bus brakes screech as the bus dropped off Susan and Brian from school, didn't hear the front door open or Susan call out "Mom?" He didn't hear Brian come stumping in behind his sister, pause to look at Bart slumped asleep on the sofa, his feet on the floor, his upper body tipped over against a pair of fat sofa pillows. Betty had needlepointed the covers on them. One of them read "God Bless Our Home." He didn't hear Brian walk over and stand at the end of the sofa, didn't hear Brian muttering as he picked up the gun, plucked the shells from the sofa. He didn't notice when Brian put the 12 gauge shotgun back into the cabinet and the shells in the drawer underneath.

Bart awoke to darkness, with only a little moonlight sneaking in between the folds where the drapes didn't quite come together. He sat up, his neck and back in a crick from sleeping in an awkward position. He rolled his head around on his neck. He had no idea how long he had slept or what time it was or even what day it was. Of course, he remembered the confrontation with King, but it seemed like years ago. He would have to deal with Brian, but not now. Later.

He got up and took his clean parka out of the hall closet, the coat he saved for wearing to church over his gray Stockman's suit when the weather was too cold for just the suit coat alone, pulled on the parka and opened the door. How many of his cows had calved while he had slept, he wondered. How many of those calves had died, and maybe the mother cows as well? He sat down on the porch steps in the crisp night air to stomp on his old boots that he had left on the porch. They were cold and stiff. He sat for a minute. Luck never lasts, he thought, except bad luck.

He went back in the house for a flashlight, spotted the dried-out sandwiches on the end table, picked them up and stuffed one each into the parka's side pockets. Down in the little pasture where the remaining cows waited to drop their calves, he walked among them, feeling the heat from their bodies steaming off into the cool night air, a little fog above each of them. They milled sluggishly. Over in the far corner, he spotted a cow with a calf that she had dropped while he'd been sleeping. The other cows gave her a wide space, but circled her, like sister sentries. The calf was fine. He flicked his flashlight over the black body, stepped closer and checked. A bull calf. Yes. He'd be a six hundred pound steer next fall if all went well, and at twenty-two cents a hundredweight—Bart's brain multiplied the numbers. That was more than a hundred dollars right there, on the hoof.

He walked through the rest of the herd, using his flashlight to check for any that looked like they might calve out in the next few hours. Their eyes glowed red in the light. None looked ready, so he walked back to the calving barn. He'd move that cow/calf pair from down in the little pasture to the corral in the morning. He walked through the calving barn, opening the stall gates and shooing the cow/calf pairs from the barn out into the corral, and when he had done and shut the corral gate, he walked back to the barn and sat down on the cot in the corridor. His stomach growled and he remembered the sandwiches in his parka pocket. He pulled them out, ate them, choking dry as they were, getting up to drink from the faucet at the end of the barn. He could go back in the house now, go to sleep upstairs in a real bed, have that conversation with Brian in the morning, but he didn't.

He lay down on the cot, pulled the rumpled dirty sleeping bag over him for a cover and went back to sleep.

15

Bit loved Sunday mornings almost as much as Friday nights. Anna was up before her husband Monday through Saturday, making sure his lunch was made, the coffee was perked, and breakfast was on the table, but never on Sundays. Tom got up first, made the coffee and breakfast before he woke Anna up, who usually was awake anyway, but luxuriating in the anticipation of eating a meal she hadn't had to cook. Well, she had cooked part of it because chili was the usual Saturday night supper, so Tom only made the pancakes that they topped with the leftover warmed up chili.

While her sisters slept in, Bit got up with her dad. He let her have a cup of coffee, half evaporated milk, which she drank sitting at the table with him for a few minutes before her sisters and her mother got up. Often, they didn't talk much, just shared the quiet in the house. This morning in mid-March, Bit saw that her dad was quieter than usual, and that often meant some new crisis. She stirred another spoonful of sugar into her coffee.

"Dad. Are you worried about Marvin moving back in with Granny?"

"Not worried. Concerned, though. She only has that little bit of Social Security to live on, but she does without things she needs to give her money to Marvin."

"Do you think he'd act better if Granny didn't give him money?"

Tom thought a minute, and said, "Probably not. He'd find someone else to support his bad habits."

"Like that girl he went up to Minneapolis with?"

"Yeah." He got up to stir the pot of chili.

"That's not what's the matter, though, is it?"

"What makes you think something is the matter? Maybe I'm just thinking," Tom said.

"Is it bad?"

The Warders had never been the kind of family that hid financial difficulty from their kids. They thought it better to be honest, even if that honesty was frightening because, if you told your kids they couldn't have something they wanted, maybe even needed that other kids got as a matter of course, they might think their parents were cruel, but if you told them the truth, that there wasn't enough money for whatever they wanted, they'd be sad, disappointed, maybe even angry, but they wouldn't feel that they had been the victims of unnecessary cruelty.

"You remember that we didn't have much of a Christmas because Bart Johnson didn't pay me the lease money on our land?"

"Yes." How could she forget? The best part of Christmas was the red transistor radio, but one of the worst parts of Christmas was that she had to dip into her allowance money and her savings money to buy fresh batteries for it. After that initial excitement of hearing the songs from KOMA that all the other kids were talking about, the cost of the batteries began to outweigh the excitement. Now she only bought new batteries once a month, and when those were dead, she didn't buy any more for the rest of the month, which worked out fine because KOMA only played the top twenty popular songs, and new ones came out about once a month, so after the first week with the working batteries, she had all the current song lyrics memorized. Another bad thing about Christmas was having to hear the other kids talk about the number of presents and the quality of presents they had gotten. She didn't envy the girls' gifts—Barbie dolls. But the gifts the boys got—a new saddle, a yellow Tonka truck or road grader, those she envied. She had her tiny moment of triumph when she told them about her red transistor radio, but her mom wouldn't let her take it to school to show it off. She brought her thoughts back to her dad's conversation.

"Do you think he'll pay it next year?"

"He could. Or he could pay for this year and not next and still be a year behind, or not pay any of it."

"Can't you take it back? Isn't there anything you can do?" She thought about her friend Susan, Johnson's daughter, who never had a serious thought in her life and likely wasn't capable of serious thought either. Susan, who always had the nicest clothes, went to the movies anytime she wanted to, got lots of Christmas presents, and said that this year her mom promised they would go to Disneyland on vacation while her dad wouldn't pay Bit's dad the lease payment he was owed.

"What would I do with it if I took it back, Bit? It's only a hundred and sixty acres, not enough to make a living on," Tom explained.

Bit frowned and took a sip of her coffee. It tasted like coffee syrup. She'd put in too much sugar.

"Can't the BIA do anything about it?"

"They could if they wanted to, but the lease officer is too busy trying to please the people who lease the land, not us Indians who own it. And he's running for reelection on the tribal council this year, so that's what he's putting his work into. Making promises he can't keep about other things."

"It's not fair," Bit said, then hastily added, "I know, life isn't fair, but I get tired of being the rabbit. Can't we just be the coyotes for a while?"

Tom laughed, and asked, "You know Granny's stories about Inktomi, the Spider?"

"Oh, yeah," Bit said, making a face. "He's always trying to pull some trick, and it never ends up right."

"He's called a trickster figure. There's lot of those. Ours in the spider, but some other tribes say coyote is the trickster figure," Tom said.

"What's that got to do with what's fair and who's the coyote and who's the rabbit?"

"Think about it. Spider always tries out some scheme and it never ends right. Coyote does the same thing."

"So you mean if we were the coyote instead of the rabbit, we might end up with nothing coming out right no matter what? Dad, you're mixing me up. So in one way, the coyote always wins because he gets to eat the rabbit, but in another way, he never wins because his schemes all turn out wrong. Which is it?"

"What do you think?"

"I think it doesn't matter if we're the rabbit or the coyote, we're going to get screwed no matter what," Bit said.

Anna, just up and dressed and reaching for the coffee pot said, "Miss Bit, watch your mouth."

Bit held out her half empty cup and Anna topped it off. Maybe more coffee would dilute the sweetness.

"Talking about the lease again?" Anna said as she sat down.

"Thinking about what I could do about it," Tom said. "You know, if that land had a wheat base on it, it wouldn't matter that it isn't butted up against some other farmer's land or not. There're leases all over this county where the farmer has to drive his tractor some miles to farm it."

"What's a wheat base, dad?" Bit asked.

Tom made a face, and said, "It's complicated, Bit. Sure you want to get bored this early on a Sunday?"

"It's about math, Bit," Anna teased. "Not your best subject."

"I get A's in all my subjects," Bit protested.

"Yes, you do, and I'm proud of you, but you have to admit that math is your least favorite."

"I want to know," Bit said stubbornly.

"All right, but your mother warned you," Tom said. "After the Great Depression in the Dirty Thirties—you know about that, don't you?"

"Yes," Bit said, rolling her eyes.

"Okay, after that, the country has a series of good years. Plenty of rain, few insect pests, good harvest, especially wheat. Farmers grew so much wheat that there was a glut on the market, more wheat for sale than the big food companies and feed companies were willing to buy. That meant the price per bushel dropped so low that it wasn't worth it for some farmers to bother harvesting it. A lot of it rotted in the field and farmers went broke. So the government stepped in and started buying up wheat at a set price and storing it. Then, to keep that from happening again, they started allotting a wheat base. A wheat farmer was paid so much per acre for *NOT* growing wheat, and was told how many acres of wheat he could grow. If he grew more than that, he lost his government payment. If he did as he agreed, he got to sell his wheat and keep the extra money. The wheat base—how many acres can be planted to wheat on any certain amount of land—is what's called the wheat base."

"How come our land doesn't have a wheat base?" Bit asked.

"It's complicated, Bit, but just trust me, we don't have a wheat base," Tom said.

"What's our land good for then?"

"Oh, it's just good for holding the rest of the world together," Tom joked.

"Dad!"

He ruffled her hair. She hated that. "It's some of the best grazing land in the county. It's got a year-round creek running across it, so there's no need to dig a well and put up a windmill. Even in a dry year it's got good grass," Tom said.

"So why don't we grow cows on it?" Bit asked.

"Here comes the math," Anna warned.

"Our land is a quarter section," Tom said. "How many acres in a quarter section of land?"

"One hundred and sixty. Three hundred and twenty in a half section; six hundred and forty in a section."

"Good memory," Anna said, getting up for a refill on her coffee.

"Now here's something you might not have heard about, Miss Know-It-All: an animal use unit. An animal use unit is the amount of grazing land it takes to feed one cow and her calf for one year. Our land will feed about one animal use unit per five acres. How many cow/calf pairs is that?"

Bit did some quick math in her head. "Thirty-two."

"Good. If you have a hundred percent calf crop every year—and that almost never happens—I mean, if every cow has a calf and every calf lives and grows up to be sold in the fall, that's thirty-two calves. Think of half of them as being steers and half of them as heifers, okay?"

"Yeah. Half boys, half girls," Bit said.

"Steers gain weight faster than heifers, and the more they weigh when they're sold, the more money you make. The average weight, though, that's about 550 pounds, say. And they get sold by the hundredweight, which these days is usually between eighteen and twenty-four dollars a hundredweight. Just to make your math a little easier, let's make the average weight of your fall calves six hundred pounds or six hundredweight, and the price per hundredweight at twenty dollars. That's going to make the payout much better than it ever is, but we're just thinking here, okay? This is just math problems. Got it?"

"Need a pencil and paper?" Anna asked.

"No, no, I can do this. Yeah," Bit said frowning, "so six hundredweight at twenty dollars is—is a hundred twenty dollars per calf when they're sold."

"Yes. Times how many calves?"

"Thirty-two. Times a hundred twenty dollars." Here she had to think harder, calculating in her head so her mother wouldn't have the satisfaction of handing her a pencil and paper. "Three thousand eighty hundred forty dollars. Wow! That's pretty good. We could live on that, couldn't we?"

"Hold on a minute," Anna said. "That's your gross, not your net profit."

Bit was puzzled, finally.

Tom explained. "Gross profit is what you get before you pay any expenses, and raising cattle is an expensive business. What if one or more of the cows doesn't have a calf? That means your calf crop percentage is not one hundred percent but maybe ninety-five. Now that's not bad, but suppose the cows got some disease where they lost their calves, so you only get an eighty percent calf crop. That's disaster. But just for the sake of argument here, let's go with the hundred percent calf crop. You've still got to pay for feed to get them through the winter, when there's snow on the ground and no grass for them to eat. You either have to devote some of the land to growing hay or buy it. If you're growing it, then that cuts into the amount of acres left to graze cows on, and there's the expense of the haying equipment. You need at least one tractor, a mower, a rake and baler, and a hay sled to move the bales off the land and into a barn or stackyard near where you're going to feed the cows. Farm equipment is expensive, and it breaks down, so either you have to pay for parts and fix it yourself or pay one of the farm equipment shops in town to do it. Suppose one or more of the cows gets sick or hurt. There are vet bills. Then you have to pay a trucking company to load up the calves and take them to market. You have to figure that cows can only have calves for a set number of years, so you have to keep back some of your heifer calves for replacement cows, or trade some with another neighbor, or buy them. You have to have so many bulls. If you don't have any bulls, you won't have any calves. For thirty-two cows, one bull should be enough, but you need two for insurance, so while you have to have bulls to get calves, that means those bulls count for a cow/calf unit each where you can't use land for grazing for one cow and her calf. Automatically your number of calves, even with a hundred percent calf crop, is dropped to thirty instead of thirty-two. How much less is that you'd get for gross when you sold the calves?"

"Two hundred and forty dollars," Bit said. "All right, all right, I get it. So what you're saying is that our one hundred and sixty acres can't grow enough calves to make a living."

"That's right, and we are talking about a hundred percent calf crop every year. There will always be bad years," Tom said.

"Enough math for one day," Anna said. "Tom, are you going to make pancakes or shall I?"

As Tom poured out the batter into neat circles on the sizzling griddle, Bit asked, "So there's nothing we can do with that land? It really is good for nothing but holding the rest of the world together?"

"I'm thinking, Bit. Maybe there's another way," Tom said, flipping the pancakes. The day before he had a long conversation with Bennie Black Hawk at the gas station in town. Bennie had prompted the conversation when he reminded Tom that Bart Johnson hadn't paid any of the other Indian landowners the lease money that was due to them either, and that he was thinking of backing another candidate in the upcoming tribal elections, a woman who might see that the guy in charge of managing leases lost his job. The woman had a nephew who wanted the job, and he might not be any better than the guy already in there, but a change couldn't be worse. Tom remembered then that previous thought, that maybe taking the leases away from Johnson might not be a bad idea, even if they couldn't lease it to anyone else. They'd get no lease money either way. Maybe Johnson would pay up this year. Maybe there would never be another problem, but Tom didn't count on good things happening. He had an idea. He'd have to work on it some more, maybe get Bennie Black Hawk to do some of this famous horse-trading campaigning, get the other Indian landowners to agree. He knew this last bit was going to be the hard part, but Bennie was a canny old politician. If there was something to trade to get something better, Bennie would figure it out. Tom had run his idea past Anna when they got home from grocery shopping on Saturday after the girls had been sent off to bed. She told him that she'd support him, whatever he decided, but not to tell the girls yet, especially Bit.

"No sense getting their hopes up," Anna said.

When the pancakes were done, Tom set the platter on the table, and the chili, still in its cast iron pot with the big red-handled serving spoon, on a folded kitchen towel in the middle of the table. The rich aroma woke the other girls, or maybe they just had enough sleep, so they sat down to breakfast all together, Connie and Patty squabbling as usual. The last of the chili had been scraped from the pot, the last pancake eaten, and all three girls were squabbling now over whose turn it was to wash the dishes, when someone knocked on the door, and when Anna answered, Marvin stood outside, his hat in his hand.

"Morning, Auntie Anna. I'd like to talk to Tom. Please," he said.

Anna's eyebrows went up, suspecting Marvin had gotten into trouble again and wanted to borrow money that they didn't have, but she let him in, and poured the last cup of coffee from the pot, grinds floating on the top.

Marvin's long-fingered hands took the cup and sat it carefully in front of him, but he didn't add milk or sugar. He had quietly said hello to Tom, glanced at the girls and said no more. Anna knew he had something to say or something to ask but didn't want the girls to hear. "All right, girls, go find something to do outside. I'll do the dishes this morning," she said.

They looked astonished but grabbed their jackets and bolted out the door before she could change her mind. She put the teakettle on to heat water, stacked the dirty dishes in the big tin pan, and sat down, waiting for the water to heat. "What's up, Marvin?" She asked.

Tom gave her a grateful glance. The sooner Marvin could be persuaded to ask whatever impossible question he had, the sooner he might go back to Granny's house. "I've been thinking," Marvin began, glancing up at Tom and quickly looking away. Marvin had magnificent brown eyes, thick black hair, and a chiseled jaw. A handsome man, most women would think, except for his attitude. That and his bandy legs ruined the total effect.

Tom made an effort to listen without prejudging.

"I've been thinking about getting a job. I think I need to stand on my own feet. I might go get a grant from the tribe. You know, go to that diesel mechanic school down in Oklahoma," Marvin said. He picked up his coffee cup, sat it down as if he didn't know what to do with it.

Well, which is it, Tom wondered, get a job or go to mechanic school, but he let Marvin gather his thoughts and go on. He suspected the words Marvin uttered weren't his own, but maybe Granny's. Maybe she'd finally decided Marvin needed to grow up.

"I need a skill. I want to go to school, but I think I need a job first. Save up some money for the trip," he said.

At least he isn't asking me for the money to travel down to Oklahoma, Tom thought, which Tom didn't have to give him and wouldn't give him anyway. He'd been around that pole before: loaned Marvin money for something important then found him drunk in town and the something important long forgotten.

"So, I was thinking . . ." Marvin continued.

Oh, here it comes, Tom thought.

"I was thinking that you might put in a word for me at the refuge."

There it was. Tom dreaded the idea of riding to work in the mornings with Marvin, of trying to get Marvin to do whatever job King assigned him without having to ride herd to make sure he wasn't embarrassed when Marvin didn't do what he was told, or did it so badly that King had to fire him. Marvin was undependable, a con artist, a liar. A year ago, Marvin wanted to learn to play the guitar, so Granny had talked Tom into loaning Marvin his old six-string, the one Tom had saved to buy years ago, and truthfully, rarely played anymore because he was too tired at the end of the day and television was just easier. Marvin took the guitar and disappeared. Tom got it back just before Marvin took off to Ft. Pierre with the girl, but it was missing all the strings but one, the neck had been cracked, and something sticky that wouldn't come off marred the back of it.

Anna caught Tom's eyes, pleading to give Marvin another chance. There was a job opening at the refuge, just like every year when King put on a couple of temporaries to get through the spring and summer work. With a sense of dread Tom said, "I'll see what I can do."

16

Bart Johnson woke up in stinking sheets and not because Betty hadn't bothered to change his bedding, which she hadn't, but because for the past twenty-four hours Bart had been in bed, alternately shivering with chills or burning up with fever. He'd thought he was lucky, that he had escaped the flu earlier in the winter when everyone else had been sick, but a lone germ or two out there somewhere had jumped on Bart. He should get up, get a shower, change the bedding. He knew that would make him feel better, but he couldn't dredge up the energy. He allowed himself to sink back into fever dreams, a mixed-up mess of joyful scenes, where a younger, happier version of himself danced with a beautiful woman who wasn't Betty, in an impossibly green field with colorful flowers like a Disney movie. He wanted those dreams, but he paid for them with the other kind, where he was herding his kids across the yard in an oncoming summer storm, wind howling, the sky overhead colored in weird shades of poison green and bruise-colored purple. He didn't know where he was taking the kids, why they were outside running across the yard. In reality the Johnsons didn't have a storm cellar, and the kids in the dreams weren't his kids, but who they belonged to, the rational part of Bart's mind couldn't decide.

At the head of the stairs, the master bedroom was truly the master only bedroom now that Betty had moved into the spare room down the hall. Acting as a sound conduit, any sounds in the living room below funneled up the stairs and directly into Bart's bedroom. Betty had yelled down the stairs often over the years for Bart to turn down that television when she had gone to bed earlier than he.

As dreamers will do, Bart incorporated the conversation from the living room into his dreams, upsetting the pleasant ones when his beautiful partner declared, "That duck is too dry" and "Lillian, you should never wear green, promise me." It seemed to him that the good dreams melted into one of the bad ones as he struggled to stay asleep, to recapture the dance in the field. When he woke he felt like he was still dreaming as the voices went on, tones rising and falling, making nonsensical comments. He sat up and took a sip of water from the glass by his bedside, realizing that if women sat and talked down in his living room, that it must be Wednesday, club day, and Betty's turn to host. With an effort he sat up, slung his legs over the edge of the bed and stood up. His head spun; his knees wobbled. He grabbed the edge of the nightstand as he sat back down, sighed and lay down again.

He walked the small pasture the next day, still shaky and feeling only half awake because he'd had to forgo his usual three cups of morning coffee. Instead, he drank a cup of unsweetened tea with a piece of dry toast while standing at the kitchen counter, looking out the window. The kids had already left for school and Betty was off to town. He had been concerned that while he'd been sick in bed, one or more of his cows had died trying to birth their calves, or that their newborn babies hadn't survived, but of the five cows still left in the small pasture, one had a healthy-looking heifer calf at her side and the other four placidly stood chewing their cuds as if they might not calve for another week.

He went back to the house and upstairs, thinking about going back to bed, but when he had taken off his shoes and pants, he couldn't lie down on the sick stench of bedding. He dressed again, stripped the bedding, sheets, blankets, and all and carried it down to the washroom just off the kitchen. By the time he had loaded the washer, he felt weak and ravenous. The refrigerator held a chocolate pie with a piece missing, a bowl of green Jell-O with carrot shreds embedded, and another bowl of something that looked like fruit cocktail with whipped cream stirred in and tiny marshmallows on top. The pantry shelves were nearly bare, likely the reason Betty had gone to town. He took out two cans of chicken broth that Betty hadn't used for making the Christmas turkey stuffing, cranked the cans open and dumped them in a pan. When it was steaming, he soaked up the broth with buttered slices of bread, feeling energy seep back into his body with each bite. As he put the dishes in the sink, he saw Betty's Impala coming up the lane, watched her park in the driveway, get out and open the trunk. He hated that red car. It looked like something a teenaged boy would drive, he thought. Betty struggled to open the gate with her arms full of bags of groceries and come up the front steps, boosting a slipping heavy bag back into her arms with a knee. He opened the door for her. She gave him a look as she passed into the kitchen.

"You might at least help me bring in the groceries," she said.

Bart stared at her a minute, then the washer shut off. He moved the batch of wet sheets to the dryer, started another load with the red blanket, and switched the dryer on. He remembered how happy Betty had been when he'd bought her the dryer a year ago, one of the first ladies of the club that didn't have to string clotheslines inside a porch or in a basement in the winter.

Betty sat another pair of full grocery bags on the table with a thump. "Is there more?" Bart asked.

Betty unloaded a bag of tinned vegetables and started stacking them in the pantry. After a minute she said, "Yes."

Bart fetched a bag of potatoes and another full brown paper bag from the Impala's trunk, slammed it shut and noticed how clean the car was, when the last snowstorm had left mud streaks on everything. Betty had taken it in for a wash in town.

The Chinese elm tree by the front porch stood hazed in pale green. Bart turned and looked out across the land, which also held a nearly imperceptible haze of green. This long winter was ending and maybe this would be a better year, he thought. Maybe that one year was an oddball, a mere wrinkle in the otherwise smooth texture of his life.

"About time you lent a hand," Betty said as he set the groceries on the kitchen counter and began unloading them. Bart leaned both hands on the counter holding back the words that wanted to come out.

"What do you mean by that?" he said in a level voice as he turned around, leaning against the counter.

She didn't speak as she walked back and forth, taking a glass bowl down from the cupboard, loading oranges, apples, and bananas, her mouth pinched shut.

"Lend a hand? I've been laying upstairs sick in bed for two days, and no one in this family bothered to bring me so much as a glass of water, so I'm wondering why you didn't lend me a hand."

Betty took out an apple, switched it for an orange so the fruit in the bottom alternated: orange, apple, orange, apple. She sniffed, stepped back to admire her handiwork, added another layer of apple, orange, apple, orange, and plopped the hand of bananas on top.

She hadn't taken off her jacket yet, a light blue wool coat that stood out slightly from her body. She looked a little thicker around the middle, but her pregnancy wasn't showing yet. Bart had always been secretly proud that his wife had kept her figure, even after bearing two children, while his friends' wives had let themselves go, gotten frumpy and tired looking.

"You know what it feels like? It feels like I don't exist. No one would notice if I wasn't even here. You and the kids—you'd just go on with your life. You'd set three places at the table as if that was how it had always been," Bart said.

Betty took off her jacket and draped it over the back of a kitchen chair. No, she didn't look thicker around the middle; that had been an illusion created by the jacket. She walked back and forth, ignoring Bart as she put away the groceries.

"Why don't you answer? It's because that's the truth isn't it? That's the way you feel? You wouldn't notice if I was gone," Bart said.

Betty took several packages of butcher-wrapped meat from a bag and took them to the refrigerator.

"What's this?" Bart said, snatching a flat package from her hand. The black marker writing on it was illegible.

"Bologna," Betty said. "Can't you read?"

"Why are you buying meat? There's a freezer full of good honest beef out there." Bart gestured toward the back room where the chest freezer sat next to the washer and dryer.

"Pork chops, sandwich meats, chicken. We don't raise any of those," Betty said, snatching the package of bologna from his hand.

Bart snatched it back, ripped it open. His stomach felt like it could hold a sandwich. He shoved her aside and got a jar of mayonnaise from the refrigerator, got the fresh loaf of Rainbow, and started to make himself a sandwich.

"You're making a mess," Betty said, as he dropped a glob of mayonnaise onto the counter.

"That's all you think of me isn't it? I make messes when I'm around, so you'd rather I wasn't around," Bart said. He waved the sandwich at her. "Where do you think this comes from?"

She looked at him as if he were crazy.

"The money to buy this? Where do you think it comes from? 'You might at least help bring in the groceries,' that's what you said. You stupid fool; I pay for the groceries. I'm the one laying on the floor in a cold barn, helping a cow deliver a calf, so I'd have the money to buy those goddamned groceries. I didn't see you out there lying in the shit with your arm shoved up a cow's twat. No. That was me!"

Betty put her hands over her ears. "Stop it! Stop it! I don't want to hear that kind of talk," she said. "You're disgusting."

"Disgusting? Disgusting? That's how you save a calf's life. Do you know how many calves I've probably saved by shoving my hand up a mama cow's twat?"

She sat down at the table, whimpering, her hand still over her ears.

Bart yanked her hands down from her ears. She cowered back in the chair. "For once you're going to listen," he said. "I've got two hundred and fifty cows out there, and this year, we may have two hundred and fifty live calves. Those calves are the reason you've got what you have—that new car that you didn't need, those presents you bought for Christmas, the clothes you buy. Sticking my hands up a cow's twat is what makes sure you get all the things you want, and you don't want to know about it? That's too disgusting for you? We've got a kid, a half-grown man who should have been out there helping me. YOU could have been out there helping me. Even Susan, she could have brought me some hot coffee down to the barn. I'm all alone in this. I'm just the cash register. You might at least help me bring in the groceries. That's what you said."

"You leave the kids out of it, especially Brian," Betty said.

He let go of her hands and laughed, took his arm and swept the bowl of fruit from the table. Apples and oranges bounced across the linoleum floor.

"Oh, so now you're going to start knocking stuff around? Does that make you feel like a big man? What are you going to do next, rape me?"

The dryer buzzer went off. As if programmed, Betty started to get up, but Bart pushed her back in the chair. He dumped the clean sheets into the laundry basket, shoved the red blanket into the dryer and the blue blanket into the washer, and started it going. He could see Betty's back as she sat at the table, her hands flat on the table in front of her.

He picked up the tumbled fruit, thinking that the apples would likely have bruises now, put everything back in the bowl and set in in the middle of the table. "I'm sorry about that night," he said. "I shouldn't have—I shouldn't have done that. That was a mistake."

Betty glared at him. "A mistake? That wasn't a mistake. That was a vicious, criminal act. I'll never forgive you, you son of a bitch."

Bart felt the epithet like a slap to the face. Betty never cursed. She said ladies didn't use bad language.

"What about the baby?" Bart asked.

Betty didn't answer. She shoved her chair back, scraping the legs on the linoleum floor. She walked out of the kitchen into the living room and sat down in her lady chair.

Bart sat down and ate his sandwich. He took the clean sheets upstairs and made his bed, opening the window a few inches to air out the room. He heard the school bus stop on the main road and a few minutes later he heard Susan chattering away to her mother.

Spring was truly here, Susan was saying, she knew because the gophers were back. They were going to dig more holes on the baseball diamond, Susan said, and she hoped that the teacher wouldn't let the boys chase them down and beat them to death with the baseball bats like she let them do last year.

Bart wondered why Brian hadn't come home on the bus with Susan but decided that Brian might have decided to stay overnight with a friend of his in town. Nobody told him anything anymore.

He had checked on his cows one last time for the night and was walking back to the house when a new black Ford Thunderbird slowly drove up the lane and parked in front of the house. In the dusk Bart couldn't see who was driving, but he wondered who could possibly show up this close to suppertime. Maybe Everett Speir, the Ford dealership owner in Jackson, who had been trying to pitch a new car to Bart for several months.

The driver's door opened, and Brian stepped out. Bart walked up and stopped. Brian grinned. "What do you think? She's a beauty, isn't she?" Brian said. He started walking around the car pointing out the rear seats—the original Thunderbird had been a two-seater, but this new model now seated four.

Jesus, Spier had hit a new low, using Bart's kid to sell a car.

"Supper's ready!" Susan called from the front porch.

"Look, Dad," Brian went on, "this new model has three taillights like Mom's Impala, not the two on each side like the old models. Neat, isn't it?"

"Brian," Bart said, a suspicion growing, "why are you driving this car?"

Brian moved to the other side of the car, looking over the low roof at Bart. "It's mine," he said.

"Yours? How?"

Brian didn't answer. He shuffle-footed for a minute, turned to glance at the fields behind him as if there were something of intense interest there. "It's just mine," he said.

Bart quick-stepped around the back of the car grabbing Brian by the shirt front. "Give me the keys," he said.

Brian's arms dangled, his eyes wide. "Why?" Brian asked.

"Give me the keys, or I'll rip your pants off and go through your pockets until I find them."

Brian's hand fumbled at his pants pocket, inserted his hand and came up with a ring of keys. He lifted it over his head, brought back his arm and flung them, jingling as they hit the gravel. Bart released Brian's shirt front. "Pick them up," Bart said.

"Do it yourself," Brian said.

Bart took a deep breath, walked over to where the keys shone in the blue yard light, snatched them up, walked around to the driver's side and got in. Brian stood there as Bart drove off.

Everett Spier came to his front door sock footed, his usual tie gone and his white shirttail hanging out over his dress pants. "Bart, how are you doing? Come in, come in," Everett said heartily, as he glanced past Bart at the Thunderbird crouched at the curb.

"Everett. We need to talk."

"Sure, sure thing. Come in," Everett said as he stood aside.

Bart stepped into the thickly carpeted entrance hall, felt his feet sinking into the depth of it, thinking in the back of his mind, beneath his pent-up anger, that the rumors were right: the carpet in Everett Spier's house was so deep a person sank into it. Expensive carpet, paid for by the buyers of his vehicles, of which Bart was not going to be one. If he had ever considered buying Brian a car, it would not be a Ford. There were two kinds of car buyers in the county: those who swore by Fords and the others. Bart was a Chevy man himself.

"What do you think you're trying to pull?" Bart demanded.

"I have no idea what you're talking about," Everett said, "but if you'll just come in and sit down, I'm sure we can get this figured out."

"You know what I'm talking about. Brian. That car sitting out there," Bart said, hooking a thumb in the direction of the street.

"Yeah. So what?"

"So what? So Brian is a kid. He isn't of legal age to sign a contract, and you—you greedy son of a bitch, you let him sign it. What? Did you think I'd be too embarrassed to complain?"

"Bart. Bart, calm down. I didn't—"

"Don't say you didn't! You did! What do you think, I'm blind? I'm crazy? I wouldn't notice my own son driving a brand-new Ford Thunderbird into my own dooryard?"

"You need to listen—"

"No! No, you need to listen to me! Brian is not keeping that car. I'm not paying for that car. It's going back on your lot as of now and that contract is going to be torn up," Bart yelled.

He felt like throwing the keys on the floor, but the picture of Brian came into his head, a picture of Brian throwing the keys at him. He grabbed Everett's hand, stuffed the keys into the man's palm and closed his fingers around them. "There! This is done. You've got your fucking car back and that's the end of it. You hear me? Never try to pull that again!"

"Will you listen to me now?" Everett pleaded. "Brian didn't sign the contract."

"What?"

"Well, not alone. He's under eighteen so he had to have a co-signer."

Bart knew what was coming, but he had to ask: "Who?"

"Your wife. Betty. She cosigned for it this afternoon," Everett said.

Bart's shoulders slumped. He dropped his eyes. The carpet was very light beige. It would stain easily.

Everett held out the keys.

Bart looked at them and said, "I don't care if Betty did cosign. I'm the one who makes the payments, and I'm not making the payments. You try running that contract through and I'll have a lawyer on your ass."

Out at the curb Bart realized he didn't have a way to get home. He looked down at his work shirt and jeans with the torn knee, his battered work boots. Even though it appeared spring had come, the night would be chilly and he wasn't wearing a jacket. He started walking. Two blocks north and one east, he opened the outside door and walked down the steps to the Legion basement. From the sounds of crashing, he knew the Thursday night men's bowling league must be playing. He opened the door and looked into the brightly lighted lanes, saw no one he wanted to see, closed the door and walked across the hall to the Legion Club bar.

A huddle of four or five men sat on stools at the bar, turning to see who had come in the door. It wasn't Wednesday, so there was no cattle auction crowd, and it wasn't Saturday, shopping day, but Gary sat on one of the middle stools.

"Gary," Bart said, ignoring the other men. "I need a ride home."

Gary gave him a curious look. Bart expected a vulgar remark or jibe, but Gary only arched an eyebrow and slid down off the stool. "All right, man. Let's go."

Gary didn't rattle on with nonsense on the way out through the dark countryside, either, but about halfway out, just as they passed over the Little White River bridge, he looked over at Bart and said, "You heard, I suppose."

Bart roused himself and asked, "Heard what?"

"She's not pregnant."

Bart let that sink in a minute before he asked, "What?"

"I said she's not pregnant."

"Who?"

"Jesus fuck, man. Who do you think? Mary Ann!"

"What?"

"Mary Ann! Goddammit, Mary Ann. Keith's girl."

Bart wondered why Gary had brought up the local gossip about a waitress, but before he could speak, Gary continued. "I was leaving Pearl. I didn't want to, that woman has given me my three boys, but Mary Ann—she was just a bit of fun, you know? A quick piece of ass, getting a little strange to keep the old equipment oiled. And then she got pregnant. Or said she was. After a while it just felt right, Mary Ann and me. She made me feel like I was young again, like anything was possible, like back when we used to play football in high school. Remember that? You and me? All the girls from Kadoka and Phillip coming around after the games? It felt like that again.

"We were going away together. I cleaned out the bank account, left a note for Pearl. You know, I don't know why I left her a note, but the woman gave up a lot for me, you know. She could have been something, but she married me. We got as far as Mission, me and Mary Ann. Stopped at the Frontier station for gas and Mary Ann went inside to get some pop, and when she came back out she had blood all over the back of her dress. Scared the hell out of me, but she just stood there looking at me, holding those two bottles of grape pop. I told her to get in the car. I was going to take her to the hospital; there isn't one in Mission, you know, and it's a long way from Mission to Winner when someone is bleeding to death, but she just stood there, and finally she said she wasn't having a miscarriage. She'd never been pregnant. She said she made it up, and when her mom overheard her talking about it, she just—she just let it go on. She loved me, she said. She said she was sorry."

Bart was shocked. He didn't know what to say as Gary beat his fist on the steering wheel and sobbed, "I loved her. I loved her," and Bart didn't know if Gary meant his wife or Mary Ann.

17

Tom found to his surprise that he liked having Marvin working on the refuge so far. He'd lost some of the fear that Marvin would screw up and Tom would be blamed for whatever it might be. Marvin quietly did what he was told, no matter how menial the job. He was slow, but after a few days Tom decided maybe he did his work slowly on purpose, just trying to make sure he did, whatever it was right the first time. Marvin didn't seem scared, just determined. When Keith missed a couple of days work and the little cat tractor was down but needed to shore up the perimeters of the swan pen, Marvin quietly went to work and fixed it before Keith came back. Tom thought maybe Marvin's idea of going to diesel mechanic school wasn't just some random idea after all; maybe Marvin really had an aptitude, so Tom was willing to concede that Marvin might turn out all right after all, even though he had been worried about putting Marvin to work with Keith.

Keith had lost his sullen attitude but went about his work with a hang-dog attitude, still touchy, as if ready to fly off the handle at any moment. If Marvin didn't mess up, Keith might make a big deal out of nothing, something that Marvin did or failed to do that would get Marvin fired and Tom would still end up looking bad for recommending his wife's nephew for a job. Tom tried to keep a lid on it by taking his lunch down to the equipment building every day, making small talk, distracting Keith with little bits of humor.

Keith didn't take to it much, but it might have helped because he grudgingly admitted that Marvin was a dab hand of a mechanic.

When Keith called in on that Friday in early April, Tom thought he had probably come down with a case of late winter flu, but Findley, who took the call, said it was a family matter. Everyone knew that it was something to do with Mary Ann and her condition. Tom expected King to be upset because the little cat tractor was down again for repairs and King wanted it up and running, not just to keep the perimeter of the swan pen in good repair but because it was spring. Spring meant that all the earthen dams and dikes that kept the system of small lakes and ponds on the refuge within their banks needed to be reviewed for damage from spring runoff and muskrats that dug tunnels into the dams and dikes weakening the structures. The cat was needed for that work. King was annoyed, but too busy to complain as much as he might have done. He was leaving that Friday for a weekend regional meeting of refuge managers, and he expected to be grilled by the higher ups from D.C. about the swan project. Not King's favorite topic, especially since he had left the entire project to a graduate student intern and a former maintenance man with no formal higher education.

For weeks, even months, Tom had been asking when King wanted to schedule a day to capture all the swans for a wing clipping. King put him off with vague responses the first few times Tom asked, so after a few weeks Tom tried going through Findley and Carl to make the request, but then they, too, stopped asking when King lashed out at them. The swans were flying. Most of them within the pen, but Bill and Martha, ever the escape artists, were persistent escapees. Usually they stayed close to the pen. Tom hoped they would attack the shiny knocker on King's door again, hoping it might encourage King to a wing clipping, but the birds were uninterested.

With the coming of spring, snow runoff and a couple of early rainfalls kept the road ditches full, the system of small lakes near the top of the dams and dikes, and the flat stretches of land inches deep in water. The swans had consumed all their favorite roots within the pen, but the ditches and seasonable runnels of water still contained the roots in plenty. The Friday morning that Keith called in with his family matter, Tom and Marvin drove in from the west entrance along the muddy road and discovered Bill and Martha half a mile west of their pen at the headquarters building in the road ditch, happily tugging roots from the muddy bank.

Tom honked his car horn as he approached the pair. They raised their heads, still chewing on roots, long muddy strings hanging from their beaks, but they didn't move out of the ditch. Tom and Marvin banged on the roof of the car with their hands. Bill and Martha looked at them as if they were playing some game with unknown rules. Tom got out of the car and ran at the birds waving his hands and shouting. They hesitated, got out of the ditch, and stalked to the middle of the road. As the person who fed them, who had sat by their pen for hours almost every day for months, they saw him as a food source, as a useful part of the scenery, but they liked the natural food they had discovered better than the grains Tom fed them. Martha flapped her wings at Tom, turned and walked back to the ditch. Bill followed.

Tom picked up a handful of pebbles from the road, slinging them at the birds. Bill turned and ran at Tom, hissing like a goose as he flapped his wings. Tom flung up his arms again, waved them up and down like wings as he shouted, "Go home, you fools! Go home!" Bill hesitated, turned and walked up the middle of the road calling back to Martha, who ignored him. Tom pitched more pebbles at Martha, and after snatching a last mouthful of roots, she clambered out of the muddy ditch and ran after Bill. Tom walked up the road herding the swans as Marvin followed, beeping the car horn. After covering the half mile to the pen, shooing the big birds inside and securing the gate, Tom and Marvin were ten minutes late to work.

King was just coming out of his house carrying a suitcase, hurrying to the official vehicle he would drive to the meeting in Sioux Falls. Tom caught up with him as he was opening the pickup door. "Boss, we have to clip the swans' wings. Right away. Bill and Martha are getting out of the pen almost every day, flying through the gaps, and the others are flying inside the pen. They're going to spread out all over the county if we don't clip their wings. Even if no one shoots them, they'll nest outside the refuge where we won't have any way to track them. They got out last night, and I found them half a mile from here on the west road," Tom said. He knew the timing wasn't good, knew that King was likely to find a way to make this Tom's fault, but he had to try.

King stood, taking off his down jacket and pitching it into the pickup cab. "So, Bill and Martha again, is it?"

"Yes, sir. They aren't digging out under the fence. They're flying out."

"Yeah. All right. When I get back." King said as he climbed in behind the wheel.

"The day you get back," Tom pressed. "I'll get the clippers ready and tell everyone to expect it. Next Tuesday?" It would take all the employees all day to herd the big birds into a corner of the pen, catch them one by one and hold them down to clip their wings. It would have been so much easier just to keep their wings regularly clipped and much harder now that they could not only run to avoid capture but fly as well. It was going to be a real cowboy roundup now unless they used the cannon net.

King stared out the windshield. "Not Tuesday. I don't get back until late Tuesday night. I'll be too tired out on Wednesday. Make it Thursday," he said. He turned the key and started the pickup.

"All right. I'll tell everyone," Tom said, and stepped back as King shut the pickup door and drove off.

Sitting on his plywood square, Tom observed two pairs of swans that appeared to be making a nest, two of the pairs that he had observed mating in the previous weeks. He wondered why it took swans so many attempts to make babies, when for humans, once was often enough, as many a sobbing pregnant teenager knew. Bill and Martha could have been displaying nesting behavior, but it wasn't obvious. They seemed affectionate, but whether that was true swan behavior or only Tom's imagination, he didn't know. They didn't look ashamed at being caught outside the pen. Perhaps both of those emotions—affection, shame—were only human emotions that animals didn't feel. Perhaps Tom had been alone with them for so long that he had begun thinking of them in human terms, become too close to them to be objective, a form of Stockholm syndrome, even though Tom had never heard of that term nor had anyone else in Jackson County.

Near noon on Friday the call came through. King would never make it the district meeting of refuge managers. He had stopped for a late breakfast in Mission, and twenty minutes after he left the café his government-issued pickup truck had crashed into the back of a slow-moving tractor. A farmer had pulled his tractor onto the highway to travel only half a mile to his next field to avoid being bogged down and stuck in the still-wet earth that would surely happen if he had to drive across one field to get to the next. The jolt of the pickup hitting the back of his tractor at 60 miles per hour had thrown the farmer from the tractor and onto a steel culvert that ran under the road breaking the farmer's neck. King survived. His face was cut up from hitting the windshield; several ribs were broken or cracked and his upper torso was severely bruised from his body trying to arch over the steering wheel, and his right wrist was shattered, probably had hit the dash. The highway patrol assumed King had eaten that heavy meal, gotten groggy, and fallen asleep at the wheel. There were no skid marks on the highway to indicate King had braked.

Findley couldn't say who had called; he was too upset to remember, he told Tom and the others, but he had written down a number to call back for more information. He wasn't as upset about King's accident or the dead farmer as he was nervous that he would be in charge of refuge operations for much longer than just a few days. The caller said—it must have been someone from the hospital, the tone of the caller and the speech patterns indicated a hospital administrative type—had said that King was unconscious, sedated, and might have head injuries. No, she couldn't say when he might be released.

Claude Sauer's evening weather report was bad news. The old adage that if March came in like a lamb it would go out like a lion wasn't quite true this year, because this prediction for a not uncommon late winter, early spring blizzard was on its way, but the general trend held. Findley left early to pick up groceries in Jackson, tiding himself over in case the storm lasted more than twenty-four hours. He would drop Carl off at his tiny basement apartment in Jackson. When Tom and Marvin left the headquarters building at their usual 3:30 quitting time, low-bellied gray clouds hung over their heads, looking close enough to touch. Only a half mile west on the access road still inside the refuge, tiny hard flakes of snow ice seeds began dropping. Slow and lazy the flakes fell for only a minute or so before the bigger flakes came down. Within the space of seconds the windshield went white, the flakes falling so fast that the wipers couldn't keep away the buildup, and immediately the wind rose to a gale driving the snow from the windshield, then back, away and back. Tom's car bucked and hesitated with the first blast, but like a sturdy obedient horse, tucked its head down in first gear and went on with Marvin watching the edge of the road to keep them out of the deep, water-filled ditches. The usually fifteen-minute drives from the refuge headquarters to Tom's house in the tiny village of Taylor took two hours. In his front yard, already eddying with wind-driven drifts, Tom shut down the car engine and sat for a few seconds, feeling the tension in his neck and shoulders relax. Marvin said "See you later," as he bailed out of the car and ran for his mother's house next door, head down against the stinging snow. Yellow light from the small front window of Tom's house spilled through the maelstrom of snow like a beacon.

The air inside the house smelled hot, not from temperature but from the spices Anna put in the Friday night chili. Her chili was good, and while it tasted like Tom thought chili should taste, it wasn't like the chili he had eaten in California when he was waiting to be shipped overseas during the war. That was thick. Anna made hers, always had done, with a quart of tomato juice, ground beef, spices, and precooked brown beans, something that she could continue doing in spite of their tiny food budget because she had grown most of the ingredients herself: the juice came from a Mason jar, canned from the previous summer garden; the spices she had on hand; the beans from the last crop that she had left on the vines to mature. The only expense was the hamburger, and by cutting it from a full pound to half, she kept up the Friday night chili tradition.

They did not watch television. The storm had blown the antenna off station and the wind kept it there, but it wouldn't matter anyway, because reception during storms—winter or summer—was so poor that the picture would make the characters on the screen look like they were moving through a blizzard of their own. They might have attempted to watch anyway, but the power had gone out.

Tom put the kerosene lamp in the middle of the table. They ate supper while the cold seeped through the uninsulated walls, and Anna's quilts, draped over the windows to help keep out the cold, undulated and bloused as wind gusts forced their way through cracks around the window frames. After supper Tom read aloud from a Louis L'Amour paperback that he had read to them before. The familiar story comforted.

The wind howled throughout the night until sometime near dawn on Saturday when it ceased as suddenly as it had begun and the entire world was hushed and silent in a deep blanket of white down. Tom wouldn't be going to town today, hadn't planned to go. Anna had told him that she didn't need anything from town. He knew it wasn't true, that there were dozens of things she needed and wanted, but there was no money to buy them and no sense in going to town just to socialize with the people who did have money for what they needed.

He worried about the swans. They needed supplementary feed. Findley and Carl were supposed to feed them over the weekend, but he wasn't sure if they had gotten back to the headquarters. He was worried about the two men. More than a few times people in this harsh country had started out in a blizzard, never arriving at their destination, found later stuck in a snowbank, frozen to death.

What if the swans had flown from the pen, some instinctual bird habit telling them to move south until the blizzard passed? Ducks and geese sometimes did that, he knew, taking off for their northern breeding grounds in early spring, flying north until a snowstorm came up, moving a few hundred miles south to a small lake or a gleaned field with spilled grain still there hidden under the snow, then back north again when the blizzard ended. Maybe trumpeter swans had the same migratory waterfowl instincts. Perhaps these birds, though, these birds had been in captivity so long they had lost those urges.

He tried to read after breakfast, but Louis L'Amour wasn't comforting anymore. He paced until Anna said, "Why don't you take Marvin and see if you can get to the headquarters? At worse you'll run into a snowbank you can't get through, but it's something to do."

At eleven o'clock Tom put a pair of snow shovels and a thermos of coffee in the back seat, and with Marvin riding shotgun, they drove slowly out of the yard. Overhead, the sun shone as if it were another spring day, but the warmth didn't touch the ground, the sun rays impotent in the face of earth's weather. At the end of the little lane that accessed the main road to the refuge, a medium-sized drift had accumulated, but with ten minutes of shoveling, Tom drove through the narrow gap he and Marvin had dug.

Snow covered the road unevenly, falling in a regular ten-inch layer in places, drifted two to five feet deep in places but rarely so deep in other places, and in yet others, no snow at all where the wind had scoured the roadway completely free. They had to stop twice to dig through deeper drifts, but mostly Tom knew from living with high plains winters most of his life, he knew that if he kept the car in second gear and moving at a steady 35 miles per hour, he could plow right through the even layers and any drift less than two and a half feet deep. His strategy worked until they hit the west access road into refuge headquarters, where a series of drifts, one after the other, covered the road from north to south. The car ploughed through the first two drifts, but stalled at the next one. He restarted the car, backing it out of the drift. Marvin and Tom got out, tackling the drift with their snow shovels. Two hours and five more drifts later, they reached the refuge headquarters.

Drifts had piled up to the very top of the swan pen fence and over. If the drifted snow had packed enough so the big heavy birds didn't sink, they could walk through sagging gaps and right over the fence, but they hadn't tried. Tom saw them huddled together in the lee of one of the nesting pyramids where they disdained to nest. Counting as best he could with the birds flocked together, he thought they were all there. He saw Bill and knew that wherever he was, Martha would be nearby. If Martha had left the pen, Bill would be gone as well. He walked down to the equipment shed, breath gusting out in the cold air, and together they fetched buckets of grain from the big metal bin in a side shed, walked back up to the pen, up a snowbank, and dumped it onto the bright white snow below as Tom called out to them, imitating their squeaky, single-note call.

They milled in among the flock of birds who were reluctant to leave the communal warmth but slowly came across the frozen creek to feed. Tom fetched an axe, went into the pen and chopped several holes in the ice, taking turns with Marvin swinging the heavy blade. When they had opened several holes for the swans to water, Tom said, "I suppose we'd better get the snow shovels out and knock down these drifts," nodding at the drifts over the edge of the pen.

"No. I'll get out the cat," Marvin said.

"I thought the cat was half torn down?"

"I fixed it yesterday. It'll go," Marvin said, and looking around at the rising wind stirring the loose fallen snow, he added, "I think I should plow out that west road too. If we want to get home."

"All right."

While Marvin drove the cat tractor around the pen, knocking down the snow drifts and pushing the snow away from the pen, Tom took the key from the hook above the office building door and let himself in. The interior wasn't much warmer than outside, but at least the wind wasn't blowing. He looked out the window. The wind had kept rising, then abating, then rising again as it swirled the already fallen snow into what some people called a horse turd blizzard—what happened when it had stopped snowing but the wind blew around the snow that had already fallen while the sky overhead was still clear, the sun shining down into this odd white world.

Tom went to the telephone on the counter near the front door. The dial tone surprised him. He looked at a number penciled on the wall and dialed. This was a party line, the only kind of phone service available in the country, and sometimes people on the phone just yakking to their neighbors had to be asked to relinquish the line for a more important business call from someone else on the same line. Sometimes the yakkers yielded with good grace, sometimes not. Tom supposed that the quiet on the line was because the lines were down farther out in the country.

"Hello."

"Carl?"

"Yeah, he's here, just a minute."

"Wait. Findley? Is that you? This is Tom."

"Tom? You at the headquarters building?" Findley knew Tom didn't have a home telephone, but Tom could have been calling from the little store near his house, which did have phone service, if the lines weren't down there too.

"Yeah. Me and Marvin got here an hour ago, but the west road in is pretty well blocked with drifts. We did a lot of digging," Tom said, adding, "Marvin's plowing the drifts from around the swan pen, then he'll go plow out the west road, but no telling how long it will stay open. You're staying at Carl's, I guess?" Of course Findley was at Carl's. Findley was a nervous kind of guy, not very good at what he was supposed to do, Tom thought, but he'd been raised on the Wyoming high plains and knew better than to start off for anywhere in the middle of a blizzard.

The sound of the cat engine receded as Marvin drove down the west road, then built to a higher pitch. Marvin had the cat pushing through a snowbank.

"Yeah, Carl's place. The storm came in so fast and hard yesterday. Carl offered to bunk me here. It's free, but—" here his voice lowered to near whisper, "but it's not ideal, you know?"

"I know," Tom answered, but he didn't know. He'd never been to Carl's place. "I've got the swans taken care of so there's nothing pressing here. The wind's come up again. That west road could be blocked again as soon as Marvin puts the cat back and we go through." He meant this latter as a hint for Findley and Carl to stay put without seeming to tell Findley what he already knew.

When he had hung up the phone he went out again, locking the door and rehanging the key on the hook, walked down to his car, got in and started the motor. In a minute, heat rushed from the interior vents. He reached in the back for the thermos of coffee.

Within minutes the cat had pushed through more drifts than Marvin and Tom had dug through in an hour. Marvin kept the throttle down, the cat moving forward slower than Tom's car, but the cat was heavier, didn't need as much momentum. The v-blade pushed the snow out to the sides. Even at that slow rate of speed, the action of the blade and the wind sent tumbling whirls of snow flying past the cab on either side. He had reached the halfway point where the road was more or less clear of drifts for the next couple of hundred yards when he saw a man in knee-high rubber boots bundled in a long dark parka with the fur-trimmed hood up, dark glasses that looked like welding goggles on his face. The man stood at the side of the road and, hanging down from his gloved right hand, a long gun.

18

Bart stood outside by the big pole that held the television antenna aloft, his bare feet freezing in his fur-lined moccasins, as he wrenched at the pole trying to turn it in the direction of the broadcast station at Hay Springs, Nebraska. The pole had gotten just enough melted snow between the pole end and the block it sat upon to freeze within minutes after the wind had blown the antenna off-station. Now it was stuck. He had attached a pair of Vise-Grips to the pipe pole for leverage and at last, leaning his weight into it, as the ice binding the pole to the block broke, the pole spun, carrying the antenna with it. He brought it back pointing southeast.

The Johnson family had been lucky. The power hadn't gone off, and throughout the cold night of blizzard, the basement furnace had kicked off and on, mostly on. This morning as Betty fried eggs and sausage, Susan had gone to the living room with her bowl of sweet cereal, switching the television on to Saturday morning cartoons, but got nothing except static and distant unintelligible voices. When she'd complained, Bart flung on a coat and went outside, still in his slippers. With the antenna aimed right, he started back into the house, quickstepping through the foot and a half of snow. He heard Mighty Mouse, *HEEERE I COME TO SAVE THE DAY!* as he came through the door. That ought to wake Brian up, he thought. He could use the kid's help this morning to fork hay over the fence into the wooden feeders in the little pasture for the mother cows and their calves.

When Bart got home from returning the Thunderbird to Everett, Betty had met him just inside the door, expecting Bart to be furious, violently angry, but he felt as if all emotion had been drained like lancing a boil. Everett had caught the worst of his anger, but Gary's raw emotion on full display, so out of character, so unlike the crude insensitive brute that Bart hated, sometimes tolerated, and sometimes used as a surrogate outlet for his own emotions had left him empty. Gary crying because of a woman—that was an unnatural event. Gary didn't cry; he made women cry. Bart wondered if he had misjudged the man all these years. This Gary was a different man than the one he thought he knew most of his life, and if Gary was different, then Bart could be too. He knew that Gary thought he was weak, or that's what Bart presumed, but maybe that, too, was wrong. Who was Gary? And who was Bart?

The Bart that came home that night was not the Bart his wife expected. She had been worried, expecting that Bart might harm his son.

"Now, Bart, before you do anything you'll regret, let's talk about it," Betty said, her hand on his shirt sleeve, pleading.

"There's nothing to talk about, Betty," he said quietly, heading to the kitchen. He had missed his dinner. He didn't want to eat, but his stomach told him that if he didn't eat before he went to bed, his gnawing gut would keep him awake. Confused, Betty followed, watching as Bart got the carefully wrapped bowls of leftovers from the refrigerator, took a plate from the cabinet, and loaded it with a spoonful of this, a spoonful of that.

"If you'll wait a few minutes, I can heat that up for you," Betty offered. If Bart was eating now, that meant he wasn't going to lash out immediately, that he might let it go. The longer he waited, the better for Brian.

"I'll eat it cold," Bart said, sitting down at the table with his plate and cutlery he'd fetched from the drawer by the sink. He didn't want to know what Betty had been thinking when she went to the Ford dealership, picked out one of the most expensive cars on the lot and signed a contract without consulting him. He knew why she hadn't consulted him, would never have agreed, but surely she didn't think he'd allow Brian to keep the car? She'd been thoughtless before, poor at managing money, downright silly with her ladies' club meetings, but she had always seemed rational. Her pregnancy was the only thing that had changed, but she'd been pregnant before and the most foolish thing she had done those other times was to get upset when he didn't eat a second piece of the cherry pie she'd made. A new Thunderbird for Brian—who hadn't done anything to deserve it and everything not to deserve it—that was strange. Was she planning to take the kids and leave him, got Brian the car as a last minute way to dip into his bank account? He snorted inside at the very idea of a bank account. His balance gave him enough leeway to make it through until he sold the calves in the fall, but it was borrowed money. He was living on borrowed money.

He loaded his fork with cold mashed potatoes, but didn't put the bite in his mouth. He'd eaten half the plate of food and didn't even know what he'd eaten. He put down the fork. "Betty. We're broke."

She looked at him as if he'd just said "Betty, the sun is purple."

"Did you hear what I said? I said we're broke."

She picked at a hangnail on her left thumb, and said, "What are you talking about? I was in the bank just a few days ago. We have a healthy balance. Why? What did you buy? More hogs? Will that check I wrote at the grocery store bounce?" She was frowning at him now.

"I haven't bought anything. Certainly not a new car. Betty, you graduated from high school, surely you can add and subtract. Surely you can do simple math. The simple math is last year too many of the calves born died. We had twenty percent less animals to sell last fall, and the market price was down too. Less animals, lower price, but the same expenses as always equals less money. Can't you see that?"

"Of course, I graduated from high school, you know that. The same year as you. And we got married the June after," she said.

"Let me make this as simple as I can," he said. "If you take in less money than you spend, you're broke." He looked at her and saw what Susan would be in another twenty years. Did that mean Brian took after him?

"Well," she began, a little less certain, "well, you'll make it up. You always do."

Bart took his plate to the trash can, scraped off the food and put the plate in the sink. He stumped up the stairs to his room. He lay in bed a long time thinking before he had finally slept.

Susan had been complaining about the television when he came downstairs, awakened by the smell of frying sausages. Back inside after righting the antenna, he stamped the snow from his slippers and said to Susan, "Where's Brian? He too old for cartoons?"

She shrugged as she took another bite of Sugar Smacks.

"Brian's went out. Ages ago," Betty said, when he went to the kitchen.

"Where?"

"I think he's hunting rabbits. Saving up for a car," Betty said as she put a platter of sausages and scrambled eggs on the table.

"It will take a lot of dead rabbits to buy a new Thunderbird," Bart said, as he walked back into the living room and opened the gun cabinet. The .410 shotgun was there, but his 12 gauge was missing. He should have known better than to trust Brian. He should have put a lock on the cabinet. As soon as he could get to town, as soon as the roads were clear, he had to buy a lock. And make a visit to the bank.

Brian came in an hour later, his face red from cold, put the gun into the cabinet, took the shells from his pocket and put them in the drawer. He was breathing hard, hands shaking a little.

"Don't take your coat off," Bart said, as he put on his own heavy chore coat. "Come on."

Brian didn't protest when Bart took him by the coat sleeve and forced him out the door onto the ice-slick front porch. Down the steps and halfway to the equipment barn, Bart finally let go.

"Where are we going?" Brian said, his voice weak, close to whining.

"To work," Bart said. He pulled his gloves on. "Keep walking." He whistled as Brian walked ahead of him, his head down.

After Bart forced Brian to get on the Allis Chalmers, he climbed up beside him and ordered the kid to start it up. When they had together gotten the tractor down to the dwindled stack of alfalfa hay bales and backed up to the hay sled, Bart shoved the kid out of the tractor seat. "Hitch it up," Bart ordered. "And once you've got that done, start loading bales."

Bart thought he would have to get down off the tractor and force the kid to do it, but after a moment, Brian started lifting bales from the stack and slinging them onto the low trailer. Bart watched, counting the bales until Brian had loaded forty of them. He ordered Brian onto the hay sled and drove the tractor himself down parallel with the fence to the little pasture where close to 250 head of cows stood on the other side, a few of them lowing with their heads up in the air, steam coming from their nostrils and open mouths.

Bart jumped down onto the hay sled, reached in his pocket for a pair of wire cutters, handed them to Brian. "Lift each bale up so it balances on the top of the fence rail, cut the three strands of wire, hold onto the wire, and push the bale over the fence into the feed trough," Bart instructed. Again, Brian hesitated, but just before Bart was set to hit him, the kid took the wire cutters. "Make sure no wire get over into the trough."

"Cows won't eat wire," Brian mumbled.

"No, but if it gets out into the pen, it can get wrapped around a leg or a hoof and cut off the circulation. If we notice it in time, it's hell to catch the cow and get it off. If we don't notice, it can cut off the circulation and cause a cow to lose a hoof." He felt like saying, "and you would know that if you've ever stepped outside the house even one time to lend a hand," but he didn't.

Feeding the cattle, getting the hay sled back to the stackyard, stackyard and the tractor back to the barn took a lot longer time than if Bart had done it by himself, but that was part of the problem, he thought. He'd been doing everything by himself for too long because it was easier that way. He took the axe from the back of the barn where it hung on pegs with other tools, and said, "You're not done yet." They walked back to the pen where the cows shoved each other and shuffled for position in front of the hay feeders. The water tank stood a little farther down, in front of the windmill. An ice crust several inches thick had formed on top with a layer of snow on top of that. Using the ax head turned sideways, Bart shoved and scooped most of the snow off the ice, stood back and swung the axe. It hit the ice with a solid THUNK, sending slivers of ice flying. He stood back and handed the axe to Brian. "Now, you do it," he said.

Brian took the axe, slid his hand up the handle, hefted it in both hands. He turned, attacking the ice with a fury, repeated blows, one after the other. Ice crystals sprayed out from the heavy blade. Bart stood back until Brian had opened a wide hole water gushing over the top of the ice crust.

"All right," Bart said. "Go put the axe up and come back to the house. I'll check after while. The axe better be back with the rest of the tools."

Bart watched Brian walk away with the axe cocked over his shoulder like a shotgun. He thought Brian looked just like Bart himself had looked at seventeen.

On Monday morning the county snowplows came by early, so Bart's pickup only had to buck some little drifts to get down the lane to the main road. His truck did just fine. Bart went first to O'Keefe's Hardware and bought a padlock and a hasp set. Mrs. O'Keefe took his money at the cash register and gave him his change. "Locking up some valuables, Bart?" she said, her smile showing a gold tooth in front.

"Something like that. Gotta keep the rats out of the corncrib, somehow," he answered. He didn't have a corn crib. He hadn't seen a rat, live or frozen, in ages.

At the bank, Bart had a quiet word with the Angie Wicker, the soon-to-be old maid teller, whose poker-faced expression gave no indication that his request was anything out of the usual. People came in every day to take their wife's name off the checking account, you would think. On the way out, Bart said a quick hello to Richard, who was just coming in the door as Bart was leaving.

"Sorry, Richard, I have an appointment to keep," he said, forestalling one of Richard's hunting stories. He sat in his pickup thinking about what he had just done. Angie Wicker would tell everyone in the bank, and that might be as it should be. His change order was bank business. The partners—Richard and Jerry Don—would have to know, and Mrs. Reichart, the older woman teller, and Angie might not be a tattler, but rumors were that when Mrs. Reichart's brother was about to get an overdraft, she had held the check that would do the deed until Bob Reichart could get into the bank and make a deposit. Oh, for sure, it wouldn't be half a day before everyone in the county would be speculating about the state of Bart and Betty Johnson's marriage. Richard would probably add to the conversation himself, telling everyone that Bart said he had an appointment, didn't have time to talk about hunting, so where was that appointment? With one of the two attorneys in town to start divorce proceedings? He turned the key and started his pickup.

"I think I'll give them something to talk about," he said to himself, as he put the pickup in gear and drove over to the office of the *JACKSON COUNTY NEWS*, right next to the post office. He walked in greeting the young high school student who stood behind the counter, one of the mayor's kids, maybe? He wasn't sure. Anyway, a pretty girl working in the newspaper office as part of her business practices course. "I want to place a classified ad," Bart said, leaning on the counter a bit.

The girl took in his felt Stetson hat and asked, "Something in the Lost, Strayed, Stolen section?" That section always had two or three ads, and usually there was a hand-drawn picture of the brand the animal carried.

"No, I have something else in mind," he said. "I think it would be under legal notices."

She handed him a square piece of pink paper and a pen. "Just write it down. Twenty-five cents a word."

He took the paper and pen and printed out his ad, counted the words, reached into his back pocket and took out his wallet, handing her a five-dollar bill.

The girl's lips moved as she counted. "Fifteen. That's exactly five dollars, no tax. We stand the tax. Or if you run the ad three times, it's ten dollars instead of fifteen."

Bart took another five from his wallet. The girl wrote "3tp" beneath Bart's printed words. "That's just for our bookkeeping. It means run the ad three times and it's paid for, so we don't bill you," she said. "Do you need a receipt?"

"No, thank you."

"Is there anything else, Mr. Johnson?"

As he walked out of the newspaper office, Anna Warder was coming out of the post office, and for a moment he thought of pretending he didn't see her, but it was too late. She gave him a pleasant smile and said, "Hello, Mr. Johnson, how are you?"

He tipped his hat. "Never been better, Mrs. Warder."

He whistled to himself as he drove home. The ad he had placed read:

I, Bart Johnson, will not be responsible for debts
contracted by anyone other than myself.

He'd thought about that, sitting in his pickup outside the bank. Betty couldn't write checks anymore, but any merchant in town would extend her credit and he would have to pay it or be embarrassed. Well, if he was going to be embarrassed it was going to be because he did it to himself. Couples who were on the brink of splitting the sheets often put dueling ads in the legal notices of the newspaper, and merchants DID pay attention to that. Betty couldn't write checks and now she couldn't run up bills all over town. He'd had to run his face at the bank last fall with Jerry Don to get the loan he needed. He wasn't going to humiliate himself asking for another loan to cover Betty's extravagance.

As he drove up in front of his house, another thought came, and he groaned aloud. Betty couldn't write checks anymore, couldn't get cash at the bank, couldn't get credit anywhere in town. He knew she would be going to Jackson later in the week to buy groceries coming home mad and empty handed. If she couldn't write checks or get cash or credit, then he, Bart, would have to do the shopping himself. Or dole out cash to her every time she went to the store. He checked his wallet. He had seventy-eight dollars, more than enough for a week's worth of groceries. He smiled to himself as he put the money back in his wallet.

19

Marvin had no recollection of plowing out the rest of the west access road to the highway or of turning the cat around and driving back to headquarters. Tom watched with concerned curiosity as Marvin drove the cat erratically, bumping into the snowbanks the cat's blade had piled on either side of the cleared path through the snow. The cat moved too fast, so fast that Tom thought Marvin might crash the vehicle into Tom's car. He leaped out just as Marvin brought it to a halt less than ten feet from Tom's car, the motor still growling like a giant yellow beast set to pounced with Marvin partially slumped in the cab over the steering wheel. Tom ran, climbed the short steel ladder and yanked open the cab door.

"What the hell is the matter with you? Are you sick? Drunk? What?"

Marvin turned his head, his dark eyes blank looking at Tom's angry face. Tom climbed up another step, shook Marvin's shoulder, and said with a bit more compassion, "What the hell? Are you okay? Sick?"

Marvin lifted his trembling hands, looking at them as if they were part of someone else's body suddenly grown onto his own.

"No. No. Not sick. Just—something happened," he said, his voice low and shaky as his hands.

Tom clung to the side of the cab, uncertain, looked down at the snowy ground. First thing he had to get Marvin out of the cat and make sure it was out of gear and turned off so he didn't accidentally ram Tom's car or drive on across the frozen yard and crash through the fence of the swan pen. "All right. All right. Let's get you out of there. Come on; I'll help you down."

Just when Tom thought Marvin had gone deaf and Tom would have to manhandle him down out of the cab, Marvin's hand switched off the engine. For a moment Tom thought it was still in gear because the big machine gave a lurch forward a foot or more when the engine died. He leaned over Marvin, looking at the gearshift. It was in gear. It wouldn't move any farther. "Come on, Marvin. Let's get you out of there."

Marvin acted as if he had no bones, as if he were a bag of meat with little volition of his own. He turned his body in the seat, his pants catching on a wire sticking out at the edge of the cushion, poking through the double layer of jeans and thermal underwear underneath, but he didn't feel the tip scratch his thigh. Tom noticed, shoved Marvin back a few inches and bent the wire down in a loop. He pulled at Marvin, almost fell off the short ladder when Marvin's weight landed on Tom's upper torso.

"Help me, Marvin! I can't carry you and me too! You're going to knock us both off of here," Tom said.

Marvin's hand caught the side of the cab. He pulled himself into a crouching position. "Get out of the way. I'm coming down now," Marvin said.

Tom hopped down, his boots crunching on the snow packed down by the cat's treads. Marvin clung a moment at the top of the ladder, half turned to come down backward, missed a step with his foot and half fell, half leaped. Tom braced himself as best he could on the slippery snow, caught Marvin's weight and staggered back, trying to prop Marvin into an upright position. Marvin gathered himself, pushing back against Tom's chest and stood upright, swaying. Tom grabbed him by the arm propelling him around to the passenger side of Tom's car, opened the door and shoved him inside.

The car's heater had warmed the interior to a temperature well above freezing but not nearly warm enough. "Get your hands in front of the vent," Tom said. "I don't know what the hell happened out there, but I think you're in shock. What the hell? Did you see a ghost?"

Marvin peeled off his gloves and after a minute held his hands, still shaking in front of the heater vent. He shook his head, fractionally, from side to side.

"What happened?" Tom pushed insistently.

Marvin took a long shaky breath and said, "He shot at me. He shot at me."

"Who? Who shot at you? Wait, never mind," Tom said. He reached over the back seat retrieving the thermos of coffee, unscrewed the lid, poured it full, and handed it to Marvin. "Take it with both hands. Don't spill it; it's still hot."

Marvin took the cup, lowered it carefully to his lap with both hands, staring ahead at the cat looming above Tom's car. The wind had risen higher, stirring the already fallen snow into gusts, tiny white tornadoes swirling across the headquarters yard. White snow filling the air made a band reaching several hundred feet above the ground while the sun shone overhead.

Tom looked at the cat. Looked at the horizon. If they didn't leave soon, the wind would fill in the track Marvin had plowed. "I think I want to go home," Marvin said.

"Sit still. Drink the coffee and calm down. If someone shot at you—whoever shot at you isn't out there now in this horse turd blizzard. I'm going to put the cat back in the equipment barn. You'll be all right until I get back. We'll go home. You hear?"

Marvin raised the thermos lid of coffee, took a sip, nodded, and said, "I'll be all right until you get back."

"All right. Don't get out of the car," Tom cautioned. "There's nobody out there hunting you. Okay? Okay?"

As he opened the car door a gust of wind-driven snow hit him in the face like a shower of tiny pebbles. He turned his face away, walked to the cat, climbed the short ladder to the open cab door. He backed the cat until he had room to turn, drove it down to the equipment shed. Marvin had left the big roll-up door open. Snow had already drifted inside, a white uneven layer forming on the greasy concrete floor. He cut the motor, shut the overhead door. The wind came at his back as he walked back to his car. Already the drifting snow had covered the windshield and started a drift across the road that Marvin had plowed.

"Marvin, we've got to go now," he said, as he put the car in gear. He switched on the headlights, but on high beam they only illuminated the swirling snow, obscuring the way ahead. He dimmed them and drove away. "Tell me what happened. I'll listen while I drive."

Marvin's hands had stopped shaking. He sipped the almost cold coffee. Tom aimed the car down the lane between the snowbanks.

"I was halfway through the road, just about. There was someone standing beside the road, so I stopped. He had a long gun. I thought he might be someone out in the blizzard that had got his car stuck in a snowbank. I stopped to help."

Tom tried to listen and pay attention to the road ahead. He passed through some of the initial drifts on the road, drifts he and Marvin had shoveled out earlier, pushed wider by the cat. They were starting to form again, but only a foot or so deep. He drove on.

MARVIN HAD LOOKED DOWN THROUGH THE OPEN DOOR of the cat at the man, heavily bundled in a dark parka, insulated overalls, knee-high rubber boots, the laces encrusted with snow and ice. Over the purr of the cat's engine, Marvin called, "You stuck in the snow? Need a lift?"

The figure turned sideways, turned back. Marvin could see an amused expression on the oval of face inside the parka hood. "No. I live just over there," he said, gesturing over one shoulder.

"What're you doing out here?" Marvin asked.

"Hunting. Rabbits."

Marvin shifted uneasily in the cat's seat. "You're on refuge land. You must have gotten confused in the snow. Is the fence down? You might have crossed over and not known it," Marvin said.

The figure shifted the gun to the other hand. "No. I crossed the fence," he said.

"You said you're hunting rabbits. It's not right to hunt on the refuge," Marvin said.

"I haven't shot any rabbits yet."

"You're not supposed to shoot anything on refuge property."

The figure looked ahead of the cat as if he could hear a car coming, but there was none. He looked back the other way and walked up to the cab, looking up at Marvin. Marvin saw his face, recognized that the figure was tall as a man, but was not a man. Just a kid. That Johnson kid, he thought. "Maybe you should take your gun and go home," Marvin said.

"Maybe you should mind your own goddamned business."

"You're not supposed to hunt on refuge property. I think you're not supposed to even carry a gun onto refuge property. Didn't you see the signs? It says so on the signs."

"I can read," the Johnson kid said. He lifted the gun so it cradled across his arms. Marvin saw it was a shotgun. He didn't know what gauge.

"I think you should go home now," Marvin said.

"I go when I want to." He lifted the gun, swiftly, pointing it at the road ahead and said, "Bang!"

Marvin wondered how big of a hole a shotgun blast at close range would make in his body. He eased his foot off the clutch just a little. The cat eased forward, but now the Johnson kid was standing at an angle to the cab. If he swung that gun up and to the right just a little . . . Marvin let out the clutch. The cat jerked to a halt; the engine stalled. The Johnson kid swung the barrel of the gun up to point directly at Marvin and said again, "Bang!"

Marvin's hand flicked the switch, gave the cat some gas. The engine roared back to life, but without his foot on the clutch, it jerked forward a foot or so and stalled again.

The Johnson kid laughed, kept the gun pointed at Marvin, repeating, "Bang! Bang! Bang!"

Marvin jammed his foot on the clutch hard, cranked the engine, and when it caught, the cat moved down the road west heading toward the open place where there were no snowbanks only foot-deep snow with the fading tracks Tom's car had made when they drove in earlier.

"Bang!"

Marvin heard the boom, much louder, the real shotgun discharge. He ducked his head so his chin nearly touched the top of the steering wheel, hearing even over the purr of the engine, the sound of shotgun pellets pinging off the metal of the cat's body. He had gunned the motor, kept going west as fast as the cat would travel, snow fishtailing up behind. He heard a second loud bang, and glancing in the side mirror saw the kid breaking open the shotgun, ejecting the spent shells. He drove on.

BOOM! SNOW EXPLODED INTO THE AIR AS TOM'S CAR HIT a snowbank that had drifted back across the road three feet deep. The car slowed, stuttered, but went on, and then they were out on the flat area where there were no drifts and even the layer of snow already deposited had begun to be swept away by the wind. Ahead of them in the car headlights low beams, the wind had swept a dark stretch of road some fifty feet long, but beyond that, nothing was visible.

"All right, Marvin. You're all right now. Keep talking," Tom said, knowing he would not hear most of Marvin's words. He needed all his concentration to keep the car on the road, not wander off into the deep invisible ditches on either side. His hands gripped the wheel so hard they cramped. He squinted his eyes and drove on until ten minutes later the car boomed through another snowbank but a lower one. Tom increased his speed—from thirty-five to forty-five. Another ten minutes later they reached the main road running north and south, so the wind swept down it in a nearly straight line. Patches of ice showed here and there, but the blacktop prevailed. He drove home.

Stopped in front of his house, he could see his front porch drifted over with snow, fading tracks showing where someone had come in and out of the house, probably Anna or maybe Bit going out to check on the chickens. "Tell me again what happened after you drove away," Tom said.

Marvin absently twirled the empty thermos lid on his left thumb. "I drove away going west. The cat blade just kept on clearing the road, like it didn't care what just happened," Marvin said. "When I got out to the main road I turned around to drive back."

"Weren't you scared that kid would still be there with the gun?"

"Yes. I drove slow so I could see if he was up there waiting. I didn't see him."

"With all that blowing snow, he could have been just off the road where you wouldn't see him until you were right there," Tom said.

"I didn't think of that," Marvin said, his eyes wide. "But I know shotguns. I know you have to be pretty close to get killed. The pellets spread out after a few feet. As long as he was at least fifteen, twenty feet away, and me up in the cab—well, he might miss."

He might not miss, either, Tom thought. Even if you were twenty-five feet away, a shotgun blast could still do a lot of damage. Game birds were killed with shotguns at a much greater distance usually, but the birds were smaller, so fewer pellets could do more damage. Besides, all a hunter had to do was bring one down. The hunter or his dog, if he hunted with one, could finish the job. He picked shotgun pellets out of his mouth many times before when eating a pheasant drumstick.

"He wasn't there. At the place where I saw him. But I was scared, I drove as fast as I could to get past that place," Marvin said.

Tom put a hand on Marvin's shoulder. "You did just right. You're alive. We'll let King—or Findley—know about it on Monday. That kid is a menace. Go home now. Granny probably has a hot meal for you. Eat and go to bed, and we can talk some more tomorrow, if you want to," Tom said, but Marvin didn't move to open the car door.

"What else? You didn't run over the kid with the cat, did you?"

Marvin looked at him quickly. "No! No. I didn't see him after I drove away." Still he sat without making a move to get out of the car, twirling the thermos cup by the handle on his thumb.

"What is it?" Tom asked. "Something you're not telling me?"

Marvin nodded, lowering his chin to his chest. "I wet my pants," he whispered.

Tom suppressed a laugh. "So, what? If it was me, if it had been me in that cat, I would have be-shit myself," he said.

Marvin gave him a little grin. "Maybe I did that, too," he said.

Another blizzard blew in on Saturday night lasting until mid-evening Sunday, while Tom fretted and worried about his swans. He had put out extra food; they had shelter; the big birds were used to similar weather in the years they had spent as a species a little farther north up at Red Rocks, but he felt as if he was the only one at his refuge who had any depth of caring about them. Yes, Carl did his part, as much as a graduate student intern who was only temporary help at LaCreek could give or even feel any ultimate responsibility for. His project had been migratory waterfowl, ducks primarily, especially the blue-winged teal, a species that often over-wintered at LaCreek. He was using those birds as the basis of his thesis that, according to Carl, was almost complete. The swans for Carl were fascinating, but he hadn't been willing to throw out all the work he had done on teal and switch to the trumpeter swans. He was due to finish out his internship in another few weeks, go back to his university and move on with a few stories to tell of the trumpeter swans, but no long-term investment. King was angry and indifferent; Findley anxiety prone about everything and unwilling to go around King's authority to make decisions. Oddly enough, to Tom's thinking, Marvin was the most interested of all refuge employees, and beyond Marvin, Bit.

Tom had hoped Marvin would work out, but half expected he wouldn't, that he would go off on a drinking binge one day and simply not show up, but Marvin did show up, asked questions about the swans, listened to Tom's answers, and asked more questions, much like Bit, who even as a kid with kid concerns pestered Tom with questions. Had Bill and Martha made a nest? Had the others? How many pairs? How many nests? If there were nests, could he see the eggs?

Tom worried that the late snowstorm might end any nesting inclinations that the birds might have. He worried if they would be all right without additional feed until he could get out there to give them more. He worried even more that the Johnson kid might hike all the way to the headquarters, to the swan pen, and shoot the birds. He might get away with it, too, with no one there to see him or stop him. He didn't think that would happen—it was at least a three mile hike through deep drifts to get from the Johnson place across country to the swan pen at headquarters, but he hadn't thought the kid would ever again bring a gun onto the refuge property after the time they had confiscated his gun and King had talked to Bart Johnson, but the kid did do that—shoot the swans and no one was there at headquarters, if no one saw the kid come and go, it would be impossible to prove it. Shotgun pellets didn't tell criminal investigators what gun they came from, only what gauge the shotgun had been. Half the men in Jackson County owned shotguns in a variety of different gauges.

On Sunday afternoon the wind stopped abruptly and a weak yellow sun came out through thin clouds. Tom put on his insulated coveralls, his tall rubber boots, coat, hat, and gloves and dared the roads from his small village into Jackson. The road ran mostly north to south so the wind had scoured out any deep drifts and the short stretch that ran east to west close to town had been plowed out by the country road crew. He drove down main street, then down the side streets where the snowplow had buried most of the cars parked on the street. He stopped, clambered over a drift to Carl's apartment, and knocked.

A slide of snow from a small drift in front of the door slid into Carl's small stuffy living room when he opened the door. Magazines and books littered the coffee table, stood in tall stacks on the floor. Findley sat up among a pile of rumpled blankets where he had been napping on the ratty tweed sofa.

"Tom," Carl said in surprise, "what brings you out on this miserable day? What's up?" He closed the door. Tom stood just inside, his boots shedding melting snow on the small rug.

"I'm thinking that we need to get out to headquarters tomorrow," Tom said.

"Really? I doubt if the roads will be cleared that far out for a couple of days, man. No way can my car make it through those drifts," Carl said, "or Findley's either. We were going to wait at least another day before we tried it."

"I've got an idea," Tom said.

"Why are you so anxious to get to work? In this miserable weather, too," Findley said, as he picked his glasses up from the end table and put them on, pushing them into position with his middle finger, a gesture that Tom knew wasn't a subtle insult but only Findley's unconscious habit.

Tom told them about Marvin's encounter with the Johnson kid. "Oh, Jesus," Findley said, disentangling his legs from the blankets as he sat up on the end of the couch. "I thought that shit ended when King talked to his old man. Now that King's in the hospital, I suppose I have to go talk to Johnson."

"I think we should report the kid to the sheriff," Carl said emphatically.

"Do you really think so?" Findley asked. "It's Marvin, who is the sheriff going to believe?"

"What do you mean by that?" Tom demanded.

"Nothing, nothing," Findley stammered, "it's just that, well, Marvin has a reputation. You know that. What would the sheriff think? Who's he going to believe if the Johnson kid denies it?"

Tom held still, taking a deep breath. He said, "Marvin is a drunk, yes. And maybe he tried to burgle a place once, but that's done. He's not a liar."

"I wouldn't say he's exactly an upstanding citizen. Not a reliable witness. He's—he's—"

"He's what? What are you trying to say, Findley?" Tom demanded.

Carl interrupted. "Hold it, hold it. Let's let King decide whether or not we go to the sheriff."

"When's King coming back? And will he be in any shape to do anything?" Tom asked.

"We got through to the hospital on Friday afternoon. They told us that King was doing as well as can be expected, should be well enough to release on Monday, but if the weather was bad they were keeping him until it cleared up. He's not to drive, even though they said his pickup wasn't damaged so bad it can't be driven." Carl continued.

"So at least two of us have to go get him. One to drive him back in their car, and one to drive the refuge pickup back," Tom said.

"Yeah," Findley said, reluctantly adding, "I guess I should go talk to Johnson. King won't be in any condition to go anywhere, even after he gets back." He bit at a hangnail on his thumb.

"Don't worry, Findley," Tom said. "You won't be alone. I'll go with you."

Findley didn't look like that comforted him very much. "We need to get out to headquarters tomorrow. No telling what that kid might do if no one is there. I'm sure he and everyone else in the county know King's not there. His house is sitting there empty and those swans are, well, the swans are sitting ducks," Tom said. He'd been standing since he came in the door. He had started to sweat beneath his heavy clothes in the overheated apartment.

"I've got an idea," he added, continuing, "the state boys will have the plows out tomorrow. We can follow the plow out to the refuge turnoff. And I know old Cutler. He's a crusty old fart, but he might be convinced to plow the road up to headquarters."

"You think? What would it take? A twenty?" Findley asked.

"No. Just a good reason for him to do it," Tom said.

20

For the first time in weeks, Susan sat at her little desk up in her room doing her homework. After the double storm that had hit over the weekend, the sun had come out raising the temperature high enough that the efforts of the basement furnace to warm the second story rooms had prevailed. The ability to do her homework in the warmth of her room was Susan's test of spring. She finished the practice sheet of math problems, folded the notebook paper neatly in half the long way, and opened her American history book to read the assigned chapter. The only trouble with working in her room was the smell.

At first, nearly undetectable, her imagination she thought, the smell only grew stronger. She had checked under her pillow for a dead bird or other animal, under the bed, in the closet, but found nothing. The day before the first of the two weekend storms she had mentioned it to her mother who had promised to come up and check it out. Betty hadn't been in Susan's room for weeks, not since Christmas, when Susan had said she wanted the kids to clean their own rooms, put away their own clean clothes, not have their mother doing it. When Susan dutifully complied, Betty took it as a sign that Susan was growing up, taking some responsibility that she wished her son would take. Betty had gotten distracted by other worries, so she didn't follow up on her promise to come check out the smell until after the second storm when the power was out and she couldn't see well enough to do much of anything else.

Betty has sniffed around the room, the closet, the corners, under the bed, and said, "Well, maybe there's something." She didn't want to dismiss Susan entirely, not now when Susan was growing up so nicely. The room was cold as ice with the furnace struggling to keep up, so she wasn't anxious to spend much time there looking for something that she didn't think existed.

"If you notice the smell getting worse, we'll get your dad to come up and take a look. Maybe a bird or a mouse crawled in between the walls and died," Betty said, and Susan accepted that idea as a possibility, since she found nothing that Brian could have done.

Today, though, the smell was back and worse when the furnace kicked on. Susan stood up and reached for the window above her desk to push it open a few inches, but the wooden frame had swollen from the damp. She got up, went around the desk and leaned over a little, putting her back into pushing at the stuck window. The smell of putrefaction or something worse boiled up from her feet. She stepped back, turning her head and waving the air in front of her nose. She looked down at the floor at the end of the desk. The furnace vent. The smell came from the vent. She waited a few minutes until the air flow stopped, stepped closer and looked at the vent, but, of course, there was nothing to see but the six-by-eight-inch rectangular vent with the brown paint a little chipped from years of footsteps, brooms, damp mops, and furniture being slid across it and back. Maybe her mother was right or partly right. A mouse or a bird had gotten into the vent, not between the walls, and died. She stood up and got a ruler from her desk, pushed the desk lamp a little closer to the edge so the light shone directly down onto the vent. She would have to unscrew the vent cover and take it off, but then she saw there were no screws. She pushed the edge of the ruler under the vent corner and pried up, but it slipped off. She tried again glad that her teacher had insisted upon a metal ruler, not the plastic kind. By pressing down on the ruler as she shoved, it went under the vent corner. She got a thumbnail under the opposite edge and pried the vent cover out. The lamp light shone down several inches into the darkness of lint buildup, but at the edge of the hole back up in the vent, she saw something light, nearly white. She sat back on her heels. She really didn't want to fish a dead bird out of the furnace vent. She sat back on her heels, thinking. She could wait until her mom came home from the grocery store or her dad came back from wherever it was he had gone, but if it was a dead bird, maybe Brian hadn't put it there; maybe it got in by itself. She remembered the ugly family fight the night she found the dead bird under her pillow. She didn't want a repeat.

She picked up the ruler, leaned over the vent and reached inside with the ruler. The tip just caught the white thing, and by twitching the ruler, she moved it out directly under the vent opening. The smell that came up nearly gagged her. Socks didn't fly into furnace vents and die. Brian had to have put it there, but why did it stink so bad? His feet smelled; her mom said that was natural, but this wasn't dirty foot stink. This was rotten meat smell, a smell she remembered from a time when she'd walked out into the pasture to pick some wildflowers and came across a calf that had been dead for more than a week in the heat of summer.

It had to come out of there. She held her nose with one hand and fished at the sock with the tip of the ruler, but every time she tried to lift it out, the sock slipped off. It was heavier than a sock should be. She got up, took a compass from her desk, and lay down on the floor, shoving most of her arm with the compass on the end, down into the vent. She stabbed the sock but instead of feeling like it went through cotton sock, it felt like she plunged the point into a chunk of meatloaf. She held her breath and lifted the heavy sock from the hole, scooting backward with her feet, dropping the putrid mess on her floor. She shoved farther backward until she sat propped against the end of her pink bedspread covered bed, put her hand to her mouth and quickly snatched her hand away. The stink clung to the hand that had held the compass. She sat a minute, her head turned away from the mess.

She stood up resolutely, went to her desk and tore out two pieces of notebook paper, placing them on the floor so they overlapped a little, took the compass, poked it into the sock and lifted it onto the paper. It lay there like a dead sock, a sock that had been dead and rotting for days. Part of the white material was crusted black, over something lumpy inside, a greenish ooze soaking parts of the sock. What had he put in there? Maybe parts of a rabbit he had killed, maybe a lump of raw hamburger, but it didn't matter what, it was dead and she had to get it out of her room.

She covered the mess with more sheets of notebook paper, shoved the ruler underneath and pulled the bottom pieces of paper over the top ones, mashing the edges with her foot until she had the thing encased in paper like a poorly wrapped Christmas present. Carefully she picked it up with both hands, and holding it out in front of her, carried it down the hall, down the stairs, out though the back door, not minding that the air outside was chilly as the sun was going down. She stopped at the lilac bushes, just beginning to show a green tinge, dropped the packet and shoved it under the bushes, covering it with dead leaves that she kicked over the top. Her hands stank. She imagined she stank all over. She ran back in the house, upstairs to the bathroom, peeled off her clothes and got in the shower. When she got out, she realized she hadn't brought clean clothes with her into the bathroom, so she wrapped a towel around herself and went down the hall to her room.

When she had dressed, she heard someone downstairs. Looking out the window, she saw that neither her mom's Impala or her dad's pickup were there. Brian. Brian was downstairs. She was furious. She wanted to tell him off. She started for the door but stopped herself.

No. Telling him off would do no good. He would do something worse next time. She didn't want to tell her mom or her dad, didn't want to be the match lighting the fire of another family fight. There had to be something she could do, but the best thing to do for now was to pretend all was well, that she hadn't noticed the stink in her room. She went downstairs.

Brian stood in front of the gun cabinet, lifting the frame that held the glass doors off and setting it carefully on the floor. He walked over to the sofa picked up the shotgun and put it back in the cabinet and was leaning over to lift the frame back in place when he saw Susan watching him from the foot of the stairs.

Ignoring her, he lifted the frame back into place, hammering it at the corners with a closed fist. He pushed the hinges back into place at the sides, retrieved the pins from the top of the cabinet, along with a screwdriver and hammered the pins back into the hinges with the butt of the screwdriver. Susan watched.

Brian leaned against the corner of the cabinet, staring at her. "Got something to say?" He asked.

"You're not supposed to take out a gun without asking Dad," she said.

"I didn't. See?" He flicked the silver padlock on the front so it bounced against the wooden frame.

"You did. I saw it all. You didn't have to break the padlock."

"You didn't see anything, because if you did see something you shouldn't have, and if you did tell someone what you saw, you wouldn't like what happens next."

His tone of voice didn't sound threatening, didn't match the words he spoke. "I could do whatever I want to do with you," he said, and this time he spoke the words in a low growl, as he took a step toward her. "I can make you disappear so no one would ever know where you went."

Susan took a step back, feeling the newel post at the end of the stairs against her back. Brian stopped and turned to look out the window. His dad's pickup drove up to the yard and parked. The stock rack was on the back and a black pony shifted inside. Brian turned back to Susan, placed a finger across his lips, and said, "Shhh."

Susan ran past him and out the front door, down the porch steps and out to her dad's pickup just as he stepped out with a grin. "Guess what I have for you?" Bart said.

Susan looked over her shoulder, ran up to Bart and hugged him around the waist. Confused at this unusual show of affection, he put his own arms around her, hugging his daughter. "If I had known you'd be this happy, I'd have got you a pony long before now," he said, tilting her chin up.

Her eyes stared at him. She wasn't smiling. "What's wrong? What's the matter?" he asked.

A big grin split her face, and she said, "Nothing, nothing at all. I'm so glad you bought a pony. Is it mine?"

Relieved, Bart led her around to the back to the pickup, started to unlatch the rear pipe tailgate. "I didn't exactly buy her—it's a mare. That's a girl horse, you know. I traded something to Curtis Bradshaw to get her. His kids got too big for this little Shetland, and he didn't want to keep her around eating her head off."

He opened the tailgate wide. The pony stood uncertainly, her head down, looking out through the tangled mane over her eyes. Her thick winter coat gave her the appearance of an odd, four-legged teddy bear.

"Dad, it's too far down from the truck to the ground. She can't get out," Susan said.

"No, it's not. It's only a couple of feet. She'll jump out like a grasshopper. Come on," he said, making kissing noises at the pony, who didn't move. Bart jumped up into the back of the pickup, took the pony by the halter and tugged her forward. At the edge of the pickup bed she hesitated, gave a little hop, and landed on the ground. Bart stood beside the animal, still holding onto her halter. "What are you going to call her?" Bart asked.

"Oh, her nose is as soft as velvet," Susan said, smoothing her hand over the place between the animal's nostrils. She moved her hand lower, allowing the pony to sniff her. "I don't know what to call her. Doesn't she already have a name?"

"Maybe. I don't know. But you can give her a new one," Bart said.

No name came to her. She was happy. She was scared, and the pony, as wonderful as it was to have a pony at last, only confused her. If disgusting things and fear could drop on her from nowhere, so could good things, and while good things were better, of course, abrupt changes, surprises, were unsettling. She wanted her parents to be the way they were last summer, just normal like other kids' parents. She wanted her brother to be the way he had been before, annoying in an absent way, but not someone to fear.

"Never mind. You'll think of a name eventually. Here, hold onto her halter for a minute," Bart said, drawing his daughter closer to the pony and placing her hand on the sidepiece of the halter. He fetched a lead rope from the pickup, snapped it onto the ring at the bottom front of the halter, reached down, and lifted Susan onto the mare's back.

"She's not as high up as Linda's horse," Susan said. She had ridden double behind Linda when she spent the night at the Bakers' house, and envied Linda, whose family raised quarter horses and Angus cattle. Linda competed in rodeos, too, and had trophies to prove it. "Dad, could I ride her in a rodeo?" She asked.

Bart chuckled. "Well, maybe in the rodeo parade, but I don't think this little pony will win any barrel racing contests. If you joined 4-H you could show her at the county fair, though," he said.

Bart led the pony, with Susan holding onto to the mare's mane, down to the equipment barn and back. "I think I'd rather wait until tomorrow to ride her by myself," Susan said, sliding off the short pony.

"All right," Bart said, a little puzzled that his daughter, who had begged for a pony for a year, seemed to lack enthusiasm. "We'll put her in a stall in the calving barn. There's a saddle and bridle, too, in the pickup. I'll help you get her feed and water, and you can brush her coat out. She'll start shedding now that the weather is getting warmer. Brushing her will help get all that old dead hair off."

Bart left his daughter down in the calving barn, brushing the pony, and walked back up to the house. Brian stood leaning against the pickup with his hands jammed in the front pockets of his jeans as Bart approached. "Where's mine?" Brian asked.

"You want a pony?"

"You take away my Thunderbird and get the brat a pony?"

Bart stood with his legs apart, bracing himself for the argument. "An expensive automobile and a Shetland pony are not the same," Bart began. "You and your mother went behind my back to get you a car that you never did a lick's worth of work to deserve."

"The brat did work?"

"She's a girl. She helps out her mom in the house. She's eleven years old. You're seventeen. That's another big difference."

"There's NO difference! There's no difference! Doesn't matter if I don't do anything around here; she doesn't do anything either. Mom understands me. She appreciates me!"

"What the hell is there to appreciate?" Bart demanded, his fists on his hips. "The fact that you were born? Any pair of animals can have a kid, that doesn't give you the right to anything other than life."

"Are you comparing me to an animal?"

Bart closed his eyes and tilted his head back. He should never have started the argument. He should have walked away without answering no matter what Brian said. "I've been working. I've been helping feed cows. Goddamned cows. Rotten cows. Rotten, stinking cows!"

"Brian, you think a week's worth of work around here is worth a new Ford Thunderbird? You have a mighty high opinion about your worth," Bart said. "What are you going to do with yourself? I mean, you're coming up on your last year of high school. You messed up and didn't take the college entry tests, not that it would have done you any good, because I can't imagine what you might study in college, anyway. I've never seen you take an interest in anything except shooting a gun, and there isn't any career for that, except one that I can think of. I think the army might be a good place for you. Teach you some discipline." He stalked off to the house, leaving Brian standing beside the pickup. He had just opened the door when Betty's Impala pulled into the driveway, the car door opened and she got out, slamming the door hard behind her. She stopped when she saw Brian standing beside his dad's pickup.

Bart watched the two of them talking. They spoke quietly so

he couldn't make out the words. Betty touched Brian's arm, then walked to the gate. When she saw Bart standing on the porch, his hand on the door, she rushed the last few feet up the sidewalk, onto the porch, screaming, "You *BASTARD! YOU BASTARD!*" He took a step back from the rush of her rage. He wondered what Brian had said to make her so furious, but Betty reached into her purse and took out her checkbook, holding it by one end and shaking it in his face.

"You've cut me off! I can't even get credit at the grocery store! I had a week's worth of groceries piled on the checkout counter, and the clerk—that old busybody Clara Pffeifer—she just stood there and said, 'That will be cash, Mrs. Johnson. We don't take your checks or credit.'"

Inwardly, Bart smiled at her humiliation, but he kept his face impassive.

"I had to leave the groceries sitting there. Well, I wasn't going to walk around the store putting everything back with all those people in there staring! You can bet I marched right over to the bank and you know what happened there!"

"No, what happened?" Bart said.

"You *BASTARD!* You know exactly what I'm talking about! You took my name off the checking account, and that smug bitch, that *BITCH*, she stood there saying, 'I'm sorry, Mrs. Johnson, I can't reinstate your checking authority without your husband's permission.' and there were *PEOPLE* there, staring at me! I went back to speak to Jerry Don and he told me to calm down. Like I was a little girl! He offered me a cup of coffee."

"Did you take it?" Bart asked.

"No! *NO*, I did not. Do you know what he told me?"

"I have no idea," Bart said.

"He *SAID* that the bank is a business, and they do not get involved in domestic disputes!"

Bart had nothing else to say, so he stood there while Betty breathed hard as if she had been running, her chest heaving. "I tell you what, Mister," Betty said, poking the checkbook into his chest as if it were a weapon. "Tomorrow you are going right back to the bank and put my name back on the account."

"No," Bart said, "and I'm not going to change the ad I put in the paper either."

Betty looked at him, her eyes questioning, "What ad?"

Bart recited it: "I, Bart Johnson, will not be responsible for debts contracted by anyone other than myself." He pulled his wallet out of his back pocket, thumbed out three twenties and a ten, and held them out to her. "Go to town yourself. Here's grocery money."

She snatched the bills from his hand and started through the door, turned around and threw her checkbook at him. It bounced off his face and hit the porch floor. He leaned over and picked it up.

She did not come downstairs that night. She did not cook supper. Susan made egg salad sandwiches. The egg salad was a little dry and bland.

Susan was sick the next day, and while Brian was at school, her mom was in town, and her dad was outside, she crept into Brian's room. He was supposed to clean his own room and put away his laundry, but he didn't and that sloppy teenage boy tendency to keep a messy room was the only normal thing about him, Susan thought. Clean clothes were piled on top of the dresser, several laundry days' worth. Dirty clothes scattered across the floor, bed unmade, the closet door half open with a belt draped over the door, a shirt hanging from the doorknob. A half-finished plastic model of a car sat on the desk on top of the instructions, a tube of glue on the floor. Susan thought that she couldn't make the room any worse than it already was unless she was willing to find a dead animal and hide it somewhere. She wasn't willing to do that. She couldn't imagine retrieving that disgusting sock from under the lilac bushes and hiding it in Brian's room. She lifted the edge of the bedspread and peered underneath. More dirty clothes shoved beneath, dust bunnies on the hardwood floor, a quarter, and a shoe box. She snagged it with a finger, slid it out, and took off the top.

Chocolate cupcakes, the kind sold two in a pack with a soft marshmallow center and a squiggle of white frosting across the top. She sat on the floor staring at them. There was a rumor going around school that some of the high school boys had heisted some of these and some other stuff—doughnuts too, she had heard—from a delivery truck parked behind Jackson Grocery. She didn't think Brian had been part of that; he wouldn't have taken the risk of being caught. He did things on the sly—sneaky, not boldly in daylight, but he wouldn't have been the least bit shy about taking some of the stolen stuff when it was offered. She could tell on him. Maybe her parents would send him off to Plankinton.

Plankinton, South Dakota, that's where the state boys' reform school was located, and parents threatened their misbehaving sons with that when their kids got up to some pranks. Susan had never heard of any kid who really got sent there. She hoped Brian might be the first one really sent to Plankinton.

She left the box on the floor, got up and went out to the head of the stairs. No sound. Her mother hadn't returned and her father was still outside. Susan walked back to the bathroom. She rummaged through the medicine cabinet until she found a blue and white box of laxatives, the kind that came in little chocolate-flavored squares but very, very bitter. She broke off a square, pushed the rest back in the box.

Back in Brian's room, she carefully lifted the sealed cellophane on the back of a two-pack, unwrapped the cupcakes and flipped one over. The bottom had a little indent where the marshmallow had been inserted. She poked the square of laxative into the opening, put the cupcake back beside the other one and rewrapped them. A drop of model car glue sealed the package back.

He'll notice the bitter taste and spit it out, she thought. No, he ate like a dog, taking big gulps, scarcely bothering to chew. It would go down. With four packs of the cupcakes in the box, it might take him a few days to get to that one loaded cupcake, but eventually he would eat it. She hoped he ate it in the morning just before he went to school and shit himself in class. That wasn't likely, she knew, but she hoped, even knowing what she had done was petty, but she didn't feel bad about it. This was a prank. The things Brian did were—criminal.

She went back to her room, got into bed, and picked up the book she had been reading for school. She was partway through one page when she thought about her pony. Her pony, which came on the same day she had seen Brian putting the gun back in the cabinet. Brian was furious about the pony, she knew, and when Brian wasn't happy, he did things, and sometimes he did things even when he was happy for no reason. What might he do to her pony?

21

On Monday, Tom and Marvin followed Cutler on the snowplow. The plow went slow, but Tom didn't mind so long as he got to the headquarters building without the need to dig through snowbanks to get there. At the refuge road turnoff, Cutler swung the snowplow onto the access road and kept going. Cutler hadn't asked for anything in return for plowing out the refuge road, except he'd put on a significant look when Tom asked for the favor. No telling what that meant, Tom thought. Old Bennie was good at figuring out what two different parties to an argument wanted and giving each of them enough of their desire so they would agree to a third thing, the thing that Bennie wanted. Tom envied that ability in one way, but in another, it made him uneasy. He didn't know if he wanted to see that deeply into other people's motives because he thought most of their motives were dark and unworthy. Better to know they had those motives and stay the hell away from them. Cutler probably just wanted a free beer the next time he and Tom happened to be somewhere together where beer was sold.

At the headquarters, Cutler turned the big plow in a circle, waved, and took off at speed down the single lane road he had just plowed through. Watching the plow drive away, Marvin asked, "How come he don't move over and plow another lane? So's two cars could pass each other?"

"Don't know," Tom said, "probably figures that one lane was good enough. If he plowed two, he'd expect a double favor."

Findley and Carl had gone to bring King home, and with Keith still out, and no telling what he was up to either. Marvin had no supervisor to assign him duties down in the equipment barn, so he helped Tom carry buckets of feed to the swans, who flocked behind them as they entered the pen and walked to the feed troughs, dug the snow out of them, and dumped in the grain. They chopped holes in the ice. The air already felt much warmer at eight o'clock, as it should in mid-April, and as the weather warmed, the swans would soon reject the grain, seeking roots to eat, and since there was none of those left inside the pen, they would be flying over the fence and digging under, escaping to search the road ditches and banks of the small lake system.

The birds were all banded; that is, each one had a small number and code stamped metal ring fastened around one leg for identification, but that didn't protect them. If a bird was killed and if the person who found that bird knew enough to send the band back to the refuge, the bird could be identified as an individual, but that did nothing to protect the bird from being killed in the first place. The refuge personnel banded other migratory wildlife sometimes. A project a few years earlier had been meant to see how far and where ducks might migrate, but only a few bands had ever been returned. If a bird froze to death in an upstart blizzard or got killed by predators and no human was there to see it, was the bird really dead? Without a returned band, perhaps some migratory waterfowl were immortal, but not swans. Every one of the few trumpeters left was a precious rarity.

Tom shared his plywood square with Marvin as they watched the swans. Down in the far south corner of the pen, a pair of swans stood together on a higher part of the ground where last year's grasses still stood, rust brown against the rapidly melting white snow. The birds twined their necks together as if to begin another mating dance, but then they stopped, and began kicking at the snow with their flat black feet, doing a shuffle dance. One of them, the female, turned a circle, bending the stems of the old grass, circling, bending them again as they popped back up, until at last she sat on the grass, fluffed her wings, and became very still. Tom made a note on his yellow lined tablet: NEST?

Marvin sat very still. Finally, he said, "I wonder what that Johnson kid was doing out in a snowstorm carrying a shotgun."

After a while, Tom said, "You know, Keith caught him before on refuge property. Carrying a gun."

"Was it snowing?" Marvin asked. He pulled off his gloves. His hands didn't shake.

"No. Early in the morning, before the school bus would've come by."

"Had he killed anything?" Marvin asked.

"He didn't have any dead birds. Or rabbits. But it wasn't cold enough for rabbit hunting then. It was last fall before you came to work here."

Tom thought he heard a faint sound, a gurgling, as if the creek water ran under the ice chewing it away from below. After a while he said, "His old man, Bart. I never thought he'd be like that, you know, not control his kid. I thought he was an honorable man for a white guy. He leased my land for seven years. Always made the lease payment. No more, no less, no fuss."

Marvin nodded wisely, and said, "Some people can fool you. He's like Inktomi." Inktomi, the spider, who plotted and spun but always his greed and hubris undid his plot, untangled part of his web, until he was caught on his own sticky strands crying out that it wasn't fair.

"You can't fix some people," Marvin added, and Tom thought that was an odd thing to say coming from Marvin, the worst example of brokenness in his own family, but Marvin was a drunk, a weak man, not—not—not deliberately malicious. He tried to remember the last time Marvin had gone on a binge. He'd been sober since he came back to live with Granny. Maybe Marvin was wrong. Maybe some people could be fixed.

"They shouldn't be in there," Marvin said.

"Who? In where?"

Marvin lifted his chin and extended his lips in the direction of the swan pen. "Them. Those birds. It's not right to cage up a wild thing like that," he said.

"We have to. If they aren't caged up, they're going to die. People will shoot them."

"Easier to shoot them all shut up together in that pen," Marvin said.

"Yeah," Tom answered. "What can we do? If we don't get their wings clipped this week, they can fly out of the pen and off the refuge, where anything can happen." He thought about Bit's question many weeks earlier, after they had come down from the hill at Wounded Knee: *ARE WE AN ENDANGERED SPECIES, DAD?* He remembered his answer: *NOT YET*.

Over in the highest point in the south end of the pen, the swan pair both sat now, close to each other, still as sentinels on a hill.

Findley and Carl brought King home in midafternoon on the Monday. He'd ridden home sitting crosswise on the back seat of Finley's car, propped on pillows, a wheelchair riding in the trunk, the trunk lid tied down with twine because the wheelchair was not foldable and wouldn't fit in the trunk if the lid was shut. Findley wrestled the wheelchair out of the trunk just as Carl pulled up in the official pickup, and the two men extracted King from the back seat of the car like pulling a worm from a hole in the ground. King was half doped up and groggy, but where heavy pain medication made most people sleepy and quiet, King ramble and complain, berate and curse. He muttered out his blessings as Carl rolled the wheelchair over the ice-crusted sidewalk to King's front door with the shiny knocker that Bill and Martha thought interesting. He complained that the house was colder inside than the weather outside, and he was right, because no one had remembered to turn up the heat. Carl volunteered to spend the night with King, who needed help back and forth to the bathroom, so Findley left the house with relief, glad to be going home to his wife and kid after days spent in town with Carl instead of in the small house the refuge provided him, two miles from the headquarters building, a house that he would share with his wife and toddler son until, like King's wife, Findley's wife eventually quit complaining that she couldn't stand the isolation and made good on her threat to move back to Sioux Falls.

Tom waited outside King's house, leaning on the corner where the afternoon sunshine warmed the brick exterior. "He all right?" Tom asked.

"Yeah. Just pissed off at everyone and everything, worse than usual," Findley answered. "Why, you volunteering to stay with him?"

"No. You think he'll be well enough to talk tomorrow?"

"About what?"

"About that Johnson kid's attack on Marvin. About getting the wings clipped on the swans."

Findley turned away abruptly, kicking at a clot of snow, now re-freezing in the falling temperature. "Look, man. Have you no sense of decency? The man has just been through a terrible accident. He's in pain. He's on some high-class dope. He's in no shape to make a decision about anything," Findley argued.

"That Johnson kid tried to kill Marvin! He fired a shotgun at him! That's serious business. That kid is goddamned dangerous. And the swans—if the kid doesn't kill one of us, he's going to kill something else on this refuge and it would very well be one of our swans if they keep flying out of the pen where he could get at one of them. We've got to make some decisions. This is important!" Tom's face wrinkled in frustration. He took a deep breath and stepped back when he saw the fear in Findley's face, not fear of the Johnson kid, not fear that a swan might be killed, but fear of Tom, of Tom's anger.

Findley stood quietly, his shoulders hunched, looking off toward the red setting sun, casting long, blue shadow across the snow. "All right," Tom said. "We wait a day or so until King gets himself unscrambled. But if anything happens to one of those swans or if that kid brings his gun onto the refuge again, I'm going over your head. Over both of your heads."

"What do you mean by that?" Findley's face hardened.

"If you and King won't do anything about this mess, I'm going to the sheriff," Tom said, walking away.

Tom came home to a different kind of trouble. Bit had messed up again. Anna had taken her to Granny to get told another story, and Bit was sulking out in the garden, which Tom had hoping to get spaded up earlier so Anna could plant but the last two snowstorms had left the ground covered with snow. It would take a week to melt the snow and for the ground to dry out enough to dig up.

Bit sat on an upturned bucket outside the chicken pen at the end of the garden, making wet snowballs and chunking them through the wire fence at the chickens, who had been scratching away inside the pen. "You're supposed to shut them up for the night," Tom said mildly, "not torture the poor birds."

"I'm not torturing them. I'm just doing my job. Every time I scare one with a snowball, it jumps up and squawks and runs into the coop. See?" she said, chunking another ball of snow at a hen who hobbled away, half her toes missing because they were frostbitten and fell off during one of the earlier cold spells.

"Bit."

"What?" When her dad didn't respond, Bit said, "All right," got up from the bucket, and went to shoo the remaining hens into the coop. When she had done, she reluctantly shut and pinned the door and came back outside the pen where Tom stood waiting for her. "Your mom tells me you messed up again. Why did you steal a book from the school?"

"The book doesn't belong to the school! It belongs to the county library, and I didn't steal it. I was borrowing it," Bit protested.

"That's not what I heard," Tom said.

Bit sat down on the bucket again, her back to her dad. "I know. The teacher was taking this batch of books back to get a new batch, and I just kind of kept this one out. I was going to return it. When I was done with it," she said.

She had already read the book several times, but it was one of the best books that ever came from the county library. The boy, or young man really, who was the main character ran *AWAY* from the circus. He was an orphan being raised by circus people, and he had a job doing tricks on horseback as part of the show, but he had to share the spotlight with two women who he hated because they were older women, clumsy and obese, while he was the real star of the show. He asked the circus manager to let him do his own show, and when the manager refused, the boy ran away. The circus moved on without him, so the boy turned up at a nearby farm offering to work for his room and board. The farmer hesitated at first, but gave in. The farmer had a wife and kids and best of all, a horse; not a workhorse but a pet, more or less, a beautiful horse that the farmer couldn't bear to part with. The young man worked hard and grew attached to the farmer and his family. He even taught one of the farmer's kids how to train a pig to do tricks, but the boy had fallen in love with the horse, and when his work was caught up and no one was watching, the boy took the horse out into the pasture, where he thought no one could see him and practiced his circus tricks on the horse. The farmer's kid that had the trained pig caught the boy at it, and in return for not telling, made the boy promise he would teach the kid trick riding, and . . .

Well, it was about the best book Bit had ever read. She didn't want the teacher to return it to the library, she wanted to keep it, but that would be stealing, so she borrowed it. She sneaked it out of school under her jacket. She wasn't going to keep it. She planned to return it the next day and made it seem like the book had fallen down behind the table where the books were kept and so got left behind. Once she had it home, she hit upon the perfect answer: She would copy the book. It would take a while, but if she was careful no one would know she had the book. She was hiding in the outhouse carefully printing the words from the book onto sheet after sheet of notebook paper until her hand cramped. She was so deep in concentration that she didn't hear when her mom opened the door. When Anna had asked what she was doing in the outhouse with a book and her notebook, Bit was so startled that she almost dropped the book down the toilet hole in the shit.

Her mom had not understood Bit's explanation, or if she did, she seemed worried that other people, the teacher, might not understand it either. Bit was led by the sleeve of her jacket across the yard and through the gate to her grandmother's house to hear another story, this one about Inktomi scheming to steal something and his plans had, as usual, gone horribly awry. Bit would rather have taken another punishment, even a spanking with the old rusty pancake turner that her mom used to clear the ashes out of the heating stove. She hadn't been spanked but once with that turner, one time when she had messed up when Granny had been off in Ft. Pierre, too far away to give a storytelling punishment.

When Bit finished her disjointed explanation, Tom said, "I guess you must like the story a whole lot if you were willing to copy it all out by hand. How many pages long is it?"

"Two hundred and five," Bit answered.

"How many have you copied so far?"

"Only sixteen," Bit said mournfully.

"You know, if you look in the front of any book, it tells right there the name of the company that published it. Sometimes it gives the address of the publishing house too. Have you looked?"

"No. Why?"

"You might write a letter to the publishing house and see where you could buy a copy of the book, and how much it costs. You have a little money saved up, don't you?"

A seed of hope began to germinate in Bit's mind. "I might not have enough money," she said, but that wasn't all that concerned her. If she could afford the book, then she would have to decide if it was worth the money she would have to take out of her horse buying fund. Was it better to have a book about a horse, or to have a real horse?

"You won't know if you don't write that letter and ask," Tom said. He put a hand on her shoulder. "Come on. Your Mom has supper just about ready."

As Tom followed Bit up the path to the house, he wished that his other problems were that easy to solve, but then, he hadn't really solved Bit's main problem—the problem of getting a horse. At more than an acre, the lot where their house sat was big enough to support a horse, with maybe some supplemental feeding, especially in the winter. It bothered him that he struggled to provide his family with just the bare necessities, no possibility of any extras. He thought of Bart Johnson's family, who had everything they needed and more, but Bart still didn't make his lease payments. He remembered what he had told Bit, trying to live by his own words : You can't expect life to be fair.

22

The first Wednesday in May, Bart went to the livestock auction knowing he would see his neighbors there. In the spring, when it was time for all the new calves to be branded and vaccinated and the bull calves castrated, each rancher picked a day to do the work and on the appointed day, neighbors showed up to help. Bart had wanted the first Saturday in May, but the Bakers had already announced their branding for that day, so he wanted the following Saturday, the day after school ended for the year. He'd tried calling neighboring ranchers several times to reserve the date, but some kid on the party line had left their own phone off the hook so he couldn't call anyone.

In the muddy parking lot outside the auction barn, Bart stopped everyone still lingering outside to announce the branding at his place, and except for Gary everyone said they'd come help. Gary was preoccupied, giving a vague excuse without saying what he had to do instead. Bart—and everyone else—knew what the trouble was. Rumor had it that Pearl had threatened to leave him and, worse yet for Gary, his boys, big and dumb as they were, had taken her side. The eldest had said he was ashamed of his dad, and the day after he graduated from high school he planned to enlist in the army. Rumor also had it that Gary had taken a room at the weekly rate in the Jackson Motel.

Gary had lost his swagger. He followed Bart into the sale barn, speaking absently and quietly about the animals passing through the ring below, but he wasn't making his usual off-color remarks. Bart had heard another rumor as well: that Keith had threatened Gary for shaming Keith's family, which shouldn't have given Gary any pause, since he was a lot bigger than Keith, but Gary seemed afraid of something.

The first animals sold were cows that had lost their calves and were unlikely to produce another, old bulls, and a few of last year's calves, now yearlings that had been missed when others of their age had been sold the previous fall. A good number of bucket calves came through, quickly snapped up by an unusual number of wives attending the auction. Calves whose mothers had died or didn't have enough milk to raise them could be fed by a bucket with an oversized nipple attached. One of these made a nice 4-H or FFA project for a kid or extra spending money for a farm wife at the end of the season. Bart had tried to get Betty or even Brian interested, but neither had shown any inclination to feed slobbering bovines twice or even more often every day including Sundays. He should have considered such a project for Susan, he thought. Now that she had her pony, she was taking an interest in the other animals as well. She even asked if she could help with the branding, and when he asked what she wanted to do, he was surprised that she didn't say she wanted to bake a cake for the dinner the wives always cooked for their working men folk, but she wanted to ride her pony and help with the cattle. Still, he restrained himself from bidding on any of the calves. No sense pushing the girl. Pushing never worked; he'd learned that lesson with Brian.

When the auction was over, Bart asked Gary down to the Legion Club for a drink. Bart talked to a couple of the other neighboring ranchers—how many calves did he have to brand, what time did he want them out at his place, what the ladies might fix for the dinner, even some jokes about calf fries, usually a subject of prurient interest and good for a few raw jokes from Gary, but he was silent, sitting on the outside position of the booth in the corner near the hall back to the bathrooms. He even turned down another drink when Russell Baker offered to buy a second round, sitting with his head down so he didn't see when the door opened and Pearl walked in.

Most of the women in Jackson town and Jackson County were nominally religious but would still take a drink now and then, maybe more than one drink if they belonged to the Lady's Aid Club. Rarely did any Jackson woman come into the Legion club It wasn't ladylike. Not particularly religious, Pearl was nonetheless a teetotaler and was no longer a member of the club.

Just inside the door of the Legion Club bar, she paused while her eyes adjusted to the dim light. All the men turned their heads to stare at the unusual sight of any woman, and Gary's teetotaling wife especially, walking into the Legion Club bar on a Wednesday afternoon. Bart nudged Gary, and whispered, "Gary, look out. Pearl's here."

Pearl turned right and walked up to the bar, set her handbag on top and leaned over to speak to the bartender, a useless exercise since the bartender never remembered who had come in or even who he had just served. He'd learned discretion as the first rule of self preservation.

Gary, at the opposite end of the barroom, stood up in a crouch and shuffled quickly down the hall to the men's bathroom. The bartender served Pearl a Coke in the can with a glass of ice. After she had carefully poured the soda so it didn't fizz over, sipped it down an inch from the top of the glass, she poured the rest into the glass, swiveled her bar stool around, and surveyed the room. The men did not meet her glance, but their conversations became labored and slow. Pearl looked and sipped. When her glass was halfway empty, she stood, took her purse from the bar top and walked over to the table where Bart sat with Russell Baker and a couple of other men. They looked up at her as if surprised to see her.

"Hello," she said, "have any of you seen Gary?"

They looked at each other, shaking their heads with those blank expressions that every woman can read.

"Well, he was at the livestock auction," Russell Baker said, giving the answer that was not all the truth.

"May I sit down?" she asked.

"Sure, sure," Bart said heartily with a pleasant little smile.

Instead of sliding into the booth beside Bart, Pearl pulled a chair over from the nearest table, placed her purse on the floor and sat down, carefully smoothing her dress over her knees.

The men couldn't think of anything to say until at last Russell cleared his throat and said, "There were a lot of bucket calves went through the sale today. Are you raising any this year?"

"No," Pearl said, dabbing at her lips with a white handkerchief patterned with purple flowers. "I believe I've lost interest."

"Oh, you should keep an interest. Lot of good money in raising bottle calves, especially if you have three or four," Russell said. "My wife got a pretty penny for hers last fall. All that individual care, you know, they grow bigger than the ones left on the mama cows. She paid for all of Christmas with her calf money."

The other men continued the conversation with a friendly disagreement over the virtues of bucket calves versus ones raised by mama cows, but Pearl had nothing more to contribute. She looked over her shoulder when the door to the outside corridor opened to admit another man, but it wasn't Gary, so she sipped more of her soda, and when she set the glass down on the square cardboard coaster, she noticed that there were four men at the table, but five glasses, and one of the glasses was still half full of beer, a few bubbles still rising from the bottom of the glass. She looked around the booth from man to man to man to man, stood up and said, "I know where Gary is."

Carefully she placed her chair back at the adjoining table, straightened her skirt, walked down the hall to the men's room, opened the door and walked in where Gary stood, leaning over the sink counter, a look of surprise on his face. She didn't say anything. She swung her handbag hard. Gary dodged but too late. His head struck the mirror behind the sinks. He leaned over the sink, blood dripping from his temple mingling with the water from the leaky faucet.

Gary stood up and asked, "Why did you do that?" Pearl didn't answer. She was bending over fiddling with the buckle on her shoe. Gary reached out, half blinded by blood, to take a paper towel from the dispenser, and when he leaned over a bit to keep the blood dripping into the sink and not on the counter top, turning on the faucet to wet the paper towel, she hit him on top of the head with the stubby heel of her shoe. She hit him again and again, as he put both hands over his head. After several blows she stood back, gasping, and glancing up noticed that the mirror was broken.

Outside in the booth, the men heard nothing, said nothing. After a few minutes, only a few, Pearl came out of the men's room, walked to the bar at the opposite end. The room was so quiet that everyone heard her say, "I broke the mirror in the men's room, and I want to pay for it. How much?"

The bartender stopped polishing the bar top with his bleach-smelling rag and said, "No charge, Ma'am. That's been broke a long time," and went back to his polishing with a little grin.

Pearl walked over to the table where Gary had been sitting. She stood looking down at the men, but none of them met her eyes. She picked up the half full glass of beer, tilted it up and drank it down, slamming the glass down on the table. Bart flinched. None of the men said anything until Pearl walked out the door.

Russell Baker said, "Holy shit." The other men nodded.

"I suppose someone ought to go check on him," Russell added.

23

Keith was back at work. He was still cantankerous, likely to fly out at the least provocation, but he had lost that air of gray misery. Tom welcomed the reversion to the norm. He knew how to deal with that Keith. Carl was gone, back to university. King had been hobbling over from his house to the headquarters building every day. Findley hadn't told King about Melvin's encounter with the Johnson kid, so on the second day King was in his office, first thing in the morning, Tom knocked on King's doorjamb.

King's office was a mess, file cabinet drawers half open, piles of paperwork stacked on the desk and in the cracked leather seat of the chair in front of the desk. He looked up at Tom, grunted, "What do you want," and went back to sorting through the stacks of paper.

Tom leaned on the doorjamb. "We had an incident while you were in the hospital, right after that last round of blizzards," Tom started. King continued methodically sorting through the stacks of papers as Tom recounted what had happened.

When Tom had finished, King leaned a hand heavily on the last stack of papers he had gone through and said, "What do you want me to do about it?"

"I thought we should go have another talk with Bart Johnson," Tom said.

After a while, King said, "Let me think about it."

"When?" Tom asked.

"When what?"

"When will you decide what to do about it?"

"When I'm damned good and ready and not before. Is there anything else?"

Tom took a couple of steps into the room, leaned both hands on the back of the chair, and said, "Yes. The swans need their wings clipped. It's long past due. They're flying out of the pens and some of them, maybe most of them, might take a notion to fly north. It's spring. I expect that's what they used to do."

"I expect that's probably true, but it isn't my problem anymore," King said, returning to shuffling papers.

"We could lose half the flock," Tom argued. "They go back to the wild, they're endangered from hunters, accidents, and what all else."

"I never wanted those goddamned birds down here in the first place," King said. His eyes were bloodshot and his hands shook. Tom wondered if King had been drinking, but he wasn't close enough to smell alcohol on his breath.

"But they're here now. They're our responsibility," Tom continued.

"Not mine," King said with a grim smile. "You know what I'm doing here?" He waved a hand over the piles of paper on his desk, encompassing the rest of the office.

"No."

"I'm getting all this paperwork in order, making sure all the reports are up to date, and you know why?"

"I don't know," Tom said.

"Because I'm retiring as of the first of June. I'm a short-timer now. I'm going to ride this horse on down and walk away."

Tom asked, "When did you decide this? Why?"

"I put in for retirement before I left on that goddamned ill-fated trip to the meeting I never got to. I was going to tell everyone when I got back, but it doesn't make any difference. The new guy will be coming on board a couple of days before I leave. And why? You want to know why?" He didn't wait for Tom to respond. "I never wanted this assignment. I was promised a job in D.C. That's what my wife wanted, and you can see she didn't want to come out here with me, and I can't say as I blame her. Who'd want to come out to this godforsaken goddamned wilderness? Nothing but old farting farmers and Indians and none of you are worth a spit. I thought if I did a couple of year's stint out here, I'd have paid my dues; someone upstairs would notice and I'd get that transfer. My wife would go with me. I'd do a few years in Washington and have a nice retirement, but I finally faced up to facts. I'm not getting a promotion. I'm not getting a transfer. My wife is not coming back, and she goddamned sure isn't coming back as long as I'm out here. It's politics. It's all politics. I don't vote the way the bureau thinks is best for Fish and Wildlife, well fuck Fish and Wildlife. I'm done. I'm out of here. Now you know, so go do whatever the hell you want to. Clip those birds' wings, clip off their goddamned heads for all I care."

Tom stood up straight. "I thought this place mattered to you. The refuge. You went over to Bart Johnson's when we confiscated his kid's gun on refuge property," Tom said.

"Yeah, yeah, well that was kind of personal to me. I suppose the kid's attitude pissed me off some."

"What he's done this time is worse. He threatened Melvin, shot at him even."

"That's Melvin's story. Where's the proof?"

"More than twenty dents in the back of the cat from shotgun pellets. Several little round holes in the back window too. He didn't make it up. He was scared shitless."

"That could have come from rocks bouncing up from the road," King said.

Tom shook his head. "No. Neatly spaced, perfectly round indents in the metal frame? No. Rocks are irregular shaped. They don't make marks like that."

"How do we know it was the Johnson kid? Could have been anybody."

"Out walking in the middle of a blizzard carrying a gun on refuge property? We should have called the sheriff," Tom said.

"Tell you what. If you catch the kid on refuge property again, or there are any other suspicious incidents, then I might do something. Otherwise, tell it to the new guy," King said grudgingly. He added, "Get a couple of locals to help out with clipping those goddamned swans' wings. I'll authorize a day's salary at regular rates."

Tom walked away, disappointed that King would do nothing about the Johnson kid but relieved about clipping the swans' wings. He stopped at Findley's office and told him of King's decision. Findley agreed he'd run an ad in the paper for day labor and set the date to do the work for Saturday, 14th. As he walked down to the swan pen Tom saw three swans sitting on nests, their mates nearby.

On Saturday the 7th Tom and his family went into Jackson for their weekly shopping. Tom went to the Frontier station for his usual Saturday chat. Bennie Black Hawk was there. Before Tom could get a pop from the machine, Bennie took him by the arm and led him outside. The warm spring sunshine had brought out all the ladies in their flower colored spring dresses, walking up and down the street, going in and out of stores, stopping to talk with friends, some of them they hadn't seen much over the long winter. Bennie waited to speak until a group of shouting kids had run past on their way down to the little park.

From beneath the brim of his winter black felt hat, Bennie peered up at Tom. He smiled, revealing teeth that were far too white for a man of his age. "We've got a candidate," Bennie said quietly. "Rebecca Richards."

"For what?"

"Potato Creek District, of course," Bennie said. "She'll run against Ronald Two Elk this fall. We get him out, then Rebecca will make sure Ronald's nephew gets fired as tribal lease agent. This is that idea of yours. You know? You told me about it a couple of months ago, and I thought about it."

"She can't fire him all by herself," Tom said. "It would take a majority of the council or I guess the tribal council president could do it all by himself."

"I know. But guess who's sleeping with the tribal council president?"

"Oh, I'd guess Rebecca probably is," Tom said.

"I don't gossip about such matters," Bennie said primly.

"Well, suppose Ronald Two Elk's wife finds out about him and Rebecca. Do you suppose he would still be disposed to follow anything Rebecca said?"

"That's only one plan. I have another one in case the first one doesn't work," Bennie said.

"Bennie, I know you're trying to help, and I'm not saying it wouldn't work, but I've thought about this too, and look, even if Rebecca gets herself elected—"

"She will," Bennie interrupted. "I've got the votes in her district lined up."

"How?" Tom asked with a frown.

"Potato Creek needs a new school bus. I promised them two new buses," Bennie said proudly.

"You can't promise that!" Tom said. "How are you going to get that done? The budget is already set, and the new school buses are going to White River District."

"I promised something else to White River District in return for giving up the new school buses. I asked—"

Tom held up his hand. "I don't want to know what all horse-trading you did. Okay. Suppose Potato Creek gets the new school buses. Suppose Rebecca gets elected. Suppose she gets Ronald Two Elk's nephew fired and a new guy in as leasing agent. Suppose he either makes Bart Johnson pay up or cancels all his leases. What am I and all the other landowners going to do with a piece of land that's too small to make a living on?"

"I've got a plan," Bennie said. "Come on down to the café and have a cup of coffee with me. I'll tell you about it."

Tom and Bennie sat at one of the tables with cups of coffee in front of them, surrounded by other tables seating half the farmers and ranchers who had come to town on Tight Shoe Day. Ladies sat at a few tables drinking iced tea, a strict separation of the sexes, not by fiat but by custom. The café owner hated Saturday, when the café was nearly filled with customers, but the customers only bought ten cent a cup coffee or ten cent a glass iced tea, and most of the people left by noon or came to town after noon, so few people bought lunch. He managed to break even on the day—usually—by offering fresh hot cinnamon rolls served with a double pat of butter. The men often bit. Most of the ladies were dieting. Some of the men with bellies lopping over big belt buckles, should have been dieting.

Tom and Bennie just had coffee. Bennie stirred a third spoon of sugar into his cream rich coffee. "What's your plan?" Tom asked.

Bennie leaned forward across the scuffed and worn Formica table top. "You know my allotment is just west of yours," he said. "No water unless I dig a well. No creeks."

Bennie still referred to his land, not as just his land, but as his allotment, a term going back to something called the Dawes Act passed in the late nineteenth century. That law broke up Indian reservations from joint ownership by all members of a tribe, allotting each head of household and each adult unmarried child a piece of land. The pieces were called allotments.

"Yeah," Tom answered. "Mine's dry on the west half that butts up against your land, but the creek is the east boundary. The northeast corner, where the creek runs north into the refuge, that land is all swampy. Water table is close to the surface."

"What's the worst weed in the county? In the state?" Bennis asked with conspiratorial smile.

"What's weeds got to do with anything?"

"Just make a guess," Bennie insisted.

"Oh, I don't know, Russian thistles, I suppose. Tumbleweeds. Maybe cheat grass."

"Wrong," Bennie said, pointing a finger at Tom. "The worst weed is sunflowers. Well, maybe not the worst, but it's right up there."

"I know wheat farmers hate getting sunflowers in their fields. They say the sunflower seeds and stems and such getting into their wheat harvest lowers the quality. They get paid less per bushel, but I think it's more than that. I think they don't like the way sunflowers look, sticking up above the wheat," Tom said, keeping his voice low because half a dozen wheat farmers sat next to them at two tables pushed together.

Bennie chuckled, his laughter a low wheezing sound. "They ought to be growing more sunflowers and less wheat," he said.

"Weeds? You think farmers should be planting weeds? The County Weed Board would disagree. Think how much work and money they put into spraying the road ditches to kill the damned sunflowers!"

"Not wise, not wise," Bennie said wagging his finger from side to side.

"All right, Bennie, quit teasing me along here. Why should farmers in Jackson County, South Dakota, be growing weeds? Excuse me, sunflowers."

"I read a lot. Did you know Russians started growing sunflowers years ago?"

"What for, shortage of weeds?" Tom asked, pausing and leaning back in his chair as the teenaged girl who waitressed after school and on Saturdays refilled their coffee cups.

"Would you gentlemen like cinnamon rolls?" she asked with a smile.

"No, thank you," Tom said, thinking about the change he had left in his pocket. Bennie pondered a moment looking at Tom as if he hoped Tom would pay the ticket, but when Tom looked disinclined, Bennie shook his head with a mournful expression. When the waitress moved on to the next table, Bennie added more sugar to his refilled cup of coffee.

One of the men at the next table said something to the waitress and the men all laughed.

"Russians grow sunflowers because the seeds are good to eat all by themselves, and because of the oil they get out of them when they're smashed," Bennie said. "There's a market for that."

"Yeah. In Russia," Tom countered.

"But there's a growing market in this country," Bennie said, stabbing his finger on the table for emphasis. "Russian farmers brought the idea with them when some of them moved to Canada, and now they've started moving into North Dakota and started growing them up there. We've got better winters down here—well, a little better. Flatter land, too. I think. Easier to farm. We take our land back and farm it ourselves."

"That's your big plan? We get our land out of leases to white farmers and ranchers and we start growing sunflowers? Bennie, that's the most cockamamie idea I ever heard of," Tom said. "Only about three fourths of my quarter section is farmable. I couldn't make a living when I was using all the land to run cattle, so how am I going to make it only farming a hundred and twenty acres? Besides that, it doesn't take much special equipment to run cows, but think of all the equipment it takes to farm. We'd need tractors and the equipment to go with them—plows, harrows, seeders—and a combine harvester. You know how many thousand one of those cost? Just to use it for what, one week out of every year? Then I suppose we'd need a grain bin to store the sunflower seeds and a truck to haul it to market? That's probably twenty thousand dollars of equipment right there. You think the bank is going to loan that much money to an Indian farmer with no collateral other than his land? Even if old Jerry Don or Richard was willing to grant the loan—"

Bennie held up both hands to stem the flow of Tom's words.

"Hold it. Wait. Listen," he said.

Tom stopped talking, but he crossed his arms and looked out the window.

"Suppose we only had to buy one set of that farm equipment? Okay, maybe two?"

"One for you and one for me? That's right back where I started my argument from," Tom objected.

"No, no. Will you just listen?" He leaned back in his chair and muttered to himself, "These young people. No respect for their elders."

Tom uncrossed his arms and took another sip of coffee. The cup was down to the last and gritty with grounds that had escaped the filter on the commercial machine. "All right, old man. I'm listening," Tom said.

"You know how many allotments are out there? I don't mean all over the whole county, I mean down there either next to mine and yours or nearby? Well, there's eleven of them. Bart Johnson has all eleven of them under lease. Some of them are little pieces, 40 acres or less, but altogether it's about 900 acres or so. Supposing we form a co-op. A business, what you call it? A corporation. That's it."

"And? I still don't think the bank would loan us the money for farm equipment, except they might. Then after all the Indians got to fighting among ourselves and didn't harvest enough sunflower seeds to feed a ground squirrel, the bank would swoop in and take all the land that we'd put up for collateral, and lease the land right back to Bart Johnson," Tom argued. "Or someone just like him. Or sell it outright."

"Who says we have to borrow the farm equipment money from the bank here in Jackson?" Bennie asked.

"Any other bank would be the same," Tom said.

"Who says we have to borrow from a bank?" Bennie retorted, and then, seeing that Tom's patience was about worn out, he hurriedly added, "I've been reading up on stuff. There's a thing called a government small business loan. And if that doesn't work, there's other loan programs through the feds."

Tom closed his eyes wearily. "Bennie, I appreciate your thinking and working on this," he didn't say scheming but that's what he thought Bennie was really doing. "I don't see it makes any difference where we borrow it from. I see the whole project getting bogged down in fighting among the landowners, half the people not doing their share of the work, and the same thing happens in the end."

"It would be a corporation, don't you see? Each landowner has a vote, but they don't all work at farming it. There's a board of directors, see, and they appoint one or two of the most trustworthy landowners to do the work. That way there's no fighting over who's not doing their fair share of work and the two people running the place just get on with it. Most of the landowners don't want anything to do with the land anyway. They don't care about it except for that annual lease check they get. The reason they don't sell it is because Bart Johnson can't afford to buy it, and why should he? It's cheaper for him to lease it from the landowners. As long as we make the lease payments to the landowners, they'll let us alone to make the money and they'll get more money from their share of the farming profits. The people who do the actual work, they'll get a salary, and then the profit from the crops gets divided up among the landowners. So they get their lease payment PLUS a share of the profit. See? Everybody wins."

"So who's going to be the two 'trustworthy' landowners who run the operation?" Tom said with a sideways glance at Bennie.

Bennie grinned.

Someone rapped on the window. Tom turned to see Anna and the girls standing outside, and he knew it was time to go home. "I think there's a whole lot of things you haven't thought of yet. And a whole lot of things you've thought about but aren't telling me," Tom said.

"Just think about it," Bennie pleaded, as Tom stood up and took the check to the cashier.

On the way home, Anna chatted about news she'd heard in town while Patty fell asleep in the back seat, her face smeared with chocolate. Connie made annoying sounds imitating the sound of the car engine traveling down the road, slightly muddy in low spots from the last snowmelt. Bit stared out the window, adding in her head the nickels she had accumulated in the mayonnaise jar at home, agonizing over whether to buy the book or keep the $2.98 the publisher's letter had told her was the price. She wondered how much $2.98 would buy of a horse? One hoof? A tail?

Tom listened to Anna and demonstrated the talent that all men have: making supportive comments in the right places, so their wives assume their husbands are paying attention. Of course, the wives knew their husbands weren't paying attention, but they let the men think they had pulled a fast one.

Bennie's sunflower scheme didn't get Tom excited. He had never been a farmer. He supposed back in the day he would have been a buffalo hunter, but he'd been turned into a herder of slow buffalo, placid domestic cattle. What if the eleven landowners formed a corporation, just like Bennie had suggested, but instead of growing sunflowers they raised cattle? What about raising buffalo?

24

On Thursday morning Brian Johnson heard the school bus come and go, then his dad's pickup left, and a few minutes later, his mother's car. He turned over in bed and sat up feeling much better now after a very bad night. He had awakened early in the morning, at what time he didn't know, but it was still dark outside. His stomach cramped, gurgled, and churned. He barely made it to the bathroom where he sat for long minutes on the commode, sweating and straining. Barely had he gotten back into bed when the urge hit again, and then again, and when his mother got up at six a.m. she had helped him back to bed, wrinkling her nose as she sprayed the bathroom with room deodorizer.

"Isn't Brian going to school today?" Susan had asked at breakfast. Her mom hadn't answered, even when Susan persisted with, "Mom? Where's Brian? How come he gets out of school and I have to go?"

Finally her dad lowered the pages of the *JACKSON NEWS* and said, "He has the shits, Susan, and probably deserves it. Probably pigged out on something after school yesterday that didn't agree with him. I know it wasn't something he ate for supper cause none of us are shitting our guts out."

Susan's mother set the skillet in the sink with a bang. Susan barely suppressed a laugh, and all the way to school she smiled.

Before she left, Brian's mom peeked in his door and asked if he needed anything. She was going to town for groceries. Bart had doled out sixty dollars, peeling twenties off the roll in his pocket with a wet thumb, slowly, one at a time. Bart hadn't said where he was going, but Brian thought he was probably going to the vet's in town to get vaccine and other stuff needed for the branding on Saturday. Brian hated being sick, but in a way it was a blessing. He got a day off school and he was pretty sure his dad wouldn't force him outside to do any work later this afternoon. Neither his mom nor his dad would likely return until midafternoon. He glanced at the alarm clock on his bedside table. It read 7:45.

Dressed and downstairs, he opened the refrigerator and drank directly from the milk carton, long slow gulps. His stomach felt okay, not gurgling but sore, like it needed soothing. He put the carton back and closed the door, opened it again and took out a block of Colby cheese, cut off a healthy chunk, rewrapped the block and put it back in the refrigerator. He walked into the living room munching on the cheese, looking out the window. Yes, both his parents' cars were gone.

He walked over to the gun cabinet, took the screwdriver down from the top, and with the flat end pried the pins from the hinges and carefully put them on top of the cabinet. Bending his knees he grasped the handles on the front, lifted the doors while pulling them slightly out at the bottom. When he had the cabinet open, he sat the paired doors aside and took out the 12 gauge shotgun, leaning it against the sofa and took a handful of shells from the drawer. Carefully he lifted the doors and set them back in the opening, flipping the hinges together at the sides. He wouldn't bother putting the pins back in until he brought the gun back. The 12 gauge belonged in the farther slot to the left, nestled in against the green felt in the back and behind the edge of the cabinet door. Anyone glancing at it wouldn't notice it was gone unless they looked closely, and why would they? The padlock was still firmly attached on the front.

He opened the door and stepped out onto the porch. A warm breeze blew, ruffling last year's dead grass along the verge of the driveway out to the road, but beneath the dead stuff, new green grass showed. His dad would make him mow it in another couple of weeks. Down in the little home pasture a couple of mother cows stamped their split hoofs and switched their tails. Already the flies were back. Stinking cows.

He went back into the house, shoved the shells into his front pocket, and shouldered the gun. With weather so warm he wouldn't need a coat. He struck out across the backyard at an angle, down a slope to the place where an old building had once stood but had weathered gray, rotting into the earth. His dad said it might have been an old homesteader's cabin, but Brian didn't believe it. Maybe the Indians who had owned this piece of land years ago had built one of their little huts, back before they sold the land to Brian's grandfather, or great-grandfather, he couldn't remember which. He went on, walking down the creek bank where the water still ran deep from snowmelt and a spring rain a couple of days past.

During the winter he could cross the frozen creek anyplace, but not anymore, not without wading nearly to his waist. He walked until he came to a place where an old cottonwood tree had fallen across the creek after the water had eaten out the bank beneath its roots. Balancing on the trunk and holding on to protruding branches that still put out a few green leaves, he crossed, walked up the far bank, and crossed the fence onto the refuge property.

He walked across grassy land, feeling the squish of the ground beneath his boots, a sogginess that would continue until the hot summer winds of June and July would lower the water table. The dead grasses reached nearly to his waist, swishing against his jeans as he passed through them. A hen pheasant whirred up nearly beneath his feet, startling him so much that he almost dropped the gun. Recovering quickly, he raised it to his shoulder and pulled the trigger, but heard only a click. He had forgotten to load it. Cursing, he stopped and thumbed two shells into the breach, clicked it shut and walked on.

A couple of hundred yards farther on he came to the west road leading east to refuge headquarters and west out to the main road. A deep borrow ditch filled with water blocked him from the road. He walked east fifty yards to where the ditch narrowed, gave a mighty leap, and jumped across onto the road. He walked east. Overhead, airplanes sketched white lines across the spring blue sky, and farther ahead, in the borrow ditch on the right side of the road, a pair of swans swam, stopping to stretch long necks, partially submerging their heads beneath the water, tugging at the roots of plants growing deep into the muck of the ditch.

Slowly he approached, walking carefully in the middle of the road. He paused once and looked both ways up and down the road, but saw no one, no cars, heard nothing but the light breeze ruffling the old-growth grasses and the intermittent low honking sounds of the swans arguing over who got the best roots. He gave a low whistle just to see what the birds would do. One of them ignored him, but the other one paused, turned its head to look at him, then resumed digging and tugging at the arrowroots. When he was less than fifty feet away from them, he flung up his arms, waving the shotgun and shouted, "Boo! Bang!"

The birds stared at him, then climbed slowly out onto the roadbed, turned and looked at him. He walked closer. One of the birds dipped its head at the other as if playing tag, while the other drew back a bit, stepping from foot to foot. Brian raised the 12 gauge, fitted it carefully to his shoulder and fired.

When the shot came, Bill raised his head in time to see the red flower blossom on Martha's breast, watching as she slumped and fell, the puddling blood darkening a patch of gray-brown road dust. Bill stepped aside, avoiding the spreading wet, looking for the source of the sound, and when he heard no further shots, he tentatively moved closer to Martha, poking at her with his beak, poking again, then again, nudging, silently pleading for her to get up, but she was still and silent as a light breeze ruffled her feathers. He lifted his head, stretched his long neck, fluttered his wings as he strutted back and forth, back and forth and around Martha crying out, "oh Oh, oh Oh, oh Oh."

Brian raised the shotgun again, pointed it at Bill, and said, "Boom," pretending to be knocked backward by the recoil. As he walked up to the fallen swan, Bill moved away, darting his head from side to side. Brian yelled "Boo!" and Bill jittered away, backward, wings flapping. Brian nudged Martha with the toe of his boot.

The kid leaned over, grabbed Martha by the neck, and hoisted her twenty plus pound weight so the body hung over his back, blood dripping from the wound in her breast. He cradled the shotgun in his other arm. Without looking back at Bill, the kid walked away down the road. For a hundred yards or more Bill followed, crying out, louder and louder, until the kid leaped the borrow ditch at the narrowest point, awkward with the heavy swan over his shoulder, caught his balance, and walked off across the field. Bill paced on the road side of the ditch, calling and calling, flapping his wings.

Overhead, a meadowlark sang. Some said it sang Go see the preacher! and the bird always sang to people coming home from a night of sinning. Others, less religious, said it sang Wee willie winkie. The bird didn't care what people thought; it sang for its mate, for the joy of being alive on a warm spring morning.

Brian walked across the grassland, feeling no joy of the morning. He felt no sorrow or remorse, only a kind of private and personal satisfaction. He was one of only a handful of people still living that had ever killed a trumpeter swan, a unique creature among his own kind. That was more than enough for him.

At the creek he looked a long moment at the old cottonwood spanning the running water, dropped the bird and ejected the second shell from the shotgun. He left the swan and carried the shotgun across the creek, propping it against a hummock of dead grass and old weeds growing over a heap of dirt probably kicked up by a badger long gone now. Back across the creek, he hoisted Martha over his shoulder and, step by step, crossed again. His stomach felt gurgley again, so he sat down on the old badger hump with the bird at his feet, reached into his pocket for the small chunk of cheese he had shoved there, and sat quietly for a few minutes, just resting and eating. He thought that if cheese plugged you up and figs gave you the runs, then if you ate a chunk of cheese with fig bar cookies, the combination would balance out in the gut. No problem. He got up, picked up Martha and walked on down the creek to the rotting gray boards of the old cabin or whatever it had been so long ago.

He used to hide things behind the rotting boards that might once have been a door, but when he tried to pull it aside, one of the boards broke off in his hand, driving a splinter between his thumb and first finger. He snatched his hand back, looked at the end of a black splinter sticking up a quarter of an inch. Closing his eyes, he bit on the end with his teeth and pulled. The top part came away, leaving a dark piece of rotting wood under his skin. His hand was sticky with Martha's dried blood. He kicked at the boards until they broke away, but the cavity that used to be behind the boards had filled up with dirt, washed there over the previous season or two. He squatted and dug at the dirt with his hands until he had cleared a hole deep and wide enough, then he shoved Martha into the hole and pushed the boards across.

Back at the house he washed the mud blood off his hands at the kitchen sink, took the dishcloth that hung over the faucet and carefully wiped the stock of the shotgun put the shell he hadn't shot back into the drawer. When he had removed the gun cabinet doors, replaced the gun in its slot, replaced the doors and pounded in the hinge pins, he went upstairs, took off his clothes, and climbed into bed where he was still resting when his mother came home later in the afternoon. She eased into his room quietly. His eyes opened when his mother's hand touched his forehead. "No fever," she said. "Are you feeling better?"

"Much better. In fact, I feel great."

"Looking forward to the branding on Saturday?"

"Oh, yes. I can't wait."

25

The refuge owned cannon net, which wasn't actually a cannon, but that's what the men who worked there called it, a kind of joke. Set on a tripod for stability and proper aim, when one of the men pulled the lanyard it boomed, but it didn't shoot a round metal ball. Rather, it shot out a net. Used for several years to capture birds for banding, mostly ducks that would sit quietly, not flying flocks, the men found it also useful for capturing the swans to be banded. They shooed the swans into a corner of the pen, set up the bird cannon, and boom! Then they could pull the pissed off birds out one at a time.

Tom had the cannon ready, the net with the corner weights to make it fly out and expand, stuffed into the wide barrel. While he waited for the appointed day, he nervously watched the birds, flying but mostly inside the pen, not through the gaps and over the perimeter fence. If King had let him, Tom would have gone into the pen with Marvin and maybe Carl, and tried to fix the sags in the fencing across the top, but as it was, Tom felt lucky to have gotten the concessions he did. A couple of times when he came to work in the morning, two or three of the swans had flown over the fence, but they usually hadn't gone far, so he was able, with Marvin's help, to shoo them back through the gate, strutting and complaining. Bill and Martha were the worst offenders.

On Thursday morning when Tom and Marvin drove into work on the west access road, they spotted Bill and Martha, way off the reservation, paddling in the ditch, stopping to tug at arrowroots. Tom slowed the car. He and Marvin leaned out the car windows shouting and pounding on the sides of the car, but Bill and Martha ignored them. The men got out of the car and rushed the birds, waving their arms and shouting. Bill and Martha got out of the ditch on the far side, waddling off into the tall grass, their long necks holding their heads up above the dead grasses, their eyes following the men's movements on the opposite side of the ditch.

Tom walked back west up the road, planning to circle the birds from behind and urge them back across the ditch to the road where they might be herded slowly back to their pen. As he leaped, his foot slipped on the muddy bank, and he slid slowly into the ditch water up to his knees. He climbed out on the other side, stomping his muddy boots, water dripping from his pants and walked off, cursing to himself, annoyed he had lost sight of the birds.

Ducking their heads low, the swans scurried through the tall grass. At least, Tom thought, they were heading in the right direction, back to the ditch and the road, but when he got back to the road the birds were not ahead of him. He turned to look behind him and saw Bill and Martha's heads sticking up above the tall brown grass thirty feet behind him. He tried circling them again, but they ducked back behind him.

Marvin leaned on the car and laughed. "You should go back to herding cows. You're no good at this," Marvin said.

"Shut up or help," Tom said.

"What do you want me to do?" Marvin asked.

"Get in the car. We have to get the bird cannon."

Tom started the car, put it in gear, and drove down the road, east toward the headquarters building. When he looked in the rearview mirror, Bill and Martha had returned to the ditch.

Back in the equipment building, Tom looked at the bird cannon. There was no fence corner out on the road, no place where he could stop the birds until the net shot over them. He looked at the net he had so carefully stuffed inside the day before. As he and Marvin were getting back into the car, King came out of the office building. Instead of his usual uniform with the Bureau of Fish and Wildlife patch sewn onto the left sleeve, he wore a pullover knit shirt and baggy khaki pants. A wisp of his thinning brown hair lifted in the light breeze. "Where are you going?" he asked.

"To capture Bill and Martha," Tom said. "They've flown out and they're down there on the west road in the borrow ditch."

"Leave it alone," King said. "They'll be back. We've got a personnel meeting."

"Can't it wait? We need those birds back in the pen right now," Tom argued.

"They'll come back on their own," King said. "We need to talk about getting the new guy informed. Refuge policy and procedures here. What we've done so far. What stuff we've had to put off. The budget submission was due a month ago, and Findley hasn't got it firmed up yet."

Tom didn't see why he should ever be included in budget discussions. King never took any of Tom's suggestions anyway, but he shut the car door and followed King back into the office.

Findley ran through the budget, giving figures and reasons for the figures, pausing after each section for King to comment, but King didn't. He sat silently, his face impassive, and that made Findley even more nervous than he usually was, filling the silence with repetitions of his justifications for the figures he had cited.

Tom saw the hands of the wall clock advance from 7:10 to 7:20 to 7:45, then 8 and past. He thought about the bird cannon, how he could set it on the tripod. The net only shot out about fifty feet maximum, so he'd have to be close to the birds or the boom of the gun would frighten them into running even farther, too far for the net to reach. He'd done a little net fishing as a kid on one of the smaller ponds and gotten pretty good at swirling a net over his head and casting it so it landed flat on the water. If he could get close enough to the swans, if he could swirl the net without frightening them farther away—

"Tom. You got anything to add?" King asked.

Findley looked from Tom to Keith as if in search of a lifeline. The hands on the clock pointed to 9:45.

"I think you've summed it up very well," Tom said. "Keith, you got something?"

Keith shook his head without a word.

King stood, tugging at the crotch of his khakis, and said, "All right. Meeting adjourned. And when the new guy gets here, remember: not a word. Got it?"

Tom didn't know what he wasn't supposed to talk about, but he didn't suppose the new guy would ask him to comment on anything anyway. He beckoned to Marvin and walked out.

In the car, he tugged the net out of the bird cannon as he explained to Marvin. "Okay, I need you to get behind them and shoo them toward me. I'll just kind of hunker down in the road until they get close, before I stand up and pitch the net. They may spook off to one side or the other when I stand up, so you have to yell and keep them moving forward."

A couple of hundred yards from where they had last seen the swans in the ditch, they saw Bill, running back and forth in the road and flapping his wings, looking south. Tom eased the car closer to the bird and stopped.

"What's he doing?" Marvin wondered.

"I don't know. Where's Martha?"

They got out of the car and slowly approached Bill, who ignored them, continuing his monotonous pacing and calling out. Tom spun the net, flung it, and watched it settle over Bill, who gave an unnatural squawk, tried to leap up, tried to flap his wings, but only entangled himself in the web of net.

Tom bundled the heavy, complaining bird tighter into the net, bent his knees and lifted. "Open the back door," he directed Marvin.

As he shoved the trussed-up bird into the back seat, Bill cut loose with a harangue of sound right next to Tom's ear. He wrapped the net as tight as he could around the bird and tried to pin its wings tighter to its body by wedging the netted package on the floorboards between the front driver's seat and the back seat. He backed out and slammed the door.

"Tom. Come look." Marvin stood a few feet back up the road, staring at a wet patch in the dirt.

Tom looked. It wasn't water, but thicker with some red gleam on the edges. His face felt hot even though the sun had gone behind a puff of fair weather cumulus.

"Think it's Martha's blood?" Marvin said quietly.

Tom squatted, dipped a fingertip into the wet and touched it to his tongue. "It's somebody's blood," he said. "And look." He pointed at shotgun pellets scattered near the drying puddle and farther out in the road, widely scattered.

Tom stood up and followed the thin trail of blood down the road, past his car, where Bill had gone quiet, another hundred yards or so up the road where the blood trail ended at the borrow ditch. He looked across where a mashed down path of weeds ran nearly straight across to the south boundary of the refuge.

"Think we ought to go over there and look for her?" Marvin asked.

Tom shook his head and said, "No. She's dead. Too much blood. We'll come back and look after we get Bill back to the pen." He turned the car around and drove. Marvin sat silently in the passenger seat. Bill rustled his wings, trying to find a comfortable position where there was none. The road blurred strangely, tilting up from right to left and back again. Tom stopped, wiped his cheeks, and said to Marvin, "You'd better drive."

When Marvin had parked Tom's car as close to the swan pen as he could, Tom got out and went to the equipment building, coming back in a few minutes with the big shears. He lifted Bill out of the car and carried him to the gate. Marvin held it open until Tom and Bill had passed through, then he came inside and helped untangle the net. When they had gotten most of it off the big bird, Marvin held him down with a knee, avoiding the snapping beak while Tom carefully clipped his wing feathers.

When they let the bird get up, he ran to the fence flapping his wings in useless attempts to fly over. "He wants to go back and look for her," Marvin said.

"Yes. There's one thing known for sure about swans. They mate for life."

King sat behind his desk, his chair tilted back and his eyes closed. Tom walked in and rapped his knuckles sharply on the desktop. Marvin lingered in the open doorway. King tilted forward with a jerk, his eyes opened in surprise. "What? What now?"

"Martha's dead."

Focus returned to King's eyes. "Martha? Who's Martha?"

"Martha the swan. Of the Bill and Martha pair. The ones who knocked on your door last fall. The main ones who kept flying out of the swan pen, weeks after I told you we had to clip their wings," Tom said. He was calm, but his voice was thick.

"Coyote get her?"

Tom laughed without humor. "No four-legged coyote would go after a healthy swan, and especially not with her mate there with her. No four-legged coyote carries a 12 gauge shotgun."

"Are you saying someone shot that swan?" King still didn't seem to understand.

"Yes! No, I'm not saying someone shot her. I'm saying that Johnson kid shot her!"

King stood up and walked around the desk, his face angry and red, his mouth set. "You don't know that! How can you know that! You can't just go accusing someone without any proof? Where's your proof?"

Close to shouting, Tom said, "Because he's been caught on the refuge before with a gun! Because he threatened Marvin with a 12 gauge shotgun and shot at him! Because there are 12 gauge pellets on the ground around a puddle of blood. Because there is a trail of blood down the road and across the ditch, heading south. Because there is a path of knocked down grass on that stretch between the road and the south boundary with Johnson's place!"

"That's not proof!"

Tom stepped close, leaning down from his taller height, looming over King. "You total fool. You incompetent asshole. You don't give a shit about any animal on this entire goddamned refuge. All you care about is a fancy ass job in Washington D.C. pushing papers and drawing a big salary so you and your wife can hobnob with the politicians at fancy ass parties and pretend you know something about wildlife. You don't know anything! You don't care about anything! You're a waste of skin, a waste of air!"

"So, are you going to hit me? Is that what it is?"

Tom took a step back. Marvin had disappeared from the doorway. "No. I'm not going to hit you. I'm going to tell you a story," Tom said.

"What?"

"Sit your ass down and listen!"

King sat down in the cracked leather chair in front of his desk, his hands clasped between his knees. He was not wearing shoes, and there was a hole in his left sock. Tom stood at one side of King's desk. "There's a story we tell about the massacre at Little Big Horn," Tom said.

King raised his head as if to speak, but stopped himself.

"After everything was over, all the people left. That's when Sitting Bull took some of his group and went to Canada. They say there were more than five thousand Indian people there, come together to socialize some, to celebrate the annual Sun Dance. Custer had about two hundred men with him. You know, they say he bragged that if he had a hundred men he could ride through the whole Sioux Nation. He had twice that many, and he lasted less than an hour. After everything was over, Custer and all his men were dead, most on top of that one hill but t others were scattered along the banks of the Greasy Grass River. When the rest of the army came up and found their dead, they saw that many of them had their ears punctured. Do you know why?"

King frowned, and said, "What the hell is this? What kind of a story are you telling me? That's disgusting shit!" He made as if to stand up, but Tom took a step toward him and King settled back, sitting on the edge of the chair seat.

"I asked if you knew why the soldiers' ears had been punctured? Do you know why?"

"How the hell should I know why a bunch of savage Indians

killed and mutilated a U.S. Cavalry troop a hundred years ago!"

"For years and years the tribes had complained about treaty violations, and the government's answer? Make a new treaty. And no sooner was the ink dry on the paper, than the United States government and its citizens violated the treaty. I don't have time to give you a list of all that shit we put up with, of all the times we tried peaceable means to resolve differences. All we wanted was to be left alone in peace, and *NOBODY WOULD LISTEN*. We thought maybe white people couldn't hear. So after the soldiers were all dead at the Battle of the Greasy Grass, the women took their sewing awls and opened the soldiers' ears so they could hear."

King's face held a look of horror. "So, what are you going to do, poke a needle in my ears?"

Tom smiled, and said, "You didn't listen. I said that the women did it. I am not a woman."

King sat up straighter. His shoulders went back, authority pouring back into him like air into a collapsed balloon, while Tom kept his eyes on him, silent, expectant.

"Well, what do you want me to do about this?" King demanded.

"Your job," Tom said.

"I've been doing my job for twenty-seven years. I was doing my job, working for Fish and Wildlife, when you were—you were doing whatever in the hell it was you did. Who are you to demand I do my job?"

"A citizen. A taxpayer. A man who cares about these animals that you are supposed to protect. That's your job."

"I do! I did!"

Tom continued looking at King's red face until King looked away. "Who's supposed to enforce wildlife laws?"

"Well, I suppose the game warden," King conceded.

"And you are the game warden. Empowered by the nature of your job as a FEDERAL game warden with more authority than the state game warden," Tom said.

"That's a technicality. I leave those duties up to Gardiner. He's the authorized state guy. That's his job."

Tom started to walk out.

"Where are you going?"

Tom stopped. "If it's Gardiner's job, then I have to report Martha's death to him."

King jumped up and said, "Wait a minute! You're not gonna bring the state boys into my jurisdiction!"

"Your jurisdiction? Yours? You just said you leave the game warden duties up to Gardiner. That's his job," Tom countered.

King threw his hands up. "All right, goddammit. It's me. It's my job. So what the hell do you expect me to do?"

"Go look at the place it happened. Write it down. Maybe take some pictures. Follow that trail and make sure it goes where I know it goes across to the refuge border. Take a picture of one of the posted signs. Go talk to Johnson again."

King walked back around the desk and sat down.

"What are you doing?" Tom asked.

"I'm going to put on my goddamned shoes if that's all right with you," King said. "Jesus Christ. You'd think we were married the way you nag."

26

Bart Johnson busied himself out in his equipment barn inventorying the rough shelves back in the walled off space in the back where he stored a variety of animal pharmaceuticals—vaccines to prevent common cattle diseases and the needles to inject them. He'd bought enough to replenish the supply he would need for Friday. He found his branding irons where he had left them propped against the wall the previous spring, took them over to the workbench and scrubbed off the rust with a piece of sandpaper. He had three irons so when one or two of them were being used, the others could be back in the fire, heating up for the next calf. Bar J—a J with a line across the top: that was his brand, and he was proud of it. Ranchers thought of the brand they applied to their livestock like aristocrats in the old country thought of their coats of arms—a mark of pride, a declaration of who you were, your family, and a legacy for your kids, not that Brian gave a shit about family or history, but Susan might.

He had let Brian out of helping out today since he'd been sick, but tomorrow—well, tomorrow he expected the kid would be out helping because the neighbors' kids would all come with their parents to help. That was just country folk tradition. The men and boys would get the branding and vaccinating and castrating done down in the pens while the women and girls fixed up a big meal for when the work was done, except Susan had asked to ride her pony and help. He said she could, but he felt uncomfortable about his baby girl being present when they castrated the bull calves. The men sometimes made jokes. He'd have to caution them before they got started.

Later today he would go down to the pens that adjoined the pasture with the cow/calf pairs. He's lost only one calf this year, damn near a record hundred percent calf crop. Mamas and babies were thriving, but he needed to move them out to the bigger pasture right away. The grass in the little pen had come on well, but with so many cattle in the little space, the grass was eaten down level with the ground as soon as a green shoot showed and he had noticed a few bare patches of earth showing through. The roots were still there beneath the surface just waiting for a good rain, but if the cattle were left on that pasture much longer, they'd kill even those roots. He'd timed the branding and all that went with it just about right.

He was out in the big corral checking that the gates worked right, oiling the hinges, when the pickup pulled into the yard. He could see the refuge logo on the side of the cab. King got out along with Tom Warder. Bart set the oil can down, closed the gate, and walked up to the men, wondering what they wanted, knowing it couldn't be about Brian and guns since the gun cabinet had been locked for months and still was. He hadn't seen Warder since the man had come dunning him months past. He supposed he ought to feel guilty about the missed lease payment, but he was past being ashamed of that; his tolerance for shame had increased tremendously since he'd had to run his face at the bank. Twice. No, Warder was here with King in an official refuge vehicle, so it had to be something else.

King kept his hands in his pants pockets as Bart walked up, so Bart didn't bother to put out his own hand for a shake and Warder stood behind King looking grim. Well, he would, wouldn't he? No doubt he was still pissed off about the lease payment. He'd change his tune come next December when Bart made up for last year and paid this year too. That near one hundred percent calf crop made it not only possible to catch up but damn near certain.

"How you doing, King, Warder? What brings you out here?" Bart asked.

King turned his head and spat off into the grass at the edge of the graveled driveway. "We've got an unusual situation, Johnson. We think you might know something about it," King said. "Or Warder here thinks so."

"And what might that be?" Bart said. King's serious face and tone of voice gave him a rising sense of anxiety.

"You know we have those trumpeter swans over there in a pen," King said, motioning with his head back toward the refuge.

"What about them? Everyone knows about that. It was in the papers, even made the national news back when you first got them down here," Bart said.

"We clip their wings ever so often so they don't fly very far. We're about to do it again," King said.

Tom ignored King's lie. The swans' wings had been clipped exactly once, when they were first brought out of their cages before they were shut in the pen last September, but he wouldn't contradict King now that the man was doing what he was supposed to have done all along.

"I don't see what you're getting at," Bart said, his anxiety growing.

"I'll get right to the point, then. Just lately a few of the swans have been flying over the fence and out of the pen. They haven't gone far, just stayed inside the refuge boundaries, but t this morning one of the pairs was out on the west access road, digging arrowroot out of the ditch like they do. Someone shot one of them."

"What's that got to do with me?" Bart's voice rose. He was indignant. Just because Brian had been caught on the refuge once with a gun didn't mean he should still be a suspect, and besides, he could prove it wasn't Brian.

"That bird was kind of a pet. The men named the pair Bill and Martha and it was Martha they shot," King went on. "See, those birds mate for life. Bill's damned upset."

Tom wished King would have stated the facts, not gone off into details about how much the birds were beloved. Shooting a trumpeter swan was illegal, a crime, and whether or not the men thought the bird was a pet had nothing to do with it. King was sounding close to apologetic, like Martha was a pet dog someone had run over.

"Look, it happened this morning around 9 o'clock or so. There's a trail through the grass across that little stretch of land between the south refuge boundary and you—your property. Trail leads over the fence," Tom interrupted.

"Where's the bird?" Bart asked.

"Not there," King admitted.

"Then how do you know the goddamned thing was even shot?"

Tom stepped forward. "Because there's blood and shotgun pellets on the road, and Mar—, the bird is gone, but there's a blood trail leading right up the road and across the ditch and right to that path of knocked down grass that comes right to your property," he said. He wanted to add you idiot but he didn't.

"Habeas corpus. Habeas corpus! Ain't that the Latin word? Means something like show me the body. If there's no body, there's no way to prove murder, and if that's good enough for a human in a courtroom, that ought to be good enough for a fucking goddamn bird!" Bart said.

"The blood and the shotgun pellets and the path through the grass leading over the fence and onto your property. The fact that your kid was caught on refuge property carrying a loaded firearm. That's not sure he did it. It's circumstantial evidence, but it means we have to investigate further," King argued. He hadn't wanted to stir into this mess, but now that he was here, Johnson's attitude was pissing him off. He'd thought Johnson had gotten the message the last time he'd been here when he'd brought Johnson's 12 gauge back.

Tom wanted to mention that Brian had been on refuge property back during the winter, that he had threatened Melvin, even shot at him, but he held back. King hadn't said anything to Johnson back then, and he sure as hell wouldn't be listening to that story now. Tom wished he'd gone over Findley's objections, over everyone's head and to the sheriff, back when it happened, or even to Gardiner, but it was too late now.

"I can prove to you my kid didn't do it," Bart said. "Come on."

Tom and King followed Bart across the yard, onto the porch and into the house where Betty sat in her lady chair crocheting another baby afghan while she watched *AS THE WORLD TURNS*. Bart whirled and pointed at the glass fronted gun cabinet with a shaking arm. "Look! Look, goddammit! See that gun cabinet?" He walked over and rattled the padlock so it clicked against the glass in the cabinet doors. "I put that lock on it last fall, the first time you came over here accusing my kid. And yeah, yeah, yeah, the little shit was guilty as hell that time, but he sure as shit ain't now. He has to ask whenever he wants to take out a gun, even to go rabbit hunting last winter, and he hasn't asked in weeks. Look! Look here!" He pointed into the cabinet. "See that? That gun in the last slot? That's the 12 gauge you brought back. It's not been out of the cabinet in weeks, months maybe."

King looked at Tom who looked uncertain. Brian and Susan stood at the top of the stairs, looking down. Betty had stopped watching the television, her ball of white cotton knit crosheen and her silver crochet hook still in her lap, but the soap opera played on.

"You got any other guns anywhere else?" Tom asked.

"No! No, goddammit, no! That's it. That's the lot."

"But you've got the key, don't you? When's the last time you took out that gun?" Tom asked quietly.

"Fuck you! Fuck you both! I have no need to kill a goddamned swan. I'm a cattleman, a beef man. I won't even eat mutton, that gray nasty goddamned meat. I don't like turkey, isn't that right, Betty? At Thanksgiving I make her cook me a ham," he said.

Betty didn't answer. She had put one hand over her mouth and the other on her bulging tummy.

King didn't say anything, and Tom didn't know how he could argue against a man's personal meat preferences. He didn't bother to point out that ham was not beef.

"Plenty of people have said they'd like to shoot one of those swans," Bart added.

"Who? When? Where?" King barked.

"Plenty of men. I've heard them talking down in the Legion Club. And why, just last winter, I think it was right before Christmas, Gary Kendall told me he'd like to shoot one of them," Bart answered.

"That trail leads right cross the refuge boundary, right toward your place," Tom said. "Were any of those men out here this morning?"

Bart stood silently for a minute. He said, "No. Not today. I've got people coming tomorrow for the branding."

"The swan is dead, Bart. The swan did not get killed tomorrow morning and then somehow go back in time to this morning at 9 a.m.," Tom said.

"No, you smart aleck son of a bitch, but I didn't kill it and neither did my son!"

Tom looked out the window. "There're a thousand places a swan could be hidden here. In any one of those buildings, or behind them. No telling where," he said.

At the top of the stairs Brian reached out and grabbed Susan's wrist. She tried to jerk away but he held her too tightly. She struggled and slipped, but he jerked her back so she didn't fall down the stairs, but only did a sort of stumble step and stopped on the second step from the top. He jerked her arm up and lifted her bodily back up to the top.

Leaning over he whispered, "You'd better not say a word to anyone."

Susan squinched her eyes shut and nodded vigorously.

Downstairs in the living room she heard her dad say, "Not without a goddamned search warrant, you're not." And then the two men said something else and walked out. In a few minutes she heard their pickup start up, heard the driveway gravel crunch as the vehicle turned and drove out of the yard.

Tom drove and King sat silently staring out the passenger side window. Tom didn't know what emotion gripped him the strongest—anger, disappointment, or grief.

After a while King said, "Are you happy now? I did my job."

"No, I'm not happy. I wonder why it took you so long to do your job," Tom said.

"Who the hell are you to tell me what my job is or when I should do it? I should have fired you a long time ago. I'd fire you right now except I don't want to fill out the paperwork."

"I know why you didn't fire me before and why you won't fire me now," Tom countered. "First off, no one else—not you or Findley or Keith or even Carl—not one of you would have done what I have—sit all day long outside the swan pen for days and weeks and months, watching those birds, writing down what I saw, learning. That's why you didn't fire me a long time ago, that and I do whatever work I'm assigned to do, and I do it right and don't bitch about it. You know how many of those yellow tablets I've filled up with what I saw? Dozens. I turned them in to Findley and at first he typed up what I wrote, but after the first few weeks he didn't bother. He just left them piled up on a corner of his desk with the ones he'd already transcribed on the bottom of the pile. So I took them home with me. You've got maybe twenty pages of typed up notes. That's it. I have the rest of it. You know what this refuge is most known for? No, it's not migratory waterfowl like it used to be. It's trumpeter swans. And I'm the one with all the information about them. I'm sure that half the colleges in this country, well, maybe not half, but all those that are studying this endangered species thing, they want to know what's in those notes I took. This new guy coming in? Is he going to care about the number of ducks we banded last year or two years ago? Is he going to care about the brood count of pheasants? I don't think so. He wants to know what we've done on the swan project, so he can use that to further his own career. You don't have that. I do. I guarantee if you did all of sudden not mind doing some paperwork to fire me, this new guy is going to hire me back as soon as your car drives off this refuge."

King stared out the window. Tom drove west on the access road from Johnson's place to the main highway, turned north for half a mile, turned right again onto the west access road to the refuge. When he got to the place where Martha had been killed, he stopped the pickup and turned off the motor.

"What are you doing? Why are we stopped?"

"I'm going to see what I can find. You stay in the truck or do what you want," Tom said, opening the pickup door.

He searched the south side of the ditch bank from the blood pool on the road west to where the blood trail stopped and the path across the tall grass began. He walked the mashed-down grass on one side all the way to the boundary fence, slowly, searching to see if Martha's body had been thrown aside somewhere, but he found nothing. He stood and looked over the fence at the land that was his but not of his use. He saw nothing. He looked to his right along the creek bank that angled off to the southwest and saw nothing but more tall dead last year's grass bent down here and there, but without crossing the fence he couldn't see if there was any blood trail. He crossed the fence.

From a hundred yards behind him, King stood on the path and yelled at Tom, "Hey, get back here! You're trespassing."

Tom laughed and said, "I can't be trespassing. This is my land."

King stood silently for a minute, put his hands in his pockets, and called out, "Is this some Indian thing? All this land is still Indian land?"

Tom ignored him and walked on. He found no blood trail but here the tall grass grew in clumps with bare dirt in between. Any blood that had fallen probably landed on the bare earth and was soaked in, leaving no trace that could be found. He walked on another hundred yards to where an old cottonwood tree, its roots undercut by the rush of water from the creek, had fallen across but wasn't dead yet. A few green leaves already grown into the characteristic heart shape clattered and clacked in the slight breeze. Tom looked, saw a few of the branches on the trunk bent and broken. He hoped to see a splotch of blood or a clinging feather, but there was none. He turned and walked back to the boundary fence, crossed it and began walking back to the road slowly, sweeping through the dead grass, looking for Martha, but found nothing. King had gone back to the pickup.

Tom got in, turned the key, and said, "I mean it's my land. I own it. Johnson only leases it, like he leases most of the land he runs cattle on."

"You mean you really got a deed?"

"I said I own it, didn't I? And Johnson is six months behind on his lease payment to me and the other landowners."

"What are you going to do?"

"Right now I'm going to go clip the rest of the swans' wings," Tom answered.

"What? That's set for Saturday. Findley hired two day laborers to come out and help," King protested.

"Tell him to cancel that. Keith and Findley and I can do it on our own. We use the cannon net, pull them out one at a time, clip them, and done. What should have been done months ago," Tom said.

27

All the way home that evening Tom drove silently and thought while Marvin sat quietly in the passenger seat. Marvin might have thought Tom was angry or grieving or trying to think of what to do next. Maybe Marvin didn't wonder at all. At the house, Marvin got out, said "See you later," and walked across to Granny's house next door.

Tom wanted to tell Anna about Martha's murder, about his suspicion of the Johnson kid, of Bart Johnson's defense of the kid, of his own lack of proof that the Johnson kid had really done it, other than the circumstances. He wanted to tell her about the ideas he had running through his head, if she thought any of them might work, or if she thought he was only chasing a gopher down a hole into a den with dozens of exit holes.

She met him at the door as she usually did, a cup of coffee waiting for him on the table instead of iced tea like she usually made for him at the end his day in spring and summer. He could tell she had some bad news from the fleeting smile she offered and the stiff, unbending tension of her body. She poured a cup of coffee for herself. He waited until she had sugared it and added the evaporated milk from the can with pink carnations on the label before he said anything, and then he reached across the table and took her hand before he said, "What is it?"

Slowly she raised her eyes to gaze at him and then she said in a low tone of voice, "I didn't know before today that one of our daughters is a con artist, and the other two are extortionists."

He choked back ironic laughter. After today he didn't think anybody's kids could be as bad as Bart Johnson's son, or the father who couldn't see what the kid was really like. He didn't express those thoughts, because then he'd have to tell her about Martha. Not yet. "They couldn't be that bad, Anna. We would have noticed something long ago, if they had become criminals," Tom said instead.

"Yes. You're right," she said, taking a sip of coffee before she went on. "I overheard the girls in a fight out behind the chicken coop. They were yelling so loud at each other that they didn't hear me coming. You know how badly Bit wants a horse? And that she's been saving her nickels for a long time?"

He nodded, and she continued, "She's found a way to make more money. She's been sneaking into the pool hall with a boy from school. I think they've been doing it for months, maybe even a couple of years, and it seems she's gotten really good at the game. So the men in the pool hall thought they could beat her—they knew she was a girl, even though she tried to hide it by putting her hair up underneath a baseball cap. One of them challenged her to a game and she beat him. Worse yet, there was money bet on the outcome. She won. I don't know how much that first time, but after that, more of the men challenged her to a game, and she kept winning. I don't know why they kept challenging her. Looks to me like anyone with sense would see her game. Tom, she's a pool shark, a con artist!"

He couldn't help admiring her ingenuity, maybe her skill, but he couldn't say that to Anna. He said, "How long has she been doing this and how come we didn't find out about it until now?"

"I don't go into the pool hall. I don't suppose you do either?" Anna asked.

He shook his head. He hadn't been in the pool hall in years, not since a year or so after he was discharged from the army, not since he married Anna and had the girls. Maybe he should have gone in once in a while, just to keep up with the local gossip, just to take the temperature, so to speak, of what other men in the county thought about instead of hanging out in the Frontier station every Saturday with Bennie and the two or three other townies and the rare distant relative or sometime friend from up on the reservation. "Looks like somebody would have said something. Why didn't anybody tell us? Why didn't one of the ladies tell you?"

"Probably didn't know about it themselves. I'm pretty sure they didn't know. Most of the women are my friends, but I'm honest enough to admit they love to gossip, just like everyone in small towns where there isn't much of anything else to do except mind everyone else's business. None of the men said anything to you?"

"Not a one. Not a peep. You know what I think? I think the men enjoyed the game too much. I think they thought it was funny, some little girl beating their tough guy friends, grown men."

"It's not funny," Anna said. "It's not a game. It's creepy, those men egging on a little girl to humiliate their own friends. Grown men, too."

"When did this start?"

"Last fall, or that's what Bit said, but I don't know if that's the truth."

"It couldn't have gone on much longer then," Tom said. "Either one of the men would have beaten her and that would have ended it, or she would have beaten all of them so none of the others would have risked a game with her. How much has the little con artist conned out of them?" Tom asked.

Anna slapped him on the arm. "Stop it. That's not funny. Tom, she has fifty-two dollars!"

He thought about that amount of money. Part of that would be her allowance, of course, but at a nickel a week for what? Maybe thirty-two weeks? That wouldn't even multiply out to two dollars. The men usually bet a quarter a game, but even so, it would take more than two hundred games to equal fifty-plus dollars. There wasn't time on one Saturday for Bit to have played that many games of pool. The only answer was that she was betting much bigger sums. Fifty-two dollars! That would more than pay the monthly light bill for five months, or the grocery bill for at least six weeks. It wouldn't be enough to buy a horse, except one who had been heading for the dog food factory, but it was getting close. He thought Bennie probably knew someone up on Pine Ridge who would sell a reasonably decent horse for less than a hundred dollars.

"All right. That's a surprise. So, Bit's the con artist, but why are Patty and Connie extortionists?" he asked but he could figure out the answer to that pretty much on his own.

"That's the fight I overheard going on behind the chicken coop. I think Connie and Patty found out about Bit's stash. Either they found it or they caught her counting it and made her tell where she got it. Then they demanded she give them half of it to keep from telling us," Anna said.

"So Connie and Patty double-dipped on crime. Either Bit gave in, which makes Connie and Patty extortionists, or she didn't give in, and that makes those two tale bearers."

"Tattle telling isn't a crime, Tom," Anna said.

"No. You're right," Tom said. He thought that killing a swan wasn't murder, but it was still a crime, and what crime would it be if Bart Johnson knew it and covered for his kid? His girls were in no danger of criminal prosecution only of being the subject of gossip for weeks or months if the ladies of the county found out. He didn't care for himself what people thought, but his girls still had to finish growing up in this place, maybe live here their entire lives. He had a vision of old ladies sitting on the front porch of the county nursing home, one turning to the other and saying, "Whatever happened to that Warder girl? You know, the one who snuck into the pool hall and gambled on the games with the men?," and the other old lady saying, "She was a wild one. She should've been born a boy." Bit wouldn't care, but still, it could cost her in ways she might not even know about.

"Did you take her money away?" Tom asked.

"No. She conned it fair and square," Anna said, getting up to refill her coffee cup.

Tom laughed, a real laugh, something he thought this morning he might not do again for a very long time.

"I don't see how we could give it back to all the men she beat," Anna added. "Besides, I'm thinking they wouldn't take the money anyway, because then their wives would find out, and the women might think ill of Bit, but they'd think even worse of their husbands. And which of them would want to admit publicly that they'd been beaten by a little girl in a game of pool?"

"Where's the girls now? You take them over to Granny's for a story?" Tom asked.

"No. Granny's got dozens of stories, but I can't think of any Inktomi story that fits this situation. Generally, I suppose, most of them would fit. You know, Inktomi schemes something but it backfires and he gets in trouble. I think this one needs a punishment beyond storytelling."

Tom raised an eyebrow. "You want me to give them all a spanking?"

"No! You know how I feel about hitting, and besides, if I was mad enough to hit them, I'd do it myself, not torture them with that awful, 'Wait until your father gets home' crap. I hoped you might have some idea for something we could do that isn't violent but gets the point across to all three of them."

"What's the point to get across?"

"Encouraging them to find better ways to earn money than con jobs and extortion," she said.

"Where are they? You lock them in the chicken coop?"

"No." She tilted her head toward the bedroom. "In there, all three of them, sitting in a row on our bed. I told them to sit there until we talked about what to do."

"Side by side? All in a row? It's a wonder they haven't killed each other!"

"Oh, no. They're sitting there trying to grow their ears longer so they can hear what we're saying," Anna said with a little grin.

"Then let's sit here a little longer while we think about the right thing to do," Tom said. "You sure one of Granny's stories wouldn't be right?"

Anna shook her head and said, "Not this time. Besides, Granny's not feeling well. I think she may have caught a late season version of the flu. And she's been so lucky not to be sick at all this past winter."

When a few more minutes had passed, Tom and Anna got up and went into the bedroom. The girls, who had been lounging backward on the bed, their feet still hanging over the edge so they wouldn't get their dirty shoes on their mom's bedspread, sat up, each with her hands clasped in front of her, like the three little monkeys: see no evil, hear no evil, speak no evil.

"Are we in serious trouble?" Patty asked, her voice quivering.

Connie nudged her. "Of course, we are dummy. They might kill us and throw our bodies down the toilet hole," she said.

"*ANAGOPTOMPE*," Anna said, but she didn't say it loud with emphasis. She leaned on the old dresser front and waited for Tom to speak.

"On Saturday morning we are all going to town just like we usually do," Tom said. "Then Bit and I are going down to the pool hall to play a game. If I win, I take all the money."

Bit started to protest, but Tom raised a hand, and said, "All except what you've saved from your allowance."

"That's not f—" Bit started to say the words she knew better than to say, but she did think better of it and stopped.

"And you are never to go into the pool hall again, unless your mother or I am with you," he added.

Anna made a face and looked at him sideways.

"Mom's a lady. She would never go into the pool hall," Bit said.

"You've gone into the pool hall, so does that mean you're not a lady?" Anna asked.

"A lady! That's one thing I don't want to be!" Bit spat out, but she caught her father's expression and said, "I like it that you're a lady, Mom. That's good for you, but that's not important to me. For me to be, I mean."

Connie and Patty had been exchanging little smiles.

"What about them? They tried to shake me down!" Bit complained.

Tom thought, *CON ARTIST. SHAKE ME DOWN*. His family

watched television too much. Looking at the two youngest, he said, "I haven't decided what to do with you two yet, but you won't like it."

"That's not fair!" Connie yelled.

"Oh shut up," Bit said.

AFTER THE GIRLS HAD GONE TO BED—EARLY, AND WITHOUT the usual complaints—Tom and Anna sat on the front step, listening to the cricket songs of spring. Tom told her about Martha and Bill, about the path of smashed grass across to the south boundary fence, about his argument with King, about their visit to Johnson and his vehement denial of any involvement in the killing. When he had finished he laid his head in Anna's lap, and she placed her hand on his temple while he cried.

28

After King and Warder left, Bart roamed the house, ignoring Betty's attempts to talk about what had just happened. He checked the padlock on the gun cabinet, gazed through the glass doors to make sure he was right that the 12 gauge was still there. He wondered if Brian had bought another gun, another 12 gauge, and hidden it somewhere on the property. There were hundreds of places a gun could be hidden just like King and Warder said. He went outside, rechecking the board fences in the corrals, testing the levers on the squeeze chute, the amount of vaccine and needles he had on hand, testing the edges of the knives for castrating the bull calves, and when he went into supper, he sat across from Betty, saw the concern on her face when she looked at Brian, the silent careful way that Susan lifted forkfuls of food to her mouth, chewed, swallowed, and repeated as if she were a robot. Brian was the only one who seemed normal.

He sat impassive, as was his usual manner, even took seconds of the coconut cake, used a thumb to wipe the last smear of frosting from the saucer, picked at a few crumbs of coconut that had fallen on the table. No one commented about what everyone had heard. No one expressed wonder at who might have killed the swan because they all knew. They just didn't know how, except Brian.

When supper was ended and the dishes done, they all sat in the living room watching that new doctor show, *BEN CASEY*, where the old guy made marks on a blackboard and then pointed at them saying, "Man, woman, birth, death, infinity." No one knew what that was supposed to mean, but the handsome actor who played the lead character looked at the symbols as if they were the key to everlasting life. After Ben Casey argued with other doctors and a patient lay dying in his bed and Ben Casey performed a last-minute surgery that saved the patient's life and the show ended and the last commercial played, Bart got up and climbed the stairs. He showered so he'd be clean enough to get dirty out in the corrals the next day and went to bed where he turned multiple times puzzling out how Brian must have done it and where the gun he most surely owned had come from, and where the gun was now, and where the swan carcass was hidden. When he got up the next day, much earlier than usual, he focused on this day, one of the most important of a rancher's year, except for the fall shipping of calves and payday, and when his neighbors started arriving in their mud-spattered or cow shit besmeared trucks or their shiny washed cars, their wives bearing covered dishes and pans, he greeted them all and made them welcome.

Betty balanced her belly in front of her as she moved about the kitchen, boiling eggs and potatoes, peeling the eggs, chopping them, cutting up pickles, adding a shake of celery seed, and stirring it all together with mustard, mayonnaise, and a few dashes of vinegar for potato salad. The sink was half full of dishes dirtied in the cooking of the potato salad ingredients and the mixing bowls and beaters and spoons for the chocolate cake now in the oven. Her apron hadn't protected the dress she wore. Splashed vinegar had soaked through perfuming her like a pickle. The two meat loafs in huge flat pats were in the refrigerator. No steak on branding day because the men always grilled it outside, and they were too busy today.

The ladies of the club had come to help, of course, and bring their own offerings for dinner: the usual green jello salad with julienned carrots inside preserved like butterflies in amber; a pair of pies, not fruit but cream pies; a Pyrex flat dish of baked beans with the sauce burnt on the edges of the pan, chopped bits of bacon half drowning on top; bags of potato chips, paper napkins and paper plates; duplicate pans of baked beans; another variety of potato salad that had olive oil instead of mayo and no one liked it but no one would say that because the maker of the exotic variety was the president of the club, Mrs. Denison.

Mrs. Denison scolded the only two under twelve-year-old kids present for running in and out of the kitchen, getting under everyone's feet. Most of the kids were teenagers because the ranching population was mostly midlifers, except for one couple, just out of high school the previous year, still billing and cooing and making their nest. The ratio of boys to girls among the offspring skewed heavily toward boys, which made the men proud of their prowess and grateful for the extra hands to work the cattle and the land, while the ladies who had no girl children envied the ladies who did, which meant that the three girls—Linda Baker, Kathy McCloud, and Susan Johnson—were equally cossetted for their gender and criticized if they didn't live up to what the ladies of the club expected of future ladies of the club. Linda and Kathy sat on the Johnsons' front porch discussing their younger friend Susan.

"She used to like Barbie dolls," Linda said, "and then she got that horse and that was the end of it. I don't play with Barbies anymore either, that's such a little kid thing, but you know what I mean."

"Yeah," Kathy said, extending her left hand as she examined her pale blue fingernails. "What do you think of this polish? Mom says it's too odd, that the only fitting color I should wear is pink. Not red. She says that's for whores."

"It's okay," Linda said, returning to the subject on her mind. "And you know what she named that horse? Melody. She doesn't even play in the band. Well, she used to, until Mrs. Bordeaux kicked her out because she never could learn to read music."

Kathy picked a bit of polish from the side of her pinkie where she had over brushed the polish, and said, "Yeah. You know what I think? I think she's playing a trick. She doesn't really care about horses. Besides, that's not a horse, it's a Shetland pony, and guess what? Her legs already hang way down below the pony's belly. In six months she'll be sitting on its back and walking along with her feet." They giggled at that image, and Kathy continued, "I really think she's only pretending to like horses and that stuff so she can hang out with the boys."

Down in the pens the men had already run all the cows and calves into the big corral. At one end a fence ran out at an angle into the middle and stopped, creating a dead pool space on one side and on the other, a funnel. One of the men on a horse would separate a calf from its mama, chase the mama into the dead space and the calf into the funnel section where it would be chased and scared into a narrower and narrower corridor with a couple of gates along the way. As a calf went through one gate, it closed behind so it couldn't go backward into the big pen, then through the next gate until the corridor dead-ended at a squeeze chute, a metal pipe affair. Once a calf had been choused into the squeeze chute, a gate would shut behind it; the man running the chute would jack a lever, which squeezed the terrified calf. When another lever was pulled, the chute turned ninety degrees on the side until the calf lay flat where it could be branded, vaccinated, and castrated if it was a bull calf.

Bart Johnson used to have to dehorn the calves, a bloody process of extracting the horns with a pair of pincers, much like pulling a tooth, but he hadn't had to do that for years. He'd sold off his Hereford bulls with horns and bought ones naturally hornless—black Angus. He was considering replacing his Angus cows with polled—hornless—Herefords, which when crossed with Angus bulls produced black, white-faced calves that the county extension agent claimed would gain weight faster—hybrid vigor or some such big word. Hornless calves sold better because everyone—ranchers, shippers, buyers—believed that cattle with horns damaged each other when packed into tractor trailers traveling to auction barns and from there to the feedlots in eastern Dakota and Nebraska.

The branding irons glowed red in the propane stove fire. A small folding table on one side held the needles and vaccines and a pair of buckets on the other—one bucket held the sharpened knives and the other was empty waiting to hold the bull testicles. Three men stood at the squeeze chute, two on one side, one on the other. One man operated the levers on the chute and did the branding, pulling an iron from the fire, applying it to the calf's left rear hip, timing it by counting one-thousand, two-thousand, three-thousand, four-thousand, lifting the iron and shoving it back into the fire to reheat. A second man did the vaccinations, rotating needles; as he emptied one into a calf, he used the other for the next calf, and at most brandings, one of the sons stood behind him refilling needles as the contents were injected. The third man wielded the knife deftly, practiced, surgical.

Back in the main holding pen, one man rode the horse that came between a mama calf and her baby, pushing the mama into the dead space, ducking and dodging the horse to keep the calf from rejoining its mama. Other men, some on horseback, some on foot, shooed the calf into the funnel while keeping the mama cow from entering. The cows, already bawling intermittently, nervous, bovine brains not recalling the previous year's terrible event, nonetheless anticipated at least unpleasantness.

Once branded, vaccinated, and castrated if they were bull calves, the calves would be turned out into the adjoining pasture. When everything was over, the cows would be turned into the same pasture. Then Bart would observe the melee as the mama cows roamed through the group and the calves did the same, bawling as they searched for the right relationship. Grateful babies found their mamas, wagged their tails as they nursed hungrily, the indignity and pain inflicted on their bodies receding. Rarely, but once in a great while, mamas had problems finding their own offspring. The confusion usually got sorted without the rancher's help, but Bart watched anyway, as a good steward should.

Before that process began though, Bart perched atop the fence just behind the squeeze chute with a mechanical counter, prepared to push a button each time a calf went into the chute, tallying, an unnecessary task because he already knew he had 248 calves—one dead and one dry cow—which gave him that almost one hundred percent calf crop. He didn't need to tally, but he did it because that was tradition, and that too was the duty of a good steward.

Bart thought he'd taken care of the worry about Susan observing the castration by putting her back in the big pen, helping to separate mamas and babies instead of at the squeeze chute, where she'd see something ladies and young girls shouldn't observe, superfluous with the man on the cutting horse and the men on foot chousing the calves into the funnel, but she didn't know that. Just as he was about to shout, "First calf," the signal to start pushing calves through the funnel, Susan came up beside him.

"Dad?" Her face was pale beneath her new straw hat with a blue ribbon trailing from the back of the crown, sweat beads on her upper lip.

"Dad," she said, "I've put Melody back in the barn. I'm going up to help mom."

Bart felt a sense of betrayal, but he hugged his daughter and said, "All right."

He yelled, "First calf!"

The branding irons sizzled. Dust floated up back in the big pen. The acrid smells of burning hair and hide and the iron smell of blood accumulated around the squeeze chute. The men laughed as once in a while a mama cow pawed more dust in the air and gave a half-hearted charge at the men taking her baby. Two of the men at the chute argued over the best way to cut a bull calf, then argued over who got to take home the calf fries, although both of them were secretly repelled at eating fried manhood, even if it wasn't human, testicles dipped in flour and spices, deep fried and turned out on a platter, tasting like chicken livers, with most of the wives embarrassed or disgusted. The cattle bawled.

Brian and one of Gary's boys tackled a calf when it came out of the squeeze chute; one of them held it down while the other climbed on its back and rode the animal a few jumps. Gary Kendall shouted at them, "Hey, you big old oxes ought to be ashamed of yourselves! I'd guess either one of you weighs nearly as much as that calf."

Embarrassed, the boys stopped riding the calves themselves, but held them down for the younger ones to give it a try. When the animals either bucked the boy off or the rider jumped off, the calves ran to the end of the corral, huddling with the other calves for companionship and sympathy.

The sun rose higher; the men sweated and drank water from the jugs placed around the fences. Dust rose higher, some of it settling in the sweat on the men's faces. Noon came and went and at last around 1:30 someone yelled "Last calf!" and Bart checked his watch. In four hours the men had managed 248 calves. His mechanical tally matched the one in his head. He was pleased.

"Hey," he called out to the men, slapping dust from their pants and their hats, coiling up the ropes they had used to swat calves through the funnel and mamas back to their corner. "We did one calf every four minutes. How about that? New record?"

"Nope," Ben Allen said. "We ran one through every three minutes and forty-nine seconds at my place last year."

"You're full of shit," Bart said, but he said it with a grin.

"No, man, ask anyone," Ben replied, "and next Tuesday is branding at my place. I bet I can set a new record."

"What, you're branding sheep now?" Gary called out.

"Nope, I got two hundred sheep and one hundred cows," Ben said.

"What's for dinner? If it's mutton, I ain't coming," Gary said, and the men all laughed.

"I'm telling you, I make more money on my sheep than the cows," Ben argued, uselessly, he knew, but he had to say something.

The cattlemen had an idea Ben was right, that they would make more money from sheep than cattle, but none of them wanted to be the next to cross the line from cattleman to sheep herder, and Ben himself still hadn't completely switched over.

They turned the cows and calves out of their separate pens into the pasture, and when that was done they walked up to the house where dinner waited outside on a motley mixture of card tables and picnic tables shoved together in a row under the cottonwood trees in front of Johnson's house. The plastic tablecloths fluttered, crackled a little in the breeze. The men washed their hands at the hydrant and sat down to eat. The women, waiting for the men to finish so they could eat and then clean up the mess, sat, one group in the living room in front of an oscillating fan atop the television console and a second out on the front porch, fanning themselves with the latest copies of *REDBOOK*, *LADIES' HOME JOURNAL*, and *FAMILY CIRCLE*.

When the men had finished eating, they moved over to lounge on the ground or sit in folding aluminum lawn chairs, smoking or picking their teeth, talking low and laughing about everything. The women and younger kids took their turn at the table, and as soon as the kids were admonished for not cleaning their plates and the ladies had cleaned their plates and drank down their second glasses of cold iced tea, Bart began to think about the dead swan again.

He looked at Gary, who looked like he'd lost some weight, hunkered over his dusty black boots, repeatedly tossing his opened pocket knife so it stuck into a bare patch of ground with a thunk. Gary wasn't talking as much now as he had down in the pens. The knife went in—thunk—Gary leaned forward and tugged it out of the dark earth, threw it again, retrieved it again. The patch he aimed at looked like a miniature plow had turned over the ground.

Gary had said back at that card party that he didn't see any reason not to shoot the swans, but Gary bragged and bullshitted a lot more back then. Could Gary have come over early, parked out on the main road, hiked across that piece of property Bart leased from Warder, shot the swan, and hiked back? He could have, but Bart didn't think so. Still, he supposed that was possible.

The ladies got up, cleared the table in trip after trip, carefully carrying nearly empty dishes and pans, two-handed, back into the house. Through the open windows they could be heard crowded into the kitchen, washing up, dividing up the leftovers to take home, examining the taped-on name labels on the dishes to make sure each wife took home the dish she had brought. The men lounged, some napped on their backs, hats over their faces. The boys wandered off down to the barn, and the four girls sat on the front porch steps. When the ladies gave the signal by emerging from the house, the men got up, dusted off the seats of their pants, and the genders joined as pairs, and family groups meandered, talking, joking, to their vehicles. Bart circulating, shaking hands, thanking.

Brian approached his dad, polite and pleasant faced. "Bob and Jack want me to go home with them for the weekend. Is that okay?" Bob and Jack. Gary's second and third boys, the ones not enlisting in the army but going back for their last year of high school next fall. Jack the oldest, but Bob who had failed a grade somewhere along the line, now joining him to graduate next spring in the class of 1962.

"Please let him go, Mr. Johnson," Jack asked, pushing his hat back on a head shaped exactly like his father's—a cement block.

"You asked your dad if it's okay?" Bart asked.

"Yeah, sure, he don't care," Bob replied for his brother.

"All right," Bart said.

Then everyone was in their car or pickup following each other like a funeral procession, down the lane to the crossroads to turn out to the main highway.

Later that evening Bart went down to the pasture to check on the cattle. The chaos had wound down with only an occasional lowing from a cow still disturbed. The restless milling and searching had ceased. A couple of cows had laid down on the cooling green grass, calves by their sides. In the bright moonlight the brands on a few of the calves showed pink or even a little bloody where the branding iron had burned too deeply. He went back up to the house, climbed the stairs and into bed, giving over the day and his worries.

He woke in the dark, someone standing over his bed.

"Dad." He sat up quickly, but it was only Susan. She hadn't come into his bedroom since Betty had moved into the spare room months ago.

"What is it? What's wrong?" He saw her tangled hair, her troubled face in the moonlight coming through the window.

"Dad," she said, a sob catching in her throat, "Dad, I have to tell you something."

29

Tom Warder had already wiped the excess shaving cream from his face, put on a clean blue chambray shirt, and pulled up his overalls straps over his shoulders. While he was outside checking the oil in the car, Anna fussed the two younger girls' hair into a condition that didn't proclaim their usual chaos, and herded them all out to the car. On the way into town Tom and Anna and Bit didn't speak and didn't hear, except as background noise, the bickering of the two youngest.

Anna wondered whether she should breach the local ladies' standards and go into the pool hall to watch the father of her children teach their eldest child the elements of 8-ball pool. Tom thought about what punishment might be appropriate and possible to carry out on two children who had committed the crime of attempted extortion. Bit thought about the seven men she had beaten at 8-ball pool taking their money and their dignity. She wondered if she could best her dad. She didn't know that he even knew how to play pool. In her memory he had never stepped foot into the pool hall, but he wouldn't challenge her if he didn't believe he could beat her. What kind of lesson would there be in that? Was there a lesson for her if she beat her dad?

When Tom parked the car in front of the courthouse, Connie and Patty flung themselves out and ran down the street to the dime store to spend their allowance. Tom and Anna and Bit unfolded from the car, Anna looking at the ladies sitting on the courthouse benches under the newly leafed Chinese elm trees.

Tom said, "Come on, then," and walked down the street with Bit a step behind. Tom nodded or said his hellos to the people they passed, but his grim expression kept them from engaging him in any conversation, and his daughter marching behind, as grim-faced as her father, aroused their curiosity. They stopped their own conversations, watched as Tom and Bit jaywalked across the street to the pool hall on the south side between the Jackson Television Repair and Sales, then past an alley, then Jack Carter's State Farm Insurance office with the sign in the window that read: Crop Insurance, Reasonable Rates. When Warder and his eldest daughter took the one step up into the pool hall, the men on the street in ones and twos and groups started moving slowly after them. The ladies clucked their tongues in disapproval that a decent man not only would allow his daughter into such a place, but escort her in, because as he reached the pool hall door, Tom Warder had stepped to one side, swooped off his hat, and bowed his daughter through the door. The ladies continued on to the benches on the courthouse lawn, where they saw Anna standing alongside one of the benches, not sitting, even though there was space enough for two more women on the white painted bench.

June Baker rushed up to Anna and asked, "Did you know your husband just took your daughter into the pool hall?"

"Yes," Anna said simply.

The ladies stared. June's mouth opened; her eyes widened. At the far bench a couple of older ladies fanning themselves with the heavy, eight-by-ten-inch cardboard poster advertising the month's upcoming movies at the Inland Theater stopped fanning themselves.

One of them muttered, "Well, I never," and the other nodded in agreement.

Anna hitched her purse higher on her shoulder and walked away down the street, crossed and entered the pool hall. The ladies watched her and watched the movement of their husbands and brothers and sons moving toward the pool hall slowly like molasses warmed enough over the kitchen range to pour over the lip of the pitcher.

Tom Warder approached Bob, the proprietor, who stood leaning his forearms on the scarred wooden counter raw jawing with a couple of the men that Bit had beaten. Bit walked to the farthest back pool table, took down a cue, and stood waiting. Tom flipped a quarter at Bob and said, "One game."

Bob handed Tom a wire basket with pool balls and a rack in it, and said, "Okay." He picked up the quarter and dinged the cash register. The men who had been talking to Bob exchanged glances, and by unspoken agreement ambled to the back of the room, standing by the corner that led into the restroom where they could have the best view of the table. The four men at the front table and the two at the middle table put down their cues, abandoned their own game, and followed. The rest of the men, the ones who had been standing around or sitting at the three little dining tables surreptitiously adding whiskey from hip flasks to the bottles of pop they had bought from Bob, followed those men, standing so their heads were between the heads of those in front. Two older men, men who had been hanging out on Saturdays in the pool hall years before Tom Warder went off to war, nodded their heads and smiled at old memories. The clock behind Bob's counter top read 12:00. High noon.

"That quarter was the last of my pocket change," Tom said. "Give me a nickel."

Bit fished in the front of her jeans pocket and brought out a dime.

"That'll do," Tom said. He flipped the coin up. Like mice watching a circling hawk, the bystanders' heads rose, following the spiraling coin. Tom snatched it from the air, slapped it on the back of his left hand and said, "Call it."

"Heads," Bit said.

Tom moved his hand and showed her. Tails. He said, "You break first. Rack 'em."

Bit put the rack on the table. She took the balls from the basket, placing the first ball of the rack on the foot spot, a stripe ball in one corner of the rack and a solid ball in the other corner with the 8-ball in the center. Tom tried a couple of cues, picked one and put the other back in the wall rack.

The air in the room felt close and stuffy and smelled of the fresh sawdust on the floor and the sweat of the close-standing men. Bit wiped a bead of sweat from her forehead with the sleeve of her outgrown flannel shirt, the orange one with cowboy print that she had insisted upon when Anna had taken them to Our Lady of Lourdes rummage basement the previous fall to buy school clothes. She removed the rack from the balls, stepped back, and took a breath, leaned over the table and shot the stick over the arch of her left hand hitting the end ball with a solid clack. The balls rolled randomly; the solid green number 6 slowly rolling toward a center side pocket, slowing, slowing, balancing on the edge, hesitating until it toppled through with a clunk audible in the room of silent watchers.

Bit looked at her dad, who nodded and stood back. She walked around the table looking for the best shot that would set up the cue ball for the next solid colored ball. The number 2 blue? No. The number 1 yellow, if she leaned just right. She leaned, shoved the stick gently. The cue ball kissed the yellow, glanced away and nearly bumped a blue striped number 2, but the solid yellow flowed six inches into an end pocket. If she could keep this up, and if her dad had been bluffing—her stomach felt queasy, and her mouth was dry. The rest of the balls, the solid ones, were all difficult shots. She concentrated, walked around the table figuring the angles on various bank shots. The men shifted their feet, but nobody talked. She set herself, tapped hard with her stick, watching as the cue ball caromed off the side, skipped past the maroon striped 7 ball, pushed the solid 2 blue, which hit the red 3 and knocked it into the pocket, but in passing the blue bumped the 8-ball. It rolled a few inches, stopping well short of any pocket, but she didn't have any other easy shots. She took a chance on the orange 5 with no result, stepped back and looked at her dad. The old men in the pool room looked at Tom, measuring if the old gunslinger still had what it took.

Tom chalked his pool cue, stepped up to the table and without hesitation sent the yellow striped ball into the corner pocket, then the maroon striped 7 into a side pocket, followed quickly by the red stripe, the green stripe. He almost sent the 8-ball in, but at the last second it stopped, poised on the lip of a pocket, while the crowd held their breath as if even one puff of air from an unguarded nose might push the ball in. Tom hit the cue ball hard along the side of the table. The 8-ball jumped the pocket; the cue ball skittered over the hole, hit the 8-ball, which hit the blue striped 2, which fell into the end pocket. The cue ball spun away towards the center. The black 8-ball meandered to a stop in the center while the crowd let out a collective sigh.

Two of the men in the front row looked down and between them, ready to be outraged when they were shoved aside. Anna stepped between them into the front row. The men behind reshuffled to get a good view. Bit saw her mom, a wave of embarrassment coloring her face red. She couldn't do it, not with her mom watching. She couldn't continue the game, but she wouldn't need to as, one after the other, the striped balls continued to fall gently or smack hard into the pockets. Tom seemed to dance to a tune only he could hear. It might have been something by Marty Robbins. Maybe it was "El Paso." Could have been "Big Iron." *NO ONE DARED TO ASK HIS BUSINESS, NO ONE DARED TO MAKE A SLIP*. Before each ball dropped, he was assessing the table, circling and dropping over in a crouch for the next shot and the next until the only ball left on the table was the ivory cue ball.

The old men who remembered Tom from before the war, back when he was a kid, recalled Tom Warder's father coming to the pool hall, standing silently at the door until his son looked up. Old man Warder never said a word, just stood and looked. Tom, then a gangly sixteen-year-old, put down his pool cue, took out his wallet and paid the bet, forfeiting the game. He followed his father out the door and never came back.

Bit put her pool cue back in the wall rack. Tom did the same, retrieved the balls from the table, put them in the basket and returned them to Bob. The men who had never seen Tom Warder play pool murmured and marveled and looked at his back, but no one congratulated him. They wouldn't have known what to say. Tom put one arm around his wife and one around his daughter and walked out. He said, "Let's go get our groceries and go home."

As he was putting the brown paper sacks of groceries in the car trunk, Bennie Black Hawk hailed Tom from across the street. Tom waited until Bennie crossed. Bennie never mentioned the 8-ball game at the pool hall, saying, "It's good. She's going to run."

"All right," Tom said.

Bennie slapped him gently on the arm, "You'd better be thinking about how to manage a buffalo ranch."

"Buffalo ranch?"

"Yes. Buffalo. That's what we're good at." Bennie gave him a wink and a wave and walked off. Tom slammed down the car trunk.

Halfway home, Bit asked, "Dad, how did you learn to play pool like that?"

"Same way you did," Tom said, and then, meeting her eyes in the rearview mirror, he added, "And I used to play a little when I was in the army. That's how your mama got her engagement ring." Anna lifted her hand to her mouth to hide her smile.

Bit brought her mayonnaise jar of money to the kitchen table, sat and counted out the nickels, dimes, quarters, half dollars, and wrinkled Georges, then divided it into two piles, mourning the eminent loss of half her savings and the near impossibility of saving enough to buy a horse.

Tom raked half the money into a pile, fetched a small paper sack from the cupboard, and dumped the money into it while his younger two daughters eyed him with a mixture of curiosity and fear. "Here's what we're going to do," he said to Connie and Patty. "We're going to use this money to buy some bum lambs, and you two are going to raise them. We'll sell them at the auction barn this fall, and you can use half the money to buy some new clothes or whatever you want, and we use the other half to buy more bum lambs next year."

Bit crossed her arms and smiled. Connie and Patty hated any kind of work done outdoors. They argued and fought against taking care of the chickens and weeding the garden and now, twice or even three times a day, they would have to mix up powdered lamb formula with water, funnel it into bottles, and feed the lambs. They would have to watch the animals for signs of scour—virulent diarrhea that could kill a lamb within thirty-six hours, dose them with medicine, pull weeds and grass to throw over the fence into the pen that Tom would build, make sure they were in their shelter and shut up for the night so no roaming dogs could get at them. Bit didn't know that her dad had already had a conversation with Ben Wheeler, who said that he had bum lambs—lambs whose mama ewes didn't have enough milk for them or rejected them or had died—but that the ones he was bottle-feeding himself were already past the risk of scours and well started. They would be a little more expensive than just born lambs, but Ben was so excited that someone else was willing to raise sheep, he offered to sell well-started lambs for newborn prices.

While Connie and Patty moped over their dad's decision, Bit was still unhappy that she had to part with half her savings, even if it meant her sisters' share didn't give them any real satisfaction. "Bit, I think you should have a real job," Tom said.

"I'm a kid, dad," she protested, "I'd work if there was work to be had, but no one's going to hire me."

"Would you be willing to run a lawnmower? Trim bushes? Pull a few weeds maybe?"

"Sure, but who do we know with a lawn? And where would we get a lawnmower anyway?" She didn't understand what her dad was getting at. It seemed to her that perhaps taunting her was part of her punishment.

"There's a lawn and bushes and trees at the refuge headquarters building. Everyone hates taking care of it. I think the new refuge manager might be glad to hire someone to take on the job. There's a lawnmower and all the tools you need," Tom said.

"How much?" Bit asked. "And how would I get out there to do the work?"

"I take you out on Saturday afternoons."

"That means you would be working five and a half days a week," Bit said.

"I think I can trade half a day on Friday for half a day on Saturday. Three dollars. I think that's fair to start."

"Three dollars a time? Once a week?"

Tom heaved a sigh. "Yes, Bit. Three dollars a time. Once a week."

GRANNY DIED THAT NIGHT OF CONGESTIVE HEART FAILURE, a condition that the doctor up at Pine Ridge Public Health Center had failed to diagnose. Marvin was drunk at the funeral on Wednesday, so drunk that he nearly fell out of the pew in front of Father Clifford, just as the good priest entered the church from the back, walking up the center aisle to the altar, swinging the censer with the two little scrubbed clean altar boys walking in front. On Thursday Marvin left a note on Granny's kitchen table saying he was hitching back to Ft. Pierre to look for his old girlfriend.

After the ceremonies were over, after he had comforted Anna and tried to explain death to his two youngest daughters—Bit had withdrawn to the garden, sitting for long hours kicking at the dirt—Tom returned to work and his older grief, of watching Bill restlessly wander the pen calling out for Martha.

30

Bart heard the alarm go off, faintly buzzing beneath the layer of top sheet, one blanket, and pink chenille bedspread. He had put it under there thinking that he would hear it go off but no one else would. He shut it off, rolled out of bed and sat up. The sky beneath the half lowered roll-up shade showed still dark at 4 a.m. He dressed, propped pillows beneath the covers so anyone looking in his door would think he was still there asleep. He felt like he had when as a teenager he had done the same thing to sneak out after curfew. He went downstairs and outside, squatting down behind the lilac bushes in deep darkness. This was the third day he had gotten up early, sat outside until well after sunrise, walked down to the barn and back as if he had been doing something vitally important down there.

When Brian came home after his weekend with Gary's boys, he seemed his usual self, at times sullen and withdrawn, at other times laughing with the rest of the family at some silliness on a television variety show—*ED SULLIVAN, GARRY MOORE*. Bart watched the kid and listened, and every morning he got up very early and waited outside behind the lilac bushes. If Brian got out a gun and sneaked out of the house, Bart would follow him. He knew Brian had killed the swan. Bart hadn't been surprised when Susan told him how Brian got out the 12 gauge. He had felt around on top of the cabinet where he found the screwdriver. A careful examination of the wood finish around the hinges revealed a few tiny scratches where the screwdriver must have slipped when Brian was prying out the hinge pins. As he examined the gun cabinet, Susan had stood behind him sobbing, begging her dad not to do anything that would let Brian know she had told on him.

Bart wanted to hit the kid the minute he came home from Gary's place, wanted to yell and rant, wanted to take the kid into the sheriff's office himself. Bart didn't know what the penalty might be for killing a trumpeter swan, but he had heard stories about people who had been sent to Leavenworth Federal Prison for similar crimes. He didn't know if that's what they would do to Brian. He didn't think so, but they might. The kid wasn't eighteen yet, and still in high school. He thought Brian would likely get off with a stern warning and remanded to Bart's custody until he turned eighteen, and what the hell good would that do?

He couldn't fix the kid. Brian was broken beyond repair, and besides, the kid might do something worse and since Bart was his dad, who would get in trouble the next time? Bart worried that he could be sent to Leavenworth or maybe the South Dakota state pen himself. What could he do? He kept thinking about possible solutions and the army kept coming back as a possibility. The kid liked killing things? Then put him in the army where men were trained to kill things, supposed to kill people. He might come out of there with some discipline, some direction, and while a stint in the army would be temporary, the kid would be somewhere else, not here, for a few years. Except the kid wasn't old enough to enlist. Bart would have to sign for him, something he would gladly do if that option arose, if he could overcome Betty's certain objections. For now, though, he wasn't going to confront Brian directly; no, that would give away that Susan had told. He had to protect her. So he set his alarm for 4:00 a.m. He had thought about waiting downstairs to catch Brian taking off the cabinet doors and getting out the gun, but he wanted to see where Brian went after he got out the shotgun, wanted to see if Brian might reveal where he had hidden the dead swan.

He was tired. The smell of lilacs just blooming around him and the cool ground and the still dark sky acted as soporifics to an already tired mind. He didn't know how much longer he could go on doing this—getting up early but staying up as late as usual, so Brian wouldn't suspect anything. He brought his knees up, folded his arms over them and rested his chin on his forearms. He might have dozed off a minute. The sound of the front screen door creaking open roused him. Brian came out of the front door easing the screen back. He stood a minute looking out, the shotgun a long dark shadow at his side. He couldn't be planning to stay out very long, couldn't be planning to go far. It was spring, early summer, and the alfalfa was about ready for first cutting. Brian knew his dad would be up early, checking the hayfield to see if the dew had dried enough so the hay wouldn't rot in the windrows formed by the rake after the mower had passed over.

Bart guessed that Brian would go far enough from the house so a shotgun blast wouldn't be noticed, but near enough so he could get back before sunrise. As Bart watched, Brian walked slowly down the steps and around the corner of the house heading north. The house sat on the very northern edge of the land Bart owned, but beyond the fence began the quarter section of land he leased from Tom Warder and beyond that boundary, the refuge.

Bart got up and followed, stopping every hundred feet or so to listen, to make sure that Brian hadn't turned off one way or the other away from the refuge boundary line, making sure he hadn't stopped. When he listened, Bart could hear Brian's steady footfalls continuing in a direct line north. Bart followed. He saw a darker shadow in the night vanish over the edge of the bank above the creek.

Brian walked carefully east along the creek bank stepping over hummocks of dirt, debris left behind from the spring flooding, and a few branches and twigs fallen from the overhanging trees above. Except for his own footsteps he heard nothing but a few chirps and cheeps from sleepy birds just beginning to rouse for the day. A hundred yards or so short of the old cottonwood tree that had fallen across the creek, he came to the abandoned former resident of an ancient pioneer or original occupant of the land, set the 12 gauge against the bank and squatted to pull aside the weathered boards. The dead swan stank, but he pulled it out of the cavity by one withering foot. After nearly two weeks the swan felt lighter, it's body fluids decaying and dissipating into the surrounding earth, but the feathers were still intact, a white blotch in the darkness.

An ancient cedar tree, dwarfed by wind and weather, grew at the lip of the bank where Brian had passed over and down into the creek gully. Bart paused, grasping a branch for balance, and leaned out. He saw Brian, a darker spot in the darkness moving up the creek to his right. His feet felt the smooth earth beneath where footsteps had killed the grass creating a path over the edge, and knew this must be a regular path that Brian had taken. Ahead the shadow stopped and collapsed into a rounder shape. He thought he saw Brian digging at something in the bank, and remembered the old structure weathering away into nothing. He saw a lighter spot at Brian's feet, measured the distance up the creek and walked along the bank to another place where the action of water had worn a shallow gully leading downward.

Ignoring the stink of decaying flesh, Brian reached out and stroked the wing at the top where the primary feathers emerged and with a swift tug pulled out a feather, stroked it across his nose and his cheeks. It was soft. He tugged out another and another; feathers that would have been difficult to remove when the bird was alive came out now with a gentle tug. He could start a club with his friends, giving a feather to each of them as a kind of membership token. Something struck him a powerful blow knocking him to the ground on his side. Stunned and confused for a few seconds, when he lunged for the shotgun, another blow knocked him down again onto his back, and then a foot pressed down on his chest. He was lying on the ground with his head pointed toward the creek, off balance with his feet higher up than his head and a rock pressing into the back of his head. "You lying little bastard," Bart spat at him. "What the fuck to do you think you're doing?"

Brian raised his head and stared up, his father's face nearly invisible in shadow, but he knew the voice. He tried to roll over on his side, but the foot came off his chest and the toe of a boot caught him beneath the chin snapping his head back onto the rock. He closed his eyes and lay still hearing his father breathing as if he had run full out for a mile.

He turned his head and spat out blood. His teeth had clacked together on his tongue.

Bart raged at his son, his words confused coming out without order or sense or logic. He said, "You've been a disappointment from the day you came out of the chute. Lazy, sullen, disobedient, defiant. You back talk me. You pull disgusting tricks on your sister. You lie and cheat. You know, I put up with it. I tried to be patient. I kept hoping you'd outgrow it, that you'd take an interest in this place, this ranch that your grandfather started and I keep trying to build into something more. I was doing it for you, for your future, but it's clear that it's a future you want no part of. I've tried patience.

I've tried understanding. I've tried being tough, and none of it, none of it has made you into half the man you should be at your age." He paused, searching for words, the right words, the words that would make Brian see what he'd done, make him straighten up, become a decent human being, the son Bart thought he'd begotten.

Brian turned his head and spat blood again, and said something that gargled and garbled.

"What? You got something to say for yourself?" Bart demanded.

Brian spat once more and spoke. "I said, we're both criminals. I killed a swan. Big deal. But you. You're a rapist."

The pressure on Brian's chest eased as Bart leaned his weight back on his other foot. Had Brian been awake that night? Had Susan?

Brian pushed with his feet, trying to heave himself upright, but with his body angled downhill his feet got no traction, and he slid a little until Bart's foot came down again hard, squeezing the air out of Brian's lungs with a propulsive *HUFF*.

"Yes. I did that," Bart said, his voice thick, "I did it, and I'm ashamed of it, and I'd like to make it right with your mother, but I don't know how, and she doesn't help it any. I don't think there's a way to make it right between us. There's too much water run under that old bridge. She's a fool. I married a fool. I thought a pretty farm girl who knew how to cook would be a great wife, and I loved her, but she's a fool, and we hatched a fool, and god help me, now there's another fool on the way. I hope to god it's a girl like Susan, not another boy like you. I can't handle the one of you, let alone another."

Brian muttered, "And all I did was kill a stupid old bird."

"What? What! You half-witted little asshole. No, I'm wrong—you're too stupid to be a half wit, you're a quarter wit, if that. Somebody is going to find out and when they do, I can't protect you, not even if I wanted to, which I sure as hell don't, and the thing is, the thing is, it's going to be on me, too, not just you. You're underage, so that means they'll hold me responsible. You'll probably get away with probation or something like that, but they just might send me to Leavenworth."

"What, you're not going to threaten me with Plankinton?" Brian's voice held a sneer within it, a distraction while he dug his heels in and shoved himself a little toward the creek.

"God, what happened to me? What happened to my family?" Bart questioned, his face raised toward the sky, as if really asking some superior being for answers. The sky had gone lighter in the east and more birds awoke, chirping and hopping in the cottonwoods and dwarf cedars.

Brian brought his knees up, shoved hard with his feet, arched his back and rolled from beneath Bart's foot. Off balance, Bart stumbled backward, caught his foot on the dead swan and fell against the broken boards of the rotting homesteader cabin. He caught himself with his left hand, driving a splinter or an old rusty nail into the side of his palm.

Brian's momentum kept him rolling toward the creek, but he fetched up against a two foot tall tangle of brush. He shook his head to clear it, pushed himself upright and rushed to retrieve the gun. He could say it was an accident. He could say he heard something behind him and when he turned to look, he stubbed his toe on a dead branch, and as he fell the gun went off. He reached the spot where he'd propped the shotgun, reached into the dark shadows of the bank, but the gun was gone, and then his father was standing in front of him, the long dark shadow of the shotgun hanging from his father's arm.

"You were going to shoot me," Bart said.

Brian said, "Are you going to shoot me?"

"I ought to. I ought to save myself and everyone else a world of trouble but no, I'm not going to."

"What are you going to do?"

"I don't know what to do," Bart said. "I never did know. I kept hoping something would come to me, some idea. Or that you'd change. Neither one is going to happen."

"So what then?"

"If I was a religious man, I'd pray."

"Pray for what? Forgiveness? A miracle?" Brian inched toward his dad, but Bart took several steps away to the creek bank, looking to the east as the sun kept creeping up ready to burst over the horizon.

"I don't know, maybe this kid on the way, maybe it'll be the making of this family. The better son," Bart said, squinting at the narrow rim of red easing up the horizon, sending the first rays straight down the creek as if the creek was a natural Stonehenge on summer solstice. Silver and gold glinted along the slow flowing water in the creek, which would soon diminish to no flow at all, only a series of widely spaced mud holes full of tadpoles. "Your brother."

"My brother?" Brian asked. "My son."

A minute passed before Bart turned to look at his son. "Your brother, my son," Bart said with a frown. "My second son."

Brian laughed.

"What? There's nothing funny about this. Nothing funny about any of it; for crissake, stop it!" Bart said sharply, but Brian continued to laugh.

"But, oh, god, it's so funny, so fucking funny!" Brian managed to say between bursts of laughter, then he laughed harder, continuously.

Bart stepped forward, and with one hand grabbed Brian by the shoulder and shook him, yelling, "Stop it! Stop that! Are you crazy?"

Brian took a deep breath, calmed himself, leaned back against the bank, and said, "My son. I'm going to be a father. You're going to be a grandfather."

Bart gaped at him, stunned with the enormity of it all, as Brian began laughing again. "You stupid old man. Who's the fool now? Huh? I'm going to be the father, and it's going to be another boy just like me," Brian taunted.

Bart raised the shotgun and pulled the trigger.

Epilogue

Bart

When he looked down at the bloody wound in Brian's chest, he wondered if the judge would let him join the army instead of going to prison, but that option never arose. He thought about turning the gun on himself, using his foot to pull the trigger, lying there beside Brian and the dead swan, but he didn't want Susan or even Betty to see this. Instead, he unloaded the second shell from the gun, clambered back up the creek bank and walked, numb, back to the house where Betty was in the kitchen making breakfast. He smelled the bacon.

He went to the phone, ordered the Baker girl off the line in such a fierce tone of voice that she hung up without an argument, and then he called the sheriff. While he was waiting for the sheriff to arrive, he had an idea that might work.

Gary

Pearl had enough of Gary's physical and verbal violence, especially after a shoving incident that turned into a black eye, a broken nose, and cracked ribs. In the summer of 1962 Pearl packed a single suitcase, called her sister, and six months later started a new life in Omaha, where she tended bar at the local VFW Club. Their oldest son, who had joined the army in the spring of '61, decided to make a career of it. He was killed in Viet Nam during the Tet Offensive in 1968.

Gary, drowning his sorrows at the Legion Club, enjoyed his conversations with Verda, the waitress, who didn't mind listening because she was about to quit her job. She had discovered her husband had had a life insurance policy that she didn't know about; the policy paid off, and she planned to move to Denver where the pool of men was deeper and broader, but after a couple of weeks, Gary was so kind, so understanding, and they had so much sorrow in common, she married him, and within six months, the proceeds from the insurance policy were spent, and Verda discovered she had sold her soul for a mess of pottage.

Betty

Betty didn't attend her son's funeral because she was in Jackson County Hospital. She had lost the baby, as the women of the club put it, in the Midwestern manner of avoiding the mention of death, as if the baby had been born, wandered out of its crib, and disappeared somewhere out on the prairie, never to be seen again. That summer she took up with an itinerant farmworker, a man fifteen years her junior, who came through Jackson County as part of the annual harvesting crew moving north from Texas to Canada, operating the combine harvesters that circled the wheat fields like gigantic grasshoppers, chewing and gobbling the golden stalks, hoarding the grain in their gullets and shitting out the straw and chaff behind in dusty clouds. She didn't take Susan with her when she left, but the rumors said Betty was living with her lover in Tulsa, Oklahoma.

Tom

He liked the new refuge manager, a youngish man with two children and a pretty wife. The new guy complimented Tom on the treasure trove of information that he had documented, but slowly he took over the daily observations and operation of the swan project himself, along with the new intern, a big blonde Swede-looking kid from the University of Nebraska. By that November Tom was back in the equipment barn with Keith, rebuilding the motor on the cat. When the tribal council elections were held, Rebecca Richards won the seat for Potato Creek with Bennie Black Hawk's help. She promptly talked the council into firing the tribal leasing agent and installing her own cousin, who promptly canceled all of Bart Johnson's leases. It took another year before Bart got all his cattle off the leased land, but by that time Rebecca had ended her affair with the tribal council president, who fired Rebecca's cousin. Bart Johnson didn't get his leases back, but the landowners couldn't agree on what to do with their property, or who to put in as manager of the land cooperative. Bennie's dream of a buffalo ranch slowly fell to dust.

Bit

Her ambition in life was to own and live on a big old ranch in the middle of nowhere, but she knew she could never buy or even lease enough land for that dream. The only way she could get that would be to marry the heir of a local rancher. She might have considered one of them. She got a crush on John Goodall in high school when she was the only girl who took classes in agriculture. That was tough. She loved the animal science and plant science she studied during the first two years even while she put up with whispers and derision from all the students. (The ladies of the club still said to themselves that Bit Warder should've been a boy.) For a while she thought John liked her, but if he did, he quickly lost interest when one of the yellow-haired cheerleaders, who didn't know anything about artificial insemination in cattle and didn't want to know, smiled at him one afternoon at a baseball game.

Bit went to college, paying her way on scholarships and part-time work as a waitress on campus at the University of South Dakota. She got a teaching credential and a job teaching elementary school in Casper, Wyoming, but in the summer of 1974 her father, Tom Warder, died of a heart attack at the ripe old age of fifty-three. Bit got a teaching job at Jackson High School and moved back home to take care of her mother, whose health had taken a downturn. Bit's sisters had married and moved away, one to Florida and one to Texas. Like so many people who come back to their hometowns after years away, it seemed to Bit that everything had shrunk—buildings, streets, even the distances between places. Most of her generation were gone, moved to greater prosperity and interest, but the ones who stayed had the same shrunken attitudes as their parents and as their parents before them. After two years back in Jackson, Bit convinced her mother to leave. Together they rented a condo in Dallas, Texas. While dancing at Billy Bob's one night, Bit met a man. He was homely as a mud fence in a rainstorm, but funny and smart and in 1977 they married. Bit moved to his family's ranch south of Weatherford, Texas, where she helped her husband raise Santa Gertrudis cattle and paint horses. She preferred the tobiano ones.

Susan

After Susan's mother left, after her father lost the leases on the ranch, Bart rented a small house in Jackson for himself and his daughter and took a job running the city garbage truck. Susan grew up and married one of the Baker boys and is now the president of the Lady's Aid Club while her father continues his day job on the garbage truck and his hobby of bending his elbow over the bar in the Legion Club.

Bill

The trumpeter swans, under the care of the new refuge manager, nested, raised babies, and eventually flew from the pen and into the wild where their numbers grew until their species became not unendangered but less endangered. Bill's grief over the loss of Martha never went away, only receded into the past. He lived another three years on the refuge, sometimes flying out of the pen back along the road where Martha had been shot. Just a non-sentient bird, he never knew that the boy who shot Martha was reported to have shot himself in remorse and bled to death beside the decaying body of Bill's beloved.